****

Into the War

Rise of the Republic – Book Three

By
James Rosone

****

Illustration © Tom Edwards
Tom EdwardsDesign.com

Published in conjunction with Front Line Publishing, Inc.

Manuscript Copyright Notice

ISBN: 978-1-957634-06-7
Sun City Center, Florida, USA
Library of Congress Control Number: 2022902546

Table of Contents

Chapter One
Planetfall

Near Planet Intus
RNS *Midway*
Alpha Company 1st Battalion, 3rd Delta Group

Captain Bryan Royce stilled his mind and steeled his resolve. After nearly two months in transit and training nonstop on the *Midway*, the first human soldiers were about to land on the planet Intus, a world that had once been a Primord colony, now controlled by the Zodarks.

The Prims had tried to take it back several times unsuccessfully. When the humans had joined the Altairians' Galactic Empire, the GE had assigned the Earthers to work with the Prims to retake the planet. As their first real military campaign with their new allies, it was a test to see how well humans could work within the coalition and be a viable partner.

Royce stood in front of his company of ninety Deltas and one hundred and seventy combat Synths. "This is a hot drop, everyone," he began, his voice booming. "When the ship drops out of FTL, they're going to burn to get us in orbit—that's when they'll release our Ospreys. Accompanying us will be a single squadron of F-97 Orions. They'll be with us until we HALO, then they'll escort the Ospreys back to the *Midway*.

"Once the Ospreys get us within thirty thousand meters of the surface, we'll free-fall from there. This'll be our first HALO jump onto a hostile planet and our first jump as a combined human and Synth fighting force. Everyone needs to stay sharp, heads on a swivel."

The Deltas nodded, listening intently.

"I don't think the Zodarks have weapons capable of targeting us individually during our drop, but that doesn't mean they won't try," Royce continued. "Platoon leaders and sergeants, it's imperative that once we get on the ground, you move to hit your primary objectives ASAP."

Royce then turned to 001, affectionately called Adam. "Once we're on the ground and identify their defenses, I need your squads to stand by to assault the ion cannon. Is that understood?" he asked. Adam was the C100 designated to be the overall leader for the combat Synths assigned to his unit. The one hundred and seventy C100s were broken down into squads intermixed with Royce's four platoons.

The Deltas had found that the best use for the C100s was direct assaults. The Synths weren't the best at scouting and surveillance like trained Deltas, but they were beasts when it came to direct-action missions. So, the Deltas were more than happy to find the Synths targets to attack and stand out of their way.

"Understood, Captain Royce," replied Adam emotionlessly, the single blue light where eyes would normally be tracking from right to left.

Royce turned back to the rest of his company. "Once the *Midway* recovers our drop crafts, they'll pull out of orbit and join the rest of the fleet in battling the Zodarks. Remember, once those ion cannons on the surface are taken out, that's when the fleet will send in the rest of the orbital assault ships and disembark the Republic Army soldiers. There's a full division of RASs coming in the first wave, but we need to take those planetary defenses out first. Hooah!"

"Hooah!" shouted the Special Forces operators. They were just as eager as he was to get this show on the road.

"Everyone, form up on the flight deck in sixty mikes," Royce ordered. "We'll load up and be ready to deploy as soon as the *Midway* drops out of FTL. Is that clear?"

"Hooah!" came the single-word reply to his question.

The Deltas filed out of the briefing room to their individual platoon rooms to finish getting ready for the mission and packing a few last-minute items. Mostly, they needed to make sure they had enough extra power packs and ammo for their rifles. Should they get cut off from the rest of the fleet, they had to make sure they could hold out on their own for a little while.

Royce inventoried his own patrol pack one final time. He had extra food in there, along with two water purification pods. He'd never liked the idea of relying on just one purification pod—if it somehow got damaged, he'd be out of luck. A person could live without food for a while, but not water. Next to ammo, it was the most important thing to pack.

Hearing some hooting and hollering, Royce cinched his patrol pack shut, draped it over his shoulder, and headed out of the supply room to the hangar. The soldiers were already filing into the sixteen Ospreys and twenty dropships anchored on the sides of the *Midway*.

Fortunately for Royce's company, they had drawn the short stick to HALO onto the planet as opposed to being dropped closer to the target via the dropships. Technically, his company had the more dangerous job, but they were also less likely to get blown out of the sky by a lucky hit to a dropship. The downside to his units having to HALO in was where they were landing. The ion cannon was heavily fortified, but one section was left partially exposed. That section butted up against a heavily wooded area that offered no optimal landing zones. Hence, the HALO insertion.

As Royce climbed into the back of one of the Ospreys, he watched the row of soldiers and Synths strap themselves in. He couldn't see their eyes or faces—not with their helmets on—but he knew his human soldiers were nervous. The C100s never showed *any* emotions; they were ready to execute orders, whatever those orders might be, regardless of the consequences.

This was a unique mission for the Earthers—a lot different from their past missions. This wasn't a mining colony on some faraway planet they were trying to capture. This was a Zodark-controlled world: one with a substantial military force on it.

Gazing at the timer in his HUD, Royce anticipated the *Midway* was about to drop out of FTL. It wouldn't be long now until their Osprey began its journey to the surface—assuming their ship didn't get blown up before they got into orbit.

"Captain Royce, prepare to launch," came a voice from the flight operations control deck of the *Midway*.

"Stand by, people," Royce told his soldiers. "We're dropping out of FTL any minute now." He hoped his other lieutenants were doing all right, keeping their men and women pumped and ready for action.

"*Midway* is dropping out of FTL...now," the woman's voice from flight operations told Royce.

Moments later, the main thruster came online and the *Midway* lurched a bit, doing its best to get into a high orbit over the planet before they unloaded their human cargo.

The minutes continued to tick by. The rest of the soldiers crammed into their shuttles and dropships, waiting for the final go order. Suddenly, the *Midway* shook. Then Royce felt the ship change course a couple of times, probably dodging something.

It felt like time stopped as they waited to launch. The *Midway* shook a few more times. At one point, it felt like a sledgehammer hit the ship, the way it jolted everyone. All Royce and the other soldiers could do was sit tight and wait, hoping the fleeters could get them in position so they could execute their part of the mission.

"Stand by for launch," one of the pilots said over their platoon coms.

Royce gripped his straps, then felt a sudden jolt as the Osprey catapulted out of the *Midway* into the blackness of space.

"Hang on. It may get a bit bumpy," the pilot said, tension in his voice.

Royce patched his HUD into the cockpit so he could see the same view as the pilots. This was an option typically only available to the platoon or company commanders. What Royce saw made him wish he'd stayed ignorant of what was going on around him.

The blackness of space quickly filled with the image of this lush green-and-blue planet—but all around that beautiful planet were bright flashes of red and blue light arcing through the area around their Osprey. The pilots were doing their best to deftly dodge the incoming fire and the enemy fighters rising up from the planet to meet them.

One of the pilots pointed to something down on the planet. A second later, Royce saw a bright bolt of light emerge from where the pilot had been pointing as the energy burst headed in the direction of the *Midway*.

Those must be the ion cannons we're supposed to take out, Royce realized.

Switching to a different video feed, Royce caught a glimpse of the *Midway*. The ship accelerated out of orbit now that it had dropped its human cargo. It looked to be taking a pounding from the ion cannon located on the planet's surface.

From what Royce could see, the dropships were descending rapidly towards the surface. The F-97 Orion starfighters had the Zodark fighters fully occupied, which was a good thing as far as he was concerned.

Returning to the view the pilots had, Royce saw a small Zodark corvette get blown apart maybe fifty thousand kilometers to their right. A Prim destroyer had pounded it with a handful of lasers, cutting it apart.

Then what looked like a lightning bolt shot out from the planet below and slammed into the Prim destroyer, ripping a huge gash in it. The allied destroyer tried to angle away from the planetary ion cannon.

The Osprey suddenly broke through the upper atmosphere, and Royce's heart skipped a beat. Small ships or fighters materialized out of the clouds, sending blazing energy beams right at them. The pilots flying the Osprey made a series of wild twists and turns as they ducked and dodged the incoming fire. The Orion starfighters flying escort duty dove into the enemy formations, their guns blazing.

"We're sixty seconds out from jump altitude. Prepare to get the hell out of here," the pilot yelled urgently over the radio.

Royce observed his company in the back of the craft. They were all holding on to something tightly or gripping their rifle like someone was trying to take it away from them. He could tell they were scared, and rightly so. The world around them was lighting up with laser fire, and all they could do was sit tight and wait to either jump or get blown up.

The crew chief stood near the rear ramp of the bird, his magnetic boots holding him in place as he lowered the ramp. They were finally near the jump location.

As the pilots approached the drop zone, the Osprey, which had been in a near-constant dive, pulled up hard. Everyone in the back grabbed for something to hold on to as they fought against the sudden change in g-forces from the maneuver.

The Osprey leveled out seconds later, and the pilots switched the jump light from red to green. "Get the hell out of the bird!" the crew chief roared at them.

"Time to go!" yelled Royce over the platoon net.

With no hesitation, he stood up and launched himself without fear into the wide-open air. As he fell away from the Osprey, he craned his neck around and saw the rest of his platoon doing the same. They were emptying out of the rear of the bird with disciplined speed.

Royce pulled his arms in tight and straightened his legs, making himself as aerodynamic as possible. His HUD told him he was picking up speed as he ticked down the altitude at an alarming rate.

Turning to catch one last glance behind him, Royce watched the Osprey angle practically straight up to head back into space and get out of there. He then saw an Orion starfighter blow two enemy fighters out of the sky, moments before that same fighter exploded from a direct hit

8

by a third enemy aircraft. The starfighters were doing their best to cover the assault force while the Ospreys bugged out of the area and back to the *Midway*.

Returning his gaze to what was happening in front of him, Royce saw he was about to enter a cloud bank that had been obscuring his view of the surface. As his body raced through the clouds, moisture droplets pelted him and misted up the view through his face shield. A few minutes later, he was out of the cloud cover and saw the lush green tropical ground below getting much closer. Checking his HUD, Royce saw he was one minute away from his parachute automatically opening. He'd be on the ground in two minutes.

Off in the distance to his right, the giant ion cannon fired off another laser-like bolt, sending another ball of energy into orbit at one of the fleeters' ships.

Royce reviewed his blue force tracker; all but one of his soldiers were showing green. The one soldier showing red had apparently been shot by an enemy fighter on the way down. Royce felt relieved he had only lost one Delta. He had known there might be enemy fighters in the area, but he really had no idea how many.

"Preparing to deploy the parachute," an automated voice told him, moments before the chute attached to the rear of his exoskeleton combat suit opened. The steering cords dropped down for him to grab. Royce latched onto them quickly and angled his glidepath to a thinner section of the trees identified in their mission brief.

As he approached the ground, Royce scanned his surroundings. The trees appeared similar to palm trees on Earth. Ferns covered the soil, intermixed with other bushes and smaller trees. As he came closer to the ground, Royce realized the trees were taller than he'd expected.

Nearing the surface, Royce released his drop bag so it hung below his feet. He pulled down hard on his parachute cords, causing the chute to grab as much air as possible in a last-second maneuver to slow him down. As he came to the tree cover, he detached his chute, just like he had done a hundred times before in the simulators. His body free-fell into the trees. As his HUD alerted him he was near the ground, the small rockets built into the sides of his boots ignited, slowing his descent. Seconds later, his feet touched down on his third alien planet in five years.

With his feet firmly on the ground, Captain Royce released his rifle from his chest rig and followed his drop cord to his patrol pack. With his rifle and patrol pack ready, he looked around for the rest of his platoon.

Using his HUD, Royce got a quick view of the situation. All around him, his Deltas landed and prepared themselves and their equipment for action. He saw on the blue force tracker his squad leaders forming them up as the platoon sergeant got them ready to move.

Captain Royce linked up with the lieutenant, who was ready to roll as well. "Lieutenant, let's move," Royce said.

Just then, his first sergeant trotted up to him with the company comms specialist. The RTO was their direct link to the *Midway* and the fleet above them. He was followed behind by Royce's first sergeant.

"Captain, we lost one soldier in the drop," the first sergeant confirmed. "The other platoons are on the ground and moving to their objectives."

"Thanks, Top. Let's get moving," Royce replied. "We're racing against the clock now to get those guns taken offline."

Lieutenant Karen Williams barked to her platoon, "First Squad, get us eyes on that cannon. Third and fourth squads, get those terminators ready to attack once we find them some targets. Second squad, deploy our drones, and let's move."

Williams was a new addition to Royce's company, fresh from Delta school back on Earth—part of the new replacement crop intended to transition the C100s to a support position with the Deltas. The Special Forces community was still playing catch-up after the battles in the Rhea system—and it didn't help that the Altairians had demanded they triple their forces in a short timeframe, either. The combat Synths were filling the gap, but no one liked the idea of running independent Synth units. The Earthers still didn't fully trust autonomous AI units.

As the platoon and company level drones deployed, their radar and lidar waves sent detailed pictures of the area around them. The place was thick with vegetation and animals, and the terrain had some slight rises in elevation. In short order, the drones would expand the perimeter. As the other platoons' drones linked up with each other, it would provide Royce with a comprehensive view of the entire area.

First Squad took off at a quick trot to the ion cannon, their HUDs guiding them. As the Special Forces soldiers moved forward, the operators let the drones scout ahead to identify any potential adversaries or obstacles as they advanced. Steadily, the platoon of Deltas advanced toward the enemy base ten kilometers away.

"Able Six, Archer Actual. How copy?" came the call over the battalion net.

Royce ducked under a low-hanging branch as he tried to keep up with everyone. Using his neurolink, he connected to his radio. "Archer Actual, Able Six. Send it."

Suddenly a weird monkey-like animal jumped from one tall tree to another in front of Royce. *What the hell was that?*

"Able Six, I see your position. I need you to move three clicks to the northwest. Hold your position at this waypoint," Major Hopper said as a spot on the map flashed on Royce's HUD. The position was four clicks away from their current destination. "That's a good copy," he responded as he hopped over a fallen log. "You want the platoon or the company to relocate to that position?"

"The company. Out," Hopper quickly replied.

Royce could tell Hopper was busy. He usually wasn't that short with his answers. It was one of the problems with all the integrated technology an augmented super-soldier dealt with. Between the cybernetic implants, neurolinks, and an integrated HUD, it was challenging not to get inundated with information and fall flat on your face as you moved through unknown territory.

Telling his neurolink to sync him up with the company, Royce sent the adjustment to their orders and the new location. Each platoon leader sent an acknowledgment moments later. The blue force tracker showed everyone adjusting their positions on the map as the contingent of operators headed to the new location.

Moving deeper into the forest, Royce noticed the trees became bigger and taller. The base of some of these trunks had to be more than ten meters in diameter. His HUD told him the trees were between two hundred and even three hundred meters in height in some parts. It was truly awe-inspiring, even more so than the banyan-like trees he'd seen on New Eden.

When the platoon came within a kilometer of the new waypoint, Royce heard something that sent a shiver down his spine. No matter how many times he heard the loud shrieking battle cry of a Zodark warrior, it still caused him to tense up.

Those guys are close, Royce thought.

Seconds later, Royce heard the lone sound of a Zodark blaster. Then a cacophony of M85 and M90 rifles opened up on the Zodark.

Royce picked up the pace, trying to keep up with the platoon. They rushed to their comrades, who were now in the thick of the fight.

"Able Six, Able Two," said Second Platoon leader. "We have two dozen Zodarks spread out in a nearby cluster of trees one hundred meters to our front. Requesting Able One flank their position to our right. How copy?"

Royce sent a message through the neurolink or NL for Lieutenant Williams to direct her platoon to flank the enemy. It was a good call, moving her people into an L position—it would prevent the Zodarks from running away.

Royce sent a message to his RTO and the first sergeant to follow him. They broke off from Lieutenant Williams's platoon to assist Second Platoon—it sounded like they needed the help, given the volume of fire happening.

As they rushed toward the fighting, red bolts of light sliced through the forest toward Royce's soldiers. Some of the fire came from up in the trees, some closer to ground level. The Special Forces soldiers threw a lot of slugs and blaster bolts right back at the enemy.

Since they weren't confined to the close quarters of the ship or worried about punching a hole in something important, the Deltas with the M85s used the magrails on their rifles while the SAW gunners tore into the enemy with the blasters. In general, the Special Forces soldiers tended to favor the magrails over blasters. Unlike blasters, the railgun slugs could punch through obstacles at an incredible range. The blasters, however, had a higher cyclic rate of fire, which was why the Squad Automatic Weapons or SAWs only came as blasters.

When Royce closed in on the fighting, he stopped next to a tree and brought his own rifle to bear. His HUD had found a pair of Zodarks situated some eighty meters up in a tree, shooting down into a group of his soldiers. They'd found a knot or branch to serve as a platform from which to pick off the Earthers.

One of the Zodarks extended his body just beyond the branch he was hiding behind to fire on someone. In that instant, Royce's targeting reticle illuminated green, and he fired. A couple of slugs crossed the distance in a fraction of a second, slamming into the upper chest and neck of the Zodark soldier. The massive blue beast fell backward and out of the tree, and his four arms flailed as his body fell to the ground below.

Seconds later, a rocket flew out of the position Royce had just shot at. It shot down into the forest and slammed into a clump of fallen logs and underbrush his soldiers had been using for cover. The explosion threw one of his soldiers into the air, a leg clearly missing from his body. Two other Deltas cried out in pain from the shrapnel hitting them.

A nearby Delta soldier fired his 20mm smart munition up into the tree where the rocket had originated. A small explosion blossomed in the moss and tree leaves. A single figure was thrown clear of the position, swinging his four arms to grab at something, anything as his body fell to the ground. The wounded Zodark landed with a thud and a loud shrieking noise, calling out to his comrades.

"Captain Royce, I'm showing several fast-approaching vehicles from the direction of the Zodark base," announced the RTO, who was dual-hatting as a drone operator. "They'll be on our position in a couple of minutes."

"Lieutenant Anders, we have enemy inbound reinforcements," Royce barked over the platoon net. "Deploy your C100s, and let's end this!" Royce liked to let his platoon leaders take the initiative and deploy their forces as they saw fit, but his junior officers weren't picking up on how fast changes were happening.

"I'm on it, sir," came the swift reply.

Two dozen C100s moved past the Deltas, weapons up, and fired into the trees. As the automated killing machines went to work, the Zodarks shifted their fire to the Synths, recognizing them as the immediate threat.

A new noise rattled through the forest—Royce thought it sounded like an airplane as four hovercraft-like vehicles zipped into their line of sight. On top of each of the vehicles was what appeared to be a turret, each manned by a Zodark soldier firing a rapid-fire weapon at the C100s. Around a dozen Zodark soldiers emptied out of the rear of each vehicle.

The hovercrafts continued to lay down suppressive fire on the human and Synth soldiers as the Zodark soldiers charged right into the C100s with their shortswords drawn. One of the Deltas fired his 20mm smart munition at a hovercraft, scoring a direct hit on the front of the vehicle, causing it to veer out of control and slam into a tree. It collapsed to the ground below, out of commission.

The newly arrived Zodarks were now intermixed with the two dozen C100s Royce had just ordered forward, cutting them apart with their shortswords. Those electrified eighteen-inch blades had a way of slicing right through the armored shell and combat suit of the C100s. In a close-in fight, those handheld weapons were more dangerous and effective than their blasters were, and the enemy knew it.

"Holy crap! Those Zodarks are cutting our terminators apart," called out the platoon sergeant.

"Everyone, shift fire to support the Synths," barked Lieutenant Williams. "Take those Zodarks out!" Her voice was a bit shaky; she was unable to hide her nervousness at the changing situation.

The terminators adapted, switching from using their rifles to their own shortswords to battle the Zodarks. In a close-in, dirty fight like this, it was best to just use a tried and tested weapon—a blade that could be rapidly wielded to slash, stab, and deflect, just like the Zodarks.

Royce realized if they didn't take those Zodarks out fast, they'd wipe out a good chunk of his C100s for this mission.

Damn! We need them for the assault on the ion cannon.

Lifting his rifle up to his shoulder, Royce aimed at the cluster of four-armed beasts. He allowed the targeting AI built into his HUD to sync with his rifle and assist him in placing some well-aimed shots.

Zeroing in on a Zodark, he squeezed the trigger and saw the beast's head explode from the impact and sheer velocity of the slug as it slammed into its head.

Moving to the next beast, Royce watched it swing its sword down and slash at one of the C100s. Its glowing red blade cut a deep gash into its armor as the terminator did its best to deflect and attack the Zodark. Royce fired another round, hitting the Zodark right in the face and ending the fight.

In minutes, most of the Zodark fighters had been wiped out, but not before they managed to take out sixteen of his twenty-four combat Synths. A few minutes went by with periodic sniping by both sides until all fell silent. The remaining C100s moved through the area, scanning for any survivors and remaining threats. They'd synced themselves to the drones above to get a better situational awareness of their surroundings.

Royce received a quick message over his NL from Lieutenant Anders from First Platoon. *We've cleared the area of Zodarks. I've got six KIAs, seven wounded.*

Copy that. See if you can get your wounded moving, Royce replied. *If not, then we need to set up a triage location until we can arrange a medical transport back to the* Midway.

A quick check of his blue force tracker showed Lieutenant Williams, the Second Platoon leader, had taken minimal casualties: one KIA and two wounded. Royce had lost twenty-three out of the one hundred and seventy C100s he had for this mission.

Lieutenants, we've spent too much time dealing with this ambush, Royce said over the NL. *We need to get back on the move to support the assault on that ion cannon. The RA is supposed to show up in fifty-two mikes. We don't have a lot of time left to take that base out. If you have wounded soldiers that can't move, then get them collected up and placed in a single location. Leave a medic and a couple of C100s behind to guard them, and let's move.*

"Able Six, Archer Actual," crackled the radio in Royce's helmet.

"Archer Actual. Send it."

"Bravo Six is engaging the objective. Charlie Six is also joining the fray. How soon can Able Company get involved?" asked Major Hopper, a hint of annoyance in his voice that they weren't ready yet.

Royce could hear explosions and blaster fire in the background of the radio call. The major was already in the thick of it. This little Zodark ambush had cost Royce's unit fifteen minutes.

Royce sighed. "We're fifteen mikes out," he replied over the battalion net. "I've got nine WIAs we're leaving behind for medical transport and seven KIAs. I'm also down twenty-three C100s."

"That's a good copy. I'm sending the coordinates of your wounded to the *Midway*. They'll send a medical transport down to collect them when they can. Also, be advised, we've got Reaper support from the *Midway* inbound. Out," came Hopper's hurried reply. More explosions and blaster fire could be heard at the tail end of the response.

Switching over to the company net, Royce announced, "Able Company, the rest of the battalion is engaging the ion cannon now. We've got Reaper support inbound to support their attack and a medical transport on the way to pick up our casualties. We need to really pick up the pace to the objective. I want First and Third Platoons to lead the assault. Second Platoon will be held in reserve. Fourth Platoon, get your heavy weapons and mortars set up as soon as we're in range. Let's move, people!"

Chapter Two
Sector Five

Planet Intus
Zodark Base

Zooming in as far as his HUD's magnification system would allow him, Major Jayden Hopper scanned the fortified position known as Intus Five. The massive ion cannon was surrounded by a large, heavily armored base. Every sixty seconds the planetary defensive weapon unleashed another powerful energy burst skyward. The longer this weapon stayed operational, the more damage it inflicted on the fleet of ships in orbit around the planet.

From time to time, a hypersonic missile or magrail slug tried to penetrate the facility's protective bubble. Each time, a streak of light swatted the threat from the skies before it could cause any damage.

"What about that spot over there?" asked Captain Jaycik Hiro, Hopper's S3 or operations officer.

Hopper shifted his gaze to where Hiro pointed. The base itself was still shrouded in dense tree cover, making it hard to see inside it or identify weak points in its defensive line. But the Zodarks had done something conniving by clearing five hundred meters of trees and underbrush directly in front of the perimeter of the base. They'd created the perfect killing field, making any direct ground assault costly.

"I see it, Hiro," Major Hopper replied. "Yeah, I think that is probably our best bet. Have Bravo and Charlie Companies assault that position when it's time. Make sure that area is saturated with smoke before they attack. It's imperative that we give them as much cover as possible."

Kneeling down on the ground, Hopper motioned for Hiro to look at a three-dimensional topographical map of the area. Pointing at the side of the facility Dog Company was approaching, he said, "Send a message over to Captain Channer that when it's time to launch his attack, he needs to make his maneuver look convincing. We want the Zodarks to believe the main assault is going to come from his direction. I want our artillery to lay smoke rounds across the frontlines facing him. If we can trick the enemy into believing the main assault is coming here, then when Bravo and Charlie launch their assault, they'll have a better chance of breaking through."

Captain Hiro nodded as he noted several positions on the digital map and motioned for the master sergeant from their artillery support unit to relay the positions to the gun units.

Hopper reviewed the map to locate Able Company. Captain Royce's unit had recovered from an ambush on their way to the objective, but not before it had slowed them down. Hopper wanted to wait on launching the main assault until they were in position, but they were running short on time. They needed to take that ion cannon down before the rest of the Republic Army showed up.

Hopper turned to find his RTO/drone operator, Sergeant Ivan Prolov. "How long until those Reapers arrive on station?" he asked.

"Five mikes," replied the sergeant. "The Orions are still working on clearing a path for them."

Sergeant Prolov's helmet visor was backlit with the various drone feeds and communication channels he was monitoring. For all intents and purposes, the RTO/drone operators were practically nonexistent during a battle as they managed the visual and communications support for the company or battalion commanders.

"All right, Captain Hiro," Major Hopper finally said, letting out a deep breath. "Send the order. Launch the assault, and let's plaster the area with artillery fire."

Off in the distance, they heard the thumping sound of the heavy artillery guns. A little closer to their position, the mortar teams joined in. Round after round sailed toward the enemy base. Streaks of light stabbed out from inside the base, intercepting many of the projectiles. Some managed to detonate over the base, filling the sky with dual purpose infrared-inhibiting smoke and chaff clouds. The specially designed chemical clouds and chaff canisters would make it difficult for the Zodarks' laser- and radar-guided defensive systems to accurately target and engage the incoming artillery rounds.

As more and more of the specially designed ordnance exploded over top of the enemy base, the mortar teams pounded the base with their high-explosive rounds. At the same time, the artillery units intermixed their rounds with both air and ground burst smoke rounds. In a matter of minutes, the base quickly became blanketed in thick white and gray smoke.

Captain Channer from Dog Company launched their attack, and a wave of forty C100s rushed forward toward the Zodark lines. When they reached the halfway point, the second wave of forty C100s advanced. Meanwhile, the remaining C100s and the human soldiers did their best to lay down covering fire for them.

All hell broke loose across the Zodark lines as the C100s reached less than a hundred meters from the enemy. Artillery and mortar rounds continued to pound the Zodark ranks, adding further chaos and confusion. The C100s were now practically in the enemy trenches. Nearly half their numbers had been wiped out, but the ones that were still operational were tearing into the enemy soldiers.

"It's working. They're shifting reinforcements to the north," called out Sergeant Prolov, who was clearly zoned in on the display in his helmet as he manned the drones.

Hopper watched the map display as the drones continued to provide real-time data updates to it. The green dots that represented the C100s were now intermixed with the red dots, the Zodarks. The fight was turning into an all-out melee.

Captain Hiro announced, "Bravo and Charlie are launching their assault now."

Zooming out on the map, Hopper saw his other two units launching their attack. The first two waves of the assault were comprised of two hundred C100s. The killing machines were moving rapidly, closing the distance between themselves and the enemy, their human minders hot on their heels.

Thump, thump, thump.

The mortar teams sent more high-explosive rounds at the enemy. Now that the artillery unit had thoroughly saturated the place with smoke rounds, the mortar teams made more use of their smart rounds. When the shells flew over the enemy base, the targeting computers compared the images below with preprogrammed targets they had been given. When the smart rounds found what had previously been identified as a bunker, the rounds would angle in for the kill. Because the area was covered in infrared-inhibiting smoke and chaff clouds, the smart rounds couldn't use their active targeting system. They had to rely on the passive memory system to find their preprogrammed targets.

Hopper watched as the first three mortars flew over the enemy lines and darted down at various points. One of the smart munitions struck a bunker that housed a heavy weapon that was raining blaster bolts down on his company. Another struck one of the blasters that were intercepting the magrail slugs being fired down from orbit. A third mortar landed amongst a cluster of Zodarks who had been preparing to charge his soldiers. It killed and wounded many of them.

"Incoming fighters!" shouted Sergeant Prolov out of nowhere.

"What?!" was all Hopper was able to say. A loud shrieking sound from an engine suddenly pierced the sounds of the battle.

Seconds later, a pair of sleek black aircraft zoomed fast and low over the northern side of the battlefield. The fighters fired a steady stream of blaster bolts across Dog Company on their approach before they flew over their positions. As they swooped over them, a string of small objects fell from their fuselage before they zipped out of the area.

The black objects falling from the enemy aircraft exploded in a series of long, thunderous explosions of flame and shrapnel across much of Dog Company's positions.

Holy crap! What the hell was that? Major Hopper thought in horror. This was their first time seeing or experiencing Zodark fighters or their close air support units like this.

As the fireballs rippled across the forested area, Hopper watched dozens of his blue icons go from bright blue to a dull blue, letting him know they'd been killed. Many others flashed on and off, indicating the individual soldier had been injured.

Jesus, they nearly wiped out the entire company, realized Hopper.

"Patch me through to the *Midway*," Hopper barked to his RTO.

A second later, a commander in the flight operations on the *Midway* came on. "This is Commander Hue. What can we do for you, Major?"

Hopper observed the face of the commander; he was nervous and stressed. Clearly, the *Midway* was still battling it out around the planet with the rest of the fleet.

"Commander, I just lost most of a company of Deltas from an enemy aerial fighter attack. Where is my air cover and my medevacs? My Deltas are getting cut to pieces down here!" barked Hopper angrily.

"I'm sorry to hear about that, Major," said Commander Hue, clearly pulling up some information on his screen. "I'm showing a flight of Orions just now coming on station over your area. They just greased those enemy fighters you're talking about. We've got six Reapers inbound to start an attack run momentarily. Do you need me to dispatch additional medical transport?"

"Yes, send additional medical transports and a med team to my location. I'm also requesting my reserve unit of Deltas and C100s to be deployed. How soon can you have them down on the ground?" demanded Hopper over the roar of the battle going on around him. With nearly an entire company wiped out, he needed Easy Company and his reserve unit of C100s on the surface yesterday.

"Uh, um, Major. We're still in the thick of it up here right now. I can order the transports to head to your position now, but I can't guarantee they'll make it," said Commander Hue. "If you can give us maybe another twenty or thirty minutes, things should be cleared up enough for us to start offloading the rest of your battalion." The offer was less than convincing.

Major Hopper took a deep breath, trying to still his rising anger. "Commander, we need to get this ion cannon taken offline in thirty-two minutes. I need those reinforcements *now*, not in thirty minutes, not in an hour. Order the transports down and do your best to cover their descent. Archer Actual, out!"

Hopper disconnected the video feed and returned his attention to the battle still unfolding in front of him. Hearing the sound of a jet engine, he looked up and smiled.

A single Reaper swooped in from high up in the clouds. It unloaded a barrage of antimateriel rockets along the Zodark lines, facing the side of the line Bravo and Charlie Companies were charging into. The entire line of Zodark positions erupted in flames, black smoke, and shrapnel.

A missile shot out from the Zodark lines and chased the Reaper. The attack aircraft did several extreme maneuvers, barrel-rolling and popping off some flares and chaff canisters in an attempt to spoof the missile. None of it worked. The missile edged itself within a dozen meters of the Reaper before it suddenly blew out a blast of shrapnel that tore the rear half of the aircraft apart. Moments later, the pilot ejected from the destroyed aircraft before it disintegrated into a flaming fireball.

Two more Reapers swooped down and plastered the part of the base where the Zodark missile had emanated from. They also raked the enemy position with their blasters and dropped a pair of two-thousand-pound bombs, tearing the area apart.

With a gaping hole in the Zodark fortress, Hopper pushed his company commanders to get their units in the breach before the enemy could plug the hole. The reserve element of C100s now raced ahead of his soldiers into the breach. Many of them were cut down, but not before they inflicted some damage inside the enemy positions.

At least two platoons of human soldiers followed them into the fortress. With his soldiers and C100s inside the enemy base, they now worked to roll up the northern and southern lines in an effort to collapse their defenses. Then they'd be able to get inside the inner perimeter protecting the ion cannon and take it out.

"Sir, Captain Royce's unit is finally in position," said the S3, Captain Hiro. "Do you want them to continue to attack the east side of the base, or should we shift them around to go in and support Bravo and Charlie?"

"That's actually a good call, Hiro," said Hopper. "Send Royce the FRAGO and tell him to haul it over to the southern side of the base and go in through the hole Bravo and Charlie created. I need Royce's unit to push past them and into the inner part of the base and take that damn cannon out."

The fighting inside the Zodark base grew in intensity. Oftentimes it devolved into hand-to-hand knife fights at close range. Twenty minutes into the fight, two of Hopper's three companies had made their way into the inner section of the fortress. It didn't take them much longer to capture the enemy ion cannon, removing it as a threat to the human fleet in orbit above.

Shortly after the ion cannon fell silent, two medical transports landed near Major Hopper's command post. Once the transports had landed, the influx of medical personnel went to work treating the wounded.

A few medics made their way over to where Dog Company had been located. They had the grisly job of sorting through the carnage to find the wounded soldiers and get them moved to the transports. Many of these soldiers had severe burns and shrapnel wounds from the enemy air attack.

While the medical transports tended to the wounded, eight Ospreys landed, offloading Easy Company and an additional two hundred C100s. The combat Synths were deployed in a wide-arcing perimeter around the ion cannon and battalion. If the Zodarks wanted to try and take the position back, they'd have to get through a couple of layers of defenders.

Twenty minutes after the Deltas had secured the ion cannon, the first wave of Republic Army soldiers landed. They brought their main battle tanks with them, along with infantry fighting vehicles and mechs. As more and more of the planetary defenses were taken down, the battle transitioned to rooting out the remaining Zodark military camps and installations throughout the planet. The first battle to secure a beachhead had been won; now they needed to win the war to liberate and secure the planet.

Chapter Three
Task Force Intus

Above Planet Intus
RNS *George Washington*

Captain Fran McKee read the damage report with a bit of concern. The fleet had taken a heavy beating during this engagement.

We need those new warships the Altairians are helping us build, she thought.

Turning to her XO, Captain McKee ordered, "Commander Yang, make sure we have some Vipers shadowing the Zodark withdrawal so they aren't regrouping on the far side of a planet without us knowing." McKee was functioning as the operational fleet commander until Admiral Halsey showed up with the transports carrying the ground invasion forces.

"Yes, ma'am," came the quick reply from Yang as the new order was sent out.

Turning to her operations officer next, Captain McKee directed, "Ops, order the flight deck to launch their fighters and support the Deltas on the ground. Send medical transports down to evacuate the wounded as well. No reason to make them wait any longer than necessary for help."

Returning her gaze back to the damage control board, McKee saw the three sections that had been red were now yellow. McKee sighed in relief as she realized the fires were under control, and the hull breach in section two alpha was sealed up. She'd lost two primary turrets and three secondary turrets in the engagement. It would take some time to get all the weapon systems operational again, but at least their superweapon, the plasma cannon, was still functioning and able to bring the pain when needed.

"Coms, how long until Admiral Halsey's group arrives?" McKee asked next.

Lieutenant Branson searched her screen for the answer. "Five minutes," she replied.

McKee nodded in approval; things were moving right on schedule. Her task force had jumped into the system three hours ago and cleared a path for the Special Forces ships to land the first wave of ground forces.

That was a key part of her task force's mission. The Special Forces soldiers needed to take the planet's ion cannons offline. Once they were down, the orbital assault ships could drop the hundreds of thousands of soldiers that were coming in the second wave with Admiral Halsey's fleet.

True to their word, the Prims had jumped in their fleet to support the humans. Their ships were smaller in number but more capable than the Earthers. At least until the Earthers' new ships came out of the yard.

Now that the Deltas had taken down the ion cannons, the Prims would jump in their own troopships and assist the Earthers in taking the planet back. The battle to retake Intus and the system was on. Now the question was how fast each side could take territory and build up its defenses to hold it.

"Captain, Admiral Halsey's fleet is arriving," her operations officer announced.

Watching the monitor on the bridge, Captain McKee saw dozens of ships blinking into existence a million or so kilometers away from her own ships. Staring at the screen, she almost did a double take when she saw how many ships were arriving—forty transports and orbital assault ships in all, far and above the largest human fleet assembled in one place.

"Captain, Admiral Halsey sends her regards," Lieutenant Branson said, relaying the newest communiqué. "Her fleet is moving toward the planet now. She's asking that we break off from our current position and establish a screening position for the transports."

"Acknowledge the order," McKee ordered. "Send the new instructions to the task force. Move to Beta formation. We'll keep the *GW* near the planet, and in the middle of the fleet in case the Zodarks show up."

A flurry of activity took place as the task force of battleships and cruisers moved to the outer edge of the cluster of transports and orbital assault ships moving into position above the planet.

With the next phase of the operation in Admiral Halsey's hands, McKee was settling in to relax when, out of nowhere, alarm bells blared.

"We've got a wormhole appearing!" yelled Lieutenant Cory LaFine anxiously.

"Holy crap!" exclaimed Lieutenant Arnold, her operations officer. "That Orbot battleship from earlier just jumped back and brought eight

Zodark cruisers with him. They're emerging one million kilometers from the transports!"

No, no, no, this can't be happening! McKee thought in shock. *I was sure we'd destroyed that ship.*

Captain McKee stood up. "Send a flash message to the task force to target all weapons on those Zodark cruisers," she directed in a loud, authoritative voice. "Weps, focus everything we have on that Orbot battleship. Let's finish it off this time, especially now that their shields appear to still be down. Navigation, move us into a blocking position to protect as many of the transports as we can."

A flash message from the *Voyager* popped up next to McKee's chair. "Captain McKee, I'm ordering the transports to FTL out of the battlespace. Buy us some time to get away until you can clear the battlespace again!" shouted Admiral Halsey. Her face contorted with fear and anger at what was unfolding around them, and alarm bells blared in the background.

"We're on it, Admiral," McKee replied quickly. "This is the same Orbot battleship we fought earlier. It's already beaten up from our previous battle. Admiral, get the transports to align behind the *GW* if you can. We'll do our best to help shield them from the enemy." The message ended seconds later as the admiral went to work on getting the transports out of there.

"Weps, get us a firing solution on that Orbot ship and engage," McKee ordered forcefully. "Focus all our primary and secondary turrets on them. Get that plasma cannon focused on its engineering section."

Moments later, the primary and secondary turrets of the *GW* opened fire, sending dozens upon dozens of slugs at the enemy vessel. Their pulse beam batteries, Havoc antiship missiles, and torpedoes opened fire next. The entire area around the *GW* lit up with fire as the Earthers attacked the most formidable vessel of the enemy alliance.

Watching the monitor in front of the bridge, McKee had a hard time seeing all that was happening. Then she remembered that Admiral Hunt used to use the three-dimensional overview from some of the surveillance drones. Sitting down in her captain's chair, McKee pulled her foldable monitor up next to her chair and tapped on the screen, pulling up the view she needed of the battlespace.

First, she noticed her battleships and cruisers rapidly closing the distance to get in range of the Zodark cruisers. That was a good thing.

The Orbot ship, however, apparently saw what she was doing with her vessel and was maneuvering to get below the Earth ship, giving them a better line of sight on the human fleet.

McKee turned to her helmsman. "Lieutenant Donaldson, match the Orbot ship's movements. Keep us between their ship and the transports. They're trying to slip underneath us so they can get a better shot at our transports—we need to buy them more time to get out of the area."

"I'm on it, Captain," replied Donaldson.

"Brace for impact!" barked one of the operations crewmen.

The ship shook hard and shuddered as the Orbot ship's primary weapon sliced a deep gash into the *GW*. The helmsman conducted an emergency maneuver as he moved the ship out of the path of the laser that was boring a hole in their armor. Countermeasures were launched.

"Where's my jamming?" yelled McKee's XO.

"I'm trying, but they're burning through it," came the terse reply of the electronic warfare officer. "We're in too close to each other for it to work."

"Firing the plasma cannon," announced the weapons officer.

The main monitor briefly whited out and then readjusted as the plasma bolt shot out from the *GW*. In the blink of an eye, it plowed right into the Orbot ship. With its shields down, the plasma bolt blew a hole ten meters wide and a hundred or more meters deep. Debris blew out the hole as the Orbot ship vented atmosphere, sucking dozens of Orbots out into the vacuum of space.

The *GW* shook violently a second time as the Orbot ship's primary weapons hit them again. The *GW* shook so hard from the hit, everyone grabbed for something to keep from falling. McKee checked the damage control board; red and yellow lights flashed on different sections of the ship, reflecting the serious damage from this last hit.

McKee caught a glimpse of two Viper frigates as they swooped in and unloaded a barrage of plasma torpedoes and Havoc antiship missiles into the Orbot ship before they were both blotted from existence.

The Orbot ship maneuvered out of the way of the plasma torpedoes heading its way. It managed to evade six or seven of them, but another dozen slammed into various sections of the ship. The enemy ship was too close to the human fleet to allow it much time or space to get out of the way of the devastating weapons.

All but one of the Havoc missiles was intercepted, but the one that got through delivered its five-hundred-kiloton warhead against the armor of the Orbot ship. The blast carved a several-meter-deep gouge along a quarter of the ship. Had the ship's shields still worked, it might not have taken so much damage from the nuke, but the ship had lost its shield generator during the earlier battle before it had warped away.

The fighters the *GW* had launched earlier to help the Deltas down on the surface now joined the fray, attacking the enemy vessels as well. Their blasters and magrail guns couldn't inflict a lot of damage on the Orbot or Zodark ships, but they were an additional threat the enemy had to contend with.

"Launching the bombers now," announced her Ops officer.

The flight deck at the bottom of the ship scrambled their wing of unmanned bombers. They headed to the Orbot ship and released a volley of plasma torpedoes. The bombers then turned around to land and rearm on the *GW* before flying back out to repeat the attack run.

Streaks of laser light flicked across the darkness of space. The Zodark and Orbot ships tore into the orbital assault ships, as well as the massive transports and freighters ferrying the human and Prim armies intended to capture the planet.

As she continued to watch the battle unfold, McKee mentally willed more of her bombers and torpedoes to hit the Orbot ship. A streak of light reached out and cut one of the orbital assault ships in half, and then another light beam ripped apart one of the massive freighters.

"Damn it! Get us into a better blocking position to keep that Orbot ship from hitting those transports!" McKee roared. "Every weapon and ship we have must tear into that damn ship *now*."

The cruisers and battleships in her task force shifted their fire from the two remaining Zodark cruisers to the lone Orbot battleship. The volume of fire slamming into the enemy ship was tremendous. Slug after slug penetrated deeper into the armor and into its hull. Plasma torpedo after torpedo hammered the ship, causing huge fountains of molten metal to erupt out of the ship before the coldness of space froze it back into a solid state.

In minutes, the Orbot ship experienced a series of explosions on the rear half of the vessel that rippled through to the front. Seconds later, the entire ship blew apart in a bright flash of light. Debris from the explosion flew out in many directions, some of it slamming into nearby ships.

Turning to her weapons officer, McKee ordered, "Have the entire task force shift fire to those two remaining Zodark ships. Vaporize them *now*!"

The large plasma cannon on the *GW* traversed toward one of the Zodark cruisers. The enemy ships were picking up speed to get out of the area. As the cruiser turned to accelerate away from the *GW*, the plasma cannon fired. In a brilliant flash of light, the enemy cruiser blew apart. The rest of the task force made short work of the last Zodark cruiser.

McKee shook her head in dismay as she reviewed the battle that had just taken place. The enemy vessels had jumped into the middle of the fleet, slashing and dashing as much as they could before her task force of battleships and cruisers could stop them.

"Ops, how many ships did we lose?" McKee asked, dreading the answer as she knew it would be high.

Before her Ops section could answer, the video display next to her captain's chair popped on, and Admiral Halsey's face appeared. "Captain McKee, that was some quick thinking and good shooting. I'm ordering the fleet that hasn't jumped away to continue with the landings. We need to get our forces offloaded as quickly as possible. Please disregard my previous order about screening for the fleet. Intersperse your task force as best you can to prevent another raid like that. I've sent a message to the Altairians as well. They said they're dispatching two cruisers to assist us. We should expect them to show up within the next hour."

McKee nodded in acknowledgment. "Yes, ma'am. Do you still want my air wings to support the Deltas and the RA landings?" she offered. "I'd like to send some medical shuttles down to pick up their wounded if possible. Many of them have already been waiting hours for help."

A short pause ensued as the admiral gazed off in another direction, calculating her response. Finally, she replied, "That sounds like a good plan, Captain. Proceed. Halsey out."

The screen went black.

Seeing her bridge crew intently focused on their tasks, McKee stood up and walked over to her operations section. "Ops, send a message down to Flight Ops," she said. "Tell them to reposition our fighters and bombers to support the Deltas and the RA as they land. Tell the medical transports to start picking up the wounded down on the surface and bring them back to the *GW*."

"Yes, Captain, right away," Arnold replied.

McKee used her communicator since she was out of range of the neurolink, pinging her chief engineer. "Commander Lyons, how bad is the damage?" she asked. "How soon can you complete repairs?"

A minute went by before she got a response. "Captain, we took some hard hits. The starboard launch tubes on the flight deck are offline. Deck five has a hull breach in section H. I'm trying to get that area sealed up and repaired. We also had five more primary turrets go down, along with three more secondary turrets and the starboard torpedo tubes. It's going to take some time to get everything back online."

McKee sighed before she replied. "OK, Commander, keep me posted on that hull breach."

"Will do, Captain. But please do keep in mind, this is going to take days to repair, not hours. Lyons out."

Before he signed off, McKee could hear a lot of shouting and alarms going off in the background. Lyons was clearly busy, and a lot was going on. She knew he was probably deploying his small army of synthetic repair workers to the hull breach. The team of Synths could operate on the outside of the ship and throw together some temporary patches. Those humanoid repair workers had saved many ships during this war.

Using her communicator to contact the medbay, McKee asked, "Dr. Michaels, what's the situation like down there?"

"How do you think it's going, Captain?" the doctor responded sharply. "We've been in a battle. I've got casualties. People are dying down here."

Dr. Lane Michaels was the lead doctor on the *George Washington*. He was a brilliant surgeon and medical practitioner, but he was also a staunch pacifist. After being drafted a couple of years ago, he'd begrudgingly accepted a posting to the *GW*. He'd been selected to be the lead doctor on the ship because of his experience as an attending physician at the University of Chicago Hospital. Despite his position at the famous teaching hospital, his prominence within the community, all the work he was doing in Chicago, and his position as a pacifist, he had been unable to avoid the draft. He was often unable to hide his bitterness at the position he'd been placed in.

"It's bad up here too, Doc," McKee answered calmly. "How many casualties are down there?" she pressed.

A moment went by before he replied, "Roughly two hundred and thirty injured. Another three hundred or so were either killed or spaced during the hull breach. I was just told we have six medical transports inbound with more than two hundred wounded humans and Prims from Intus." Dr. Michaels paused. "Are you evacuating the wounded from the planet already?" he asked. "We're not ready to receive them yet."

Trying to maintain her composure, McKee responded, "Dr. Michaels, we have thousands of soldiers down on the surface battling the Zodarks for hours. Many of them require trauma care. They're inbound, and you're going to treat them."

She then cut off the transmission, not wanting to argue with him further. He had a job to do, and so did she.

Chapter Four
New Allies

Planet Altairius

After months of traveling across the galaxy, Rear Admiral Miles Hunt and his small entourage had finally arrived in Altairius, the Altairian home world and the center of the Galactic Empire.

Hunt stood in awe of the beauty of this new planet, admiring the view from the windows on the observation deck of the ship. In orbit around Altairius were several orbital stations and space elevators, while hundreds of smaller commercial spacecraft darted between the stations and the planet below. The planet had several vast continents surrounded by bodies of water. Even from space, one could see massive cities dotting the coasts of the continents.

"It's beautiful, isn't it, Miles?" Lilly asked as she wrapped her arms around her husband.

He smiled as he turned his head to his wife. "It sure is, but not nearly as beautiful as you."

Lilly blushed. "Oh wow. That was cheesy, mister. Tell me you didn't stay up all night working on that one," she joked as she poked him in the ribs.

Miles chuckled. "Oh, I was up all night all right, but it wasn't working on some corny joke," he joked back.

Lilly shook her head and laughed, then suddenly turned very serious. "I suppose this is the part of the trip where you'll be gone a lot?" she inquired softly.

Miles squeezed her as he replied, "I think so, but I'll do my best to keep that to a minimum if at all possible. I also talked with Handolly about the spouses on board. He's arranging for some day trips and other activities for everyone. It's part of their cultural exchange program." Hunt couldn't completely conceal a hint of jealousy at the spouses' itineraries—touring the Altairian worlds sounded like more fun than his schedule.

"What will you be doing while I'm gone?" Lilly inquired as she stared out the viewing window.

Miles shrugged his shoulders. "Probably drinking from a firehose. It sounds like us Earthers have a lot of catching up to do if we're going to be a serious spacefaring species and member of this Galactic Empire."

Lilly kissed him on the cheek. "I'm sure you'll do fine," she responded.

The two of them stood there taking in the view a little longer before going back to their room to pack their few belongings in preparation to leave the ship.

****

A few hours later, Hunt stood next to Handolly as they prepared to teleport to the surface, the transportation method preferred by the Altairians over shuttles or space elevators. Hunt mentally prepared himself to spend the next few days being awed by the Altairian technology and advancements.

Though he did have some doubts about the new alliance, he kept them to himself. He'd had to prioritize preserving his species and their way of life. Despite many attempts to speak with the Zodarks, the only peace terms the Zodarks would agree to were Earth's complete surrender. That wasn't something Miles or the human race could ever accept.

When Hunt and Handolly materialized on the surface, they appeared in a promenade or gathering place. Hunt was taken aback, for the first time seeing multiple races of aliens walking about freely like it was normal for many alien races to interact and live amongst each other.

Handolly saw the astonishment on Hunt's face. "It is different to witness so many races in person. It is a lot different than seeing them in videos and pictures, is it not?" he asked in his normal emotionless, formal way of speaking.

Hunt didn't respond right away. He just nodded slightly. He found himself watching, and then staring at, an unfamiliar type of alien. It had a long face with large lavender eyes that had catlike black pupils. It didn't have any hair. Instead, its skin appeared reptilian, covered in what weren't scales but were more like a tough, leathery version of a lizard's skin. The alien stood roughly the height of a shorter human and scurried past him like it hadn't even noticed him.

Without any eyelids, it was always hard to tell Handolly's mood, but Hunt thought he detected a hint of amusement in his voice as he explained, "That is a Prodigal. They are a trading race. Terrible warriors, but exceptional traders and shipbuilders. They are actually the species building your new flagship right now."

Miles just shook his head. Everything here was so different, so foreign to everything he'd known up to this point.

"Come this way, Miles. We have much more to show you," Handolly said as he escorted Hunt.

The two of them continued to walk across the promenade until they came to the entrance of a building several hundred meters tall. Despite the height of the building, it was still tiny in comparison to the buildings surrounding it. Miles used to think the towering buildings of New York City were big—these buildings dwarfed those. They went right up into the clouds.

Hunt and Handolly came upon two doors that were three meters wide and ten meters high. Several guards inside the building snapped to attention as Handolly approached. Once inside, Miles's eyes went wide as saucers. He barely kept his jaw from falling to the floor. On either side of the interior walls were enormous columns made of marble or a similar material. It reminded him of ancient Greek columns he'd seen in pictures. The bases of the columns stood at least a meter tall and two meters wide before the columns reached up to the ornate ceiling, reminiscent of a baroque exhibit Miles had studied in a museum back on Earth. The columns reached at least fifty meters to the ceiling and the decorated arch beams that held the ceiling up.

Realizing that in his moment of awe, Handolly had strolled ahead of him, Hunt walked briskly after him to catch up. The long corridor continued for over a hundred meters before it opened into an even larger room.

"Handolly, what is this place?" Hunt asked in wonder as he continued to take in everything around him. Periodically, he spotted a door or two between the columns, presumably leading off to another room.

Handolly turned to his human guest as he replied, "This place, Miles, is our palace: the seat of government for the Galactic Empire." He paused before adding, "The rooms you see on the sides are offices for different departments in the GE. The room we are about to enter is the Grand Hall. It is where we host celebrations and parties for Galactic Empire members."

Hunt let out a soft whistle as they entered the Grand Hall. "What are we doing here?" he asked.

The two of them walked over to what Hunt assumed to be an elevator. "I am taking you to your first Galactic Empire meeting," Handolly said as he gestured for Hunt to get on the platform.

Moments later, the glass tube moved skyward. As they moved up, the tube lifted out of the lower portion of the building, giving them a full panoramic view of the city as they traversed upward.

When they reached their destination, Hunt had to chuckle when he heard a chiming sound before the door opened. *Millions of light-years away, and elevators still make a familiar ding when you reach your floor*, he thought. *I guess some things transcend species.*

The two of them walked off the elevator and down the corridor, which was equally grand as the corridor on the ground floor. They eventually came to the entrance of a large room at the end of the hall. As they approached the door, Hunt heard voices—many types of voices speaking many languages. Then he saw a large round table in the center of the room.

As soon as they entered, everyone stood and acknowledged Handolly. They then collectively turned and eyed Hunt skeptically. He was, after all, the new alien species: the unknown human.

Handolly introduced Hunt to twenty new races of species Hunt hadn't known existed. They all talked at him in their own languages, leaving Hunt to wonder what they were saying. A second later, an Altairian walked up to him with a small autoinjector device.

"Do not be afraid," the Altairian said calmly. "I am going to inject a universal translator into your inner ear. It will allow you to understand everything that is being said."

Before Hunt could ask a question or protest, the Altairian had placed the device next to his right ear and injected something into it. A second later, the process was repeated in his left ear.

Hunt could hear the people sitting around the table clearly now. A few of them laughed at his realization that he could now understand them. A few others grumbled, annoyed that their meeting was held up to greet an inferior species that was being allowed to join their alliance.

Turning to face Hunt, Handolly said loud enough for the others to hear, "Admiral Miles Hunt, this is the Galactic Empire war council. The council meets regularly to discuss the overall war effort and to coordinate our member objectives. It is through this coordinated effort that we have been able to hold the line against the Dominion. This," Handolly said as he pointed to an empty chair, "is where you will be seated. However, right now, you will accompany me to another room, where Bjork from the Primord Union and I will bring you up to speed on how the Galactic Empire operates, our enemy, the Dominion, and your species' function and position on the war council."

A couple of members seated at the table stood and walked over to greet Hunt before Handolly and Bjork walked with him to a room nearby. It was the first time Hunt had seen a Primord—Bjork looked almost human to him, with a few exceptions. He was approximately the same height and had the same number of limbs, with similar hands, but his ears were pointy, his nose was long and angled, and his skin had a light gold tint.

When Hunt and his two minders entered the room, they took a seat at a small circular table to talk.

Bjork was the first to speak once they sat down. "Do you prefer to be called by your military title, your given name, or your surname?"

Hunt smiled as he replied, trying to be as amicable as possible. "My friends call me Miles."

Bjork smiled. "I am glad the two of us can be friends. My name is Bjork Terboven. I am considered an admiral among my people, but for the purposes of the Galactic Empire, I currently serve as a senator on both the war and political councils."

"It sounds like you have a busy job," Miles commented.

Bjork shrugged his shoulders. "Being, as you would say, 'dual-hatted' allows me to know what is going on across the Alliance to better serve my people. You should consider doing the same. It will serve your people best."

"I will have to inquire about that," Miles replied. "It may not be my decision to make. There are those more senior than I am that may choose to place me elsewhere."

Changing the subject, Bjork asked, "Do you want to know why our tables are in the shape of circles?"

Miles tilted his head. "I don't think I had thought about that," he responded. "Please, tell me."

Bjork lifted his head up slightly. "The tables are circles to represent each of us as equals. When a species joins the Galactic Empire, they become equal within the Alliance. As you saw earlier, the Alliance has a war council. We also have a senate. Each species is required to send five representatives to serve in the senate. Three of the senators are required to be on Altairius to be a part of the senate while the other two are required to be back on their core worlds. This ensures both the core worlds and the senate are represented by the citizens of the Empire."

"Is there a leader in the senate?" Miles asked, genuinely curious. "Someone that ultimately governs the Galactic Empire?"

Bjork smiled briefly. "The senate elects a chancellor who serves as the governing head of the Galactic Empire. The chancellor's term of office is seven years. There are no term limits, though the chancellor needs to be reconfirmed by majority vote every seventh year unless a vote of no confidence is proposed. However, these are political questions you are asking, and what Handolly and I are here to talk with you about are military questions. The ambassador that accompanied you on the trip will handle the political aspects for the Galactic Empire for the humans unless you become dual-hatted like me."

Miles blushed slightly. "My apologies, Bjork. I'm sure Ambassador Nina Chapman will bring me up to speed on all of this at a later date. This is all new to me, and I'm just trying to do my best to understand. We humans have a saying on Earth, 'drinking from the firehose.' It means a person is taking in more information than they can absorb."

Bjork turned to Handolly. "Perhaps we should give him a knowledge injection," he suggested.

Turning to Miles, Handolly nodded. "I shall send for one."

"Whoa—what do you want to inject me with this time?" Miles countered in protest.

"Fear not, Miles," Bjork said cheerfully. "The Empire has studied and observed the human species for a long time. We know a great deal about your physiology and genetic makeup. We've extensively studied the human brain as well. It is actually an incredible neural network. Its ability to learn and absorb information is truly remarkable. The challenge you humans have with your brain is accessing instant recall of all the information you are continually absorbing.

"When your species employed neurolinks and some cybernetic implants like the ones you currently have, you more than doubled the intellectual ability of your species. However, what we are going to inject you with is a chemical compound that will allow you to absorb, analyze, and understand faster. We have a lot of information we need to impart to you, and not a lot of time to do it, I'm afraid."

A minute later, another Altairian with a small white case walked over to their table and opened it, pulling out a small autoinjector.

"I am going to inject a knowledge booster," the pale white alien explained emotionlessly. "It will not hurt, and its effects will be felt immediately." The Altairian placed the injector on the side of Miles's neck and pushed the button.

Miles didn't notice any effects from the knowledge booster immediately. They finished their meeting rather uneventfully. However, for the next two weeks, he was inundated with information about the Galactic Empire: the species that were a part of it, where they were all located, who they were battling, and everything there was to know about their adversary, the Dominion. It was a lifetime of information being fed to him in a short period of time. Had he not been given that knowledge booster shot, Miles knew he would have forgotten large chunks of it or been unable to absorb it as quickly.

After the incredible experience of the knowledge booster, Miles insisted that all the humans who had accompanied him on this journey be given it. Those five hundred and ten humans needed to absorb an enormous amount of information. Then they needed to be able to take that information back with them on the new human flagship currently under construction.

****

Standing on the observation deck, Miles and Ethan Hunt were transfixed by the image of the ship before them.

"It's enormous, isn't it, Dad?" Ethan commented.

Miles's son, Ethan, had agreed to come with him on this journey to the Altairian home world and capital of the Galactic Empire. It had given the two of them a significant amount of quality time together, and an opportunity to develop a new kind of adult-to-adult relationship while sharing in this incredible experience of traveling across the galaxy.

Miles had been learning more about the GE and the humans' new role within it. Meanwhile, Ethan had spent his time at the Altairians' equivalent to Space Command Academy or Command Staff War College. He had learned a lot about how the Altairians fought their starships, and how they maintained, repaired and built them.

Miles snapped out of the sea of thoughts that had been swirling through his head. "It sure is," he replied. "I just hope we can figure out how to build them ourselves, and that it won't take us years to train our people how to use them."

The Altairians and a few other species had given the Earthers a lot of new advanced technology. The trick had been getting that technology integrated into their society and having enough people who understood how to use it.

"I asked that question the other day at the Academy," said Ethan. "I was told the Altairians will be sending a training cadre to help us get our own schools up and running. What we really need is for everyone on Earth to get the knowledge booster, or maybe they can give us the ability to make it ourselves. I don't think it's possible to impart this level of sophisticated technology to our people without it. We just aren't as developed as a species as they are otherwise."

Miles nodded. "I agree, Ethan. I've spoken with Handolly about it as well. He agrees. They're going to program the medical replicators they're providing us with the ability to create the serum."

Miles shook his head in amazement. "I cannot believe it's been twelve years since we went to the Rhea system and discovered the Zodarks. Had we not done that, I don't know that the Altairians ever would have contacted us."

Ethan shrugged his shoulders. "I suppose; it does seem like a lifetime ago. Heck, I've only been an officer now for five years. I feel as if I've been in Space Command my entire life."

"Imagine how your old man feels," Miles said with a chuckle. "The technology changes I've seen in human space flight since I first joined to now would boggle your mind." Miles reached over and placed a hand on his son's shoulder. "I'm glad I get to experience this with you. For a little while, I wasn't sure if you'd come with me."

Ethan laughed at the comment. "You mean pass up a chance to travel millions of light-years to an alien capital to see dozens of new alien races? Yeah, like I would turn that opportunity down, Dad. I'm just glad you asked me."

The two laughed again as they continued to stare at Earth's newest warship: a gift from the Empire to the people of Earth.

Chapter Five
War of Consequences

Planet Intus
1st Orbital Assault Battalion

Private Paul "Pauli" Smith ripped open the meal ready to eat or MRE pouch and squirted its contents into his mouth.

Yum, spaghetti mush, Pauli thought sarcastically.

It took him five full mouthfuls to finish off the disposable pack. Pauli looked around and saw a patch of loose dirt near his foot. He grabbed the knife off his chest rig and tore at the dirt a bit, pulling some of it away with a gloved hand. He placed the empty food container in the hole and buried it. The pouch would degrade over time now that the inside of it had been exposed to oxygen.

"Hey, Pauli. You doing OK?" asked his battle buddy, Amy, her face covered in dirt and grime. Private Amy Boyles was one of the replacements to join his battalion after the battle to capture New Eden nearly two years ago. She was from Maine while he was from Texas. Their accents made quite the pair, but the two of them had been assigned as battle buddies ever since her arrival.

"Yeah, I'm fine," said Pauli. "Any word from the sergeant on when we're pulling out of this place?"

Following the initial assault to the surface, their battalion hadn't seen any action. They'd been tasked with pulling perimeter security for an engineering battalion building an airstrip and a series of large hangars and storage facilities. As far as Pauli was concerned, that suited him just fine.

Amy shook her head. "Not yet. Maybe we'll get lucky and get to pull garrison duty in that Zodark fort the Deltas captured or here at this airbase the engineers are building."

Pauli shook his head. "I wish, but not likely. The 1st OAB is a combat unit, filled with the best warriors from across the Republic. The brass would never let us be relegated to garrison duty."

"Best warriors from across the Republic," Amy said sarcastically with a laugh. "You know you sound just like Major Monsoor, don't you?"

Walking up to their position, their squad leader Sergeant Travis Atkins barked, "Hey, enough with the chatter. We're pulling out in five mikes. Grab your gear and get ready to saddle up."

Sergeant Atkins was a bit salty after getting demoted a grade. When the militaries of Earth had re-formed into the new Republic Army, a major streamlining of the NCO and officer rank structures had taken place. Some folks had been promoted while others had been demoted to fit within the new structure.

Staff Sergeant Atkins had found himself demoted to sergeant when his grade and the grade above his were eliminated. The new rank structure for the ground pounders consisted of private, corporal, sergeant, master sergeant, sergeant major. That meant four previous enlisted ranks had been removed. Not only was Atkins pissed about being demoted back to sergeant, a *lot* of lower enlisted were ticked about being demoted back to private. The officers hadn't fared much better, having lost several of their own grades. However, the officers were still paid better, and now fewer grades meant it was going to be even harder to rise to the higher ranks.

"Help me up, Pauli," Amy asked as she finished attaching her rucksack to her shoulders.

Pauli reached his hand down and pulled her up. The two of them walked over to where the rest of the platoon had formed up.

In the distance, they could still see the smoldering ruins of the massive ion cannon as it towered high above the fortress surrounding it. The fort had taken a beating during the initial attack; an engineering battalion of construction Synths was hard at work repairing the place.

As they approached the rest of the soldiers in their unit, Pauli spotted their captain. Captain Trubinsky had climbed up on a rock so he could be seen by everyone as he addressed them.

"Listen up!" Captain Trubinsky bellowed. "The major has been given a mission, which means *we've* been given a mission. In thirty mikes, we will be picked up by some Ospreys. They'll ferry us eighty klicks to a Primord city the brass wants us to help the Prims liberate.

"Fleet intelligence says there's a Zodark base nearby. It was hit with a couple of orbital strikes during the initial invasion, so it's unknown how many Zodarks may still be in the area. Fortunately for us, we're only responsible for clearing the surrounding area of Zodarks while the Prims liberate the city. In addition to the Prim units we'll be working with, a C100 battalion is on standby to assist us in clearing any heavy Zodark resistance."

The captain surveyed the soldiers in front of him before adding, "Our platoon leaders and sergeants will brief you on the rest of the details. First OAB, this is our chance to get in the fight—let's not let the major or the Prims down. Hooah!"

"Hooah!" came the single-word reply.

The captain hopped down from his perch and walked over to a large clearing not far from them. A squadron of Reapers and troop transports were arrayed in nice neat rows, their mechanics and ordnance technicians crawling over them.

"Come on. Let's go, Pauli," Amy said nonchalantly as she trotted to the makeshift flight line.

Forty minutes later, the Osprey lifted off the ground and flew over the ruined fortress. From above, Pauli could see how heavily fought over this place had been. He'd heard rumors a company of Deltas had been nearly wiped out by an enemy air attack during the assault. He hadn't even known the Zodarks had close-in air support. If a company of augmented superhuman soldiers could be wiped out, he thought nervously, how was a company of regular human soldiers like them going to fare?

As Pauli flew over the forest, he appreciated the beauty of this planet—at least the part of it he'd seen. It reminded him of an old classic movie from a hundred years ago called *Avatar*. The trees on Intus reminded him of the ones he'd seen on New Eden, but they were even more spectacular. There were a host of unique birds and flying creatures that flew above the trees. In the distance was a mountain range, which was impressive to say the least. It spanned many miles to the north and tapered off as it ran south. Near the tops of the mountain was snow, which he had never seen on another planet before.

I wonder what's on the other side of that mountain range, thought Pauli.

The Ospreys, packed full of soldiers, flew on for about thirty minutes. Just as the soldiers in Pauli's squad were starting to relax, the pilots flying them to this Prim city suddenly dove the transport toward the ground and picked up speed. Pauli had flown in many assault transports before, so he wasn't alarmed by the sudden movement. He figured they must be getting closer to the objective, so the pilot was just trying to wake them up and come in nice and low.

"Oh my God!" yelled someone as they pointed out the window to something a few hundred meters to the left.

By the time Pauli swung his head over to see what they were getting all excited about, the Osprey carrying part of the Fourth Platoon and their captain was blown apart. A string of red laser bolts shredded the craft before it could get out of the way. Then red lightning bolts slashed out toward their own Osprey, zipping through the air where they had just been moments before.

"Hold on!" one of the pilots shouted over their helmet radios.

The door gunner seated behind the pilot fired his weapon wildly at some unseen enemy, probably just trying to let whoever was shooting at them know they could fire back.

"Over there!" yelled another soldier.

A split second later, an F-97 Orion zipped right over their heads, laser cannons blazing away. In the distance, they saw an explosion and then a fireball descending to the ground below. The Orion starfighter banked to the north and fired another string of laser shots at another unseen enemy.

The soldiers in the Osprey held on for dear life as the pilots made wild dives and course corrections. Red laser bolts zipped past and around them as the pilots deftly maneuvered out of the way.

These pilots must be pretty damn good, thought Pauli. He had no idea how the guy had managed to evade so many laser bolts.

The ground below them was rapidly approaching as the pilots continued to drop altitude. A voice in their helmets yelled, "We're going to set down fast and hard. Once we're on the ground, everyone out!"

At that moment, Pauli didn't care how far away they were from the objective. He just wanted to get off this flying contraption before they got blown up. At least on the ground, they had a fighting chance. Up here, their lives were in the hands of the pilots and blind luck.

The Osprey leveled out; dirt and chunks of trees flew into the air around them as several laser bolts plastered the ground around them. The pilot pulled up hard on the nose, bleeding off their speed in seconds.

Pauli watched a black object zip past them as it turned to the left and climbed. A second later, several streaks of light flew out after the enemy fighter, and it fell to the ground in a fiery wreck as their Osprey landed on the ground with a hard thud.

"Everyone out!" yelled the crew chief to the rattled soldiers.

Pauli twisted the harness clip, releasing the straps holding him in place, and bailed out of the Osprey. The rest of his squad was out moments later, and the pilots applied power to the engines and got the hell out of there.

Lying in some thick grass with his rifle pointed in front of him, Pauli glanced at his HUD with a sigh of relief. The display wasn't showing any ground threats near them. The sky above them was still roaring with high-altitude dogfights, but the ground around them appeared to be safe.

"Everyone up! We're going to rally on the lieutenant's position and continue on with the mission," barked their sergeant.

Pauli noticed Amy appeared a bit rattled. "Hey, it's OK. We made it. We're on the ground now."

Amy gave him a sheepish smile. "That was close, Pauli. Fourth Platoon didn't have a chance."

Pauli shrugged as he walked, following their sergeant. "That's how it is, Amy. When it's your time, it's your time, and nothing's going to stop that."

Amy trotted to catch up to him. She was a good five inches shorter than him. His long legs allowed him to take some big strides.

As the two squads of soldiers walked behind their sergeant, no one really said much. They were all a little numb from their near-death experience. Half the platoon was technically cherries, replacements from the losses the battalion had taken on New Eden. This was their first experience in combat, and it rattled the new soldiers to see how quickly their lives could be snuffed out. It reinforced how fragile life really was in the grand scheme. One minute you're alive; the next, you're dust before you even knew what happened.

Amy saddled up next to Pauli as the two squads folded out into a loose wedge formation. "Is this what it was like on New Eden?" she asked.

Pauli barely turned his head to face her. "Hey, watch your pacing, Amy. Don't bunch up."

"I'm just trying to ask a question," she shot back as she slowed her pace to create some distance between the two of them.

They were regular Republic Army soldiers, so they didn't have neurolinks like the Special Forces or senior military officers had. They had to communicate the old-fashioned way, by talking.

They walked for a little longer, until they came to a clearing and linked up with the rest of their platoon. The lieutenant told them to take five while he and their sergeant figured out where the rest of the company was and who was in charge since the captain had been killed.

Amy sat down next to Pauli. "Sorry about back there. I shouldn't have bunched up on you like that."

Pauli sighed. He wasn't mad; he just didn't want to get smoked by a Zodark because his battle buddy wasn't following the standard operating procedures.

"It's OK, Amy. There's a reason we don't bunch up like that on patrols. If we present ourselves as an easy target, then chances are a Zodark will take a shot at us. I'd rather not give them any more reason to shoot at me than I have to."

With eyes full of fear, Amy asked, "What was it like on New Eden? You know, when you first landed."

Pauli snorted at her persistence. She'd asked him that a few times, and each time, he'd found a way to change the subject. It wasn't something he liked to think about.

"Let's just say this has been a cakewalk so far. Hopefully, it'll stay that way," Pauli said as he fidgeted with his rifle.

"I don't think the Deltas would describe it as a cakewalk," she countered.

Pauli took his helmet off when he saw some of the others do the same. He ran his hand through his closely cropped hair as he scratched at his scalp. "When we landed on New Eden, it was pure chaos. We lost half our platoon in the first five minutes. By the end of the day, there were only sixty-two of us left from the entire company. Sixty-two out of two hundred and sixty—it was a bloodbath. These Zodarks fight like animals. They're vicious, and they're fast as hell. When you see one, don't hesitate. Just pull the trigger and kill 'em, 'cause they won't waste a second trying to kill you."

Just then, their platoon sergeant, Master Sergeant Jason Dunham, walked over to a cluster of them. "Listen up, everyone. We're twenty-two clicks from the Prim city of Oteren. Intel says there's supposed to be a Zodark outpost somewhere in the vicinity. The fleeters hit the place with an orbital strike a few days ago, and the Orions paid them a visit earlier today. The latest intel we have is the contingent assigned to it bugged out of the base before all that happened, so they're supposedly held up in the foothills just north of the Oteren."

The lieutenant walked over at this point to join their platoon sergeant. He added, "We're going to move out on foot and link up with Charlie Company on the outskirts of the city. Tomorrow at 1200 hours, a Prim unit is going to be airlifted in to join us. They'll liberate the city while we patrol the foothills nearby and go Zodark hunting."

Many of the soldiers who hadn't fought the Zodarks yet nodded their heads excitedly. They were eager to get in the fight. The veterans like Pauli knew better.

Fourteen kilometers later, Pauli's dogs were killing him. He'd learned long ago that an infantryman had to take care of his feet. Pauli realized he wasn't doing a very good job of that, and his feet were letting him down as a consequence.

He hated ruck marches. Long treks across uneven terrain hauling a hundred pounds of gear and weapons weren't exactly his idea of a fun time. Throw in an unknown number of Zodark soldiers somewhere out there in the dark on a foreign planet more than a hundred light-years from home, and Pauli was really hating life right now.

He tried to recall what that Delta operator had told him back on New Eden. *Embrace the suck, soldier*, he remembered. *Well, this sucks—no two ways about it.*

Gazing into the sky, Pauli lost himself in the beauty of the two moons. One was a little more than halfway into the sky, the other appeared to be a little further away, just above and behind the first. The largest one had a bluish-purple tint to it, while the smaller one that was further away was more reddish in color. It was a strange contrast. He wished he could snap a picture of it and send it to his folks back home.

Pauli found himself wondering if humans would ever be allowed to settle down on Intus after the war. *This place is really beautiful*, he thought.

"Everyone down!" came an urgent voice over their helmet communication system.

Pauli didn't hesitate. He hit the dirt just in time to see dozens of red laser bolts reach right out for him. The bright flashes of light zipped over his head and body, right where he had been just seconds earlier.

"Contact, eleven o'clock!" shouted someone a little further ahead of Pauli.

Pauli flicked his selector switch off safety, then fired a handful of blaster shots at whoever was firing at them. Meanwhile, one of his friends crawled up to his right with their M90 squad automatic weapon. He set up the SAW and opened up where the enemy fire was coming from.

As the two of them were shooting, their HUDs displayed threats to their front and to their left side. Pauli searched for his battle buddy, Private Amy Boyles.

"Boyles! Get the hell up here," he yelled to be heard over the growing roar of the battle.

A few seconds later, when she hadn't joined him, Pauli turned around to see what the problem was. He found her curled up in a fetal position, screaming and crying as laser bolts flew over her head. Pauli stopped shooting and crawled over to her. He pulled his face up close to hers. "Amy, snap out of it," he said calmly but forcefully. "I need you to remember your training and help return fire."

Amy opened her eyes when she heard his familiar voice. She seemed to calm down a bit, and she finally relented and nodded her head.

"Amy, it's OK to be scared, but I need you to follow my lead," Pauli said. "I need you to grab your rifle and crawl over there with the rest of our fire team. The enemy is a few hundred meters away from us in that tree line over there." Pauli pointed to where he wanted her to fire.

When she nodded again, he turned around and crawled back to the rest of the fire team.

When Pauli reached the firing line, Corporal Yogi Sanders grunted. "Pauli, when Amy gets over here, we need to bound forward and take up a flanking position in that cluster of trees over there," he directed, pointing to a position a hundred meters to the left.

"We're on it," Pauli responded.

Private Rob Anders, who was operating the SAW, sustained a near-constant barrage of fire on the enemy positions. The SAW sliced through small trees and ripped the area apart. As Rob laid into the enemy, Amy crawled over to Pauli and tried to explain her sudden breakdown.

Pauli waved it off. "I need you to stay low and follow me while Rob continues to keep their heads down," he directed.

Pauli and the three others ran while keeping their heads low to the edge of the tree line. While they were making their move, the squad nearest the Zodarks continued to lay down suppressive fire at the enemy while another squad flanked the Zodarks on the opposite side. If the squads positioned themselves correctly, they'd form an L-shaped formation enclosing the Zodarks. Then they'd be able to cut them apart with the crossfire.

As they moved closer to the tree line, Pauli's HUD showed more and more of the enemy markers winking out. By the time his fire team had gotten in position, there were only two Zodarks left shooting at them. They broke contact and ran deeper into the woods.

"Everyone, stand down," the lieutenant ordered. "Stay where you are and stay frosty. We're going to get some drones up and see if that's all of them or if there are more in the area we haven't accounted for."

Crouching next to a tree, Pauli scanned the area around them. The little radar unit built into their smart helmets and HUDs was good at identifying threats as far out as two thousand meters, depending on how thick the vegetation was. When the AI was able to link and share its own image and data with the rest of the platoon, it really created a good picture of their surroundings.

Pauli turned to his battle buddy. "You all right, Amy?" he asked.

She didn't say anything at first, her eyes hidden behind her HUD. Her voice quivered. "I think so."

Five minutes later, their lieutenant told them the drones showed the area was clear. The two Zodarks appeared to have gotten away. The lieutenant didn't have their drones pursue them. He ordered them to set up a perimeter around their positions for the time being.

As they walked back to where the rest of the platoon was, Pauli confronted Yogi. "Hey, what the heck? Why didn't the LT have our scout drones up earlier? They should have spotted that ambush before it happened."

Yogi shrugged his shoulders. "Probably because most of our scout drones got zapped with the captain and half of the Fourth Platoon. You know that platoon carries our heavy weapons and scout drones. He probably wanted to conserve the few we had left for the Prim city."

That...is actually a good reason, Pauli realized. He hadn't considered that. Master Sergeant Atkins had probably told the LT to conserve the drones.

Atkins was one of the veterans from New Eden. Pauli didn't particularly like the guy, not since Atkins had passed him up for corporal, but Atkins was a solid NCO. He knew his stuff.

By the time they got back to the platoon area, they could see the sun rising. Third Platoon had moved to their position, and so had First Platoon. Their platoon was now going to pull rear security for the company.

A group of soldiers ahead stood in the two-lane road, staring down at a body. Pauli went over to see who it was. As he got closer, he saw a pool of blood had formed on the road. When he saw the dead soldier's face, Pauli recognized him as one of the cherries. He'd joined their platoon fresh from basic training a few weeks before they'd headed to Intus.

Pauli shook his head. The poor cherry hadn't had a chance. The blaster shot had hit him in the neck and torn a big chunk out of it. Pauli hoped he had died from the shot and not drowned in his own blood.

Walking back to his fire team, he found Amy and motioned for her to follow him. When they got closer to the dead soldier, Amy slowed down. He reached over and grabbed her arm, giving her a good yank, pulling her to him so she could see the body.

He leaned in close so only the two of them could hear. "This is what happens when you freeze up, Amy," he said strongly. "This could have been me, or anyone else in our fire team. You can't freeze up like that; you can't start crying and go into the fetal position either. People die because of mistakes. People die because they're in the wrong place at the wrong time. You need to stick to your training and listen. Do as you're told and kill the enemy as soon as you see them. Got it?"

Shock and terror covered Amy's face. She nodded silently. The lesson had been learned, and she wouldn't soon forget it.
****

Hatteng City, Intus
Third Army – Second Expeditionary Group

The greenish waters along the edge of the city glimmered in the morning light. It was a beautiful contrast to the glass skyscrapers and the emerald-green tree-covered mountains to the west of Hatteng City, the capital of Intus.

Before the capture of the planet by the Zodarks, it had boasted a population of thirty-two million residents. The Prims estimated the population to be closer to half of that after the occupation.

The Prims and the Earthers had liberated the city on the second day of the campaign. It was a big day for the Prims and the remaining residents. Millions of people had come out to greet their liberators and celebrate the end of the Zodark reign of terror.

The Prims and Earthers had also lucked out when the Zodarks opted to retreat into the mountains and densely forested areas nearby and not take the fight to the streets. They were thankful for no civilian casualties in any of the cities they'd liberated. Instead, the Zodarks had methodically retreated into the countryside, areas of the planet that were a lot more defensible than the cities. It was going to make rooting them out a lot tougher.

General Ross McGinnis gazed out the floor-to-ceiling windows on the eighty-seventh floor of his army headquarters. It gave him an excellent view of the city and the mountains off in the distance. He knew the Prims were moving a large ground force into those mountains to dig the Zodarks out. This was the part of war that was always the hardest, searching for an enemy that decided to fade away into the countryside rather than stand and fight.

"General, you really shouldn't be up here," said one of McGinnis's aides. "At least not until the Prims have made sure the city is fully under our control."

General McGinnis turned to the young captain and nodded. "I know, I couldn't resist the opportunity to see the mountains with my own eyes." He sighed. "Let's head back to the bunker."

The two of them made their way to the basement of the building, which had been turned into a temporary command center. As they entered, General McGinnis scanned the cavernous space, impressed with how quickly his staff had turned the place into a fully functional command center. They had only captured the city a day ago. In the short time they'd occupied the basement of this massive building, his staff had already tricked out the place with computer screens, cabling, and operators manning the various terminals.

The general spotted the large map table and walked over to it. In the center of the table sat a large holographic terminal, which currently displayed a floating image of the planet surrounded by an enormous fleet of starships in orbit. Hundreds of smaller ships headed down to the surface, while others were flying back to the fleet.

It was a massive undertaking, capturing a planet. Once the fleet had cleared the area of enemy warships, the Primords had begun the painstaking process of retaking what had been a colonial world of theirs for the past three hundred years. The Prims were offloading more than a million ground soldiers to help fight the remaining Zodarks scattered throughout the planet.

"General, Brigadier General Lucia said to inform you that his entire division has deployed to the surface along with their equipment," said one of McGinnis's staff officers. "He's asking for orders. What would you like me to tell him?"

"Pull up a map of the area where they are," General McGinnis ordered.

A map display of the Prim district Oteren appeared. Eighty kilometers from the district capital stood one of the ion cannon fortresses. The area surrounding the orbital defense weapon had been turned into a gigantic military encampment now. A battalion of engineers had built a large airbase to support the hundreds of Ospreys and Orion starfighters brought down from the heavy transports in orbit.

Further away from the military encampment and closer to the Prim district capital, a string of red icons was displayed along the foothills and in the forested area a few kilometers west of the city, representing the known enemy positions.

McGinnis turned to his operations officer. "Tell General Lucia to deploy his battalions as he sees fit to secure the district and support the Prim operations."

The operations officer nodded. "Should we provide him with any special instructions on how to use the C100 battalions that are arriving?"

McGinnis paused for a second as he thought about that. During the first few days of the invasion, they had taken a lot of casualties. At this point in the operation, he wanted to find a way to prevent further losses if at all possible.

"Instruct him to use his C100s as often as possible when carrying out direct attacks on a large Zodark force to reduce the casualties in the campaign," McGinnis directed. "I want him to integrate the C100s into the fight a lot more than they have been."

The operations officer nodded in acknowledgment He instructed his staff to disseminate the new instructions to the various division commanders. At this point, they were four days into the campaign, and they'd already offloaded four of the ten divisions they'd brought to Intus.
****

Oteren, Intus
1st Orbital Assault Battalion

Pauli reviewed the contents of his MRE #17: beefsteak with gravy and mushroom sauce. Amy walked over and dropped down next to him. "Hey, you want to swap meals?" she asked. "I got cheese tortellini."

Pauli raised an eyebrow at the suggestion and proceeded to open up the freshly warmed beefsteak packet. After a long night of marching, he was particularly hungry. He had opted to eat one of his large MREs as opposed to the smaller squeeze pouches he ate to tide him over when he was hungry.

"You know, Amy, the tortellini isn't so bad if you heat it up," Pauli replied. "It comes with a disposable heater."

"I know it does, I just don't like the smell it makes when it's heating up the food," Amy remarked.

"Damn, girl. Beggars can't be choosy," Pauli said with a chuckle. "You should count yourself lucky we can use the heaters. When we first landed on New Eden, we didn't know much about the Zodarks or the equipment they used at the time. For all we knew, the heaters could have shown up on some thermal equipment, so we had to eat these things cold when we were out on patrol."

Amy stuffed a forkful of cold tortellini in her mouth, trying to hide her obvious disdain for the dish. "Pauli, what did you think of those C100s?" she asked. "I thought they were a myth until I saw them with my own eyes."

"Why would you think that?" Pauli asked, left eyebrow raised skeptically. "You've been in the battalion for nearly two years. We've been using C100s for a while now."

"Duh, they don't exactly talk about that stuff back on Earth," Amy said, defending herself. "I hadn't even seen a photo of one of them until a week ago during the briefing before we landed here."

Pauli shook his head. "Wow, Ames. Sorry, I really thought people from back home would know a bit more about what's going on out here."

Amy snickered. "How long have you been gone from Earth, Pauli?" she pressed.

Holding the last of his beefsteak in front of his mouth, Pauli answered, "Um…four years, I think."

"Damn, that's a while. How much time do you have left on your enlistment?" Amy prodded.

"How long do you have?" Pauli countered.

"You know that's a sore subject with us draftees," Amy remarked.

Pauli knew the answer. He just liked to poke fun at the draftees. If someone got drafted, they were selected for the duration of the war—just like back in World War II, one hundred and fifty years ago. When it had been learned that this space war Earth now found itself a part of never really ended, the draft board had put a ten-year service requirement on all draftees. Since space was so infinitely vast and it could take a long time to move from one battle to another, a shorter term didn't really make sense.

Pauli chuckled. "I've got one year and one month left," he answered. "Then my six-year enlistment is done."

"Are you going to reenlist or get out?" Amy was eyeing him inquisitively as she finished off her MRE.

Pauli just shrugged his shoulders and pursed his lips. "I honestly hadn't thought about it much. I've been just trying to make it one day at a time. I figure when I get closer to that time, I'll make a decision."

"What's to think about Pauli?" Amy asked. "If I were you, I'd get out. You got a Bronze Star with V device on New Eden. You've done your part. Go back to the real world and live your life. Find a woman, get married, have kids—you know, like regular people."

Pauli finished his beefsteak and stuffed the empty pouch into the main MRE bag. He grabbed his packet of jalapeño cheese spread and put a generous gob of the mixture on several crackers before replying. "Amy, I know you may not see it yet, but what we're doing matters. If we don't fight these Zodarks out here," Pauli said as he waved his crackers and cheese about, "then we'll end up fighting them at home. Besides, by being in the Army, I've now seen two alien worlds and a couple of moons.

"I'm twenty-three years old, Amy. I've seen more in my nearly five years with the Army than most people will ever get to see in their entire lives. I don't know if I'm ready to go back home to Texas. I may just reenlist or see if I can try out for Delta and make the military a career."

Amy shook her head in disbelief. "If we survive the next year, Pauli, you should get out. I know we're doing good work out here, but you'll have done your time. There are millions of people like me, drafted to serve a ten-year hitch. Heck, you should see if you could get a residency card to live on New Eden or Alpha—start fresh on a new planet and live out the rest of your days in peace."

"Hey, listen up, everyone!" barked their platoon sergeant, Master Sergeant Atkins, as he signaled for everyone to form a half-circle around him. The man had a thick Georgian accent that sometimes made it hard for those from the Northeastern US, Great Britain or Canada to understand.

Pauli and Amy stood up, falling in with everyone else as they waited to hear what was going on.

"Captain Hiro is going to take over command of the company," announced Atkins. "He'll still be nominally in charge of us, but I'm going to run things until we get a replacement officer. As you all saw, the C100s pushed ahead of us yesterday. They're circling around the city and into the foothills to flush the Zodarks out. In an hour, a Prim unit is going to land near our positions. They'll take the lead in liberating the city. We've been ordered to follow the C100s as they sweep through the forest on the northwestern edge of the city. Get your gear sorted and be ready to move once the Prims arrive."

With their new instructions, the soldiers went back to their areas and packed their patrol packs and rucks. Now that they'd been in the field for three days, their packs were a little lighter as they'd consumed a good portion of the food they'd brought with them. Pauli figured he was still good for another three days before he'd need a resupply.
****

Two hours later, the Prims finally arrived...late, but par for the course when it came to the military.

Pauli stood next to a tree, watching the Prim soldiers as they disembarked their transport craft. The transports were massive and relatively quiet for a large space-capable flying contraption; Pauli admired the design. The Prims' transports were a lot cleaner and leaner than anything Pauli had seen up to that point. The Prims used a different type of propulsion system than their human allies. It allowed them to hover and take off at extraordinary speeds. Pauli loved to see the technology and equipment of another alien species.

Amy poked him in the ribs. "You know what those Prims look like?" she asked with a mischievous grin.

Pauli turned his head slightly toward her, caught off guard by the question. "What?" he asked.

"The Prims. You know what they look like to me?"

Pauli shrugged and shook his head. He didn't care what they looked like so long as they knew how to fight.

"They look like elves with those pointy ears," she commented with a smile, almost like it was some sort of inside joke.

Pauli snorted at the reference. "Yeah, except for those long pointy noses. I don't think they look like elves—maybe more like Vulcans from that new version of *Star Trek*. But those noses, though, they throw all the dimensions off for me with elves."

"Whatever. They look like elves to me," Amy said as she turned to go chat with another friend who probably agreed with her assessment of what they looked like.

Standing alone now that Amy had left, Pauli continued to stare at the newcomers. He'd never seen a Prim in person before. He knew this was a Prim world, though, a colony that had been in their control for more than three hundred years.

Three hundred years...humans haven't even been a spacefaring society for half that time, thought Pauli. It still astonished him to think that there were dozens of species out there in the galaxy now allied with humans who'd been traveling the stars for thousands of years.

"Hey, Pauli. Master Sergeant wants to see you," called Corporal Yogi Sanders, his fire team leader.

"Thanks, Yogi. I'll go see what he wants," Pauli replied. He turned around and headed off to find their platoon sergeant. It took a few minutes to track him down. When Pauli walked up to him, he noticed Atkins was no longer wearing his master sergeant chevrons. He had a silver bar on his uniform.

"Ah, there you are, Private Smith," Atkins said. "Lieutenant Hiro was just promoted to captain by the major. For some unknown reason, Major Monsoor decided to make me an officer instead of one of the other platoon sergeants. I, in turn, needed a new platoon sergeant, so I promoted Sergeant Dunham. Dunham has seen fit to promote Yogi to take over the squad." Atkins paused for a second before he settled his gaze back on Pauli.

"Look, Pauli, you should've been promoted to corporal a long time ago. It was my recommendation that you be promoted instead of Yogi, but the lieutenant had other plans. Had Big Army not done this major reorg of our rank structure, you'd probably be a sergeant or staff sergeant by now.

"You're smart, you know how to soldier. You're cool as a cucumber under fire and you're a damn fine infantryman. I couldn't promote you when you should have been, but I'm promoting you to corporal now. You've earned it, and more than that, I'm proud of you. You will take over your fire team from Yogi. Continue to do a good job and help make sure these draftees don't get us all killed. OK?" Lieutenant Atkins reached into his patrol pack and pulled a pair of corporal chevrons out, handing them to Pauli to attach to his uniform.

Pauli stood there for a second, not sure what to say. He was a bit dumbfounded. "I, yes, sir. Thank you for the promotion, sir. I'll do my best not to let you down."

Smiling, Atkins extended his hand. "Welcome to the ranks of the noncommissioned officer, Pauli. You'll do fine. Now go find your squad and get ready to move out. Then send Yogi over to see me next."

As Pauli walked back to where his squad was set up, he attached his new rank to the center of his chest rig, his helmet, and the collars of his uniform blouse.

"Hey, hey. Look who just made corporal!" one of Pauli's squadmates announced. Everyone started walking up to Pauli, congratulating him on his promotion.

A few minutes later, Yogi joined them, wearing his new rank as well. He'd gone from corporal to sergeant.

Yogi motioned with his head for Pauli to walk with him. "Pauli, I know Amy's your friend and battle buddy, but you need to keep an eye on her," Yogi said quietly. "She needs to get it together. We can't have one of our soldiers freezing up like that. She'll get people killed."

Pauli nodded; he knew Yogi was right. It was now his responsibility to take care of the team. It had been different when she was just his battle buddy. Now, he was the fire team leader. He had eight soldiers to take care of.

Heck, Yogi has sixteen soldiers in the squad he's in charge of now, Pauli realized. It was a lot of responsibility. Pauli missed the days before the reorg. Back then, a squad had had six to ten soldiers. They'd increased the sizes of the squads and platoons to increase the firepower and capability of the company and battalion-sized elements that would be deployed on the starships.

"I know, Yogi," Pauli responded. "She froze up during the ambush. I spoke with her about it, and she won't make the same mistake twice. I showed her the cherry that got dusted. I told her that could happen to her or the rest of us if she freezes up again. I'll keep an eye on her." Pauli paused for a second before asking, "What do we do if she can't hack it, though? I mean, not everyone is cracked up to be in the infantry."

Pauli had known Yogi since they'd left Earth, headed for New Eden. He was one of the original soldiers that had deployed with the unit to become a true forward-deployed space force.

Yogi shrugged. "I honestly don't know. If she truly can't cut it, then maybe Atkins will be able to get her transferred to a rear unit, or maybe a non-combat job. All I know is we need everyone in the squad able to fight. We can't have someone unable to pull their weight, putting all our lives at risk. You remember what happened when Pitaki lost it back on New Eden. Half our old squad got smoked when that dickhead lost his nerve—the bastard just dropped his rifle and ran."

Yogi spat on the ground in contempt at the memory. Private Pitaki had been positioned on the far-left side of their flank during one of the last battles on New Eden. When the Zodarks had attacked, he'd lost it. Half a dozen Zodarks had penetrated the part of their lines Pitaki had been guarding, killing eight of their platoonmates before they'd been stopped. They had found Pitaki many hours later, naked and curled up in a ball next to a tree, crying.

"Let's head back, Yogi. We have to get everyone ready to move," Pauli finally said, ending the conversation.

By now, the Prim unit was on the move. They were advancing on the city, which was still four or five kilometers away. Everyone hoped the Zodarks had truly abandoned it and not left a trail of booby traps in their wake.

The radio in Pauli's helmet crackled to life. "This is Captain Hiro. We're moving out. First Platoon, take point. I'm sending the waypoints now. Unless we meet resistance, push on until we hit Waypoint Delta. We'll bivouac there for the night. Let's move."

"You heard the captain," echoed Lieutenant Atkins. "Let's roll. I want Third Squad on point."

"Let's go, people. We're taking point," Pauli announced to his fire team.

Pauli's usual point man walked in the direction their HUD guided them. The rest of the team fell in behind him. It took them a few minutes of moving before they got their spacing right. Pauli had them keep three to five meters of distance between them. He had no idea how many Zodarks were still out there, but one thing was clear—the enemy was in this forested foothill area. They just didn't know where or how many.

Two hours later, Pauli suddenly heard a series of explosions, followed by a lot of human and Zodark blaster fire off in the distance. It didn't sound close, but the fact that he could hear it meant it wasn't that far away either.

"Keep moving," Pauli said to his point man. He also changed their patrol formation, moving his fire team from a single-file formation to a wedge. He wanted them ready to lay down covering or suppressive fire if needed.

As they moved closer to the sounds of battle, Pauli's radio chirped. It was Lieutenant Atkins. "Sergeant Sanders, Corporal Smith, the C100s found an enemy encampment. That's what all that blaster fire in the distance is about. Captain Hiro has tasked our platoon with setting up a blocking force along this area."

A spot on the digital map was highlighted on their HUD. It was a few kilometers away and directly behind the enemy encampment the combat Synths were attacking.

"We're on it, sir," Yogi immediately replied.

"Good. Lead the way and find us a nice defensive position. We need to hurry, so don't dawdle. Atkins out."

Pauli told the rest of his fire team about what was happening and the change to their mission, and then he took the lead from his point man. It wasn't that he didn't trust the soldier or anything, Pauli just wanted to be the one to lead them for a bit.

As they approached the blocking position on the map, the sounds of the battle grew louder. It was clear the C100s were driving the Zodarks right to them.

"Here, I found a good spot for us to set up," Pauli announced over the platoon net.

In short order, the platoon fanned out along a copse of trees and boulders.

Pauli checked on his fire team and made sure they were ready for whatever was coming. Yogi walked up to the fallen tree Pauli had selected for himself to hide behind. "This is a good spot you found us, Pauli. Nice job."

Pauli smiled at the compliment. "Thanks. Now we just sit tight and wait to see if those Zodarks head our way or somewhere else," Pauli commented as he dropped his patrol pack against the base of the tree.

"Judging by the sound of things, I think those C100s are pushing right to us." Yogi paused for a moment before leaning down closer to him so no one else could hear him. "Pauli, I need you to keep an eye on Boyles, will you? Her little episode from the other day has a lot of people in the squad and platoon on edge. We can't have her spazzing out on us when those Zodarks get here."

Pauli nodded. "I get it, Yogi. I'll stay on it. Do you want me to place some of our mines out there before the Zodarks get any closer?"

Yogi shook his head. "No, I'm going to have Corporal Yance and a couple of soldiers from his team do it." He paused. "Hey, if those Zodarks do come our way, make sure your team doesn't open fire on them until they hit the mines, OK?"

Yogi then walked down the line to go talk with Corporal Yance and his fire team.

Pauli spotted Amy on his right, twenty meters further down the line. He sent a quick message through their HUD, telling her to set up closer to his position. He found a spot for her five meters away from him. He wanted to keep her close in case she needed help. He knew that sometimes a soldier under fire just needed some encouragement to know they'd be OK, and then they could push through their fear.

As the Zodarks and the Synths continued to battle it out, Pauli's platoon remained hidden in their positions and waited, hoping the

Zodarks might somehow bypass them or the C100s would finish them off.

The battle continued to rage on in the distance. It went on for an hour or two with little respite. Pauli wondered if there would be any Zodarks or C100s left when it was all said and done. He'd seen a handful of Reapers swoop in and plaster a few targets with some smart missiles and bombs. It was good to know they had some air power in the area.

While he was watching where the battle was taking place on his HUD, Pauli saw a warning pop up. It came from their scout drones. Lieutenant Atkins had positioned them about two kilometers in front of their lines—this would give them a heads-up if the Zodarks headed toward them. It appeared their little electronic tripwire had been tripped.

"Time to stay frosty, everyone," Lieutenant Atkins announced over the platoon net. "We've got Zodarks inbound. Call out your targets as you see them and don't let them slip past us."

Cranking his neck around, Pauli confirmed that everyone on the right flank was now pointing their weapons in the direction of the Zodarks. His squad was the anchor on the left flank for the company, and his fire team and platoon needed to hold the line or their entire position could get rolled up.

Pauli turned to Amy. "Ames, this is it. They're headed to us. I need you to stay calm and focused. Remember your training and stay in the fight. All right?"

Amy acknowledged with a nod, but her face betrayed her fear. He couldn't see her eyes as her HUD was active, but he could tell by the expression around her mouth that she was scared. Heck, he was scared too…but he needed her to do her part.

"Here they come!" came a voice over the radio.

Pauli didn't check to see who'd spoken; he just faced the direction his HUD told him the enemy was coming from. The HUD suddenly filled up with little red icons denoting Zodarks.

Holy crap! That's a lot of them heading our way, thought Pauli.

"Hold your fire until they get a little closer!" he shouted over his team channel. The enemy was still four or five hundred meters away. He wanted to wait until the Zodarks hit their landmines before they fired on them with their blasters.

Every soldier in the platoon carried a Claymore antipersonnel mine. These weren't the old-fashioned mines from the last century. These were fifth-generation Claymores—way more powerful and a whole lot more deadly.

The Zodarks moved at a good clip, utterly oblivious to the trap they were rushing into. When the first group of Zodarks hit the mines, explosions rocked the forest in front of their positions, blowing chunks of tree, underbrush, and parts of Zodarks in every direction.

"Open fire!" came the order from Lieutenant Atkins.

Pauli flicked his selector from safe to fire and opened up. The targeting AI on his HUD tracked a Zodark two hundred meters away. He sent a string of three or four blaster bolts right for the Zodark. His HUD indicated he'd scored a hit and was already guiding him to a new target to shoot at. Steadily, the count on his HUD dropped as the platoon tore into the enemy.

Just as he'd shifted fire to his third target, Pauli suddenly ducked as a string of blaster shots slammed into the fallen tree he was hiding behind. Chunks of the tree flew in the air as he rolled to a different position in case his cover didn't hold up. As Pauli returned fire, he noticed Amy once again paralyzed by fear. She wasn't moving, just staring at the Zodarks charging toward their position.

Pauli shook his head in anger, then crawled over to her position and pulled her down next to him. He dragged her closer until their helmets touched. "Amy, snap out of it! I need you to return fire. Let your HUD identify a target for you, aim at the target, and squeeze the trigger!"

Amy nodded her head and then rose above the fallen tree. She raised her rifle and fired a couple of shots, then a couple more. Then she was off to the races, firing as quickly as she could from one target to the next.

Pauli smiled to himself when he saw her get into a groove. *There, she just needed some encouragement*, he thought.

Just then, something overhead zipped right over the top of their positions. "Everyone down!" roared Yogi over the squad net.

Pauli dropped to the ground and pulled Amy down with him. A fraction of a second later, the entire world around them erupted in fire.

Even with a face shield covering his face, Pauli could feel the heat from the flames. Part of his clothes lit up, so did Amy's. Pauli immediately rolled on the ground and patted at the flames to put them out. He saw Amy doing the same and was relieved to see she wasn't freaking out. This wasn't the time to panic.

With the flames on their uniforms put out, Pauli scanned the scene and saw close to half the platoon was either dead or on fire. Many of them were putting out the flames just like he had, but many others were flailing their arms about wildly.

"Amy, I need you to grab the SAW and shoot at those bastards while I help a few of our guys out. We need to keep those Zodarks pinned down, or they'll overrun us!" Pauli yelled. He jumped up and ran over to a couple of soldiers who were panicking.

He grabbed one of the soldiers and threw him to the ground. He started putting out the fire with his gloved hands and threw some loose dirt on the flames. He then moved to the next soldier and did the same. A couple of soldiers ran over to help him while a few more joined Amy and returned fire at the Zodarks.

Pauli heard that hideous sound those Zodarks made when they charged. He knew they were about to get overrun if more of their company didn't get on the firing line. Pauli watched Amy sweep the SAW from right to left at the charging enemy—she was mowing them down, screaming like a wild animal as she did. Pauli felt proud of her in that moment; the warrior in her had finally come out.

"Get on the line! The Zodarks are charging!" Pauli yelled to be heard over the chaos happening all around them.

Pauli grabbed a wounded soldier who was moaning on the ground and practically dragged him up to a tree stump. Grabbing the soldier by his chest rig, Pauli pulled him close to his face. "I know you're hurt. We're all hurt. But those Zodarks are charging right for us. If they get in our lines, we're all dead. Keep firing, and don't stop!"

The wounded soldier just grunted and nodded. He brought his rifle to bear and fired single shots at the enemy.

By the time Pauli got back to his old firing position, he realized he was probably the only one left alive on the far-left side of the flank. His HUD identified more than twenty targets charging toward him.

Flicking the selector switch from blaster to 20mm grenade gun, Pauli fired round after round at the line of enemy soldiers until he'd expended the six-round magazine. Dropping the empty mag, he reached down, grabbed for a fresh one and slapped it in place. Pauli aimed and fired off the next six rounds at the charging horde, letting the smart AI determine when to detonate the charge to kill the most enemy soldiers possible.

Small pops of black smoke and shrapnel appeared in front of and intermixed within the Zodark lines. Many of the vicious blue aliens dropped to the ground while many more just shrugged off their injuries and continued to charge forward.

Crap, they're going to overrun my position! Pauli realized in horror.

"Amy, I need some help on this side!" Pauli shouted in hopes she might hear him.

Pauli kept squeezing the trigger, firing at the enemy. He saw several blaster bolts hit a Zodark, who went down, only to be replaced by another one. It was maddening.

When he realized their lone SAW hadn't pivoted in his direction, Pauli turned to see why. He saw Amy's body slumped over the weapon, her head missing from her corpse. He wasn't sure when she'd been dusted, but she was gone.

The enemy is now one hundred meters from your position, called out the AI in his HUD.

Pauli broke from his position and ran to the SAW. Brushing Amy's dead body aside, he grabbed the weapon and aimed it at the charging Zodarks on the left flank.

The SAW fired hundreds of shots a minute at the alien soldiers rushing toward him, cutting many of them down. A handful of the Zodarks ducked behind cover as they returned fire.

Pauli ducked and rolled to the left behind the stump of a burning tree as several blaster bolts slammed into the position he'd just abandoned. Raising the SAW to his shoulder, he sent long strings of fire at the remaining Zodarks. He hit two of them as they bounded forward to his position. A third Zodark dove out of his line of fire and behind a boulder. Several of Pauli's blaster shots ricocheted off the rock into the air.

Sensing he should duck, Pauli rolled to his right this time and came up behind another boulder just in time to see an object land near the tree stump he had just been hiding behind. He ducked back down just as an explosion went off. The concussion blast blew right over him.

At that moment, Pauli just wanted to close his eyes. He knew if he did that, he'd probably pass out. If that happened, he likely wouldn't wake up. The Zodarks hadn't exactly been known to take prisoners.

Shaking off the effects of the blast, Pauli grabbed the M90 and pulled himself up above the boulder that had saved his life. He saw six Zodarks, less than twenty meters away. Leveling the SAW at them, he cut loose a string of shots at the group, cutting all six of them down before they had a chance to react.

"Hang in there, Pauli!" came a shout from behind him as half a dozen soldiers from another squad ran past him. They charged right at the remaining Zodarks, plugging the hole in the line.

A few minutes later, the blaster fire died down. Either the Zodarks had been killed, or they'd opted to fall back and find another way around the human soldiers. In either case, Pauli half-collapsed against the nearby rock. With the enemy threat gone, he could finally stop for a moment and catch his breath.

Slumping over on his side, Pauli reached for the straw on his CamelBak. He placed it in his mouth and took a couple of long pulls of water. His body slumped further until he was practically lying on the ground. *Thank God this thing still works.*

"Hey, I need a medic over here!" came the voice of someone standing near Pauli. He looked up and found Lieutenant Atkins staring down at him with a look of concern on his face.

"You look like hell, Pauli," Atkins remarked. "Good job plugging that hole and holding the line. Damn good job. Now hang in there while we get a medic over here."

Pauli just smiled a stupid grin. His body hurt too much to do much of anything else than just lie there and do nothing.

A medic trotted up and dropped down next to him. "Hey, Pauli. Roll over and let me see your backside, will you?"

Pauli obliged and practically passed out from the pain. *Strange, I didn't feel that bad just a few minutes ago*, he thought.

"I'm going to apply some bandages on your back and give you a nanite injection," the medic said as he went to work.

"Just give me something for the pain, will you?" Pauli begged, barely audible.

A second later, Pauli felt a couple of autoinjectors poke him. He suddenly didn't feel so terrible anymore, but he was physically spent.

I'm just going to close my eyes for a few minutes...

Chapter Six
Task Force 92

Above Planet Intus
RNS *George Washington*

Captain McKee rubbed her temples; she knew she needed to get more sleep. She was having a hard time staying focused and sharp. There was too much work and too little time to do it.

All these status reports from her various department chiefs had her shaking her head in frustration. The *GW* had taken a lot of hits during the battle to secure the planet. Her people were doing their best to get it all repaired, but what they really needed was a couple of weeks in a shipyard.

Her computer terminal flashed, alerting her to an incoming transmission. She opened the channel and was greeted by Admiral Abigail Halsey.

"Admiral, what can I do for you?" asked McKee.

"Captain, I reviewed your damage report. You still have a lot of systems down. The Prims are sending a squadron of ships to Intus, along with three battleships. They've said we can send some of our damaged ships over to one of their repair yards in the Kita system. It's three days' travel by FTL, which is considerably closer than going back to Rhea or Sol for repairs. When their squadron arrives in the system, I'm ordering you, the *London*, the *New York*, and the *Midway* to make repairs in Kita.

"Since this is the first time a human ship will be making a port call in a Prim core system, our people must stay on their best behavior. Any questions, Captain?"

A smile crept across McKee's face at the chance to see a developed planet in a core Prim system. "When do we leave, Admiral?" she asked.

Admiral Halsey returned the smile. "The Prim ships are scheduled to arrive in twenty-four hours. Before you leave, we're moving as many of our wounded as we can from the surface to the ships heading to Kita. The Prims have a more advanced medical capability than we do. Their ground commander offered their facilities on Kita to our wounded, and I'm not about to look a gift horse in the mouth.

"Oh, and Captain, I'm sending you an encrypted file. Open it after our call, and you'll receive your other set of orders."

McKee's left eyebrow rose at that last comment, which sparked her curiosity. When she saw the file, she grinned. *A secret mission…*
****

As the Special Forces officer stood in front of her, Captain McKee realized she was more than a little intimidated. Damn near everyone in the Republic knew who Brian Royce was. He was a legend in the Republic—hands-down the most dangerous Special Forces operator in the Deltas. Awarded the Medal of Honor, two Distinguished Service Crosses, three Silver Stars, three Bronze Stars with V device, and five Purple Hearts: Captain Brian Royce was a real-life war hero who just didn't know when to quit.

"At ease, Captain. Take a seat. We have a lot to talk about," McKee finally said. *I hope I didn't leave him standing there too long*, she thought, trying to conceal the flushing she felt in her cheeks. Royce was a very attractive man.

The Delta captain smiled and took a seat opposite her desk. "Captain McKee, permission to speak freely?" Royce asked.

"Granted. But call me Fran when in private."

"OK, Fran. Two days ago, my company was in the thick of rooting out a Zodark command bunker dug into the side of a mountain," Royce began. "Then I receive a cryptic message from Third Group, telling me I need to pick my ten best soldiers and report to the *GW* for some secret squirrel stuff. So, here I am. What was so important that ten of my best soldiers and I were told to leave the battle and report here?"

I like this guy, McKee thought. *Direct and to the point. No BS.*

She leaned forward in her chair. "Brian, the *GW*, along with a few other ships in the task force, took some bad damage during the assault to capture the planet and the system. As such, the Prims offered us the opportunity to repair our ships at a large shipyard at one of their core worlds, Kita. They also have a more advanced healthcare system than our own. They've offered to treat many of our wounded from Intus. That's why we evacuated most of our wounded to the ships leaving for Kita—"

"Sorry for interrupting, Fran, but where do we fit into this?" asked Royce. "My men and I aren't injured."

"Brian, this is our first time going to a Prim world. Not just any Prim world, but a core world. Kita is one of their main military worlds. It has one of their largest shipyards. In light of all of this, Admiral Halsey wants your team to conduct a covert FID mission."

Brian raised an eyebrow at the idea of conducting a foreign internal defense mission on the Prim world. The Deltas specialized in FID missions—at least they had before the war with the Zodarks. However, they hadn't completed one in years, especially since the governments of Earth had consolidated into one. The closest thing to an FID they'd done in the last seven years was examining the Zodark forts and encampments to better understand their military operations.

After thinking about it for a moment, Brian remarked, "Fran, we're guests of the Prims; we're also allies. I get the need for an FID, but maybe a better approach that would allow us more access would be to just ask them. They might be completely open to giving us a tour of their facilities. If they'll allow us to tour their shipyards, training bases, and military facilities, it would give us far better access than carrying out a covert FID on a foreign planet of a society that is far more advanced than our own."

Fran almost laughed at the idea, but she just shook her head. "Brian, I think I'm going to like working with you. When we arrive in Kita in a few days, I'll approach my counterpart there and I'll do what I can to arrange that. Maybe we'll get lucky and the direct approach just might work. If it doesn't, then I'll need you to prepare your men as best you can to carry out the mission. Any questions?"

Brian smiled and shook his head.

"All right. Well, enjoy the short break. We arrive in Kita in three days once we leave the system."

Fran finished the interaction by leading him out of her office.

Chapter Seven
Changes at Home

Earth, Sol
Lackland Training Facility
US Space Command

"As you can see, we created a complete replica of the engineering rooms, along with a representation of the frigate, cruiser, and battleship for the recruits to train on," the commander explained.

Admiral Chester Bailey nodded in approval. This clever idea was helping solve the training problem they were suddenly experiencing. When the Altairians helped the Earthers build three new classes of starships to serve in the Galactic Empire, humans soon realized they had a major obstacle. They knew how to man and operate their existing warships and had a training program in place to keep them running—these new warships with integrated advanced alien technology were so entirely new and different, they needed to develop a new set of skills. The new training program needed to be targeted, effective, efficient and scalable because training time could make or break their ability to man the ships as they came off the line.

Bailey turned to the woman in charge of developing the training program. "How many students or crews are we able to effectively train on each of these replicas at a time?" he asked.

Commander Alisha Lopez guided them onto the replica of the battleship's engineering room. Then she explained, "We have five training classes simultaneously training on each replica of our frigate, cruiser, and battleship. With two replicas of each class of ship, we're able to push a total of thirty classes simultaneously."

Bailey whistled softly as he shook his head in amazement. "That's incredible, Commander. How many students or crewmen to a class?"

"For engineering, usually a typical class or crew complement is twenty," she explained. "Each class goes through six weeks of classroom training that's also intermixed with two weeks of training on each class of ship before we consider them ready for an assignment on one of the new starships."

Doing some math in his head, Bailey commented, "So roughly twelve weeks to get an engineering crewman through training?"

Lopez nodded. "Yes, sir. Exactly. It means we're pushing through six hundred Altairian-certified engineering crewmen every three months. However, I'd say it'll probably take them closer to a year on an actual ship to really become proficient in everything. There will be a lot of on-the-job training that'll take place for sure. Starting next quarter, once the other facilities open, we'll be able to triple the number of recruits we're able to train. Ideally, I'd like to have a couple of our new ships held back from fleet service to act as real-life training ships so we can run the trainees through some additional training before they are sent to the fleet and assigned a ship."

As they exited the battleship training facility, Bailey commented, "I'd love to assign some ships for your command to train on, but I think we may need to wait a few years before we're ready for that. The demands of the fleet are enormous with the optempo we're being given by our allies.

"By the way, this is a great setup for training on the engineering side of the ship. Have you established the same arrangement for other sections and departments?"

Commander Lopez looked a little disappointed that she wouldn't be able to squeeze a frigate or two out of him for her training program, but she responded, "That's a good question, Admiral, and, yes, we have. It took us some time to get them all fabricated and built, but they are all ready to go. I honestly don't think any of this would have been possible without a lot of help from the Altairians. Their trainers, training aids and tools are incredible."

Bailey just nodded as she talked and showed him more of the training rooms and simulators. He found it all very interesting. He was glad he had flown down to see the facility in person, even though he had a *lot* of other issues on his mind. The shipyards were still eight months away from completing their new frigates, which was a good thing, considering how unprepared they were to crew these new ships. Given the training numbers and the time to get a person ready to operate one of these new warships, they were only going to have the crews to operate twenty of the new frigates when they came out of the shipyard. The cruisers were another six months behind the frigates, and the battleships a year behind them.

Just stay calm, Bailey thought. *Remember, this is going to take some time to retool our navy to meet the Empire's new standards.* The

Altairians had given them time to prepare; now they just had to stick to the plan.

Bailey found himself practicing various calming techniques more and more often. There was so much work to be done with the integration of the Empire and the Earth's previous governments. Then they had a new layer of changes being imposed by their Altairian benefactors that were causing some subtle unrest among the people and within the military. It was just a lot to handle, and most of it fell on his shoulders.

Chester turned to Commander Lopez as the tour ended. "You've done a good job getting this place up and running. Now I need you to replicate this process at six other Space Command bases. Find two more in North America, one in Africa, one in Europe, and two in Asia. We need to increase the number of trained crews for this new navy we're building. Once these ships come online, we'll phase out our training programs for our existing ships. They'll be moved to the reserves or placed in mothball status once our new ships are fully operational.

"Your focus will need to be on preparing our new recruits and crews for the ships the Altairians are helping us build. I also need you to align the training schedule with the shipbuilding delivery schedule. First, we need enough crews trained to man the frigates that come online in eight months, then six months later, the cruisers are the focus, then a year after that, we need to man the battleships.

"Oh, and before I forget, Commander—I'm promoting you to captain. It's a well-earned promotion, and you'll need it as you take charge of more and more of our fleet's training program."

Commander Lopez beamed at the news. She was clearly excited to lead this training program. Bailey knew it was something she excelled at, and it certainly was critical to the future success of Space Command.
****

Jacksonville, Arkansas
Space Command HQ

General Rob Pilsner read the casualty report from the Intus campaign and cringed. The invasion was sixteen days old, and losses were still mounting. General Ross McGinnis was requesting two hundred thousand C100s and another two corps in addition to the four he already had. That was another one hundred and thirty thousand soldiers.

Pilsner sighed at the request, but he reviewed the casualty numbers again and concurred. McGinnis definitely needed reinforcements; however, Pilsner was more inclined to send *double* what had been asked for. Intus was nearly two months' travel by FTL, unless they could get an Altairian cruiser or battleship to open a wormhole portal directly from Earth to Intus.

They were already two years into this global draft, and his ground forces had just reached six million of the twenty million forces they'd been tasked to create by the Altairians. All the new training requirements from the Altairians had added two months to the four months of basic combat training a soldier already received. Add anywhere from two to twelve months of advanced specialty training, and it was apparent why it was a slow-going process to reach their quota.

Pilsner heard a knock on his door. Fleet Admiral Chester Bailey poked his head in. "Afternoon, Admiral Bailey," said Pilsner. "Come on in."

Bailey smiled and walked to his desk. The two men shook hands briefly before he took a seat opposite him.

"What can I do for you, sir?" asked General Pilsner.

"General, I reviewed the casualty reports from Intus. It appears the operation is going well," Admiral Bailey said optimistically. "I received a new request from the Prims and Altairians to assist them in liberating another colony in the same region of space. Before I agree to that request, I need to know if you think we can support another operation that'll be about the same size as this current one without shortchanging ourselves elsewhere. What are your thoughts?"

Pilsner contemplated for a moment before he responded. "Well, I'm glad the Prims and Altairians believe the operation is going well, and that we've acquitted ourselves well enough that they'd now like to include us in another operation. That speaks well of our soldiers and their performance. As to supporting another operation—yes, I believe we can support another operation if it's the same size and scope as Intus. I'd prefer to complete this one first and use the same force, but, yes, I believe we can support another invasion, or at least the Army could. Can the fleet? I heard your losses were bad."

Bailey grimaced at the mention of the fleet losses. "I won't lie and say this operation didn't hurt us in regard to ships and crews. It did. But ultimately, if the Prims and Altairians are asking us to participate in

71

another operation, I don't know that we can decline. The Prims are allowing us to cycle our damaged ships through their shipyard at Kita. It's apparently one of their core worlds. If they hadn't done that, then I don't think we'd have a fleet capable of supporting another invasion.

"What I really need to know from you is if we can still move forward with our plan to station one million soldiers in the Rhea system if we get involved in another invasion."

Pilsner nodded. "We can. It's taken us some time to get a steady pipeline of soldiers moving through their basic and advanced training, but we're finally hitting optimal levels. We've just crossed our second targeted goal, two hundred thousand soldiers graduating training each month. By this time next year, that number will be doubled."

Bailey let out a sigh of relief. "This is good, Rob. The Altairians gave us some time and wiggle room to meet our military goals, but we need to make sure we're showing constant progress. We lost thirty-two thousand soldiers on Intus. It hurt, but not as bad as it could have. I think the C100 program has really saved a lot of lives."

"It sure has," Pilsner concurred. "I know there was a lot of consternation about the program at the outset, but it's clearly been a good move. We lost sixty-eight thousand of them on Intus. I have to think we would have lost at least that many human soldiers had we not had them."

Admiral Bailey nodded in agreement. "How are Special Forces coming along?"

Pilsner shrugged. "It's our longest and toughest training program. It still takes us roughly three years to get a soldier through the entire training program. We've increased the program by twelve hundred percent, but we're *years* away from being able to really double or even triple them in size."

"OK, just keep at it," Bailey replied. "They've proven to be incredibly effective in this war against the Zodarks. Once we get our new frigates and cruisers, we will implement some new strategies and ways to leverage the Special Forces to carry out some operations behind the enemy lines."

Pilsner smiled. "I like the sound of that, sir. Just keep in mind, we only have a limited number of them right now. In another year, we'll be graduating a full three thousand new SF soldiers a month. Until then, I wouldn't risk losing a lot of them if it can be avoided."

The two talked for another thirty minutes before the admiral left.

Bailey had given Pilsner a lot to chew on. The more he thought about it, the more one part of their conversation struck Pilsner as a bit odd. Admiral Bailey had mentioned something about not feeling like he could say no to a Prim or Altairian request.

What did he mean by that? Pilsner pondered.

Chapter Eight
Planet Hopping

RNS *Comfort*
Intus Orbit

Corporal Paul "Pauli" Smith had just finished reading his book when the doctor walked up to him. "You appear to be healing up nicely," said the doctor, glancing over his electronic chart. "Do you still have any pain, muscle cramps or stiffness?"

Pauli shook his head. "Not really. I think I actually feel better now than before I got hurt, to be honest."

The doctor snickered at the self-assessment. "Well, we did just pump your body full of medical nanites," he replied.

"Hey, I have a question for you about that," said Pauli. "How are the nanites we get here any different than the nanites our medics stick us with when we get hurt?" He didn't know a lot about this stuff and was genuinely curious.

The doctor nodded and became much more serious as he explained, "The nanites the medics use are meant to stabilize your body and help keep you alive long enough to make it to a higher-level field hospital or a medical ship like the *Comfort*. The nanite injections infuse your body with roughly ten thousand robotic machines the size of white blood cells. They immediately rush through your body and identify the damage or life-threatening injury.

"First, they go to work on stopping any bleeding. Then they work on trying to repair the body as best they can. Once you make it to a field hospital or a ship like this, we give you a blood transfusion that pumps upwards of one million of these little nanites into your body. Over a few days to a few weeks, they can heal just about anything. In your case, they healed several broken ribs, a fracture in your femur, a concussion and brain lesion, and the second-degree burns on parts of your legs and arms. For good measure, they also repaired some overused calf and lower back muscles, which were probably strained from all the walking you've done and the heavy ruck you infantry soldiers carry."

Pauli shook his head in amazement.

The doctor smiled. "Corporal Smith, we're going to send you to a couple of days of physical therapy now, to make sure everything is functioning correctly. Once they've cleared you, you'll be sent back to your battalion, good as new. If you don't have any additional questions for me, then I wish you the best of luck, and I hope we don't see each other again unless it's at some dive bar back on Earth."

The doctor left to speak with the next soldier, presumably to give him or her the same speech.

****

The next day, Pauli made his way over to the physical therapy group. They ran him through a battery of tests to make sure his injured areas were, in fact, healed and functional. After being signed off as fit for duty, he was directed to a large transient bay of the RNS *Comfort* to wait for a shuttle.

The waiting room was filled with bunk beds, interspersed with some couches, chairs, and tables. Finding an empty bunk, Pauli dropped his meager set of belongings next to it. The supply section had given him a fresh new uniform now that he no longer needed to wear the hospital garb. They had also given him a second set of uniforms along with some underclothes, socks, and a new pair of boots. A rifle and combat gear would be allocated once he was back on the planet. This was, after all, a hospital ship; there wasn't any need for that here.

There were probably close to three or four hundred soldiers milling about in the transient bay. Most of the soldiers were either reading a book, listening to music or an audiobook, talking with each other, or playing a video game on one of the many entertainment systems. Pauli had to give props to whoever had set this place up. They'd done a good job of making sure the soldiers had a comfortable place to relax and unwind after they got discharged from the hospital and waited to return to their units.

Each day, at around 1000 hours and 1400 hours, a lieutenant would announce over the PA and post on a bulletin board the soldiers scheduled to leave on one of the transport crafts. Roughly fifty soldiers would leave during each announcement. As some soldiers left, more were being discharged from the hospital side of the ship and filtered into the transient hangar.

Pauli became curious. He tapped one of the fleeters on the shoulder and asked him how many wounded the ship could handle at one time.

What the spacer said floored him. Apparently, the RNS *Comfort* was able to handle up to ten thousand wounded soldiers. The ship had a crew of three hundred and twenty, and a medical staff of four hundred. It didn't sound like a lot, but apparently, the crew and medical operations were augmented with six hundred Synths.

The more Pauli thought about the medical Synths, the more he wondered why they hadn't integrated them into the Army units as medics. A nurse practitioner, physician assistant, nurse, or doctor took a long time to train. If that kind of knowledge could be imparted on a massive scale to C100 combat Synths, it could probably save a lot of lives during a battle.

"Stay in your lane, Corporal, stay in your lane," Pauli said quietly to himself. "Control the things you can control and let go of the things you can't." He'd never really been into meditation or spiritual stuff in the past, but during his tour on New Eden, he'd met a Delta soldier during one of their operations. Since Pauli had thought about one day joining the Deltas, he'd asked the Special Forces soldier a lot of questions.

The SF operator had told Pauli something that had really changed his attitude toward both life and the military. "One of the keys to making it through Delta selection and training is to find ways to reshape your worldview," he'd said. "You need to learn how to make your world small. Instead of saying to yourself, 'I just need to make it through selection or phase one of the training,' you need to shrink your view. Tell yourself you just need to make it through the next twenty minutes, or the next hour. If you focus on just trying to make it from one hour to the next, or one meal to the next, your mind and body become a lot less overwhelmed by what's being thrown at you."

The Delta had also told Pauli, "If you allow yourself to get angry at situations or people you have no way of influencing, it's just wasted energy that's going to put you in a bad headspace." He had emphasized the need to control what you can control and let go of what you cannot. At first, Pauli had just nodded at the suggestions. But as time had worn on during the New Eden campaign, he had begun following the Delta's advice more and more. Pauli told himself he just needed to make it to breakfast, then he focused on making it to lunch, then dinner, then sleep.

Within a week of doing this, Pauli noticed two changes happening. First, time was flying by. The days and weeks were no longer moving at a snail's pace; things seemed to move along at an incredible clip even though nothing had really changed. They still went out on daily patrols or sat on guard duty along the perimeter of a firebase. Still, those routine duties flew by in a blur.

Next, when Pauli had given up being angry and frustrated at things he had no control over, his entire mindset and outlook had changed. He found himself a much happier person. He was less moody and more fun to be around. He realized if he had implemented more of these changes in himself during the big reorg, he probably would have been selected for corporal then instead of having to wait nearly two years longer.

"Are you Corporal Smith?" a sergeant with a clipboard asked.

Pauli placed his book down on the bed, looked up at the sergeant and nodded. "I am. How can I help you, Sergeant?"

"The ship leaving at 1000 hours is apparently a large cargo transport. It's got room for thirty-eight more people. You'll be leaving on it," the sergeant informed him.

Pauli nodded. The sergeant was about to turn to leave, but Pauli stopped him. "Sergeant, once we leave, what base are they sending us to?" he asked. "I'm just trying to figure out how I'll be getting back to my unit."

"When we send soldiers back, the transport takes everyone to a large base outside Hatteng City," the sergeant explained. "It's the Prim's capital city on Intus. I don't know much about the base other than it's not far from the capital city, and it's a megabase they've been building. I suspect once you get there, they'll arrange another transport to send you back to wherever your battalion or company is operating." The sergeant then took off to go inform some of the others they'd be leaving as well.

Pauli had another thirty minutes before he needed to go to the hangar to catch his ride. He'd been on the *Comfort* for seven days, and two of those days had been spent in the transient bay. Pauli hoped the rest of his platoon and company were still doing all right.
****

When all the soldiers had piled into the transport, it left the *Comfort*. The spacecraft had some portholes, so Pauli could see out even while strapped into his jumpseat. He really enjoyed being able to see the planet from orbit. Intus was a beautiful planet, and seeing it in combination with the two suns and the moons in orbit made a spectacular sight.

Thirty minutes later, the transport was already on its final approach to Hatteng City. Pauli heard a few whistles as the soldiers got a good look at the capital city. Clusters of skyscrapers rose high into the sky and appeared to go right into the clouds. Pauli wasn't sure how high they were, but he imagined they had to be hundreds of stories tall.

The pilot zoomed past the city and kept them moving closer to the coast. For probably a solid two or three kilometers from the shore, the water reflected various shades of green, turquoise, and aquamarine. It was some of the clearest, see-through water Pauli had ever seen.

As they approached the human military base, Pauli was impressed with his surroundings. The Earthers had only been on the planet for coming up on a month and a half, and they'd already built this massive base. It had several runways and numerous parking ramps filled with P-97 Orions, Reaper ground assault ships, Ospreys, and other large and small transport craft.

At three different positions on the base, he spotted artillery positions—and these weren't small artillery guns either. These were the new, improved M88 Howitzers. These bad boys could hurl a 240mm projectile of one hundred and sixty pounds of high-explosives, smoke, or white phosphorus rounds up to eight hundred kilometers away. They were the ultimate heavy infantry support weapon. They leveraged a special glide technology that allowed them to loiter high above a unit for up to twenty-four hours before they ran out of power. The AI-assisted smart warhead could hit enemy targets with incredible precision once the soldiers below identified an enemy target or geographical location. Because of their incredible range, they minimized the need to have hundreds of fire support bases like they had on New Eden.

Further behind the flight line, parking ramps, and hangars were rows and rows of neatly aligned containerized housing units, which the soldiers called CHUs, pronounced "chews." Each housing unit had its own bathroom and shower facility and housed sixteen soldiers.

What really drew Pauli's attention, though, was the beach. The base was situated right on the water with a long sandy shore that extended as far as the eye could see. There were a lot of people making use of the beach and swimming in the water. Pauli hoped he might have a few days or a week here at this base before they sent him to his unit. Growing up in Texas, he used to swim often in the Gulf of Mexico along the coast.

When their transport landed and the ramp opened, the soldiers inside were greeted with the oppressive heat and humidity of a ninety-three-degree summer day. As they all filed off the transport, a sergeant was waiting for them nearby. "Head to the hangar and wait to be briefed," he directed.

Once they were all lined up inside, the sergeant called off each of their names and told them to stand in different sections of the hangar. When everyone had been divided up, he announced, "Prepare to board an Osprey in twenty minutes. You'll be delivered to your division or brigade headquarters units. From there, your parent units will handle getting you back to your individual units."

The declaration caused more than a few groans from the soldiers. They were all clearly hoping for a few days at the base and maybe an opportunity to swim in the ocean.

Pauli realized his group consisted only of himself and two other soldiers. He wasn't sure if that was good or not. Twenty minutes later, an Osprey landed not far from the hangar they were waiting in.

The crew chief walked into the hangar and shouted, "First Orbital Assault Battalion!"

Pauli and the other two perked their heads up and waved to the man. He motioned for them to follow him back to the bird.

The three of them grabbed their minimal gear and trotted after the crew chief, who was already loaded up in the craft. When Pauli and the two other soldiers climbed in, he saw that the Osprey was practically full. There were only five open seats. Apparently, they'd already picked up some other replacements, or they were moving another unit around.

The flight to Firebase Oteren didn't take very long. The Osprey flew over the base and settled down on the flight line a second later. The pilot shut the engines down, and everyone got out.

Another sergeant was there to greet them and guided them over to a reception tent. Once inside, he went over everyone's name. If they were a new soldier to the battalion, he assigned them to a company and told them to hang tight.

As Pauli listened to the sergeant call out their names and assign them to a company, he realized most of these soldiers were being assigned to his company: Alpha Company, 1st OAB. When the sergeant got to Pauli, he apparently realized he had just gotten back from the *Comfort*. "Report to the battalion commander's office and then go to supply to get a new set of combat gear," the sergeant directed.

Pauli wasn't sure why he was being summoned to the battalion commander's office, but if Major Monsoor wanted to see him, he wasn't going to keep him waiting.

As Pauli walked across the firebase, he could see they'd made a lot of progress in building it. His unit had been in the field since they arrived in the state of Oteren. He knew the brigade was building a base around the state capital, but he had no idea it had grown to be this big.

When he found Major Monsoor's tent, Pauli approached cautiously. A sergeant walked out of the tent and immediately recognized him. "Corporal Smith, I thought I saw your name on the list of new arrivals this afternoon. Welcome back! Come on in. The major wanted to speak with you personally once you arrived."

Pauli wasn't sure what all this was about, but he was glad it appeared to be something good.

The two of them walked into the tent and made their way over to a field table the major was sitting at. The sergeant announced their presence to the commander.

Monsoor smiled when he saw Pauli's name tape. "Ah, Corporal Paul Smith. I'm glad we found you. How was the *Comfort*? Did the fleet take good care of you?"

The man seemed genuinely concerned. That was a big reason why a lot of the soldiers in the battalion liked Major Monsoor—no matter how low someone was on the totem pole, the major always checked in on them. He was well liked by the enlisted and junior officers.

Monsoor must have seen the confusion on Pauli's face. "Take a seat, Corporal. I called you in here to tell you Lieutenant Atkins put you in for the Silver Star for your actions during the battle of Two Pines a few weeks back."

Pauli was shocked. "Oh, wow. Thank you, sir, but I was just doing my job—trying to stay alive and keep the soldiers in my squad and platoon alive."

Major Monsoor put a hand on Pauli's shoulder. "I know, Corporal. You did a great job; you went above and beyond in organizing the defense of that line and keeping those Zodarks from overrunning your position. That was incredible if you ask me. The medal is well earned, and so are these."

The major turned and grabbed something off his desk, handing it to Pauli. It was a set of chevron stripes. "Your lieutenant recommended we promote you to sergeant. You'll be taking over command of your old squad when you return back to your unit."

Pauli raised his left eyebrow at the mention of his old squad. "What happened to Sergeant Sanders?" he pressed. "Is Yogi all right?"

"Yes, Sergeant Sanders is doing fine," said Monsoor jovially. "He moved over to take charge of Third Squad. You'll be in charge of First Squad, unless Lieutenant Atkins or Master Sergeant Dunham has made changes. As a matter of fact, your company should be arriving back on base tomorrow morning. I'm rotating your company back to the FOB for the next month—you all have been in the field since we arrived on the planet and seen more than enough combat. It's time to give you a break and get your unit back up to one hundred percent again," the major went on to explain.

Pauli nodded and smiled at the news. He was glad his unit was going to get a reprieve soon; they'd all earned it.

"In three days, we're going to have an awards ceremony for your unit," Major Monsoor added. "You, along with a few others, will receive your awards then. In the meantime, enjoy the rest of the day and evening off. Grab some hot chow from the new dining facility and chill out. The coming weeks may get busy. I hear we may have a new mission coming down from Division."

When Pauli left to walk to the new dining facility, he paused just long enough to affix his new rank to his uniform. It felt good to be a sergeant. Lieutenant Atkins had told him if it hadn't been for the reorg, chances were he already would have made sergeant or even staff sergeant—but here he was, finally a sergeant. The added pay bump wouldn't hurt either.

Military pay after the reorg actually wasn't all that bad. Because of the reduced number of ranks and the elimination of overseas and danger pay, a private's salary was now 52,000 Republic dollars or RDs. A corporal made 62,000 RD, a sergeant 73,000 RD, a master sergeant 85,000 RD, and lastly, a sergeant major received 100,000 RD.

The typical enlistment was six years. If a soldier reenlisted, they automatically received a 5,000 RD bump in pay, regardless of their paygrade. No one would really get rich off military pay, but it wasn't all that bad either. When Pauli factored in the other military perks like thirty days of paid vacation, housing, and various schooling or educational benefits, he felt that it was a good career field.

The more Pauli thought about it, the more he realized he should try to make the jump to being an officer if he was going to stay for the full fifty years to collect a pension. Officer pay was ridiculous—take the enlisted pay and add thirty percent, and you essentially had officer pay.

Pauli walked into the tent areas where his unit was going to be staying, and he saw Yogi. "Whoa. Hey, how's it going, Yogi? I thought you weren't coming in until tomorrow."

Yogi grinned broadly. "That was the plan. Captain Hiro was apparently able to get us a ride on a couple of transports, so they brought us in early. The rest of the company went to the chow hall. But, hey—how are you, Pauli? They get you all patched up?"

Pauli dropped his gear and the few personal items he had next to an empty bunk. "Right as rain, my friend. That ship is amazing. They pump your body full of some new advanced medical nanites and let them go to work on you for a few days. Honestly, I feel physically and mentally better now than I have in years."

Yogi laughed. "That's great, Pauli. Maybe I should get shot or blown up so I can have them pump my body full of advanced nanites," he said, poking his friend in the shoulder. "My body is killing me. Nearly two months in the bush has beaten me the hell up."

"Did we lose any more people after I left?" Pauli asked.

Yogi shook his head. "Thankfully, no. But we did lose a lot of people in that attack. Half the platoon was wiped out. After you left, we consolidated the platoon with Third Platoon. We're supposed to get a bunch of replacements while we're here on the FOB, so we'll see."

Pauli nodded as he took in the information. "When I flew in, the Osprey I was on was full of replacements. I'll bet most of them are probably coming to our platoon then."

Yogi shrugged. "Well, let's go get something to eat, my friend. We can catch up."
****

Three days later, the company was standing in formation as Major Monsoor read off a list of soldiers receiving various medals and awards. It was a *long* list. Roughly half the medals being awarded were posthumous, a sad testament to the brutality and intensity of the last couple months of combat. Ironically, the first two days of the invasion had gone smoothly—they hadn't been involved in any combat. The last two months, however, the company had suffered a thirty-two percent casualty rate.

When the major stood in front of Pauli, he attached a Silver Star on his breast pocket, then he added a Purple Heart, an Army Commendation medal, an Intus Service Medal, an Orbital Assault Medal, a Primord Liberation Medal, and lastly, an Empire Primord Campaign Medal. Pauli had no idea he was being awarded seven medals. The last four were completely new—he'd never even heard of these medals.

When the major was done with the award ceremony, he told them about the last four medals. "Each time a soldier participates in an orbital assault, they will receive an Orbital Assault Medal," he explained. "The Prim Liberation Medal is given for liberating one of their worlds or colonies, the Intus Service Medal was for service on the planet Intus, and the Empire Campaign Medal, well, those are for participating in an Empire campaign."

As far as Pauli was concerned, it was just more junk to clutter up your uniform. He was sure some real-echelon pukes were probably excited as hell to receive them, but the only medals that meant anything to Pauli were the Purple Heart and the valor medals. Those medals meant he'd been in the thick of it—proof he was a real badass.

Once the major was done with his speech telling them how proud he was of them all, he announced that a special dinner was being prepared for them. Somehow, someway, he'd managed to find them a couple kegs of beer and some steaks. They were going to eat like kings and party like it was 2099 tonight. It was a nice gesture and something the soldiers appreciated. The major was all right in their eyes.

****

Two weeks had gone by with the platoon pulling FOBBIT duty—they mostly pulled guard duty along the perimeter of the base. Once a week, they went out on a twelve-hour patrol outside the perimeter, but that was about it. They were soaking in the light duty after a rough couple of months.

Then the world changed again. Three hundred and fifty thousand human soldiers and nearly twice that number of C100s showed up from Earth. The population of human soldiers on Intus had more than doubled.

The veterans knew this meant one thing—the brass was gearing up for another campaign. The big question was who was staying on Intus, and who was going? Granted, there was still some fighting happening on the planet, but most of it was isolated to a handful of pockets of resistance. It was mostly a mop-up operation, being dealt with by the Prim troops. At this point, the human soldiers were pulling garrison duty all over the planet.

Finally, word officially came down that the human soldiers would be invading another planet—not a Prim planet, but a Zodark colony. The resistance to this operation was expected to be stiff. The day after the announcement, the entire brigade was going to begin practicing orbital assaults. The dropships would arrive, and they'd load all their gear and equipment back up and return to the RNS *Tripoli*, a beast of an orbital assault ship the Altairians had helped them build. The ship could hold the entire battalion and deliver them to any planet in the galaxy with sustained operations for up to three months.

When Pauli heard the news, he shook his head. He was getting short on time. He only had ten months left on his enlistment. The last thing he wanted to do was be a part of a new invasion mere months away from the end of his tour in the military. When he got to the *Tripoli*, he'd make an inquiry with personnel and see if he could still apply for Delta school or maybe get a softer assignment to ride his time out.

Chapter Nine
Kita Shipyard

Kita, Primord Core System
RNS *George Washington*

"Would you look at the size of this place?" one of the bridge officers said to no one in particular.

"Helm, bring us into the slip our guests provided," McKee's XO directed.

The *George Washington* moved slowly towards the massive shipyard. The facility was bigger than anything they had ever seen, housing more than two hundred slips. Most of them were either full of new ships under construction or repairing the battle damage of others. It was an astronomical operation.

"Captain, we're receiving a message from the station manager," the coms officer announced. "They said to inform you that once your ship docks, a boarding party will come aboard to meet with you. They're requesting that you keep all our people on the ship for now."

McKee acknowledged the request and returned to her seat. She reviewed the laundry list of items that needed to be repaired. She was glad they were able to pull into a shipyard to get fixed up and ready for the next campaign she was sure was already being cooked up.

Once the ship docked, a detail of Prims came aboard and made their way up to her boardroom, where McKee was waiting for them along with her chief of engineering and most of her department chiefs. Bringing them into the loop of what was about to happen was the easiest way to disseminate information.

As the Prims walked in, McKee rose from her seat to greet them. She had to remember, the Prims didn't shake hands like humans, and they didn't do a slight bow like the Altairians. The Prims would raise a hand as their form of greeting. It was awkward and odd, and it kind of reminded McKee of a Nazi salute from two centuries ago.

"Captain Fran McKee, I am Admiral Stavanger. This is Mr. Hanseatic; he is in charge of the shipyard facility. We would both like to welcome the people of Earth to Kita. It is a real honor and pleasure to meet such fearsome warriors. My people have regaled us with tales of your ferociousness in battle on Intus," the Prim admiral said in an almost reverent tone.

"Thank you, Admiral Stavanger. It is an honor and a pleasure to meet you," McKee replied. "My people cannot thank you enough for allowing us to bring some of our critically wounded soldiers to your medical facilities, and for your offer to repair our ships. We are very excited to be working more closely with the Primords and to learn more about your people." She motioned with a hand for the group of five Prims to take a seat.

As the group sat, Mr. Hanseatic spoke. "I was told you would have a list of critical systems that need to be repaired. If you have this list ready, I'd like to send it over to my repair manager. He'll give me the precise time it'll take to complete the repairs of your ships."

McKee nodded toward her chief engineer. He handed over a tablet that contained the detailed list. Using Altairian language translation tech, they had converted their request to the Prims' native language.

The shipyard manager took the tablet and smiled when he saw it was already in his native tongue. He synced it with his tablet and sent it on to his own people.

The Prim admiral spoke again. "Captain McKee, if you move your injured people to the docking port, our medical technicians will transport them to our infirmary. I was also told by your Admiral Chester Bailey that you would like a more detailed tour of our industrial and military facilities. As allies, we will honor this request and do our best to help answer your questions. Perhaps some of your soldiers can tell us what makes your own soldiers so fearsome in battle. We've been fighting the Zodarks now for three hundred years. It has been a long war that has seen the front lines change many times. Everyone in the Galactic Empire is hopeful that humans will become a deciding factor in turning the tide of the war in our favor."

McKee did her best to hide her shock that the Prims been fighting their own war with the Zodarks for three hundred years—a war that essentially never ended wasn't something she had signed up for. She wondered if the Chancellor had known this was going to become the new reality for humans when they'd joined the Empire.

She smiled, putting an optimistic tone forward. "That would be great, Admiral. As a matter of fact, I have a contingent of our Special Forces with me. I am sure they would be able to provide your military leaders with a lot of information about how our ground forces fight. My officers and I are spacers. We fight starships, so our knowledge and understanding of ground warfare are very limited. We are eager to learn from your officers how to fight our ships better and how to integrate more advanced technologies into our ships and their capabilities."

The rest of the meeting went by quickly as the admiral and the shipyard manager went over a brief schedule of the next ten days. Mr. Hanseatic said it would take his people eight days to complete the needed repairs. "With your permission, we'll also provide an update to the repair Synths on the human ships that will allow them to know how to carry out some of these more advanced-level repairs," he offered.

For the next six days, McKee's Special Forces contingent would tour a couple of Prim military bases and spend some time learning about their military and how it fought. They'd also work on explaining to them the differences between the Deltas and the regular Army soldiers, and how the two groups worked together but also had distinctly different missions and skill sets.

****

Five days later, McKee was sitting in her office as one of the stewards prepared a small table with some fine china, silver cutlery, a pair of wineglasses, and food. When they had finished, they left to allow her and the Prim admiral the chance to talk privately.

The food had been specially prepared to make sure it was acceptable and safe for a Primord to eat. McKee was doing her best to impress him with some specialty dishes from Earth and some California merlot.

When it was just the two of them, they ate and enjoyed the fine wine in private. The conversation remained mostly neutral. Captain McKee was doing her best to get to know and understand Admiral Bvork Stavanger, his history and personality. She planned to write up her personal assessment of the man later that evening while the information was still fresh.

The more they talked, the more fascinated she was by him. He was an astonishing three hundred and sixty-two years old and had been in the Primord military now for three hundred and twenty of those years.

McKee just shook her head in amazement at how long he'd lived. She couldn't imagine what he must have seen over the years. *To live to be so old.* He'd been married twice; each marriage had lasted for more than a hundred years. He had had six children with his first wife and eight children with his second wife. He had an astounding eighty-four grandchildren, and more than five hundred great-grandchildren.

At first, she thought this was preposterous, but the more she thought about it, the more she came to realize that if she lived to be as old as he had, this could be her own story. She was only forty-two and still single, but heck—who knew what could happen over the next three hundred years?

As the end of the dinner came near, they finished off their second glass of wine. McKee leaned in to ask a question she'd been burning to ask. "Admiral, how long have the Primords been a part of the Empire?"

A slight smile crept across his face. "Please, Fran, just call me Bvork," he replied, almost in a comical manner. "You and I, we are friends now, and friends call each other by their given names."

Fran's cheeks flushed and she nodded.

"The Empire… or the GE as it's called…we Primords, Fran, have been part of this alliance for two hundred and ninety-one years," Bvork explained.

Fran wondered if the wine might be going to his head. No matter, she had questions, and he'd just opened Pandora's box for her. She was going to get her answers, and the answers Republic intelligence wanted.

"Bvork, you're telling me that the Primords have been at war with the Zodarks longer than you've been part of the Empire?"

Bvork nodded. "We have. We've been a spacefaring people for nearly five hundred years. We colonized our first planet a hundred years after we went to space and never looked back. As you probably know, our core system has six planets in it. We've colonized five of them. We also have colonies in fourteen other systems with a total of twenty-four colonies. Our population now exceeds one hundred and thirty-two billion people.

"You see, we first discovered the Zodarks three hundred and one years ago. At first, our relationship was peaceful. We had a small mining colony on a system near one of their systems. We interacted with them for a year, carrying out some trade and informational exchanges. Then they probed our territory. We believed they were just trying to make sure we weren't a threat, so we kept our military presence in the nearby systems to a minimum. Two years after we first encountered them, they invaded.

"The invasion was lightning fast. They captured the system with our mining colony, and the very next month, the Zodarks launched a new invasion of our other systems. The next seven years were tough, long years. We rushed military forces and soldiers to our colonies on the frontier as the Zodarks pressed us from all sides, but as you know, they fight like savage beasts. We were losing millions of soldiers fighting them. By the time we were able to ramp up the production of warships, the Zodarks had captured seven of our star systems and twelve colonies. Our eighth year into the war, we were finally able to turn the tide. We halted their advance and then pushed them back. They still control two of our original star systems and three colonies, but I'm optimistic that we'll get them back now that you humans have joined the alliance."

All Fran could do was sit there and listen, dumbfounded. "Bvork, how is it possible that this conflict has lasted as long as it has?" she asked. "How come no side has been able to achieve a victory to end it or to obtain peace? It seems crazy to us humans that with all this advanced technology, billions of people and starships, defeating the Zodarks hasn't been achievable. Why is it so hard to beat them?"

Bvork laughed. "Politics, Fran, politics. You also have to keep in mind that this war is being fought across not just systems and regions of space but entire galaxies. We are just one of the dozens of galaxies involved in this gigantic power grab. The Zodarks are not the only ones we fight. You already know about the Orbots, the half-machine, half-biological beasts. Well, there are other species of aliens we fight as well. This war, Captain, is bigger than you can imagine. We are but one very small part of this galactic war machine. The Altairians manage the overall grand strategy of this conflict. They manage the larger strategy and coordinate everything across the galaxies while we lesser species fight and implement these plans."

Fran sighed. She thought about what he'd just told her. While it made sense, something just didn't seem right. After all these years, a grand fleet or battle to win the war should have been organized, but for whatever reason, it hadn't. She didn't understand.

"Bvork, I'm just a ship captain. I go where I'm told, and I attack who I'm told to fight. Why can't we organize a large fleet of warships and soldiers and go invade the Zodark home worlds? Why can't we seek to end the war with the Zodarks and Orbots, or at least look to remove them as a threat to the rest of us?" she asked, almost pleading with him for understanding.

Bvork sat back in his chair as he silently sized her up. "Fran, this has been mentioned before. Many years ago, the Primords and another allied race, the Tulley, drew up some plans for an invasion of the Zodark core systems. Unfortunately, the Altairians learned about our plans, and they, along with another species you will soon meet called the Gallentines, summoned us to Altairius Prime. They confronted us about our plans and disallowed us from pursuing it. They told us that if we launched an invasion of the Zodark core worlds, it could provoke the Orbots, or worse, another elder species within the Dominion called the Collective. The Collective is a step above the Orbots in both technology and their physical beings. Unlike the Orbots, who are essentially cyborgs, the Collective are machines—"

"Whoa, Bvork. How is that possible?" McKee interjected. "What do you mean they're machines? And how come we haven't heard about them before?" She was blown away by what he'd just told her.

Bvork suddenly seemed hesitant, as if he'd just revealed too much. "Fran, you humans are just too new to the Galactic Empire," he said. "Maybe the Altairians haven't told you because they do not want to concern you with something that doesn't affect you yet."

Fran shook her head in frustration. "We have another naval officer, perhaps the most knowledgeable and bravest ship captain in our military, Rear Admiral Miles Hunt. He's on Altairius Prime right now. I'm sure he's probably being briefed on this. But this is important, Bvork. Why would the Gallentines and the Altairians be concerned about the Collective getting involved in preventing you from attacking a Zodark core world? Does the Collective run the Shadow Dominion? Are they the ones in charge of the enemy alliance?" Fran was practically peppering the poor man with questions. She needed answers; the humans needed answers.

Reaching for his glass of wine, Bvork finished it off. He was probably stalling as he tried to figure out how much he should tell her.

"Fran, there is a lot you do not know about this Galactic Empire. You will learn more about it in time. Right now, you need to focus on preparing your people to become a dominant military power in space. You need to grow an economy that can support this never-ending war, and you need to do your best to become as independent of the Altairians as possible. For the time being, you need to accept that you will need a lot of their help. Eventually, you will learn how to either take their technology and improve upon it or integrate captured Zodark or Orbot technology into your own. As you do this, you will be able to protect your people better, and you'll be able to think and act more independently of the Empire."

Fran knew confusion covered her face, but she didn't care. This was incredible information. "Bvork, you have given me a lot to think about. I have so many more questions I'd like to ask. Right now, I need to think about what you have already shared with me.

"Mr. Hanseatic said our ships will complete their repairs in a few more days. Would you join me for another private dinner like this before we leave?"

Bvork nodded. "I can do that. But before I leave tonight, let me tell you more about our next campaign. This is primarily going to be fought by us Primords and you humans. The Altarians, Tully, and Gallentines will not be participating.

"As you know, the Zodarks still control two of our colonies. One of them is a planet called Rass. It was the first colony the Zodarks seized from us more than three hundred years ago. It's a Zodark world at this point. Our colony had less than twenty thousand people on it when it was captured. Our latest intelligence indicates the Zodarks, and the Orbots have turned it into an industrial center and a major military outpost.

"This invasion will not be easy; they will fight hard for this planet. I'd like us to consider attacking the planet like this…"

They spent the next hour going over details of the coming campaign. It was going to be a brutal fight, but one that needed to happen. It was the proverbial punch in the face Fran thought the enemy needed.

Chapter Ten
Train Like You Fight

RNS *Tripoli*
Planet Intus

Sergeant Paul "Pauli" Smith peeled his body armor off and collapsed on his bunk. His battalion had just completed their fourth weeklong training mission. They'd been conducting orbital assaults for the last three months to prepare for the next mission. The training was intense: as iron sharpens iron, they trained like they fought.

"Hey, Pauli, your appointment with the S1 was changed to 1700 hours," Master Sergeant Dunham said as he stripped off his own body armor and collapsed on his bunk in exhaustion.

The sergeants of the platoon were spent. Pushing the new replacements and everyone else was taxing. It was tough work whipping the cherries into fighting shape. Sure, they'd learned a lot in basic training, but carrying out an orbital assault was a completely different beast to master.

"Thanks, Master Sergeant," Pauli replied. "I appreciate your help in arranging the meeting."

"Hey, anyone interested in going through Delta selection after they served six years in the infantry is my kind of crazy. I hope they take you, Pauli. You're a hell of a soldier," answered Dunham. He lay on the bunk and tried to calm his breathing a bit.
****

Two hours later, Pauli approached the office with a placard on it that said "S1, Personnel." He walked in and looked for the lieutenant he was supposed to meet with.

"Ah, there you are, Sergeant Smith," said the lieutenant with a warm smile. "Please, take a seat; I've been expecting you."

"Thank you for meeting with me, Lieutenant Tyrus," said Pauli as he pulled a chair out and took a seat.

"Master Sergeant Dunham and Lieutenant Atkins both said we needed to see you. After reviewing your service record, I can see why. It's quite impressive. A Bronze Star, Silver Star, Purple Heart, two Orbital Assault Medals, two combat tours on New Eden, and then the combat tour here on Intus. You've seen a lot in your short time in the military," she said, flipping through pages on her tablet. She paused and put the device down. "I also noticed your current enlistment ends in seven months."

Pauli nodded. "That's what I want to talk with you about. I'd like to reenlist, but only if I can secure a slot to try out for Special Forces—I want to be a Delta."

Her face scrunched up a bit. "You want to reenlist, but only if you can try out for Special Forces?" she repeated skeptically.

Pauli lifted his chin up. "I do. Is that a problem?"

Lieutenant Tyrus locked eyes with the sergeant major sitting another seat over. He shrugged and then went back to what he was working on.

She blew some air out of her lips. "Look, Sergeant, Special Forces has been ramping up its training program for the last three years," she began. "A portion of those being drafted are going immediately to SF training. It's not like it was before—you know, where you had to serve your first enlistment in the infantry before you tried out for SF. Let me check something."

As the lieutenant typed away, Pauli felt his chances starting to diminish. For years, trying out for the Deltas had been his dream and motivation to excel.

"Ah, there it is. OK, Sergeant, here's the deal. As you know, Special Forces training is three years long. You first have to make it through selection—that part is two weeks. Then you have to go through two weeks of medical evaluation to see if your body can support the physical augmentations they're going to make to it. If you pass both of those selection activities, then you're given a class number and start date for school.

"Once you start school, they give you two months of training before you begin the medical transition. I'm not going to lie to you, Sergeant. That transition is painful, and it's long. It takes two months to recover from the surgery, and then they put you through three months of phase one training, teaching you and your mind how to use your new body. If you fail phase one, you're immediately sent back to the infantry to serve out the remainder of your enlistment—"

Pauli interrupted her. "What's the washout rate for phase one and two of selection?"

Lieutenant Tyrus opened her mouth to say something, then she stopped and glanced at her computer terminal again. "Um, phase one hovers around fifty-two percent. Phase two, medical evaluation, is twelve percent. Phase three, the physical training to teach you how to use your new bodies, is six percent. Basically, for every hundred people that start the process, only thirty-nine ultimately make it. Then they have two and a half years of specialized training before they receive orders to one of the SF groups. It's a long process, Sergeant."

"It sounds like you're trying to talk me out of reenlisting," Pauli said glumly.

The sergeant major who had been working the next desk over joined the conversation. "It's not that we're trying to talk you out of it, Sergeant. We just want you to make an informed decision."

"OK, fair enough, Sergeant Major. What else am I missing?" asked Pauli.

"OK. First, because of the training length, and the time and money the Army is going to invest in you, they require a long enlistment term. They want to make sure they get their money's worth out of you," he explained.

Lieutenant Tyrus then added, "You should also know there is a stop-loss going on right now. When you first joined, everyone joined for a six-year enlistment and had to serve two years in the inactive ready reserve or the IRR. The Chancellor and the Minister of Defense activated the IRR and put a stop-loss in for all soldiers with regular enlistments. That means that while your term is technically up in seven months, you'd still have to serve two more years because you're still in the IRR, and they've stop-lossed you."

Pauli shook his head in annoyance. "So, Lieutenant, Sergeant Major—you're basically saying that even if I don't reenlist, I'll still have to serve at least two more years in the infantry."

They both nodded.

Pauli took a deep breath and let it out. *Control the things you can control. Let go of the things you can't.*

"OK, let's assume I still want to go into Special Forces," he said. "If I do, what will the term of that enlistment have to be?"

The sergeant major's demeanor softened a bit. "Well, Sergeant, Special Forces first enlistment is fourteen years. As you know, the first three years are spent on training. Once you complete training, they want at least ten solid years of service out of you. They figure you'll also end up attending some additional training schools, which is why they tacked an extra year on to make it an even fourteen-year enlistment.

"However, if you *do* join, since this would be your second enlistment, you'd be eligible for the bonus. And it's a doozy."

Pauli leaned forward. "How much?"

"Half a million RDs," said Lieutenant Tyrus. Pauli let out a soft whistle.

"You get a quarter of it if you complete the first three phases of selection," she explained. "You get another quarter when you graduate SF school, another quarter when you reach the seven-year mark of your enlistment, and the final quarter at the ten-year mark."

That's a lot of Republic dollars, thought Pauli. It was certainly more than he'd ever seen. Then again, having spent nearly his entire time in the military on either New Eden or Intus, he'd already managed to save one hundred and thirty thousand RDs so far.

"OK, if I want to join and I'm willing to do the fourteen-year enlistment, when's the soonest I could leave for training?" Pauli asked.

Lieutenant Tyrus searched her screen for the answer. "The next available selection slot we can get you is March 2116. The other slots are all taken up."

Pauli slumped his shoulders. "So, how does this work, then? I reenlist for this new fourteen-year enlistment, but I can't start training for another thirteen months?"

She nodded her head. "Basically, yes. Except that once you officially start training, they'll add however long it was between your new enlistment and the time you started training. They're pretty firm on getting fourteen years of use out of you. That's also when your enlistment bonus clock will start."

The sergeant major added, "I know this seems like a crappy option, Smith. But here's the deal—whether you enlist to try out for Special Forces, you are still going to have to serve at least two additional years after your current enlistment ends. If I was in your shoes, I'd go SF. I don't think you'll regret it one bit, and it'll be an incredible adventure. That or finish off your time and your IRR commitment and get out and never look back."

Pauli thought for a moment. "OK, let's do it," he said confidently. "Sign me up for Special Forces. I've wanted to do this for years."

****

RNS *Tripoli*
1st OAB Briefing Room

Major Monsoor observed the officers and NCOs sitting in front of him. He saw the nervousness in their faces. He was nervous too. This was a big mission.

Captain Shinzo Akio asked, "Major, what if our fleet isn't able to punch through the Zodark fleet? Will they call off the invasion if we aren't able to secure the battlespace?"

Several of the officers nodded. A few transports carrying more than seven thousand soldiers had been lost during the invasion of Intus. When the Orbot battleship and a few Zodark cruisers had suddenly appeared in the middle of the fleet, there wasn't much the transports could do to escape.

"My understanding is, like Intus, there will be two fleets," Major Monsoor explained. "The first fleet will jump into the system and move to secure the stargate. Then they'll engage the enemy fleet over the planet Rass. Once it's been cleared, the second fleet consisting of the transports will jump through the stargate and then head to the planet."

Monsoor continued, "This planet contains multiple Zodark bases. Our goal is to assault this particular ridge. It provides us a decent view of the entire valley and the enemy base some thirty-two kilometers away. Behind the ridge lies a large plateau. The brass has ordered the heavy artillery set up there. The M88s will soften the base up before several brigades of C100s are unleashed on it. After destroying or securing this facility, we'll stand by to see what the division has next for us."

"When do we leave?" asked another officer.

Major Monsoor smiled. "The fleet leaves in three days. We have to transit twelve stargates to reach our marshaling point. I was told by the captain the trip will take us four months. That means we will have a lot of time on our hands. Run your company and platoons through the simulators as often as you can. Drill into them everything there is to know about this planet and our objective. I have no idea how long this campaign will be, but what I *do* know is this won't be like Intus. This is a Zodark planet—a planet they stole from the Primords more than three hundred years ago. It's now a Zodark and Orbot military depot and industrial center. The hope is that taking this base and facility out of play will put a dent in the enemy's ability to continue to wage this war."

The meeting broke up shortly after that. Everyone clearly felt both nervous and excited about the mission and a chance to attack a Zodark military base and industrial center.

****

"I still can't believe you reenlisted for fourteen years. You are a special kind of crazy, Pauli," his friend Yogi said as they played a football game on the computer.

"Well, I was being stop-lossed, so it's not like I could exactly leave when my enlistment was up anyways," Pauli countered as his quarterback threw a forty-yard pass to his wide-open receiver.

Yogi cursed when his cornerback missed the interception and then the tackle. Pauli ended up grabbing another twenty yards before his player was brought down.

"Still, why Special Forces?" Yogi pressed. "I heard if you reenlisted in the infantry, they're offering a ten-thousand-RD bonus per year you re-up. You could have netted a hundred and forty thousand RDs for that same length."

Pauli laughed at the sum. "You know what the bonus is for Special Forces, Yogi?"

Yogi's defensive ends blitzed Pauli, and one of his players managed to sack Pauli's quarterback for a ten-yard loss.

"More than a hundred and forty K?"

Pauli turned to his friend. "Try five hundred thousand."

Yogi let out a whistle at the number. "Damn, dude. Maybe I should look at joining when I get closer to my reenlistment. That's a lot of money. I'll bet you could buy a nice plot of land on New Eden with that kind of dough."

"Maybe, but I'd actually rather see if maybe I'd be allowed to live on Intus," Pauli replied. "That planet was beautiful, even more so than New Eden."

"Yeah, but it's a Prim world. You'd probably be one of the only humans on the planet," said Yogi.

Pauli shrugged indifferently.

"Pauli, Yogi, I need you both to come with me," announced Master Sergeant Dunham as he walked into the dayroom. They turned their game off and got up to follow their platoon sergeant. Whatever was up, they'd find out soon enough.

When they walked into Captain Shinzo's office, the other sergeants in the platoon and company were there waiting for them. Pauli felt like a heel being the last ones to show up.

"Take a seat, gentlemen. We've got a lot to talk about," Captain Shinzo announced as everyone perked up. "OK, so here's the skinny. We're getting closer to our final destination. Our particular mission just got its first FRAGO. 1st Battalion, 4th Special Forces Group put in a special request for our particular battalion to assist them in a mission. This is the same SF battalion we worked with on New Eden, so apparently, their commander was impressed with our performance because he asked General McGinnis for us by name. The major was *so* excited, he didn't bother asking what the mission was." Several of the sergeants chuckled. "An hour ago, we got the mission brief, and let me just say, it's a one-of-a-kind mission to say the least."

Pauli was excited that the 4th SF Group had requested them by name. They'd fought with them for more than six months on New Eden. Heck, it was a couple of soldiers from that unit that had convinced Pauli he should apply to Delta. He was stoked to be working with them again.

"Let me guess, the mission's a real ballbuster," Lieutenant Atkins said aloud to the chagrin of the others.

Captain Shinzo grunted. "That's an understatement, Lieutenant. This mission's going to suck. It's going to be tough as hell. Honestly, I can't believe the major agreed to this. I think he forgot we aren't augmented superhumans like they are. This mission is actually so tough, the entire battalion is being outfitted with Delta body armor and equipment. The reason I called you all in is, starting tomorrow, we're going to be issued the new equipment. I need you all to drill your men relentlessly in it. We don't have a lot of time to get ready. Worse, we'll be carrying it out with entirely new equipment and weapons we're not used to using—"

"New weapons? What are we getting?" asked one of the master sergeants with a grin.

Shinzo shrugged. "Not *new* weapons per se. We're still going to be using the M85s, M90s, and M91s, we're just going to be fitted out with the SF versions of them. They're generally smaller and more compact than our current infantry weapons. They've also improved the battery packs for the blasters, doubling the number of shots they can fire. The magrail and 20mm smart grenades are also double the capacity. I think the biggest change for us is going to be the armor. It's made of a lightweight composite material, but it's also bulky and essentially covers your entire body—"

"Sorry to interrupt, sir," said Lieutenant Atkins. "If the Greenie Beanies are giving us their fancy armor and improved weapons, it means they're expecting this to be a nasty fight. What exactly *is* the mission?"

Captain Shinzo snorted at the bluntness of the question. He and Atkins had a well-known back-and-forth. Atkins was a thirty-year veteran of the infantry; he was direct and to the point, and he seldom missed much either.

"Unlike the rest of the invasion force, the Deltas go in during the first wave. For this attack, they're going to assault a Zodark military base in high orbit over the planet," Shinzo explained. "Once they breach the facility, they want our help in securing it."

The captain brought up some images of the station provided to them by the Primords. He then showed them a short video clip of how the attack was going to play out. Basically, the Prims were going to use several of their ships to disable the station's defensive weapons. Once that was done, the Deltas would land a contingent of soldiers on the outer shell of the station. They'd cut their way into it and then move down to the hangar bay. Once they secured the hangar bay, Pauli's unit would fly in and help them hold the hangar facility while more reinforcements were brought on board. When a beachhead had been secured, they'd expand further into the facility. The goal of the entire mission was to capture the station and any technology or intelligence they could use from it.

Lieutenant Atkins cleared his throat. "Well, then I guess we have our work cut out for us. We've got, what, three weeks until we arrive in the system? It sounds like everything is situation normal—nothing to see here."

The others laughed.

****

RNS *Tripoli*
Training Bay

"I think I could get used to this body armor and these fancy rifles, Sarge," one of the new replacements said.

"Just remember, this armor might keep a blaster bolt from penetrating, but that doesn't mean it won't hurt," Pauli said to his squad. "You still need to stay frosty, heads on a swivel if you want to survive. This is going to be a tough fight. We'll be confined to a starbase. This won't be like fighting on the planet surface where we can spread out. This will be tight-quarters, close-in, dirty combat with the Zodarks. You need to be ready for it, all right?"

His two corporals nodded their heads, knowing it was going to fall on their shoulders to make sure each fire team was ready.

The next two weeks were spent practicing close-in combat on a simulated starbase. They practiced clearing rooms, corridors, hangars, and anything else they could think of. They went for daily runs in their new body armor and combat rigs, carrying their modified weapons. The officers and NCOs were doing everything they could to get the men ready for what would certainly be a tough fight.

As they neared the planet Rass, the training continued to intensify. They were embarking on a mission that had never been attempted before—the capture of an enemy starbase. If all went according to plan, they'd capture the facility and learn a lot more about their adversaries.

Chapter Eleven
Task Force Rass

RNS *George Washington*
Stargate 352-NHW

"You can do this, Captain McKee," said Admiral Abigail Halsey via the holograph communication. "I have the utmost confidence in your ability to lead this task force."

Deep down, McKee felt overwhelmed with self-doubt and uncertainty. She'd lost a lot of friends during the attack on Intus; a lot of ships under her command had been destroyed. It weighed on her a lot.

"I wish we had our new warships ready," McKee commented. It was just the two of them talking privately in her office—she'd never say something like that in public.

Halsey grimaced. "We all wish we had the new ships, Fran," she countered. "We're just going to have to wait until they come online, and we've had time to get our crews trained up and ready for them. In the meantime, we keep punching the Zodarks and Orbots with what we have. Let's not forget you also have your new Primord friends here with us: Admiral Stavanger and his fleet. Heck, they've brought more ships to this fight than we have in our entire fleet. I'm sure this battle will go differently than the last one."

"Thanks for the pep talk, Admiral. I guess I needed some reassurance. I'm still having a tough time being in command of so many ships and people. It really hurts when you lose a ship and know that eleven hundred people died because you ordered them into a position that put them in harm's way," Fran lamented.

Abigail nodded her head in agreement. "Wait until you become an admiral and you have to do this on a much grander scale. You suddenly find you're responsible for dozens of warships and tens of thousands of people. You learn that no matter what you do, people are going to die. It's the nature of war. Our job is to minimize the number of losses we take and increase our chances of winning."
****

"The Prim fleet is jumping through the gate now," announced Captain McKee's operations officer, excitement and tension in her voice.

"Stand by to follow them in," Captain McKee announced as her ship and sixteen other RNS warships prepared to join the fight.

For five minutes, they watched and waited as one group after another of Primord ships led the way and jumped through the gate. Everyone knew on the opposite side was an enemy fleet waiting to greet them, so the Earthers anticipated an outright melee once they jumped through.

McKee turned to her flight operations officer. "Once we emerge on the other side of the gate, launch our squadrons of Orions immediately. We don't know how bad the battle will be on the other side. Deploy them and make them ready to assist us. Have the B-99s ready to deploy as well. I want our bombers to focus their weapons on any Zodark or Orbot battleships that may be waiting for us. It's going to be important to take those ships out first.

"EWO, I know they're going to be in close, so you may not be able to jam them as effectively as you otherwise would. Still, try to do what you can. Focus on the smaller frigates and cruisers who may not have as strong a countermeasure as the battleships. Also, make sure you're constantly deploying our SW antilaser countermeasures. Create a constant bubble of that crap around our ship, even as we're moving."

Now that McKee had given some last-minute instructions to her crew, she was ready for whatever was waiting for them on the other side. Come hell or high water, this was going to be a defining battle: one that would either throat-punch the enemy and put them on their heels or force the allies to fall back and rethink their strategy.

Finally, it came time for the *GW* and its accompaniment of two battlecruisers, six cruisers and six frigates to jump through. The squadron approached the gate and waited their turn. When the gate activated, it created a liquid shimmer inside the center of it, the signal for them to pass through. As the squadron approached, the gate sucked the ships into it. Once inside, the bridge crew watched as they appeared to speed down, up, and to the sides of some sort of tunnel. Meanwhile, all sorts of different colors of lights swirled about them for a couple of minutes as they transitioned through the gate. Although only a couple of minutes passed, it felt like an eternity. The gate ejected them out the other end and into the blackness of space.

It took only minutes for their sensors to pick up what was going on around them and to visualize the light from the nearby sun and planets

102

in the system. In fractions of a second, their radar screens lit up with dozens upon dozens of Prim and Zodark warships. They also spotted two dozen laser turrets and other weapons anchored around the gate. The gate guns were actually something new—the human fleets hadn't encountered them before.

Judging by what they saw on their sensors, the Zodark ships were pounding the Primord ships hard, trying to finish them off before their human allies could jump in and assist them. Several of the Prim cruisers were being ripped apart and exploding all around them.

Crap, what did we jump into? Fran silently asked herself.

"Target those gate guns now! Take them out before more ships jump through the gate. Then find us a target for the plasma cannon!" she commanded as the bridge crew on the ship went into overdrive trying to analyze and handle all the incoming data.

Her weapons department locked up the gate guns with their primary and secondary turrets. It didn't take many shots from their magrails to pulverize the gate guns.

Once they were silenced, they turned their massive magrail turrets on a Zodark battleship that was pounding away on a Prim battleship. The two vessels were hitting each other with brilliant stabs of light. Each laser shot cut deep into each other's vessel. Chunks of debris, atmosphere, and even bodies were being ejected from the vessels as they tore into each other.

Then the *GW* got into the fight. They hammered the enemy battleship with dozens upon dozens of sixty-inch and thirty-six-inch slugs. The enormous projectiles rattled the Zodark warship hard. The ones that penetrated through its armor and into the ship lit off their high-explosive warheads, causing further damage and destruction on the enemy warships.

"Firing the plasma cannon now!" yelled out one of her targeting officers.

The massive cannon fired, whiting out their screen momentarily. When they could see what was happening around them again, they realized that the plasma cannon had scored a direct hit on the Zodark warship, blowing a twenty-meter-wide hole clean through the ship. With the hole in their midsection and a near-constant broadside barrage of magrail slugs, the Zodark ship started breaking apart. Secondary explosions rippled across the chunks of the vessel as it began to separate into two main sections.

"Shift fire to those enemy cruisers!" called out Captain McKee. There had to be thirty Zodark cruisers battling it out at the gate with the Primord ships. They needed to thin the herd before they became overwhelmed.

With a view of the *GW* and the battle unfolding around them, McKee saw both sides of the *GW*'s primary and secondary weapons blasting away at the enemy cruisers. Their lone plasma cannon repositioned to fire on the remaining two enemy battleships.

"Release the bombers," McKee ordered her flight operations. "Focus their torpedoes and missiles on the battleships."

The F-97 Orions were soon in the thick of the fight, heavily engaged with the Zodark fighters. McKee saw two Primord cruisers explode moments later, succumbing to the volume of enemy fire being directed at them.

The *GW* itself was starting to shake more and more. Several enemy cruisers circled in on them, firing their powerful lasers. The enemy were going after their primary and secondary guns, knowing that would minimize the damage the *GW* could inflict on them.

The stargate behind them suddenly activated again. Three more RNS battleships emerged, escorted by two dozen frigates. The human ships spun up their engines to full speed as they dispersed and put some distance between themselves and the gate.

The added firepower from these ships would greatly help in the battle. The Primord ships did their best to hold out against the Zodark vessels, but more and more of them were succumbing to the volume of fire being thrown at them. The battle at the stargate was proving to be an epic battle for the ages.

As more Primord and human ships continued to jump through the gate, group after group of Zodark ships also arrived to reinforce their fleet. The vast array of ships crowded into this area of space was creating a hectic and chaotic scene to say the least. The Zodarks clearly knew if they lost this battle, then chances were, they'd lose the system.

The gate activated again, and moments later, thirty-two Primord cruisers and battleships emerged. Seconds later, the remainder of the Earth fleet jumped through. The Galactic Empire fleet now outnumbered the Zodark ships by a five-to-one ratio. Several of the Zodark ships near the perimeter of the battle jumped away, presumably back to the planet Rass and their orbital stations there.

The battle around the gate continued to rage, but it wouldn't last much longer. While the Primord and Zodark ships blasted each other repeatedly with their lasers, masers, and direct-energy weapons, the human ships made good use of their magnetic railguns to pulverize the thinner-skinned Zodark vessels.

The Zodark ships were incredibly tough to kill with a direct-energy weapon because of their use of an organic material that absorbed and dispersed the high energy of a laser. This armor technology had allowed them to dominate space warfare for hundreds of years, maybe even longer. However, when the humans had shown up using almost exclusively magrails, the effects of this weapon had been felt immediately.

Despite using what other races deemed an old, outdated technology, the human ships were pulverizing their more technologically sophisticated adversaries. The Earthers just didn't have the quantity of ships or trained crews to throw into these major battles like their allies; they hadn't been a part of this war long enough to have fully retooled their shipyards to meet the increased demand for ships, or to get their economy on a solid wartime footing. It would take them close to a full decade to be a true, fully capable member of the Galactic Empire.

"Captain McKee, the enemy ships that could warp away are warping in the direction of Rass. Shall I set a course to pursue them?" asked her helmsman.

"Coms, patch me through to Admiral Stavanger. I need to speak with him immediately," McKee directed.

It took a moment to get a response from the Primord ship. Then an image of Admiral Stavanger appeared on their main computer screens. "Captain McKee, please pass along my compliments to your ships for their incredible fighting. My ships will take one of your hours to recover our life pods and give our people some needed time to get our ships repaired. Would your fleet like to lead the assault on the planet?"

McKee thought about that for a moment; it was a great honor and opportunity that he was offering her. "My fleet can do that, Admiral. However, we need to make sure we leave some ships to maintain control of the gate. We're about to have hundreds of transports transit through the gate."

Admiral Stavanger nodded. "If you agree, I recommend we leave one of your battleships and two of my own: maybe four of your cruisers and ten frigates. I'll leave the same contingent. This ought to give us enough ships should the Zodarks opt to send another force here."

McKee liked the idea. "This sounds like a solid plan, Admiral," she said with a smile. "Let's detail off the ships. We need to secure the planet and capture those stations and other orbital platforms. I will give the order for my ground forces to initiate their part of the plan."

When the two had ended their transmission, McKee ordered her coms officer to send a communications drone back through the stargate, telling the assault force to begin their part of the operation. Once the joint fleet arrived around Rass, the real battle would start.

****

RNS *Midway*
1st Battalion, 4th Special Forces Group

Captain Brian Royce stood at the front of the briefing room as he addressed his operators. "This will be a first for us—the seizing of a hostile station. We've never done this before, so I'm not even going to pretend to tell you that this'll be a walk in the park or that it'll be tough-as-hell mission because frankly, I don't know. What I can tell you is this—we've come up with what I think is a decent plan for getting us inside the station alive."

Royce paused for a moment as he brought up several closer-up images of the station. "As you can see, there are a number of close-in point defense turrets protecting the stations. A handful of Primord frigates are going to do their best to take them out for us. What I want to show you, however, are these points here," he said, using a laser to point at the images.

"This, gentlemen, is how we're going to get into the station. Once the Prims take the close-in gun turrets, our pilots are going to fly a platoon to each of these access doors. Once the Osprey settles in over it, we're going to essentially treat this like we would any other ship boarding operation. As a matter of fact, it's just like that Zodark carrier we assaulted over New Eden many years ago.

"A breaching team in each platoon will cut their way through the access door, allowing the rest of the platoon to breach into the station.

From there, each platoon needs to do their best to reach this point here. The intelligence provided to us by the Prims says this location isn't too far from the hangar bay, which we'll need to get opened up so the rest of our force can land and help us seize the station. I can't tell you how many Zodarks are inside, but you can bet they'll have a decent contingent of them. The sooner we can get the hangar operational, the sooner we can get reinforcements moved in."

Some of the soldiers whistled, while some whispered and grumbled. This mission was just getting better and better the more they learned about it.

"Now, before we leave for this mission, four Prim commandos will be assigned to each platoon. Once we breach the station and gain access to the hangar, they'll get it unsealed and opened up. Your job is to secure the hangar and start pushing out further into the station to give us more room. I can't tell you how long it'll take to start receiving our reinforcements, so you need to plan on holding the place for as long as possible.

"Once we're inside, deploy your scout drones ASAP. Get those little buggers mapping the place as quickly as they can. We need to know what the layout of the station is and what kind of force we may be dealing with."

Captain Royce turned to look at his platoon leaders. "Second Platoon, your job is to secure the hallways and intersections immediately around the hangar once we've secured it. Establish a solid blocking force and prevent the Zodarks from sending reinforcements to the hangar bay. First Platoon, your job is to push out beyond our immediate perimeter and go hunting. You'll cause some chaos inside the station, which will keep the enemy on their toes. When you run into enemy resistance beyond what you can handle, then you need to fall back to the perimeter Second Platoon will have established and reinforce them. Hopefully, your activities will have bought us more time.

"Third and Fourth Platoons, your job is to be the QRF for First and Second Platoons. Whichever one runs into trouble or needs the most help, that's the platoon you help."

After they spent another ten minutes going over additional details about the mission, one of the platoon leaders asked, "Sir, are you confident a regular army unit should be our backup? Why wasn't it possible to get another SF company to help us?"

A few of the other soldiers grunted in agreement as they bobbed their heads up and down.

Royce sighed. "Look, I know you'd rather work with another Delta unit, but it's just not going to happen. Our battalion and the rest of the group have their own missions on the surface. The Army unit we've asked to help us is the 1st OAB. We've worked with that unit on New Eden in the past. They fought pretty well with us down there, so I'm confident they'll do just fine here.

"Now, let's start getting our gear, weapons, and ammo ready. We're going to drop out of warp in ninety minutes. Everyone, load up in the Ospreys in seventy. We need to be ready to leave the *Midway* ASAP once we're in the system and close to our objective. Understood?"

Everyone gave the obligatory "Hooah!" They'd execute their orders as best they could when the time came.
****

"Stand by. The *Midway* is dropping out of warp," announced the Osprey pilot. Royce had come up to the cockpit to join the pilots as they waited for the action to start.

Minutes later, the *Midway* did indeed come out of warp, and they were now less than five hundred thousand kilometers from the enemy station. As the area around the *Midway* populated with targets, they realized they had jumped into a real hornet's nest.

There were two dozen Zodark cruisers scattered around the battlespace, along with at least one Zodark star carrier and three battleships. There were even an Orbot cruiser and battleship here as well.

Captain Royce and the pilots noticed the *George Washington* firing its plasma cannon at the Orbot battleship. The energy weapon slammed into the ship with an enormous amount of force. It caused a massive explosion near the rear half of the Orbot ship, which led to multiple secondary explosions that rippled throughout.

Then the *GW* opened up on the Orbot ship with its primary weapons; its rows of sixty-inch magrail turrets sent strings of slugs at the enemy warship. Then the secondary weapons, the thirty-six-inch guns, turned their attention to the Zodark cruisers as they sought to cull the enemy.

The four Prim battleships moved into position to attack the Zodark battleships while the six human battleships kept their fire directed on the Zodark carrier and the Orbot battleship. The Prim and human cruisers and frigates went to work on the remaining ships. A smaller group of Prim frigates, five in total, headed right for the enemy station. These were the ships assigned to go after the station's weapons. Until they were taken down, the *Midway* couldn't launch its boarding crews to take charge of the station.

The battle around them raged for close to half an hour as the Prim ships fought their way to the enemy station. As they disabled the enemy guns, two Republic Navy battleships moved to the station, adding their volume of fire. These ships were also providing cover for the *Midway* and the *Tripoli* as they moved in on the station. Half of the *Midway*'s Delta teams were slated to assault the station: the others would be hitting objectives down on the planet. The *Tripoli*, carrying the 1st OAB, would be assaulting the station with the Deltas.

The pilot for the Osprey turned his head slightly to Captain Royce. "Best take a seat, sir, we're about to launch. This is going to get hairy as we fly into that hornet's nest."

Taking the hint, Royce climbed back to his seat. He fastened himself in and prepared for what would come next. He knew this was going to be a rocky ride.

Moments later, the Osprey shot down the launch tube and into the darkness of space. After the Osprey left the protection of the *Midway*, Royce patched himself into the pilots' camera view so he could get a sense of what was going on around them and keep an eye on their objective: the outer service hatch they'd be cutting their way into.

Brilliant flashes of light zipped throughout the blackness of space all around the warring ships. One Primord ship was firing laser shots in all directions around it as a squadron of smaller Zodark fighters dove in on it. Several of the fighters were blotted from the sky in the form of small explosions, while some of their comrades fired plasma torpedoes that plowed into the Primord ships, causing extensive damage.

While the Zodark fighters pulled up and away from the Primord ship, they practically flipped themselves around. Then they halted their speed and reaccelerated right back at the Primord ship, unleashing another volley of plasma torpedoes. The Prim ship shook violently as half a dozen more torpedoes slammed into them, causing a series of explosions that began to break the allied ship apart.

As the Zodark fighters regrouped to go after another Primord ship, a handful of P-97 Orions came in behind them, raking their spacecraft with 20mm magrail slugs. Half the Zodark fighters exploded before they even knew they were under attack. The enemy ships then darted to different positions, allowing their laser turrets to reangle to engage the human ships. They fired a series of barrages at the Orions. Two of the human starfighters exploded, but not before their pilots were able to eject from the stricken crafts.

A human frigate joined the fray, letting loose brilliant streaks of light from their close-in weapon systems or CIWS 20mm rotary guns. The incredible cyclic rate of fire of these seven-barreled liquid-propellent-fired weapons was nothing short of amazing. With every fifth round being a tracer, it lit up the darkness around the ship like Royce remembered Independence Day back home. The remaining Zodark fighters were ripped to shreds, unable to get out of the way of the torrent of tungsten projectiles being thrown at them.

Royce found himself getting lost in the battle going on around him. He snapped himself out of his observations of the battle and selected the image of the rapidly approaching station that the pilots were looking at. The facility itself was still in the fight. Scorched black marks showed the spots on the station where the Prim frigates had taken out the station's close-in laser turrets and weapon systems, which had to be destroyed so their Ospreys could attach themselves to the access hatches and cut their way in.

One of the Prim frigates zapped two more laser turrets, only to be cut in half by a Zodark cruiser that moved in. Royce had no idea how large the Zodark cruisers truly were, but he felt their Osprey was tiny in comparison. The enemy ship didn't appear interested in their little craft as it angled away from them and headed towards one of the human battlecruisers. Its main guns fired a handful of shots at the *Bishop*, which had been a sister ship to the *Rook* back in its heyday.

Amid all the craziness going on around them, their Osprey pilot deftly maneuvered them through it all as he continued toward the station. He dodged several missiles, then a couple of laser shots and lastly a Zodark fighter before it was intercepted by an Orion. With skill and a lot of luck, their pilot maneuvered them over the service hatch they needed to cut their way through. He settled the shuttle overtop it and began the process of establishing a seal so the Special Forces operators in the back could cut their way into the starbase.

Once they had a hard seal between the ship and the station, one of the crew chiefs undogged the floor hatch and opened it up. The breaching team was right behind him with their specially designed cutting torch. A Delta trooper dropped down the hatch to the surface of the station. He activated the cutting torch and began to slice the outline of the hatch that would lead them into the station.

Meanwhile, the soldiers inside the troop bay of the Osprey readied themselves and their equipment. They knew once they were inside, things were likely to get pretty crazy. No one knew how many Zodarks were in the station or what kind of nasty surprises they had prepared for them inside.

A lot of the Deltas who'd participated in the battle to capture the Zodark carrier a few years back knew from experience that this was going to be a tough fight. If it was anything like that battle, they'd be using a lot of hand grenades to clear the various rooms and corridors.

The Deltas had brought ten of their C100s on the Osprey. They'd given their group of terminators special orders for this mission—they'd essentially been directed to kill anything and everyone that wasn't human or Primord inside the station. This would be the first time they used the combat Synths in a close-in battle like this. If things worked out well, then they might use them more often in the future.

Walking past a couple of his guys, Royce made his way over to the hatch to get a look at the soldier cutting their way in. "How much longer?" he asked.

The soldier paused what he was doing as he looked up. "At least five minutes, sir. I'm moving as fast as I can. This access hatch appears to be pretty thick and it looks like they coated it with that organic material they cover the rest of their armor in."

Royce nodded; he knew the guy was doing his best. Asking him for updates every few minutes wasn't going to speed things up. They'd get inside the station soon enough.

The minutes ticked by like an eternity while the battle around the station raged on. Meanwhile, their shuttle had to sit there like a tick attached to the belly of a dog. At any given moment, they could be zapped by an enemy laser, blotted from existence. It was perhaps the most helpless feeling any of them had ever experienced.

Then the operators heard the best possible news. "I'm in! I just have to kick it free and we're in the next room."

Royce's tension and anxiety lifted, knowing that in mere moments they'd be inside the station and no longer sitting ducks on the outer hull of the starbase.

One of the soldiers nearby called out to the man with the cutting torch. "Here, let me help you out." And he jumped down to help the man get the door opened up.

The others got themselves ready and stepped out of the way to allow the C100s to get lined up to enter the station first. Not knowing what they were jumping into, they wanted to let the combat Synths clear them a path. Once the Synths deemed the initial area clear, the rest of the platoon and the remaining C100s would follow them in.

When they got inside the station, the plan was to break the C100s up into five two-man teams and turn them loose on the station while the platoon moved to secure the hangar. Once it was secured, the rest of their reinforcements would arrive and the fight to capture the station would ensue.

"Breaching," called out one of the C100s in its monotone voice as it used its mechanical leg to kick the hatch inward; the door was thrown deep into the corridor that was behind it. The killing machine practically fell inside and flailed its arms and legs out to stabilize itself. Once it was steady on both feet, the C100 immediately had its rifle up and ready for action. While the lead terminator moved into the corridor, the rest of the Synths fell in behind it.

When the first two Synths weren't immediately shot to pieces or opening fire with their own rifles, the rest of the human platoon started dropping into the corridor. Advancing towards the next door, they used a portable electronic device that did a quick scan of the locking mechanism on the door. Moments later, the light indicator on the device went from red to green, letting them know the door should be unlocked. The lead Synth pushed the door open. As soon as it did, the first group of Synths pushed their way into the next room and spread out.

It appeared the room beyond the initial corridor was attached to a warehouse of some sort. In seconds, the squads of the platoon fanned out inside the cavernous room, clearing the rows of stacked items and locating the other entrances and corridors that led in or out of that space.

So far, they hadn't stumbled across any Zodarks. Royce actually thought it was a bit disconcerting not stumbling into any enemy soldiers.

Soon enough, they'd make contact, though, and once that happened, all bets were off.

One of Royce's soldiers pulled his patrol pack off, placing it on the ground. He unzipped it and pulled out a dozen microdrones they called Dragonflies. They were only about the size of a fifty-cent piece. One by one, the soldier activated the little drone and synced them up with a small tablet attached to the left side of his forearm.

The soldiers opened the doors to each of the corridors, and the drone operator sent an equal number of Dragonflies down each exit. The drones would travel near the ceiling, hopefully out of eyesight. As they traveled further inside the station, they'd emit a small radar signal that would help them map the inside of the base. The Dragonflies also used a special electronic scanner that would allow them to see through a wall to map out the layout of the room on the other side.

While their drone operator was getting the drones going to help them build a better picture of the layout of the base, another soldier used a small scanner that allowed them to see through the walls of the storage room they were in. The device provided a more detailed version of the types of images the drones could create.

"I got something over here!" called out a couple of the soldiers excitedly.

Royce and half the platoon made their way over to the corporal who'd called out to them.

"What do you have, Corporal?" Royce asked tersely. He had a lot to juggle, now managing three platoons of people.

"Sir, on the opposite side of this wall appears to be our primary objective, the hangar. From what we can see, there are a handful of Zodarks inside the room. I think we can gain entry to the place if we go out this corridor here," the soldier said, pointing to one of the entrances, "then turn right and follow it down five or ten meters. The entrance to the hangar should be just to our right."

Royce squinted as he looked at the image. He overlaid it on top of the images the little scout drones were feeding them, and what the corporal said matched up with what the drone had mapped out.

"Good call, Corporal," said Royce. "Excellent find." He turned to his lieutenant. "Let's get the platoon moving. We need to secure that hangar ASAP. Go ahead and disperse the terminators. Cut 'em loose and let 'em cause some chaos for us while we fortify our positions."

The next couple of minutes saw a flurry of activity as the drone operator fed the terminators the layout of the station that the Dragonflies had provided thus far. The C100s synced themselves up with the scout drones and would leverage them as their eyes and ears while they moved through the station.

As the drones moved out, the platoon left the warehouse and made their way towards the hangar. They reached the hangar door and prepared to enter.

I'm going to try and unlock the door, said the platoon sergeant over the neurolink. *Everyone stand by to breach.*

The sergeant placed the unlocking device on the keypad of the hangar bay door and tapped on it a few times. The light on the electronic device switched from red to green. Moments later, the hangar door hissed and retracted into the wall.

When the door opened, a half dozen stunned Zodarks turned to see a group of soldiers standing there, weapons drawn and aimed right at them. For the briefest of moments, no one moved or said anything. Then one of the Zodarks attempted to raise his blaster up to shoot at them, and that was when the Deltas opened up. In seconds, they had cut the enemy soldiers down before they had a chance to react.

The Special Forces soldiers rushed forward, sweeping the massive facility for any other Zodarks that might be lurking behind something or possibly hiding in one of the many shuttles or fighters. It took the soldiers less than five minutes to clear the hangar and officially declare it captured and secured.

Captain Hopper sent a message back to the *Midway* to bring the rest of their troops and C100s over, along with the RA soldiers from the *Tripoli*. Now that they had a beachhead secured, they needed to flood in reinforcements before the Zodarks realized what was happening.

"Captain Royce, sir—one group of terminators ran into some stiff resistance," said one of the platoon leaders. "Do you want me to dispatch a team to help them?" The young lieutenant had just joined his company a few months back.

Royce scanned the situation on his HUD. Two pairs of C100s had run into a Zodark quick reaction force that had probably been dispatched to figure out what was going on in the hangar. Royce turned to face the lieutenant. "Yes, take Second and Third Squad to assist them," he ordered.

Pausing for a second, Royce searched the map on his HUD. *There you are*, he thought.

"The Dragonfly found our secondary target—that research lab the G2 asked us to secure if we could," Royce announced. "It's over here." He tagged the location on his HUD's digital map. "Tell First Squad to do their best to secure the lab with our remaining C100s until I can send more reinforcements from the *Midway* and the *Tripoli*. Got it?"

The lieutenant nodded and took off to make it happen, barking orders to the squad leaders.

The next incoming Osprey was supposed to gain entry into the station via one of the access hatches like Royce's platoon had. However, when several enemy fighters broke through their fighter cover, the Osprey broke off their approach to the station so they wouldn't get taken out as they sat there attached to the side of the station in full view of the enemy fighters. Since Captain Royce had signaled that they had secured the hangar, the Osprey pilot made a mad dash to get them inside and offload his human cargo.

Royce looked nervously at the shield protecting the hangar from the vacuum of space. He turned to their Primord commando. "Are you sure our shuttle will be able to land without bouncing off the shield or being ripped apart?" he pressed.

The allied commando tapped away at a control panel in what appeared to be the nerve center or control center for the hangar. The outer shield shimmered briefly and then changed colors slightly. "I just disabled the shield," the Prim replied. "They'll be able to enter now without a problem."

Captain Royce shook his head at how close they were cutting things. "Maybe you should have done that before I called for reinforcements."

The Prim shrugged. "I would have told you to wave the shuttle off if I couldn't get the shield taken down. It's taken care of now. They can go ahead and land."

Royce looked through the deactivated shield—there was just enough color to tell that it was still there, keeping the vacuum of space from sucking everything out. Outside the membrane that would now allow ships to enter, the battle was still raging; fighters circled some of the Prim and human ships. Zodark ships were being hammered by the human magrail turrets. Control over the area around the station and the planet was still being heavily contested.

While he was observing the battle, Royce caught a glimpse of an Osprey angling in towards the station and the hangar bay he was in. Watching the craft, Royce could see stabs of light from lasers darting all around the Osprey. He was surprised it hadn't taken a hit or two but immensely glad it hadn't. Nearly sixty of his men were packed in the back of that thing. Moments later, the Osprey glided inside the hangar and made its way towards an empty parking slot near them.

The craft set down not far from Royce and dropped the rear hatch; the platoon of soldiers and ten additional C100s trotted off. When the platoon leader made his way over to him, Royce told his lieutenant to hold the Synths back in reserve along with two of the four squads. The other two squads were sent forward to reinforce the units currently fighting the Zodark patrols engaging his soldiers.

For the next thirty minutes, the fighting inside the base intensified immensely. The Osprey that had brought Royce and his platoon to the station had sealed the hole they had cut into and left. They darted back to the *Midway* to load up with more soldiers and equipment.

While the fighting in the station increased, the fight outside the station also raged on. The human and Primord ships assaulting the area continued fighting the remaining Zodark ships, which just wouldn't quit or retreat. They were apparently determined to fight to the death despite being hopelessly outnumbered.

Moments later, the nose of the next Osprey carrying Royce's Third Platoon penetrated the forcefield of the hangar bay. In seconds, the craft made its way towards an empty parking spot.

Damn, we need to figure out how to integrate that kind of tech into our ships, thought Royce. He admired how all these different races had solved so many of the technical challenges of being a spacefaring race.

The pilot moved the craft to one side of the cavernous facility and then shut down its engines. After they entered the facility, a T-92 Starlifter maneuvered in next. Starlifters were the heavy-lift shuttles for moving lots of cargo, armored vehicles or a lot of infantry all at once. They were practically defenseless since they only carried two CIWS weapons, but they more than made up for it with what they could carry—up to four hundred and twenty soldiers, or twenty-six palletized pieces of equipment, six light armored vehicles, four tanks, or even sixteen mechs. They typically weren't used unless the battlespace was cleared, but in this case, they needed to land a lot of troops quickly. As the T92 set down, a second one lined up its approach and moved forward.

Once the transports had successfully docked, the ships disgorged their soldiers and additional equipment. In addition to bringing Captain Royce's three other platoons, they also brought four hundred C100 combat Synths and the 1st Orbital Assault Battalion, ready for action.

Captain Royce eyed the lead Synth and walked straight for him. "Sync up with the other Synths on the ship. They have the intel for immediate action," he ordered. He then tasked them with forming up in squad- and platoon-sized elements and ordered them to use the map information the Dragonfly drones had acquired for them to attack the various important targets on the ship.

A regular Army major saddled up to Royce, chest puffed out. *This is my operation*, Royce thought. *I'm not going to cede control of it to a regular Army soldier, no matter how special he thinks he is.*

"Are you Captain Brian Royce?" the major asked. Royce did his best to control his facial expressions. The regular Army soldiers, fitted out with the same body armor and weapons the Deltas used, were clearly uncomfortable—they didn't carry themselves the same way as Special Forces soldiers did.

"I am. I'm the Delta commander for this mission. You must be Major Monsoor. How much of your battalion is here with you?" Royce asked.

"It's good to meet you, Captain Royce. I think the last time we met, you were a lieutenant."

Royce shrugged off the comment. "Well, casualties have a strange way of promoting people, Major. I'm sure if you and I live a few more years, we'll both find ourselves promoted another grade or two."

Major Monsoor laughed. "I think I'm going to like working with you," he said. "So, what do you want my soldiers to do? I have about three-quarters of the battalion here with me right now: about eight hundred and ten soldiers. The rest will arrive on the next Starlifter, along with more of our supplies."

Royce took in the information—eight hundred and ten battle-hardened regular Army soldiers would make a world of difference. "OK, Major, let's walk over to my operations desk," he said, and the two of them made their way over to the makeshift setup Royce was using at the moment.

"We sent dozens of our little Dragonflies to get us a working layout of this place," Royce explained. "Now that I have another eighty C100s and another platoon to work with, we'll go on the offense. If you believe your soldiers are capable of clearing and securing rooms or even a level of the station, then I'd like to assign you some targets. As I get more of my C100s and the rest of my platoons arrive, we'll expand our footprint on this station to take it over."

As Captain Royce explained the plan, the two of them stood in front of one of Royce's operations soldiers. He had a computer set up on a cargo container and a small holographic projector displaying some information. He showed them the layout of the level of the station where they currently stood. Several of the Dragonflies had been discovered and destroyed, but close to fourteen were still operational, and they were working on finding ways to get to the other levels of the base.

They had a very detailed layout of the station and the number of Zodarks on their floor. One grouping of six C100s was heavily engaged. Two more Delta squads went to reinforce them, but clearly that bottleneck was going to be tough to break through. The Zodarks had heavily reinforced that section and were fighting like hell to keep the invaders contained.

In the opposite direction, Royce's other two groups of C100s had gotten bogged down in two other corridors. The lone squad of Deltas that had been sent in that direction were holding the area they'd captured, but in need of reinforcements soon.

"Major, send a company-size element to support my two squads here," Royce directed, pointing. "This is a tough fight as it's mostly close quarters, but maybe some of your soldiers can figure out a way to blow a hole in some of these rooms and open up a way around the enemy position here.

"Down this hallway, I need at least a platoon or two worth of troops to assist my lone squad and four Synths holding it. Again, try to find a way around the enemy if possible. Establish one of your companies as a QRF to assist in case the enemy pushes our company back.

"Also, leave one of your companies here to hold the hangar bay. It's critical that we keep this place secured and open to keep receiving more reinforcements," Captain Royce explained as he gave the regular Army soldiers their new marching orders.
****

Lieutenant Atkins signaled for everyone in the platoon to rally up on him. When they had all formed a half-circle, he started issuing orders. "Sergeant Smith, take your squad and head over to this location here." He sent a set of coordinates on the hastily drawn map of the station to his HUD. "There's a Delta squad with four C100s holding this area. It's important that we hold it because further back, down the corridor, is a scientific lab the higher-ups want us to hold on to."

Atkins then turned to Yogi. "Sergeant Sanders, I'm sending your squad to support Smith. He's in charge, but you need to work together on this. We apparently have some exploitation teams coming over on the next transport. The rest of the platoon and I are going to make sure the area around the lab is secured while they go to work on exploiting whatever's inside. They want to scan or video as much of it as possible and send it back for analysis. If you run into serious trouble, let me know and I'll detail off another squad, but that's probably about all I can send you unless we get more reinforcements. Remember, we just need to hold out for a few more hours until a battalion of terminators get here. Once they show up, they'll help us finish taking the station. Hooah?"

"Hooah," came the single-word reply.

****

"OK, you heard the lieutenant. It's time to earn our pay," shouted Sergeant Paul "Pauli" Smith. "Let's show these Deltas the regular Army grunts know how to fight and hold our own." His little pep talk worked; his squad was pumped up.

Utilizing the HUD in their new helmets, Pauli strategized where they needed to go. He motioned for the rest of his troopers to follow him. The soldiers moved out of the hangar and down a dark and dingy corridor, a stark contrast to their own starbases, which were always well lit and clean. The Zodark corridors were also much wider than a human facility, and taller—it reminded Pauli of how much larger the Zodarks were than the humans.

As they advanced further away from the hangar, they eventually came to a bend in the corridor. When they crept around it, there was evidence of some intense fighting. The lab facility and area around it were pretty shot up, with bluish blood everywhere and the remains of five dead Zodarks strewn about.

119

The lab was being protected by a single C100, which reacted menacingly when they appeared from around the bend. Once it recognized them, it returned its gaze in the other direction, where the rest of the Zodarks soldiers were and where all the fighting was taking place.

"Come on, follow me," Pauli said to his squad as he stepped over a few dead Zodark bodies. No matter how many times he saw one of them, they were still menacing, even dead.

As they approached the spot marked on their HUDs, Pauli suddenly heard a lot of shouting and shooting. He could hear M85 blaster fire, and the two heavier blasters were tearing into something. The SF soldiers ahead of them were clearly in a fight.

A figure appeared from around the corner. It was one of the Deltas. "I was told a couple of squads were headed my way. I'm Sergeant Riceman," he said. "I'm sorry I don't have a lot of time to talk or get to know you, but we're in a hell of a fight right now. The rest of my squad is spread out up ahead trying to keep those blue monsters from overrunning our positions. Let me give you a breakdown of what I need from you."

"Sounds like a plan. I'm Sergeant Smith, but everyone just calls me Pauli. This is Sergeant Sanders, but everyone calls him by his first name, Yogi. What do you need my squad to do?"

Sergeant Riceman motioned with his head for him and Sergeant Sanders to follow him over to the side of the corridor, away from the others. "Listen, it's getting pretty hairy up there. Those damn Zodarks keep trying to charge us. We're stuck in these confined corridors, which means we can't get around them or do much of anything other than try to keep them from pushing past us."

Sergeant Riceman shared a schematic of the area, or at least a display of what the little Dragonfly drones had created for them. "Behind you is a storage room. It's just filled with some boxes. I have no idea what's in them, but that's not important. This right here is," Riceman said as he highlighted the far end of a wall in the storage room. "Plant some explosives on that wall and bust a way through it. Once you gain access to this corridor, I need your squad to push through to this door leading to this large area.

"This is where the Zodarks are basing out of to storm our positions from. Get inside there and tear them up. Use your grenades or whatever you have to—but kill them all. Once you start the action, I'll push my squad to link up with you. I only have two C100s left, so I'm going to have them protect the new opening you're going to create in that room. I can't have you leave half your squad there, and we sure as hell can't leave it unguarded."

Yogi and Pauli shared a nervous glance. This was a hell of an audacious plan Sergeant Riceman had just given them. Pauli wasn't sure any of them would survive the next twenty minutes the more he thought about it, but this was the kind of tough-as-nails mission the Special Forces soldiers were known for—impossibly tough jobs that needed to get done.

"OK, Sergeant Riceman, we've got it," Pauli said confidently. "Between my squad and Yogi's, we've got thirty-four of us. Someone from the *Midway* was kind enough to lend us your armor and versions of your own weapons. We'll do our best to support you."

"I'd expect nothing less from you RASs," said Riceman, nodding in approval. "Your battalion fought well with us on New Eden. I'm sure you'll do just as good or better on this damn station. Now, let's get to it. These animals need to be culled, and we're here to do it."

The sergeant's mouth was visible below his HUD. Yogi and Pauli could see a wicked grin on the man's face. He clearly loved his job, killing Zodarks.

Turning to the soldiers filling up in the corridor behind them, Pauli made sure his HUD was synced with both squads. "Listen up. We've been given a ballbuster of a mission by our Delta buddies. We're going to filter into this storage room over there. I need our breaching team to pull out your explosives and meet me on the western side of the wall."

The soldiers filed into the storage room. Three soldiers moved to the north wall, pulling out some small strips of explosives. When Pauli joined them, he explained what he needed them to do. The three of them talked about it for a minute. Once they'd formulated their plan, they began attaching the strips of explosives on the wall.

They started applying one line of the explosives at the base of the wall and unrolled it like a piece of tape, going up the wall about three meters high. He turned and kept rolling the line about a meter and a half to the right before unrolling the explosives down to the floor—he'd essentially created a rectangle the size of a large door. A corporal attached a small chip to one end of the explosives, then told Pauli they were ready to breach.

Pauli got Yogi's attention. "Have one of your fire teams break to the right," he directed. "They need to cover our backs while the rest of our soldiers advance on that large bay the SF sergeant told us about."

Yogi nodded and disseminated the order. Then Pauli nodded to the corporal holding the detonator.

Bam!

The explosion wasn't as loud as Pauli had thought it would be—perhaps because it wasn't a big charge, or perhaps the special armor they were wearing helped to dampen the sound. Either way, when the wall came down, Pauli motioned to his fire team leader to go.

The seven soldiers ran through the smoke and immediately broke left. They headed down the corridor, prepared to keep going until they came to the next bend or until they ran into some opposition. Once they were through the door, Yogi's fire team ran through next. They broke to the right and would do the same thing; they'd set up a blocking position to make sure no one came through and hit them from behind.

As the second team finished filing through, Pauli led the second fire team as they raced to catch up to the first set of soldiers. Running down the hallway in the new gear reminded Pauli how unused to this equipment they really were. The body armor and exoskeleton combat suit the Deltas used were both incredible and dynamic, but to an untrained person, they were hard to control. He had had to relearn how to adjust his run speed and how tightly he gripped something. It was incredible gear, but using it didn't come naturally.

When Pauli rounded the corner at the end of the corridor, he saw the fire team ahead of him had stopped at the next bend. Approaching his corporal, he asked, "What's the holdup?"

Without taking his eyes off what he was looking at, the soldier replied, "We found the bay where the Zodarks are holing up. There's a crap ton of them in there. Here, take a look."

The corporal took a step back, making room for Pauli to catch a glance.

Pauli inched forward just a bit and then pulled a small camera pen out so he could see around the corner. What he saw boggled his mind. Not only was the room filling up with more and more Zodark soldiers, he saw the strangest species he'd ever seen.

Pauli connected his HUD communicator with Sergeant Riceman. "Sergeant, we've found a way into that large bay you told us the Zodarks are attacking you from. But I need you to take a look at this. I'm zooming in to get you a better image of what we're seeing."

Pauli then made sure the camera was taking some live video shots and feeding it into the chat channel between the two of them. At first, Riceman didn't say anything. Then the private channel filled up with several new people: Captain Royce, who Pauli didn't know, and then Lieutenant Atkins and Major Monsoor.

"This is a good job, Sergeant Smith," said Sergeant Riceman. "Captain Royce, I believe what Smith found might be an Orbot. It looks exactly like the pictures the Altairians and Prims have shown us, but this is the first time we've seen one in person. What do you think, sir?"

"I think you're right," said Captain Royce. "Those *do* look like the Orbots the Altairians told us about. Sergeant Smith, can you try to give us a better view of the room? I need to see if there are more of them present."

Pauli pulled the zoom out on the camera and then slowly panned the large room. There had to be close to a hundred Zodarks in there. They were breaking down into smaller squads, with several of them appearing to be giving some orders and guidance on what to do next. There also appeared to be twenty or so Orbots.

Pauli found himself mesmerized, watching these quadrupedal biomechanical cyborgs. The lower portion of their bodies resembled a mechanical spider with half as many legs, while their upper bodies looked very similar to the C100s. They also appeared to be holding rifles and had other military-style equipment fastened to their chest. Clearly, these Orbots were soldiers, just like the Zodarks in the room.

Pauli's HUD radio chirped. Captain Royce explained, "Sergeant Smith, we have several transports inbound; they're at least twenty mikes out. I'm going to need you to do something really tough. I need you to bust in there and do your level best to kill as many of them as possible. They're clearly regrouping to launch another assault down the corridor that'll lead them to the hangar. We can't let that happen. I'll let you figure out how you want to carry out this assault, but you need to figure it out in the next couple of minutes. We don't have much time."

Pauli thought through the scenario. There was a very high likelihood they were about to get killed in the next few minutes, but there was also no other way around this situation. They needed to attack this numerically superior force and break up the attack before they could launch it. This was what the Special Forces did. These Delta operators would hurl themselves into unimaginable situations like this and somehow come out on top.

"That's a good copy, sir. We'll get it done," was all Pauli said in reply to the order.

He turned to the soldiers behind him. "Here's what we're going to do. All of you carrying an M85, switch over to your smart grenades. When we come around the corner, empty your magazine of grenades into the enemy. Make sure you blanket the place—this way we envelop the entire area. When you've emptied your magazine, drop down to a knee and reload."

Pauli then turned to the two soldiers with the M91s and the four soldiers with the M90s. "While we're blanketing them in grenades, you six need to open fire on that horde with your machine guns. Those of you with the M91s, pay special attention to the Orbot soldiers. Keep in mind, these Zodarks are damn fast. They can take a lot of hits and shrapnel before they go down. You need to hit them more than once, so don't let up once the shooting starts."

He turned back to the first group of soldiers. "Once you've reloaded your smart grenades, blanket the area with grenades again. Focus on the Orbot soldiers if possible with your second magazine, but you must hammer the hell out of them. When you've emptied your second magazine of grenades, switch back to your blasters and join the fray.

"Do what you can to move from time to time and spread out, but remember, the first few seconds of this assault are going to determine whether we live or die. We have to cut as many of them down as possible with our initial barrage. Hooah?"

"Hooah!" came the simple reply from his guys.

"We got this, Pauli," Yogi said to his friend with a nod and a look of confidence on his face.

Watching the soldiers around him, Pauli knew it was time. They were ready, and so were the Zodarks. The Zodarks were letting out their raucous war cries, a clear indication that they were getting ready to launch another attack—an attack that might recapture the hangar.

"Follow me!" roared Pauli. He let out his own guttural yell as his body filled with adrenaline.

Rounding the corner, Pauli saw a large group of Zodarks about to head down the other corridor that led to the hangar bay. He aimed his

M85 at the mass of enemy soldiers and fired one 20mm smart grenade after another until he had emptied the eight-round magazine. By this time, the rest of his motley crew had also joined the fray. They blanketed the entire area with smart grenades. Then his two heavy gunners opened up on the Orbots, sending streaks of blue light into their ranks. The four M90 gunners laid into the horde of enemy soldiers. It was almost like shooting fish in a barrel. Pauli's HUD told him there were one hundred and twenty-three Zodarks and thirty-one Orbots in the cavernous facility.

Within seconds of the human soldiers appearing out of nowhere and firing on them, the Orbot soldiers pivoted toward them and returned fire with their rifles, which released a small vapor trail that flew out of the barrels and raced to connect with a human soldier. When one of the vapor trails hit the armor and exoskeleton combat suit of a soldier, it was like someone had just hit that person with a sledgehammer. The human soldier was thrown backward, off their feet and to the ground. Pauli wasn't sure what to make of it when he saw one of his guys go down. His HUD told him the soldier wasn't dead but injured.

As Pauli finished slapping the second magazine of smart grenades into place, he shifted his fire to where the Orbots were and proceeded to send a hail of grenades in their direction. To his amazement, the cyborgs shot at the grenades—their internal systems must have identified them as the most immediate threat to deal with.

While the bunched-up Zodarks got cut to pieces by his M90 gunners and his grenadiers, only three of the Orbots had been rendered inoperable. Pauli knew he needed to call an audible quick, or they were dead.

"Everyone, switch your rifles from blasters to magrails and focus on the Orbots. Our blaster bolts are bouncing off their armor, and they're shooting our grenades before they can reach them!" Pauli boomed over their coms system.

Flicking his own selector switch, Pauli took aim at one of the Orbots just as it hit his last M91 gunner. As soon as he squeezed the trigger, the railgun projectile flew at incredible speed, slamming into the head of the Orbot he'd been aiming at. It blew right through the cyborg's helmet and exploded a mist of biological and mechanical material out the other end. The Orbot's body fell to the ground, dead.

The Orbots were now fully engaging Pauli's team. The damn cyborgs were accurate as hell and didn't miss nearly as often as a Zodark.

Pauli kept shooting at them, but he was having a hard time keeping track of the information on his HUD and staying focused on shooting at the enemy soldiers all around him. He didn't have any cybernetic implants to help him, or a neurolink like the SF soldiers did. Pauli stole a quick glance at the blue force tracker—half his squad were already KIA.

Damn! Crap! They'd only been fighting for less than a minute, and sixteen soldiers were gone. Pauli took a deep breath, centered his mind and staved off his feelings of despair.

"Sergeant Smith, my squad and a handful of Terminators are about to enter the hangar," Sergeant Riceman told him. "Hold it together for a few more minutes."

Pauli sensed he needed to duck. He dropped to a knee just as an Orbot blaster shot sailed over his head, right where he had just been fractions of a second earlier. He scrambled to a new position a few meters away and then popped up just long enough for his HUD to identify an Orbot and zero in on it. He squeezed the trigger several times and saw chunks of the cyborg's body get ripped apart. The Orbot collapsed to the ground, part of its body unable to function. It still tried to shoot at Pauli, so he sent a couple more slugs into its head.

Pauli grabbed for one of his M99 fragmentation grenades and pulled it from its quick-release holder on his chest rig. Depressing the arming mechanism on the grenade, he gave it a good throw in the direction of the Orbots. The damn cyborgs constantly moved about as they sought new cover and a way out of the human soldiers' kill box.

The M99 was the newest version of a very old weapon of war. When the Army had first encountered the Zodarks, they'd realized they were going to need a new set of weapons designed specifically for use against them. The previous generation of fragmentation grenades worked exceptionally well against humans, but they had not worked nearly as well against Zodarks. The Zodarks' skin was too tough, and their body armor was just strong enough to protect them from the older versions of the grenades. The M99s, however, packed a serious punch. They were twice as powerful as the previous grenades and had a specially designed shell that, when detonated, broke apart into larger chunks, thereby making it more likely to kill a Zodark.

When Pauli's grenade landed between two Orbots and blew up, the explosion ripped them both apart. Then, to Pauli's horror, more than two dozen Zodarks circled around his left flank while his soldiers had been focused on the Orbots.

Pauli saw all eight soldiers who had been covering his exposed flank, lying in different positions on the floor, dead. *No, one of them is still alive according to the blue force tracker,* he realized. But that soldier was unconscious and in a bad way.

"Behind us, I need some help ASAP!" Pauli yelled over the coms, hoping someone might hear him.

Yogi turned to see the chaos and then opened fire as fast as his M85 would shoot at the charging horde. Another soldier fired his 20mm smart grenades into the mass of enemy soldiers.

Pauli felt something slam into his chest hard, then another solid punch to his gut or diaphragm knocked the wind right out of him. Yogi saw him go down and made a move to come to his aid. Pauli watched in horror as his friend got hit by several Zodark blaster bolts before his body spun around and landed with a thud on the floor.

Just as Pauli thought they were all dead, Sergeant Riceman and his squad of Delta soldiers rushed through the other entrance into the large room. They charged right into the Zodarks, firing and shooting the entire time. At the end of their M85 rifles was a newly designed blade or bayonet, specially built and adopted by Special Forces and the C100s for the close-in fights they often got into with the Zodarks.

The Deltas tore into the Zodarks, thrashing and slashing as they went. The few remaining C100s went right for the Orbots. Pauli tried his hardest to keep his eyes open and lift his body up to help fight, but the more he tried, the weaker he felt. Then everything went black as his head rolled over on the floor.
****

"Take those Quadbots out!" barked Captain Brian Royce to his soldiers as they rushed into the room. The Primords called the Orbots "Quadbots" because of their four legs—now that the human soldiers had encountered them, the name was starting to stick.

Several of the C100s moved like lightning toward the Orbots, firing their weapons the entire time. After seeing what that regular Army sergeant had done with the magrails, Royce had ordered his soldiers to switch over to their magrails as well. It was the only weapon that appeared to penetrate the cyborgs' body armor.

Royce saw only a couple of the RA soldiers left shooting from the other side of the room. Most of them had been wiped out during their attack. Then an urgent alert flashed across his HUD.

System shutting down...System shutting down...

It took Royce a moment to realize who or what was saying this. It was his handful of C100s. One minute they were rushing toward the Orbots, shooting at them—the next, their metal frames were clattering to the floor with a loud thud.

What the hell just happened to my terminators?! Royce asked himself.

One of Royce's master sergeants chimed in. "Sir, I think the Orbots might have hacked into our C100s and shut them down."

Oh crap! If they can hack into the OS, they may be able to turn them against us, Royce thought, alarmed.

Royce linked himself into all the operating C100s on the station with them and the C100s on the transport that was in the process of docking at the moment. "Execute emergency shutdown, code: Bravo, X-Ray, Niner, Niner, Three, One, immediately!"

Blaster bolts from the remaining Zodarks and vapor contrails from the Orbots continued to zip all around the Deltas as they tore into the enemy ranks. The few Zodarks that were left fell back further into the station as they sought to get out of the hail of fire from the human soldiers. The Orbots, on the contrary, not only held their ground—they were working as a combined unit to engage the Deltas as efficiently as they could.

One by one, the Orbots were taken out. Their refusal to fall back with the Zodarks, or perhaps their programming not allowing them, ultimately led to their demise.

As the battle in the bay ended, several of the sergeants organized a couple of squads to pursue the Zodarks further into the station. They weren't about to let them have a chance to catch their breath or reorganize for a counterattack.

While the Special Forces soldiers continued to press home the attack, more regular Army soldiers started filtering into the area. The rest of that major's battalion had arrived, and they were now doing their best to augment Royce's unit. With his last two platoons finally arriving, Royce sent them forward to help his other squads out.

They officially had a foothold in the station; now they were going to expand their proverbial beachhead and see if they could seize the station and everything within it.

Now that the fighting had moved beyond the room, a handful of medics rushed in and went to work treating the wounded RASs and Special Forces soldiers. They'd do their best to stabilize the wounded, then get them back to the hangar so they could be brought back to the *Midway* or the *Tripoli* for further triage. The medical ships would only jump into the area after the battlespace was clear of enemy ships.

While the medics were tending to the wounded, one of the technical exploitation soldiers walked up to Royce. "Excuse me, Captain Royce?" the man asked, as if unsure he'd found the right officer.

"Yes, I'm Captain Royce," he told the geeky tech. "What can I help you with?"

"Sir, you issued a kill switch order to all the C100s a little while back. Can you tell me what happened?" the technician asked. "Perhaps there's something I can do to help solve the problem."

Royce resisted the urge to be annoyed at being interrupted by one of the exploitation techs, realizing this guy might actually be able to help him. "Sure, I can tell you what happened. I'm synced in with all the C100s; this allows me as the commander to direct them to attack specific targets or override something their AI is telling them to attack. The AI is good, but sometimes it doesn't anticipate what's about to happen, and that's where I come in. When our C100s started charging the Orbots, something happened. I received a message telling me there was some sort of system failure. In a fraction of a second, they dropped to the ground like hunks of useless metal."

Royce now motioned for them to walk and talk as they headed to the lab, which was the real reason this tech was here. "One of my platoon sergeants said something about the Orbots possibly hacking them and turning them off. I don't know why, but in that instant, I thought if the Orbots could hack into their OS and turn them off, they might be able to also turn them against *us*. I couldn't take that chance, so I issued a kill order to all the C100s on the station and the ones on the transport that just docked. I know you're here to exploit the lab, and that's critically important. But do you think you might be able to do a system check on the C100s and determine if the Orbots had infiltrated their OS?"

The tech was silent for a moment as they approached the lab. Finally, he turned back to Royce. "You're right, Captain. We need to focus on the lab first. Once that's completed, then, yes, I think we should check the C100s. Let's separate the ones that turned off from the others. If they hacked them, they'd have hacked that group first. We'll need to see if they were able to get through our firewall. If they did, that could be a problem. It's beyond my technical ability, but I'm sure someone from Walburg Industries would be able to help us figure it out."

Chapter Twelve
Battle Over Rass

RNS *George Washington*

"Damage report!" barked Captain McKee.

"Primary guns one through six on the port side are still down. Primaries eight, nine, and twelve are still down on the starboard side. We're still sitting at roughly fifty percent of our secondary turrets down on both sides. One-third of our torpedo launchers are down as well," the commander in charge of the damage control party said.

"Weps, how many missiles do we have left?" McKee asked, starting to get anxious as more of her weapon systems were going down and the battle was still raging.

"We've expended forty-percent of our ship-to-ship missiles," Lieutenant Commander Cory LaFine shouted back to be heard over the various alarms, warnings, and other noise blaring on the bridge. "I still recommend we empty the magazines on the remaining Zodark and Orbot ships while the launchers are operational."

Her weapons officer had been doing a superb job during the battle, identifying high-value ships they should engage first over others. The battlegroup had prioritized these and then focused all their firepower on a single ship at a time. He'd also been pushing for them to expend all of their nuclear warheads and missiles on the remaining ships. McKee was hesitant. She was concerned about enemy reinforcements showing up and not having missiles to deal with them.

McKee turned to her tactical section. "Commander Arnold, how many enemy ships are left and how many Prim and Republic warships are still in fighting shape?"

It took Arnold a moment to get the info she was asking for. "We have two functional battleships, three battlecruisers, twelve frigates, and ourselves. The Prims have five battleships, twelve cruisers, and fourteen frigates. They're in better shape than we are."

"How many enemy ships are still left?" asked McKee.

"There are two Orbot battleships and one cruiser. They still have that one support ship further away, but frankly, we have no idea what that thing really is or what it does," Commander Arnold explained, putting his hands up a bit as if surrendering. "It's not participating in the battle. As to the Zodarks, they have two carriers left, six battleships, a lone star destroyer, and eight cruisers. We've been popping their cruisers quickly as they are just easier to take down."

Captain McKee's battlegroup had fallen back to let the Primord ships take the brunt of the fighting. Admiral Stavanger had directed her to pull her forces back so they could work on getting their ship damage under control. He kept reminding her that space battles take a bit of time to play out. It wasn't a sprint—it was a marathon to keep your ships alive as long as possible.

"Damage control, how long until we'll have more of our primary and secondary turrets back online?" McKee asked next.

Commander Dieter Bonhauf turned to face her. "We'll have at least two of the starboard turrets fixed in two or three hours. A couple of the secondary turrets on the port side will be ready in an hour. The remaining guns are going to take a day or more."

Damn, this isn't good, McKee realized. *We're down half our primary and secondary weapons.* They needed to get back into the fight. Admiral Halsey was still waiting with the transports to bring the landing force in. McKee's mind raced as she considered what to do next. They needed to clear the path for the infantry, and they needed to do it now.

McKee faced her bridge crew. "OK, here's the plan. We'll move the fleet back towards the battle. Our battlegroup will maneuver around the edge of the enemy fleet to get in position to attack those Orbot ships. Lieutenant Commander LaFine, when you believe we're in the optimal range to attack those Orbot battleships, fire our Starburst missiles. Do your best to blind their sensors. While that's happening, fire twenty of our ghost missiles at them. Once they deploy their decoys, hit them with twenty of our nukes each. Let's take them out before they tear our Prim allies apart."

With their new orders in hand, the crew went to work getting the ship spun up and ready to enter the gauntlet once again. The other ships in the battlegroup would begin to form a battle line both above and below the *GW* to maximize the volume of fire directed at the enemy battleships.

It took some time, but the ships finally lined up to reenter the battle. The Primord ships were in the process of leaving the battlespace to reform and reengage. Judging by the movement of the Zodark ships, they were in the process of doing the same while the Orbot ships positioned themselves to meet the human fleet.

The *George Washington* led the way for the Republic. At one million kilometers, the Orbot battleships attempted to lock onto them as their smaller cruisers raced toward them to get in a better attack position.

"EWO, jam their ships as best you can," Commander Arnold called out. "Weps, have our SW missiles primed and ready to go. We have a pretty full stock of them again—make sure you have a solid screen going."

When John Arnold had been promoted to commander a year earlier, he'd moved from being the ship's operations department chief to the tactical department chief. He'd then assumed the role of XO when their previous one had been killed during the Intus invasion.

McKee gave Arnold a slight smile and nod to let him know he was doing a good job. She liked John; he was a smart, capable officer. He was also well liked by the crew, but that probably had more to do with the weekly poker tournaments he'd organized when they weren't conducting military operations.

"They're jammed, at least for the moment," said their EWO, Lieutenant Commander Robinson. "Once we cross the three hundred and fifty thousand mark, they'll be able to burn through it."

Captain McKee bit her lip as they waited. The group of Orbot cruisers had sped well ahead of the battleships. A few moments later, her EWO announced, "They're approaching three hundred and sixty kilometers. A little closer and they'll burn through our electronic wizardry."

"Lieutenant LaFine, order the primary and secondary turrets to engage the cruisers. Let's throw a wall of slugs at them. A few are bound to hit," McKee ordered. She wanted to start thinning the enemy fleet before they could get in range and go after her turrets.

Lieutenant Cory LaFine should have been a commander by now. He was hands-down one of the best weapons officers in the Republic—at least as far as Admiral Hunt and Captain McKee were concerned. However, when he'd been selected for Lieutenant Commander, he'd ended up getting in some trouble; LaFine had been caught banging the wife of a master chief. Fraternization between officers and enlisted was still highly frowned upon—fraternizing with the spouse of an enlisted person's wife, well, that usually got you kicked out of the military.

There had been a lot of pressure on Admiral Hunt, and then later Captain McKee, to drum him out of the service. But with the war heating up, they had prevailed on the board to keep him in uniform. LaFine would be assigned to the *GW* for the foreseeable future, where he could be "watched." He'd had to forgo his new promotion and start over with a new time in grade, meaning he had to stay a lieutenant another three to five years before a review board might select him for promotion. Depending on who was on the review board, he might get a pass, but if the jaded master chief had anything to do about it, he'd hound any officer on that board until they passed LaFine over again.

LaFine turned slightly as he replied, "On it, Captain. Do you want me to hit them with some of our regular Havoc and nuke missiles? I'll keep our new stuff a surprise for the battleships."

She smiled. "Yeah, that sounds like a good plan, Lieutenant. Do it."

The ship vibrated slightly as the large primary and secondary turrets fired volley after volley at the enemy.

The cruisers took evasive maneuvers once they saw the *GW* fire its weapons. The Orbots were learning quickly that they couldn't take a lot of hits from them.

The cruisers had now closed in to under three hundred thousand kilometers—close enough to burn through the *GW*'s electronic jamming signal. They fired their masers at the human ship. Unlike the Zodarks, who relied on high-powered lasers, the Orbots used some sort of highly advanced maser weapon, utilizing microwave technology.

"Firing countermeasures now!" Lieutenant LaFine yelled out when they saw them fire.

Dozens of the small SW rockets shot out from the ship; when they'd traveled twenty-five thousand kilometers, they detonated a large, dense cloud of fine sand-and-water mixture. These cloud walls generated a barrier between the ship and the incoming lasers or masers; while they still tended to burn through it, their force was greatly reduced or dispersed by the time the beam hit the *GW*.

Still, the ship shook hard from the hit. Not as hard as when an Orbot battleship hit them, but hard enough that they felt it.

McKee caught sight of the monitor as one of the enemy cruisers flew into a barrage of sixty-inch slugs all across the front and middle section of the vessel. It drifted and lost control as a series of secondary explosions rocked it. Moments later, the cruiser exploded spectacularly.

The battleships and battlecruisers of her little fleet sent a wall of slugs at the remaining Orbot cruisers. They crumpled quickly under the intense barrage. It was unlike anything McKee had ever seen. She made a mental note to review the ship formations afterward, pending they lived of course. If this new tactic worked, they might have found a new way to take on these more advanced ships. In either case, they pulverized the Orbot cruisers and turned their focus to the remaining battleships—the tough nuts.

"I'm firing the plasma cannon now!" LaFine shouted.

The heavy hitters of the Orbot fleet were still five hundred thousand kilometers out: close enough to burn through the *GW*'s electronic warfare tools, and just far enough away to maneuver out of the human fleets' magrail guns.

The monitors on the *GW* whited out briefly from the plasma cannon firing. After the screen readjusted, they watched the white ball of plasma energy head right for the lead Orbot ship as it tried to make some radical maneuvers to get out of the way. The ship was just too big, and the plasma shot moved too fast—close to three hundred thousand kilometers per second, a full three times the speed of their magrails.

When the shot hit the enemy vessel, it punched a huge hole in it, blowing debris out from the other end. That didn't always happen when shooting at an Orbot battleship. They must have found a soft spot for it to have done that amount of damage.

"Brace for impact!" Commander Bonhauf called out.

The *GW* shook hard from the maser hit. It was one of those types of jarring hits that made the fillings in your teeth hurt.

"Firing missiles now," McKee's weapons officer exclaimed.

Missile after missile fired from their various magazines. McKee had made the decision that they were going for broke in this battle. They needed to take these enemy ships out now before they opted to jump away, only to return later and plaster their troop ships like they had at Intus.

The first volley of missiles was their SM-97 Starburst missiles. These missiles would detonate about halfway to the enemy. When they exploded, they emitted a flash of light with specially designed electronic wizardry that temporarily blinded an enemy's targeting system.

This SM-97s were quickly followed by the SM-98s. These were the Ghost missiles. Once the Starburst had gone off, the body of the 98s released five dozen smaller missiles that emitted the same electronic signature as the 98s or the newer SM-99 Tridents. The Tridents were the nuclear warheads, the ones that packed the real punching power. The Ghosts packed a ten-thousand-pound high-explosive warhead, but they were nothing like the Tridents' variable yield nukes.

If the missiles were used correctly, then the Orbot ships shouldn't know what hit them until it was too late. The humans executed this completely new tactic and strategy with renewed hope of defeating the Zodark and Orbot ships.

"All missiles are away, Captain," LaFine informed Captain McKee.

McKee nodded as she turned to face Commander Bonhauf. Bonhauf had originally served in the Greater European Union Navy before the big reorg. He'd been part of a swath of GEU and Asian Alliance officers that had transferred over to the *GW* as part of the Republic integration program.

"Commander Bonhauf, how are we holding up?" McKee questioned. She was concerned with how much damage they were taking. The battleships were now starting to focus their attention entirely on the *GW*. While the *George Washington* was a large tank of a ship, even they could only sustain so much damage.

Bonhauf grimaced. "They haven't punched through our armor yet, but they're getting close. Those battleships are specifically targeting our main gun and then the primary and secondary ones in those orders. As of right now, we're down to thirty-two percent of our primary and secondary turrets on the port side of the ship. It's a good thing we emptied our missile batteries—we just took several maser hits, effectively destroying them."

McKee shook her head at the news. They couldn't keep taking a beating like this for long or they'd be in trouble. Meters and meters of their new armor were being melted right off with each of these maser hits.

"C-FO, if we launch our fighters and bombers now, how long will it take 'em to get in range of doing some damage to those battleships?" McKee asked of her Commander, Flight Operations.

Captain Anatoly Kornukov wrinkled his brow as he crunched some numbers. It wasn't just a matter of getting the airwing launched. They needed to know that the fighters and bombers were in close enough to get in position to attack the Orbot ships without having their ordnance destroyed or being destroyed themselves. If they launched their fighters from too far out, the Orbots would have enough time to zero in on them and take them out before they could launch their missiles.

He finished his calculations and responded, "We could launch now, but I recommend we have the airwing form up behind the battleships near the tail end of our battlegroup. The fighters and bombers will stay shielded while we get in closer. At our current trajectory and velocity, we should come within eighty-six thousand kilometers of each other in ninety minutes. At that point, I'll order the airwing to pop out from behind the battleships and hit them hard. Then they can duck back behind the battlewagons as we pass them by."

Captain McKee didn't respond right away. She held up a hand as she did some quick calculations of her own. The way she saw it, this meant they needed to take a pounding from the Orbot ships for at least ninety more minutes before the bombers could unload their nukes. She shook her head in frustration before finally agreeing with his plan.

The former Russian officer went into action, scrambling the four squadrons of F-97 Orions and the two squadrons of B-99 Raiders.

"Captain, the *Paris* is going down. They just lost reactor control," called out Lieutenant Commander Molly Branson, her coms officer. The *Paris* was one of the newest Republic battleships. It wasn't the new Altairian version currently being built, but it was still a solidly built battlewagon.

Sitting in her captain's chair, McKee pulled up a view of the ship. As she watched the overview of the battlegroup, she saw it wasn't just the *Paris* going down. The *Amsterdam*, *Shanghai*, and *Tokyo* were all in trouble. All three of the ships had fires raging, signifying hull breaches and venting oxygen.

As the minutes ticked by, the *Paris* eventually blew up. The captain had fortunately ordered everyone to the life pods, so it appeared that a lot of folks managed to get out before it exploded.

The Republic and Orbot ships continued to close the distance between each other. As they neared each other, the Orbots' masers became more potent and caused significantly more damage. It also meant the Republic magrail slugs were finding more and more success in hitting their targets.

"Captain, two more Orbot ships are out of the fight," one of the crewmen called out.

McKee didn't lift her head to see who it was; she was too busy focusing on one particular Orbot ship. Something about it just didn't seem right. While the battleships were duking it out, this other ship remained in the area but stayed several million kilometers away.

"Captain, our missiles are coming up on their terminal approaches," Lieutenant LaFine exclaimed excitedly.

This time she took her eyes away from her screen to see how many of them were going to make it through. Nearly a dozen missiles got zapped before they could hit one of the Orbot vessels, but two managed to connect. The twenty-five-megaton warheads lit up like a new sun being born.

When the flashes had subsided, the enemy vessel was practically ripped in half. Three more nukes managed to score hits on two more vessels, causing considerable damage.

Commander Arnold walked up to her and sat down in the XO chair. He leaned in as he whispered, "That didn't work out quite as well as we had wanted."

She crossed her arms. "How do you mean, John? Three of their battleships are destroyed, and the remaining ones are crossing the zenith of our paths. We're about to wipe them out."

"I'm talking about how we fired off over six hundred missiles and only scored eighteen hits," Arnold explained. "We've got to get better at this if we're going to survive many more battles."

Before either of them could say anything else, they were practically thrown out of their seats from a hit. Being this close to an Orbot ship meant their masers hit with a lot more power.

"Hull breach, deck two, section J," called out Commander Bonhauf gruffly. "Hull breach, deck three, section Q. Hull breach, port-side hangar deck."

The damage control board lit up with yellow and red lights, signifying multiple hull breaches and fires, and Fran knew they were in trouble.

The next forty minutes were tense as the engineer Synths fought to contain the fires and seal the ship back up. They'd had to seal off several sections, trapping dozens of sailors, to prevent the fires from spreading or further depressurization events from happening.

As the Republic battlegroup flew past the Orbot ships, they turned to their starboard side and shifted the battle to that side of their ships.

Instead of preparing their own ships to return to the fight, roughly a third of the Orbot vessels jumped away. The remaining ships appeared to self-destruct. Moments after they blew up, that odd-looking vessel that had stayed at the fringes of the battlespace jumped away.

****

One Week Later
RNS *George Washington*

Admiral Halsey and Captain McKee stood near the Walburg tech, looking over the C100 he'd been examining.

"So? What do we know?" asked Halsey.

"Well, the Orbots definitely breached this C100's firewall," said the tech, matter of factly. "Do you want the good news or the bad news?"

"Good news, please," Captain McKee remarked, crossing her arms.

"Since Royce hit the kill switch on the other C100s, the ones that were not inside the room with the Orbots don't appear to have been affected. None of the Orbots' faulty commands got transferred to the other C100s."

"And the bad news?" Halsey pressed.

"We still don't know how they did it," the tech admitted. "It's not like they inserted code—I've never seen this before. We're going to have to take the affected C100s back to Earth and do more research to find out how the Orbots overrode our firewalls.

"In the meantime, I'm going to install a special kill switch that I think will shut the C100s off if the Orbots try to tamper with them again. That way, they won't be permanently damaged."

Halsey sighed. "Great. It looks like we need to focus on using human soldiers with these freaks of nature for now. The ground troops are not going to like this."

"Sorry, Admiral," said the tech. "I wish there was something else I could do, but this is just going to take time."

Chapter Thirteen
Galactic Empire Council

Altairius Prime

As Admiral Miles Hunt sat in his seat on the war council, he marveled at how many battles and skirmishes were being waged across the universe—not just in their galaxy, but in dozens of galaxies that the Empire and Dominion spanned. It was mind-blowing to think about so many species and races out there that could travel the stars.

For the last two hours, Hunt had listened to briefings on a series of battles the Tully and the Zodarks had been fighting. Then he heard an hour-long update on the battle of Intus, the first battle the human-led Republic had fought in. He was proud to hear how gallantly they had fought, but also sickened by the losses of ships and soldiers. In the grand scheme of things, it seemed like a meaningless battle to him. It didn't change the outcome of the war, but tens of thousands of people had died.

When the account of the battle for Intus was finished, Hunt thought he had heard the last of the Republic's military exploits. He was dismayed that he wasn't able to be there in person, leading the human forces himself.

A different speaker stood up, a Primord. He gave a quick review of the battle to retake one of their former colonies, a planet called Rass they had lost more than three hundred years ago. Apparently, they had had a cordial relationship with the Zodarks for a decade, which Admiral Hunt found extraordinarily surprising. Their account of how the Zodarks had turned on them and viciously attacked them later, however, rung true with what Hunt knew of the Zodarks.

The Primord was a senator who went by the name of Bjork Terboven. Miles had gotten to know him quite well during his time on Altairius Prime. The senator had taken a liking to him, and they'd conversed many times since.

As Bjork spoke, Miles felt incredibly honored to hear about how well the Republic forces had performed in the battle. The Altairians and many of the others in the Galactic Empire had their doubts about the humans. Each victory and battle eroded any skepticism they held.

Captain Fran McKee had led the main battlegroup of Republic forces, a position Hunt couldn't help but envy. Her group of battleships and battlecruisers had managed to destroy nine Zodark vessels. More importantly, they had destroyed eight Orbot ships, including four battleships. It was an incredible victory, and one that made the Altairians and the rest of the Galactic Empire take note.

This battle's significance, however, was much more consequential. Capturing Rass would position the Galactic Empire at the edges of Zodark-controlled space. From what Hunt could gather, the GE planned to turn Rass into a launching pad to invade the Zodarks' territory.

As the group talked, Admiral Hunt became concerned about the timetable for the invasion. The representatives talked about taking several years to build up the necessary forces to invade Zodark space. However, Hunt worried that holding off on an invasion of this importance would tip the Zodarks off, giving their enemy time to position more forces to lie in wait for them or launch a counterattack.

When it was Admiral Hunt's turn to speak, he stood and cleared his throat. "I know I may be new to this group, but I am not new to war, nor am I new to fighting and defeating the Zodarks. The plan you have laid out is a fine plan, but it has a fatal flaw in it."

Several of the other representatives on the council tilted their heads to one side, but they held their tongues, waiting to see what the newcomer had to say.

"When the Empire captured Rass, it placed our forces at the edge of the Zodark space. We know that, and they know that. However, what has been proposed is that we take several years to build up our forces in the area before we attack further. This is a mistake."

One of the alliance members interjected, "Admiral Hunt, it takes time to reposition battlegroups and soldiers. We cannot move enough forces to Rass to launch an invasion of the Zodark space any faster."

Another alliance member added, "If we do not build up our forces on Rass, then we'll leave the planet unprotected. We need to restore the station we captured. We need to build up orbital defenses on the planet and position a garrison on it. There is much that still needs to be done before we can move further."

Hunt nodded politely at the information. He held his tongue, letting them say their piece, then he swooped in. "If our objective is to capture Zodark-controlled space and push them back on their heels, then I propose we launch an invasion of Tueblets now, with our current force at Rass," he announced confidently as he stuck his chin out a bit. Hunt knew he was being cocky, but he was tired of hearing plan after plan about campaigns and battles that were never going to end this war. It was as if they were fighting for the sake of fighting.

This proposal shocked and terrified several members. But the representatives from the Primords and the Tully smiled slightly. They knew what Hunt had just suggested.

One of the Altairian members exclaimed, "Out of the question!" It was the most emotion Hunt had ever seen from an Altairian. "We cannot launch an invasion of Tueblets. That is twenty-one systems away from Rass. It is practically in the middle of the Zodark core worlds. If we launch an attack like that, the Orbots will certainly come to their aid, perhaps even the Collective."

Several members whispered in hushed tones at the mention of the Collective. Hunt had seen that happen several times. It was like they were the boogeyman or something. People only talked about them in quiet corners, like speaking of them out loud might cause lightning to strike.

Hunt turned to face the Altairian. "Being twenty-one systems away from Rass and in the middle of their territory is *exactly* why we should attack them now," he insisted. "The Zodarks wouldn't expect it, and neither would the Orbots. We just destroyed eighteen of the ships they had been using to assist the Zodarks. We've succeeded in punching them in the face. Now it's time for us to land another blow, and then another blow until we knock them out of the war, or we force them to sue for peace."

Hunt felt alive and energetic as he spoke. The inner energy he felt welling up as he explained his strategy just flowed. That was, until the three Altairian members on the council shook their heads in dismay.

"This is not possible, Admiral Hunt. There are rules. We cannot push the boundaries like this without attracting the attention of the Collective," the Altairian explained. He spoke softly, like you would to a child who didn't understand the bigger picture.

"Rules? I haven't been told about any rules," Hunt countered. "Pardon me, but in the last four hours, we sat and listened to the results of one campaign after another. The problem is, none of these campaigns mattered. None of them led us one step closer to victory except Rass. We just crushed the Zodarks and Orbots there. Now is not the time to pull back—we need to press our advantage now and hit them hard. If we transfer additional forces to support them, we could launch this attack in the next six months, not three or more years."

The Altairians didn't say anything at first. The three of them talked privately amongst themselves. It was clear what Hunt had said had struck a nerve with the other alliance members. Some of them were clearly annoyed that a "lesser" species like humans would suggest such an audacious plan. A few others nodded their heads in approval—they were eager to bring an end to this war. Hunt made a mental note to talk with those members further. He was still trying to figure out how the council worked and who really held power.

Finally, the Altairian who had been objecting to Hunt throughout the meeting spoke. "Admiral Hunt, you have brought up an...interesting plan. I will say, it was not something I would have thought about, but perhaps it warrants further study. I would like to propose that we spend the next several days discussing how we could make a plan like this possible. If it can be made feasible, then we can put it to a vote. I must warn you, however—we are going to stir up a nest of raptors if we are not careful."

Hunt hadn't heard of a nest of raptors, but he guessed it meant the same as hornets or vipers. Nodding his head toward the Altairian, Hunt took his seat, and the meeting progressed. He was happy his point had been made. Maybe they'd take it seriously, or maybe they were just trying to placate him. In either case, Hunt was eager for his new starship to be completed so he could return to the war. He wanted to find a way to end it, not keep it going for another hundred or even thousand years.
****

After the meeting, Bjork walked up to Hunt. "Hello, Admiral. That was quite a speech you gave earlier."

Hunt smiled politely. "I think I probably just got myself in trouble, more likely."

Chuckling at the comment, Bjork countered, "You spoke the truth, something many on the council seem to be afraid to do with the Altairians."

The two of them started walking toward the small set of offices that constituted the Republic's working spaces. Hunt had a staff of one hundred personnel; the diplomatic corps had a smaller staff, only twenty.

Like it or not, this was a military alliance, and matters of war came first in the eyes of the Altairians and everyone else.

As they neared the door to Hunt's workspace, a Tully general walked toward them—his species reminded Hunt of a Wookiee from *Star Wars*, only their hair was much shorter and matted. They also didn't look quite as tough somehow. The Tully had a unique speech pattern and spoke in low tones. They were also extraordinarily smart. They'd been a spacefaring society for nearly six hundred years and an ally of the Altairians now for five hundred of those years.

"Excuse me, Admiral Hunt, Bjork. I would like to know if I could speak with you both…in private."

Bjork answered for him, "Sure. We were just about to enter Admiral Hunt's office. You are welcome to join us, General Atiku Muhammadu."

The three of them walked into the office space and to Hunt's office. Hunt had a very spacious office, even by Earth standards.

Hunt got down to business. "I'm not sure what's customary in this social situation here, but on my planet, in a private setting between senior military and political leaders, I would usually offer a stiff drink. I can give you some alcohol to try if you'd like," he offered somewhat awkwardly.

Bjork smiled. "I will gladly take a glass of what you call bourbon. I tried some at one of your diplomatic events, and I must say, it was aromatic and tasteful. I am actually in talks to see how I can get some of this sent to some of our core worlds. It's that good."

"Well, if Bjork says it's good, then it must be. I'll take some as well," said General Atiku Muhammadu. "By the way, the Altairians do a very good job of making sure that foods and liquids are either safe for everyone to eat or clearly labeled with what species should avoid it. It has made commerce and the ability for mixed species to eat and drink together very easy."

Admiral Hunt didn't know a thing about General Muhammadu other than that his name sounded like a name he might have heard from the Asian Alliance. The only thing Hunt really knew about the Tully was that they were brawlers. They liked to fight, and they used their big hulking physiques to their advantage in that pursuit.

General Muhammadu took the glass from Hunt and moved it closer to his nose. He took a sniff, then a small sip. His eyes went a little wide as he tasted it. "This is good, Bjork." The general then downed the whole glass in a couple of sips.

Bjork just shrugged as he caught Hunt's eye. "He'll figure it out."

"Figure what out?" the general asked as he let out a loud burp.

Hunt tried not to pass out from the stench of the general's stomach. "This is alcohol," he explained. "If you drink too much of it or drink it too quickly, it can have an interesting effect on your mind and your body. Maybe it won't hit you like it hits me, but if I drink mine too quickly, I feel...how do you say it? Buzzed. Not sure if that word translates into your language."

The general shrugged his shoulders as he held out his glass for Admiral Hunt to refill it. Hunt looked at Bjork as if asking if it was OK. The Primord nodded, smiling slightly.

After handing the general another half glass of bourbon, Hunt asked, "General, what was it you wanted to talk about? What can I, or the Republic, do for the mighty Tully?"

General Muhamaddu leaned forward as he responded. "First, call me Atiku. We are not in a formal setting. As to what you can do for me...that depends. I heard about your proposal at the council. May I speak to you about it?"

Miles felt his cheeks reddening, and not from the alcohol. He hoped he hadn't come down with a bad case of foot-in-mouth disease—not everyone on the council had appeared happy with his proposal.

Seeing his discomfort, Atiku quickly added, "I agree with what you said. This war...has dragged on for too long. There is much you do not know about this conflict or those pulling the strings. It is much more complicated than you may be able to understand."

"I keep getting that sense after each meeting," Hunt responded, "like there's a lot more going on behind the scenes than I know about. I understand we humans have only been members for so long, but it feels like there's so much to learn and not nearly enough time to learn it all."

"There will always be much to learn, Miles," Bjork replied. "Your species is young. Humans have not been around nearly as long as many of the others on the council. This war is being fought across multiple galaxies by species even more advanced than the Orbots or the Altairians, if you can believe that. The Collective and the Gallentines are two such races. In our galaxy, these two species are the oldest, most dominant species, but there are older races out there."

Hunt downed the rest of his drink and placed the empty glass down on the coffee table next to his chair. He leaned forward, sizing up his two visitors before he spoke. "The Zodarks control several planets where they have enslaved other humans, just like myself. I want to liberate them. How much grief are the Altairians going to give me if I present a military proposal to do just that?"

"Did the Altairians give you plans to build a series of ships for you?" the Tully general asked.

Hunt furrowed his brow and nodded.

"Here is my suggestion: learn how to build these ships yourself," Atiku said. "Take all the technology they've given you and figure out how to replicate it. You want to make your ships completely independent of their technological parts and components. As long as your ships are operated by their technology, their economy, the Altairians will always have a way of controlling you. I'm not saying you joined the wrong side in this war—the Collective is much worse—but the Altairians have their own designs for the galaxy, and they may not always align with our own."

Bjork interjected to add, "There is a reason why this war has been raging for hundreds of years without coming to an end. Not everyone *wants* to end the war."

Now Hunt believed he was finally getting to the truth. "I've thought that before, but why? What is to be gained by fighting a never-ending war?"

"Think about it. The Altairians don't really fight in this war," Bjork explained. "They've equipped and trained all of us 'lesser' species to fight it for them. This has given them hundreds of years of peace and stability to build, grow, and develop while only participating in minor skirmishes or maybe one or two major battles or campaigns. It isn't their population doing the dying or putting all their resources into fighting this war. *We* are, and you, now that you've joined the alliance."

"Hasn't anyone thought about creating a new alliance?" Hunt asked. "One that strives for either victory or peace with the Zodarks and Orbots?"

The Tully general shook his head. "It had been talked about in the past. The problem is, none of our races have the technological superiority to stand against the Orbots on our own, let alone the Collective if they ever showed up. It's because of our strategic alliance with the

Gallentines that we rarely ever have to face a Collective ship. If several members broke away from the Empire, we'd be entirely on our own. Without the aid of the Altairians, most of our worlds would struggle to stand up against the Zodarks and the Orbots at the same time."

Miles thought about that for a moment. "Then we need to find a way to increase our independence from them," he asserted.

"That's easier said than done," Bjork said glumly.

Hunt chuckled. "My friend, have you not seen how we inferior humans have been kicking the crap out of the Zodarks for the last twelve years? Every battle we've fought against them, we've won. They have better armor, better lasers, faster propulsion systems, yet each time we fight them, we find a way to win."

"You humans have gotten lucky, that is all," Atiku interjected.

"Really? Luck?" Hunt said, his left eyebrow raised. "Is that what destroyed eight Orbot ships in the battle of Rass? It's not luck, my friend. It's strategy. We humans are clever and aggressive. We know how to fight, and we also know how to win."

"How is it humans have developed such a warrior class of a society? I've heard stories about your military...I think they are called Special Forces, Deltas maybe."

"My people have been at war with each other since our inception," Hunt replied. "We have spent more than a million years fighting and killing each other. Humans excel at war and killing. Our history is unfortunately riddled with one battle after another. I hate to say this, but it's in our genes. I think this is particularly true of my previous country.

"Before the Republic was formed, our planet was broken down into three major factions. My faction was called the Republic. We eventually absorbed the other factions, but prior to being called the Republic, we were called the United States of America. For more than a hundred years, my country was the most dominant military force on the planet. We waged nearly endless conflict for more than two hundred years in one form or another. It was through this history of warfare that we developed a warrior ethos and class. It's allowed us to push ourselves harder and farther than any soldier we've ever encountered."

"You really think your soldiers are better than the Zodarks or the Orbots?" Atiku asked skeptically.

"Atiku, I mean no disrespect when I say this, but our soldiers called Deltas have never lost a battle against the Zodarks or the Orbots," Hunt replied. "Our people are taught through years of specialized training to fight like utter savage animals. In combat, they are fearless. They throw themselves into a battle without any regard for their personal safety. Our training program is so intense that, when the battle starts, our people fall back on that training and practically fight like AI-driven machines. Only unlike an AI, we're able to adapt to the changes in situations without missing a beat. It's what makes our soldiers true warriors."

The Tully general nodded. "Then I can see why the Altairians were eager to bring you into the Empire," he replied softly. "They want to use your species as cannon fodder in their war."

Hunt shook his head. "Let the Altairians think that if they want. What I can tell you, Atiku and Bjork, is don't ever underestimate us. We're a lot more clever than you may think. This knowledge booster shot they gave us has given us an even greater edge than I think they realize. When we're able to take it back to the rest of the people on our planet, watch out for the innovation our scientists will come up with. I read during the battle for Rass, the Republic captured the Zodark and Orbot station. My people tell me they obtained a lot of high-level critical intelligence and technology. I haven't seen everything just yet, but once the exploitation report arrives, I'll know more."

Bjork leaned forward. "You should be careful with that information, Miles. The Altairians will expect that exploitation to be shared with the council. They will then determine what should be done with it."

Hunt lifted his head up as he countered with a devilish grin. "Are you implying there should be a problem with that information being sent here? That somehow it just happened to arrive in a case of bourbon to one of your core worlds instead?"

Bjork chuckled at the suggestion. "It would be convenient, wouldn't it?"

Atiku let out a guttural laugh. "Only if it also arrived on *my* core world in a shipment of this wonderful new drink you have introduced me to as well."

Hunt smiled inwardly. He'd made some new friends and potential allies. *The counterintelligence folks were right*, he thought—the Tully and the Primords were disgruntled by the way the war was being fought. *We need time...time to get ourselves brought up to speed and time to organize our planet and build up a fleet of our own ships.*
****

Several days later, Pandolly knocked on the door to Hunt's office. His aide opened the door and announced the Altairian's arrival.

"Pandolly, it is good to see you," Hunt said warmly as he stood up to greet him. "Thank you for making the time to meet with me. I know your time is valuable and you have much to attend to."

"Likewise, Miles. It is good to see you as well. I heard you made quite the stir during the war council meeting the other day."

Hunt shrugged his shoulders. "I'm a tactician and a battlegroup commander. I'm only giving my opinion based on the battles I've fought against the Zodark and Orbot ships."

Pandolly nodded as he took a seat at one of the chairs with a beautiful view out into a courtyard with flowers and trees blooming.

"Miles, a while back, you and Ambassador Chapman had asked me if we could help you organize an expedition to free the human planets being held captive by the Zodarks. Is that still something you are interested in pursuing?"

Admiral Hunt perked up at this question. He'd been trying to push for such an intervention since their arrival nearly a year ago. He wanted to bring these human planets into the fold of the Republic and free them from the bondage of slavery.

Sitting down next to Pandolly, Hunt replied, "It is. But I get the sense there's a catch to this potential offer."

Pandolly smiled slightly, a very rare show of emotion by any Altairian. "You humans really are perceptive and clever, are you not?"

It was a rhetorical question, but Hunt got the hint. The Altairians knew he could be a problem for them at the war council.

"Miles, the proposal you presented the other day in the council—it is not that it is a bad idea," Pandolly continued. "It is actually a very good idea according to our own internal analysis. Actually, it is better than a good idea. It is the exact type of campaign that could knock the Zodarks out of the war or severely cripple them. It is also the type of operation that would certainly lead to an intervention by the Collective. While some Altairians relish the opportunity to fight them, many more of us do not believe we are ready.

"Our strategic alliance with the Gallentines is in a difficult position right now. They are heavily committed in another galaxy with another campaign. That commitment means they would not be able to come to our assistance should the Collective decide to intervene. So, here is the alternative I would like to propose to you. The Republic withdraws its request for a vote on this campaign to invade and capture Tueblets—in exchange, we will recommend a vote and put our full support behind the Republic's campaign to liberate these human planets that the Zodarks control."

Hunt sat back in his chair as he contemplated what he'd just been told. Pandolly had just given him a unique piece of strategic intelligence. He'd revealed to him why the Altairians did not want to put a vote to the Republic's plan—it'd likely pass, but it could backfire and destroy them in the process.

"You agree, then, that the plan I put forward has a real chance at changing the course of the war and even ending it, or at least for the Zodarks?" Hunt asked.

The Altairian canted his head slightly. "Yes. It would. I knew from the time I met you that you were a tactician. That is why we requested you be sent here to represent the Republic on the war council. It is also why we're willing to build a warship that, in all reality, your species is not yet ready to handle. I believe you may be the military leader many of us on the council have been waiting for. But you still have much to learn. You need to learn more about the Collective that, until now, we have kept from you."

Pandolly paused for a second before adding, "I think it is time we take a short trip and have a private meeting with our Gallentine allies. There is more they will be able to tell you about the Collective and why they are so dangerous. I know you may not understand it right now, Miles, but we have to be careful in our dealings with them. If you thought the Orbots or the Zodarks fought viciously, you have no idea what the Collective is like. They assimilate everything they touch, everything they attack.

"Tell Ambassador Chapman she is to come with you; you may also bring one individual to aid you. Pack your bags. In two days, you will accompany me, and I will show you more that you need to see and hear."
****

Altairius Prime
Republic Embassy

Ambassador Nina Chapman couldn't have been happier with this posting. After all she had endured after being kidnapped by the Zodarks on New Eden, she finally felt alive again. The four-month journey from Sol to the Altairian home world had given her a lot of time to read up on not just the Altairians, but also the other species that made up the alliance they were now a part of, the Galactic Empire. Every time she said "Empire," she either giggled or sighed internally. She liked the term Republic more than Empire. That latter term made her think more of kings and queens ruling than a democratic or republican form of government where the people at least had a voice.

When Nina had received the knowledge booster shot, it was like a whole new world of understanding had suddenly opened up. Complex subject matters became easy to understand. Remembering names, faces, places, and conversations required no effort. Her mind became like a computer, with instant recall and the ability to process everything it saw or heard. Twelve months later, that feeling of drinking from the firehose persisted—especially considering the literally tens of thousands, if not millions of years of history and knowledge there was to learn. Once Nina and her small diplomatic team had gotten themselves established and found housing, Nina had brought in lecturers to bring her staff up to speed on their new mission.

Three times a week, Ambassador Chapman facilitated a three-hour lecture from a different member of the alliance. They explained some history on their people and their planet. Those early lectures grew into a discussion of much more—like trade, industries, mineral resource management, interplanetary commerce, colonization, industrialization, evolution, and, of course, the intergalactic war that bound them all.

What Chapman found most interesting was how all these varying alien species got along. There was a sense of order to the alliance she hadn't expected. She'd learned that the Altairians had worked with each species to determine what planets were habitable for them. Each one had a unique requirement.

By working as a collective, moons and planets were given to races based on their needs. These became known as the core worlds. Most nations were allocated between six and ten core worlds. In time, the Altairians assigned new ones. Over time, this allocation process ultimately blended these regions of space and systems together with a multicultural diversification of allied races.

151

After months and months of these types of lectures, Chapman broke them down into specific topics, geared toward helping her staff learn more about their specific assignments. One of her key charges from Earth was the acquisition of technology and overall information of the Empire and the races that made up the alliance. It was a daunting task but a fulfilling one.

While Ambassador Chapman didn't work with Rear Admiral Miles Hunt often, their paths seemed to be crossing more and more as of late. Then, just last week, she'd received the oddest request. Admiral Hunt had asked for shipments of bourbon to be delivered to some of the Tully and the Primords. She found the small quantities of the orders of the brown liquid strange—only a few thousand cases. She would have expected orders of hundreds of thousands of cases.

Then, to her surprise, Pandolly had invited her on a special trip with Admiral Hunt. He wouldn't say where, only explaining that they'd be gone roughly ten standard days. He'd told her to bring a couple of formal outfits for dinner engagements and then regular work and casual clothes.

She'd tried on a couple of occasions to pry out of the admiral where they were going, but all he'd tell her was that it was someplace special, and that he'd explain more once they left. Whatever it was, it intrigued her.

When it was time to leave, Admiral Hunt and his personal aide, who for the time being was his son, accompanied Chapman. When Pandolly arrived at the meeting location, the four of them were teleported to an Altairian ship in orbit.

Chapman had teleported a couple of times already, so the novelty had worn off, but she still smiled each time she was deconstructed and then reconstructed in a new place. It was an incredible technology, one her masters on Earth were eager to acquire.

As the human delegation of three casually strolled to their quarters, Nina finally asked, "Is it safe now to tell me where we're going?"

The admiral blushed briefly at the question before answering, "Yes, I can tell you. I'm sorry about all the cloak-and-dagger stuff, but Pandolly requested that I not tell anyone until we were on our way. We're on our way to meet with the Altairian patrons, the Gallentines."

Chapman's eyes went wide at the news. This was huge. Despite her best efforts, she had learned very little about the Gallentines—only that they were even more advanced than the Altairians and the Orbots.

"This is incredible, Miles. How did you manage to get us an audience with them?"

The admiral shrugged. "I didn't. Pandolly offered it to me in a drug deal of sorts."

She lifted an eyebrow at the comment. "Really? Well, now you have to tell me more."

The ship they were on wasn't a warship; it appeared to be a VIP transport ship. The three of them walked down a hallway, at the end of which was a decorative door that led to the enormous suite they'd be staying in. The suite had three separate rooms with a shared living room in the center. The central room also had a beautiful floor-to-ceiling window that allowed them to see the stars, nebulas, and everything else around the ship. That was, when they were in between jumping through wormholes.

The three of them moved to the seating area of the living room to have a deeper conversation. The admiral sat down in one of the armchairs and leaned forward. He explained what had happened at the war council, and how Pandolly had visited him the next day and offered to allow the humans to liberate Sumer and the other human planets if Hunt dropped his campaign proposal at Tueblets.

"Really?" asked Nina. "This is a big deal, Miles. We've wanted to liberate the Sumerian home world for a very long time. Would they actually let us move forward with it?"

"Yes. Not only that—the Altairians are going to provide us the support and resources we'll need to make it happen," Hunt explained. "With that kind of offer on the table, I agreed to withdraw the Republic's more audacious plan in favor of this one."

Nina nodded in approval. This was one of the reasons she enjoyed working with Admiral Hunt. He had a good eye for the future and knew when a good deal was being presented.

"This is good, Miles," said Nina excitedly. "I think we're going to come out ahead on this deal. Bringing these other planets into the fold of the Republic is not only going to make us stronger—it's going to greatly expand our ability to become more self-sufficient in the future."

She'd been pushing privately for this mission since Admiral Hunt had first proposed it. Neither of them had had much luck. Up to this point, the Altairians had been using the Republic to assist the Primords in their battles to retake some of their lost territories, something she wasn't happy about, and she knew Hunt wasn't either.

The younger Hunt then interrupted their discussion. "Just wanted to remind you both, we're supposed to have dinner with Pandolly in thirty minutes. If you want to freshen up or anything, now would be the time," said Ethan.

They broke up their conversation and got ready for dinner.

As Chapman walked into her room, she made a mental note to ask Pandolly a bit more about the complexities of the situation within the alliance. She was curious to know why they were turning down a viable plan to bring an end to the war.

Chapter Fourteen
New Orders

RNS *Midway*
Medbay

Sergeant Paul "Pauli" Smith woke up to a rhythmic beeping noise. The sound was unmistakable. It was the same beeping he'd first heard on the RNS *Comfort* the last time he'd been wounded.

As Pauli groggily opened his eyes, his vision slowly came into focus. Steadily, his mind broke through the fog. He lifted his head up a bit and got his first glance of his surroundings. "This isn't the *Comfort* or the *Tripoli*," he remarked aloud.

"Ah, you're awake, soldier. How are you feeling?" asked a female nurse as she attended to a monitor next to his bed.

"Um, where am I?" asked Pauli.

The woman, who was maybe in her midtwenties, smiled warmly at him. "You're on the RNS *Midway*, luv. You were brought here five days ago," she explained, her Australian accent and those brown puppy dog eyes making his heart go pitter-patter.

Damn...she's gorgeous. I need to get wounded more often, he thought as his mind tried to push through the brain fog he was still feeling.

"I-I'm sorry," he stammered. "How long have I been here? I thought you said five days ago, but I think I was distracted by that beautiful smile of yours."

She tilted her head slightly and laughed. "Well, I see the drugs haven't dulled your ability to flirt," she replied. "I suppose that's a good sign for your recovery, Sergeant. But, yes, that's right. You've been here for five days. We've had you in a medically induced coma so the nanites could do their thing and get you fixed up."

A doctor walked up to his bed and grabbed a tablet at the foot of the bed. The doctor appeared to be in his fifties or sixties, maybe older—one could never really tell a person's age since the introduction of antiaging nanites into the human body.

"Hello, Sergeant Smith. I'm Dr. John, one of the medical doctors on the *Midway*. I understand your friends call you Pauli, so I'm going to call you by that name as well if you don't mind. We try not to be as formal on the *Midway* as some other ships are, being Special Forces and all," the doctor said with a wink and a smile.

Something about the man gave Pauli a pleasant feeling. Maybe it was his casual demeanor.

"We're actually pretty laid-back about ranks in the RA as well," Pauli replied. "But what happened to me? Why was I put into a medical coma for five days, and why am I on the *Midway* instead of the *Tripoli* or one of the medical ships?"

The doctor walked around the foot of the bed and took a seat next to Pauli. The nurse left at this point to go check on another patient.

The doctor smiled as he saw Pauli's eyes follow the Australian nurse as she left. "She'll be back to check on you hourly, so don't worry."

Pauli blushed but didn't say anything.

"The drugs we used to keep you in a coma should fully wear off over the next hour. You probably don't remember this, but the two of us actually had a good conversation earlier this morning. I'll do my best to re-explain it to you."

Pauli was aware that he had that dazed, confused look on his face, confirming the doctor's initial assessment that Pauli had no clue they'd previously talked.

"Your battalion was supporting 1st Battalion, 4th Special Forces Group, seizing that Zodark station over the planet Rass. You, along with eighty-two other soldiers from your battalion, were brought aboard the *Midway* when your ship, the *Tripoli*, took some serious damage during the battle. They were in no shape to treat more wounded, so everyone was brought here."

"As to your injuries—you sustained fourteen broken ribs, a contusion on your left lung, a broken collarbone, a broken femur, a traumatic brain injury, and a broken cheekbone. You had a lot of internal bleeding and swelling in your brain, so it was important for us to keep you in a coma to allow your brain and the rest of your body the time it needed to heal. As a matter of fact, you were clinically dead for a period of time on the medical transport bringing you to the ship. One of the medics worked on bringing you back and managed to keep you alive for thirty-six minutes until they were able to get you to the medbay."

The doctor paused for a moment as he checked something on the digital medical record. "Pauli, you were in bad shape when you got here. Under most circumstances, you should have died and been unrecoverable. Fortunately, being a Special Forces' ship, we have an advanced medical bay, just like the *Comfort* and *Mercy*. We were able to handle your injuries. Now that you are awake, we still need to keep you here for a few more days to let the nanites continue to repair your body."

Pauli stared at the doctor for a moment as he took in the information. He had no idea he'd been that badly hurt. Last time he'd been injured, he'd only been knocked out for a day—not the better part of a week.

"Doc, how are the rest of my soldiers?" Pauli asked. "I was in charge of two squads of RA soldiers during the battle. Is it possible to know how many of them made it and if any of them are here with me?"

"I thought you might ask that once the drugs wore off, so I looked into it." The doctor's demeanor changed a bit. "I'm sorry to report only five of your soldiers made it. The others died during the battle."

Pauli felt numb as the words hit him. This was his first squad as a sergeant—his first time being in charge of soldiers—and they'd nearly been wiped out.

"There was another squad leader with me, Sergeant Yogi Sanders. Did he make it?"

Dr. John typed something on his tablet then nodded. "He did. He wasn't in as bad a shape as you, but he's still in the medbay. At least for another day."

Pauli let a slight sigh of relief escape. He was comforted to hear his friend had made it. He and Yogi had been friends since basic training. They'd been together through five years of war, and Yogi was like a brother to him. Pauli had lost a lot of friends throughout the years; despite that, he and Yogi had always seemed to make it through whatever the war had thrown at them.

The doctor stood up. "OK, Pauli, I have a few more patients I need to visit. If you need anything, let one of the nurses know."

When Dr. John left, Pauli lay there in the bed, trying to figure out what he should do next. As the drugs continued to wear off, the memories of what had transpired flooded his mind. He also felt physically tired as his body was continuing to repair itself. While he knew he should rest, Pauli also knew he needed to take time to write some letters to the families of his fallen soldiers. Writing a letter to someone's next of kin was one of the toughest tasks he'd ever had to do, but as the soldiers' squad leader and sergeant, he felt he had to say something to the families. They deserved to hear how their loved ones had died from those who were with them when it had happened, not in some generic letter from the War Department. No one deserved an impersonal form letter like that.

Pauli asked the Australian nurse if she could bring him a tablet. Once she had, the next nine hours went by in a blur. One by one, he wrote a personal letter to each of his soldiers' next of kin:

Dear Mr. & Mrs. Locke,

By now you have probably received a letter from the War Department, letting you know your daughter died from wounds sustained in combat. I was with your daughter when she died; I was her squad leader, her sergeant. Our squad was tasked with supporting a Special Forces mission to capture a Zodark star base over the planet Rass. This was an incredibly tough and dangerous mission, which is why it was given to your daughter's unit, the 1st Orbital Assault Battalion.

Your daughter fought with bravery and distinction when she died. She led her squad in an assault against a superior Zodark and Orbot force. She never hesitated in the face of danger. She led her squad fearlessly all the way until she was killed. When she was killed, it was quick and painless. I won't provide details, but what I can tell you is she didn't suffer. She died fighting with her friends and comrades. She died as a member of the greatest battalion in the army, fighting for a cause she truly believed in. I know there are no words or acts that will bring her back to you. But know she was loved by her brothers and sisters; she didn't die alone and she didn't suffer.

I'm putting her in for a valor award. I don't know if it'll be approved, but I'll do my best to see that it is. She was a real hero.

Sincerely,
Sergeant Paul "Pauli" Sanders

When he'd finished writing the letters for the casualties from the last battle, Pauli let out an exhausted sigh. *God, I hope I don't have to write many more of those*, he thought. *I don't know how officers do it.*

After reading up on some of the after-action reports or AARs of the battle written by his surviving soldiers and some of the Deltas, Pauli's blurry recollection of the battle came clearly into focus. This would allow him to complete his next task, which was to write up individual awards for the soldiers in his squad and the others that had been part of their assault force.

As an NCO, Pauli knew it was important to recognize his people for their acts of bravery. This included those who had died. He decided to recommend that everyone in the battle with the Zodark and Orbot soldiers be awarded a Bronze Star with a valor device. He also recommended two of his soldiers for the Silver Star—they had not only fought an overwhelming number of Zodark soldiers and survived, they'd fought the equivalent of two squads' worth of Orbots.

"You holdin' up all right, Sergeant?" asked a Delta soldier as he approached Pauli's bed. From the captain bars and the name Royce on the nametape, Pauli realized he was the commander of the operation his battalion had been supporting.

"I think I'm better now, sir," answered Pauli as he tried to sit a little taller in his bed. "I guess I was a little banged up when I first got here."

"I'm glad the doctors are taking good care of you. I wanted to stop by and say I thought you and your squad did a hell of a job," Captain Royce said. "We'd never fought one of those Quadbots before. We had no idea how to fight them or what to expect. Your battle gained us some highly valuable intelligence."

"We were just doing our jobs. I only wish more of my soldiers had survived," Pauli said, sounding a bit defeated.

Captain Royce stepped a little closer. "It's tough losing soldiers, and I can tell you with certainty, it won't get any easier the more it happens."

With respect and admiration for the captain, an enhanced augmented super-soldier, Pauli asked, "As a leader, how do you handle the losses and still hold it together mentally?"

Captain Royce scanned the room for a second and spotted the rolling chair the doc had used earlier. He pulled it over and took a seat next to Pauli. "I reviewed your service record before I came to talk with you. You've been in the Army now for almost six years. You've seen combat on New Eden, Intus, and now Rass. During each battle, you were awarded a valor medal. You know why?"

Pauli felt kind of stupid at that moment and only shook his head. He had no idea why he'd been given one medal over another. In his eyes, he was just doing his job.

"In each battle, Sergeant Smith, you went above and beyond. It's going above and beyond that will allow you to handle these kinds of losses," Royce explained. "You aren't one of those soldiers or draftees that tries to shirk your duties or do just enough to get by. In each situation, you chose to rise above the others around you to either lead them or take charge of the situation. The soldiers who can't handle the losses are the ones who 'should've' all over themselves, when in reality they need to accept that they can only control the things *they* can control and need to let go of the things they cannot."

"Is that a Delta motto by chance?" asked Pauli with a chuckle. "When our two units served together on New Eden, I met a Delta soldier who told me the same thing. It's actually something that's helped me get through a lot of tough situations."

Captain Royce leaned back and laughed. "No, it's not an official motto or anything, but it is a very common phrase said in our ranks. When I was reviewing your service jacket, I also saw that you had reenlisted and signed up for Delta school."

Pauli nodded. "I did. I figure if I'm going to stay in the military, then I'd like to join Special Forces."

The captain rubbed his chin briefly as he surveyed Pauli. "You know it's a tough and very long school, right?"

"It can't be any tougher than three planetary invasions or battling thirty-plus Orbots," snickered Pauli.

Royce grunted. "Special Forces is more about conditioning the mind to overcome what the body doesn't believe it can do. The training is tough for those who don't have the mental discipline to do that. I think you'd probably excel at it.

"Oh, by the way, your company CO put you in for a second Silver Star and Purple Heart. I wanted to let you know our battalion pushed for it to be upgraded to the Distinguished Service Cross. Your switching from blasters to magrails to fire on the Orbots was a game changer for us. If you hadn't figured that out when you did, we wouldn't have known to do that right away and could have lost a lot more people during that battle. You saved a lot of lives with that kind of thinking on your feet."

Pauli felt his cheeks reddening a bit at the compliment.

"Sergeant, I actually have a question for you, and I want an honest answer," said Captain Royce. "Back before the formation of the Republic, American Special Forces had many different types of groups. Each one performed specific roles and tasks to support the overall military. You had Navy SEALs, Army Green Berets, Army Rangers, Marine Raider battalions, and Air Force Tactical Air Control Party. When the Republic formed out of the ashes of the last Great War, they combined most of these units to form the Deltas."

"Mm-hmm," said Pauli, wondering what the question was.

"With this new war against both the Zodarks and the Orbots, we Deltas are finding ourselves needing to rely on a lot more RA support than we ever have in the past. There is some talk amongst the SF community about bringing back another SF unit to help augment us Deltas."

Pauli perked up at this idea. "I hadn't heard that, but it sounds like a good plan."

"The 1st OAB has assisted 4th Special Forces Group now during two military campaigns. There's some talk about pulling your brigade out of the line and retraining the entire group as Rangers, making you guys a direct-action unit to help support our operations. As someone who isn't Special Forces and spent most of your time in the regular Army, what are your initial thoughts on something like that?"

Pauli mulled the idea over. "I'm not sure. What specifically would you want them doing that we RA guys can't already do?"

"That's a fair question. Honestly, not much. We need a support unit that can help us hold objectives or take them when necessary, while we perform more specialized missions. I think if they formed a special unit like this, they'd give you the same neurolink implants we have and probably some of the physical enhancements. A big change would probably be the armor you'd be issued—Special Forces is upgrading to a new type of armor that's able to stand up to Zodark blasters better than our current stuff. This unit would also get a lot more training on seizing objectives and performing what we call blitzing attacks—pretty much what you saw happen when Sergeant Riceman's squad charged into the room right before you passed out," explained Royce.

161

"I think it sounds intriguing," said Pauli. "It also sounds like we probably need this kind of unit because, as you said, the current Special Forces program takes roughly three years to complete. If you can train an augmented force in less time, then the Deltas could return to their more specialized roles and not have to be constantly used as shock troops."

Captain Royce smiled. "If you stay in the Army, Sergeant Smith, I think you'll go far with smarts like that. So let me pose another question to you—if your battalion and brigade is ultimately selected for this new role, would you want to stay with them? Or would you want to fall into this new role as a Ranger or Raider or whatever they end up calling them?"

"I think if my battalion became a part of Special Forces, then I'd probably stay with them and be a part of molding a new Special Forces battalion," Pauli replied without hesitation.

Captain Royce smiled at the quick reply. "I think we're going to see a lot more of each other, Sergeant. Continue to rest up and get well. We have a lot of work ahead of us in the coming weeks and months."

Chapter Fifteen
Grand Army of the Republic

New Eden
Third Army

General Ross McGinnis took in a deep breath as he stepped off the shuttlecraft. It had been a long four-month trip back to New Eden. Being cooped up on a ship for long periods had a way of making a person feel claustrophobic.

McGinnis missed New Eden. He'd spent a little over three years in the new colony. It had been a slugfest fighting the Zodarks for a while, but they had mostly been hunted down and dealt with at this point.

McGinnis stretched his back, soaking up the rays of the three suns in the afternoon sky. He let the warm rays wash over him, wiping away the stress of the last couple years of war off him. This place felt peaceful, it felt inviting…and it felt like home.

"Ah, there you are, General McGinnis. It's good to see you again," said Governor Crawley. "I was very happy to hear your force was coming back to New Eden after these last two campaigns."

The two men shook hands. McGinnis didn't usually care for politicians one bit. That said, he'd really come to like David Crawley, the Governor of New Eden. The two of them were practically two peas from the same pod. Perhaps that was why they worked so well together.

"It's good to be back home, my friend," said McGinnis. "Let's walk and talk away from everyone so you can fill me in on what's been going on since I've been gone."

McGinnis turned to his aide. "The governor and I are heading into the city. Tell everyone to get settled in for the day. Have the Chief of Staff put together a light-duty rotation with a special focus on giving as many soldiers as possible a forty-eight-hour pass to the city. Tell General Rossi I'll talk with him later today."

His aide nodded and dutifully left to carry out his wishes.

"Let's go, David," said McGinnis. "We have lots to talk about."

Crawley smiled, seemingly amused at how quickly the general had just dispensed with an enormous amount of work. "Right this way, Ross. It only took Tesla five years to get the damn factory built with a limited number of vehicles a month being fabricated, but I've finally gotten some decent vehicles for us to use."

As they walked away from the shuttlecraft and into the spaceport, they headed to a parking area reserved for VIPs.

"Tesla, eh? No Ford or GM out here?" asked McGinnis with a grin.

Crawley laughed at the question. "No, we've got them as well. I just happen to like the new Tesla. It's fast as hell, and it's comfortable."

"Eh, they all seem the same to me these days. All electric and practically nothing new or different about them," replied McGinnis.

"Oh, did I forget to mention the newest Tesla model is a hovercar?" inquired Crawley.

Stopping dead in his tracks, McGinnis exclaimed, "Shut the hell up! Tell me I heard that wrong?"

Crawley let out a deep belly laugh out. "It's real, Ross." He pointed to the car parked just outside the floor-to-ceiling window.

General McGinnis admired the car in awe. It was incredible, and larger than most of the puny cars these days. He was a bit of a car snob, and Crawley knew that about him.

McGinnis had grown up in the Show-Me State of Missouri, where his family had owned four Ford dealerships in and around Kansas City on both sides of the state. His family had been in the car business since the 1930s, so they'd been around a long time.

As he looked over the new Tesla, McGinnis thought that if he had to describe what it looked like, it resembled a 2021 Bentley Continental GT convertible—the really old first-edition model of the car that had become a legend for the Bentley brand. McGinnis's great-grandfather had been so smitten by the car and the design he had actually purchased a single Bentley dealership license all the way down in Springfield, Missouri, the only place in the state where he could get one.

Nearing the vehicle, McGinnis asked, "Is Tesla the only one with hovercars?"

Crawley nodded. "For the moment, yes. This is one of the first ones. As a matter of fact, they're only being allowed for commercial use on New Eden. I guess they want to figure out how they'll function in society before they release them back on Earth with its twelve billion people."

McGinnis gently ran his hand across the smooth shell of the body of the vehicle as he walked along the side of it and then around it. He was taking in every detail, every little feature he could as he sized it up.

"Can I drive it?" he finally asked.

Crawley laughed. "Not a chance. This bad boy set me back a good chunk of change, and you don't have a clue how to operate one yet."

General McGinnis smiled and shook his head. He climbed in the passenger seat of this new vehicle he found himself enamored with and noted how the interior looked like the cockpit of a fighter. He was ready to roll.

Governor Crawley pushed the ignition button, and the car came to life. In seconds, a digital HUD appeared across the windshield, providing them with several key pieces of data.

"Buckle up, Ross. I'm going to take you on a tour of the capital so you can see what's changed since you've been gone. Then we'll head over to the Ocean View for dinner. I've got us a reservation in a private room so we can eat and not be disturbed."

When Crawley placed the vehicle in gear, it took off. Gentle, soft, and so smooth McGinnis realized he hardly noticed they were already doing almost one hundred and sixty kilometers per hour.

With the wind blowing through his loosely cropped hair, McGinnis held his right hand out and allowed it to flow up and down with the wind, just like he used to do as a kid with his great-grandpa. He loved convertibles. They reminded him of happier times with family, back before the discovery of the Zodarks and this never-ending war they seemed to have been drafted into.

Crawley steered them to the center lane of the highway, to what McGinnis assumed was the express lane. When their vehicle entered the travel lane, Crawley turned another knob and depressed a different ignition button. While they continued to advance at a good clip, moments later, they gained altitude until they were thirty meters above the ground.

"Oh wow. Is that really it? That's how easy it is to turn this thing into a hovercar?" McGinnis asked, in disbelief at how simple and seamless the process appeared to be.

Crawley smiled and nodded. "It is. Once the vehicle shifts modes, it glides six to nine meters in the air when a small set of wings fold out from underneath the driver and passenger doors of the car. If you look down, you'll see them. They aren't very big, but they help provide the car with some lift and the flaps to raise or lower our altitude. If you turn around, you'll also see a small tail has emerged from the back, which gives us another set of flaps to steer from left to right."

"This is amazing, David. How high can you fly this thing, and how fast?"

Keeping his eyes fixed on the "road" in front of them, Crawley answered, "Not as high as you'd think. The hovercars only have enough juice to get you up to speeds of around five hundred kilometers per hour once in the air. As to altitude, again, they don't have a lot of lift or big wings, so they're constrained by those limitations. I think the maximum altitude is around one hundred and fifty meters.

"We're doing a lot of testing and safety evaluation with the Department of Transportation so they can figure out how to regulate these vehicles back on Earth. Right now, people driving north have to fly at altitudes of fifteen to twenty meters and no more than three hundred and fifty kilometers per hour. People flying west fly between thirty to forty meters. We've basically established a buffer of ten meters between each lane. Also, because we're talking vertically, we're stacking the hovercraft lanes on top of each other. This ensures we don't have any accidents in the air," Crawley finished explaining as they zipped past some traffic.

As the two of them were talking, McGinnis saw another hovercar heading right for them. He was about to point it out to his friend when he saw on the HUD that the car coming toward them was more than thirty meters above them, just like Crawley said they would be. Moments later, it zipped right over them.

General McGinnis felt exhilarated by the experience. "Damn, this is cool, my friend. So, tell me, how has the colonization been going while I've been gone?"

"It's strange, Ross," said Crawley. "Sometimes things go incredibly quick. We'll get a major construction project or housing development built. Then another project will drag on or stop altogether because we run out of supplies. We've made good progress getting a lot of manufacturing plants built; however, there are still some items we can't produce yet. We're still a few years away from having all of the facilities we need to be fully independent of Earth for critical supplies—"

McGinnis interrupted, "Have you brought this up to the Chancellor or anyone else back on Earth?"

"I have, multiple times," Crawley responded, sounding a bit irritated. "When I inquired about the supply problem, I was told most of our transports were being diverted to support a major alliance campaign.

They said it should only be a short-term problem and not to worry about it. Then when it persisted, they told me another campaign had started, and it might be a while longer until the system levels out again. I'm hoping that since your army appears to be settling back in on New Eden, it might mean our logistic network can get caught up again."

McGinnis grunted at the news; he'd had no idea his last two campaigns had practically halted the colonization efforts of New Eden. Getting this colony fully independent and operational was a critical priority of both the Republic and the Empire. New Eden needed to be a launchpad for future operations. It also needed to be able to support the war effort by building ships.

The two sat in silence as they rode to the city, and McGinnis admired the skyline. He thought they'd done a good job of developing the planet, even if they were short on supplies. They had specifically engineered these new megacities to support millions of people without overwhelming the public transportation system they were building. A network of subway tubes and delivery supply systems lay underneath the city. Instead of having delivery trucks clogging the roads, they had created a unique network of underground roads and a separate subway system to deliver food and other goods to the basements of the buildings.

Some of the finished buildings stretched to the heavens, reaching as high as fourteen hundred meters. They contained as many as three hundred and fifty floors of living or commercial space. Interestingly enough, at the hundred and then three hundred floor levels, there was a specially designed five-story gap built to provide a couple of functions. One, it gave a break in the building to allow for air to move more freely. It also acted as a firebreak should they ever need one. The gaps in the building had been turned into green spaces with flowers, hanging vines, and trees, increasing oxygen production and helping to bring joy to the citizens of this new city.

"For dealing with a supply problem, you have done a great job building the place up since I've been gone," McGinnis commented, in awe of the cityscape.

"I think we owe that to the Altairians and a small army of construction Synths," Crawley commented. "Walburg Technologies finished building a manufacturing plant two years ago. The synthetics even have their own supply and logistic system, so they bring in all their own components. They've been able to ramp up production to around

167

two thousand Synths a week, but they still can't keep up with the demand."

"How about immigration? Is that still happening?" asked McGinnis.

Crawley followed a turn in the highway in the sky before answering. "It is, but it's slowed like everything else. We're still receiving one Ark transport a month, plus maybe three dozen smaller ones. I think the immigration numbers are somewhere around ninety thousand a month—nowhere near what we need them to be. Even with the supply shortages, we're slowing down the construction of the skyline. We're building up too much capacity."

"Well, hopefully, that'll change now that we're back home," McGinnis countered. "I believe the next campaign isn't slated to start for close to a year. They want to wait until more of our new ships are finished. We have a lot of reorganization and training that needs to happen before this next campaign."

"I heard about the losses. It sounds like it was a real slugfest out there," Crawley said softly.

Ross reflected before answering. He took in some of the finished buildings and some of the ones under construction, lost in thought for a moment. The casualties from the campaigns weighed heavily on him. He'd lost more than a hundred and thirty thousand soldiers. Four times that number had been injured and, luckily, able to return to duty, but it had been a costly campaign.

"It was," McGinnis finally admitted. "Now it's time to rest and recoup as we prepare for the next one. So, how long until we reach this restaurant you were telling me about? I'm eager to eat some fresh food that doesn't come from a replicator."

"Come on, Ross, they aren't that bad," Crawley said with a laugh. "But don't worry, we're probably ten minutes away. Then you can try some fresh seafood from this new world of ours. It's really delicious, and it's healthy, according to my doctor."

****

Camp Victory
Third Army Headquarters

Lieutenant General Ross McGinnis said nothing, but he was very aware that his facial expression clearly said, "You've got to be kidding me."

General Benni Pilsner, the Army Chief of Staff, responded, "I know, Ross. Your army just got back from a brutal multiyear campaign. But you're our most battle-hardened force. If we send Army Group Two, you know it'll take a ton of casualties learning what your force already knows. AG1 is out of the question—the Chancellor won't let them leave Sol. They're on standby in case the Zodarks or Orbots decide to launch an attack on Earth or Mars."

"General Pilsner, sir, you know my force is down to seventy-six percent," McGinnis countered, frustrated. "We're not even close to being ready for another deployment. My people are worn out. They need some time to recuperate before they'll be ready for another long campaign."

"It's just the two of us, Ross. Call me Benni," said Pilsner, who turned away briefly as he took a deep breath. "Ross, I'm not happy about this request either. I don't think our forces are ready for another major campaign. I'm still trying to get the Army up to its required size, and that's taking time. It didn't help that we had two major campaigns going on, chewing through soldiers as fast as we could get them trained."

McGinnis snorted angrily at the comment. "It wasn't as if we were trying to make your recruitment job any harder," he retorted icily. "The bastards know how to fight, and we still don't have the best equipment to fight them with."

Pilsner held a hand up in mock surrender. "That's not what I meant, Ross. Your men fought bravely and did a hell of a job. You're frustrated at the rate and size of these campaigns, and I'm frustrated at the number of people I'm being told we have to draft and train every month to fight in a war that appears to have no end or strategic purpose."

General McGinnis lifted an eyebrow at that last comment. It caught him off guard. "So you think something is up with this war too?"

Pilsner furrowed his own brow and didn't say anything for a minute. Then his eyes darted to the brown liquid in a beautiful decanter on the side of the room. He got up and walked over to it. He filled two ornately decorated Glencairn glasses to the brim and brought them over to where the two of them were sitting.

McGinnis took the bourbon he'd been offered and sipped on it.

169

Pilsner gazed into the glass, deep in thought, then downed nearly his entire drink before he spoke next. "I'm not sure I like this alliance, Ross," he said quietly. "Oh, and this conversation stays between us."

McGinnis nodded but didn't say anything; he wanted to let Pilsner do the talking. As a result of being off fighting for the last two and a half years, McGinnis felt rather clueless as to what had been going on back home.

Pilsner continued, "When we joined nearly three years ago, the Galactic Empire handed us a list of economic and military requirements for us to meet as part of the GE. I don't know what all the economic requirements are, but I know some of the folks in those departments are just as stressed as I am about meeting them. From a military standpoint, we've been directed to create a twenty-million-person force over five years. I told the Altairians that was impossible because, the way our military force is structured, basic training is only part of their training—they then go on to their secondary or advanced training for their specific job. The Altairians adjusted our timeline: instead of five years, they gave us seven."

McGinnis sat there in stunned silence as Pilsner explained things. He finished off his glass and then got up to grab the bottle. He had a feeling they were going to need it. He caught a glance of the clock on the wall. It was 1823 hours. *Well after quitting time.* McGinnis poured Pilsner another glass, and the old general continued.

"Ross, we've known each other for coming up on fifty years, so I'm going to be blunt with you. I think we humans are being used as cannon fodder to fight in this war. I say this because the first campaign on Intus, while successful, had no strategic value toward ending the war. When that battle was done, they immediately invaded and captured Rass, which I concede did have some strategic value as it placed GE forces on the border of Zodark-controlled space.

"What we should have done, and what I know Admiral Hunt proposed to the Altairians through the Galactic Empire war council, was launch an immediate invasion of the Zodark territory. I saw a copy of Admiral Hunt's proposal. He pushed forward a plan to invade Tueblets. You may not know where that is on the star map, but let me tell you something about this system. Aside from it being one of their core worlds, it's also a transit hub. Tueblets, for whatever reason, has *nine* stargates in the system. Admiral Hunt planned for us to attack the system and seize control of it. In doing so, we'd effectively cut the Zodark Empire in half. From this position, we'd be able to attack their systems one by one until we captured them all or forced the Zodarks to sue for peace."

"Let me guess, the Altairians disagreed?" asked McGinnis dryly.

"They did," said Pilsner with a nod. "That's when they made the counterproposal: beginning the campaign to liberate the Sumerian home world and that dead-end chain of other planets and systems."

Now McGinnis understood why his Army group had just left the conquered territory to travel four months across the depths of space to reach New Eden again.

General Pilsner leaned forward. "What I need to know from you, Ross, is what do you need to liberate the Sumerian home world and this entire chain of systems? From what I've been told, there are eight systems with twelve habitable planets for humans. I mean, putting aside the possibility we might need to assault all twelve planets, having this many habitable planets under our control would be a huge boon for the Republic. We need room to grow. But what I need to know right now is, what do you need to make this happen?"

McGinnis sat back in his chair and gathered his thoughts. He ran through in his head what he would need versus what he'd like to have.

"First, I need my Army group brought back up to strength," he began. "Second, we need better body armor for our soldiers. Third, I need more infantry. We've got plenty of support troops, but at the end of the day, we need to take and hold ground, and I can only do that with infantrymen. Fourth, we need better ground support vehicles and more Ospreys. During the Intus campaign, once we landed the brunt of our force on the planet, we realized we didn't have nearly enough armored vehicles to move our squads around as needed. We had to rely on large-scale aviation lifts or some rather long road marches. Lastly, I need the fleet to do a better job of protecting our ships. We lost a brigade and a half worth of troops and equipment when a couple of transports were destroyed in space."

Pilsner scribbled some of this down on his tablet. He'd hand these tasks over to one of his aides later. "Let me throw something past you, Ross. General Reiker from SOCOM said he's been fielding some requests for the creation of a new Special Operations Force."

"Really?" asked McGinnis, surprised. "It already takes three years to train a Delta member. Can we really afford to make that pipeline even longer or more clogged with bodies?"

"I agree with you on the training pipeline for Deltas," said Pilsner. "We're not willing to change that around to spit people out faster. If we do that, they'll be less trained and they'll lose their advantage over the Zodarks. No, what they're talking about is training a new force—a slightly smaller force but one that could handle some of the tasks that are costing us a lot of operators."

"You mean orbital assaults and direct-action missions?" McGinnis pressed.

"Those are the ones."

"Yeah, and the Deltas are perfect for them," said McGinnis. "Their physical enhancements, increased training, neurolinks, and better body armor make them ideal for these tough missions. It's why I've been using them like that." He could hear the defensiveness in his own voice.

"I know, Ross. That's why we want to create a second SOF unit that will train specifically to perform orbital assaults and direct-action missions. If we keep using the Deltas, we're never going to keep up with the losses we're taking unless we shorten their training, which means we sacrifice their training quality. If we use regular soldiers for these missions, the losses are going to be unacceptable. We need to create a specialized unit to handle these types of missions."

McGinnis leaned forward as he replied, "Benni, I've got the 1st Orbital Assault Division. They've been doing a good job hitting in the first wave, either with the Deltas or very close behind them. We could beef up their body armor and weapons and just use them."

Pilsner smiled. "That's exactly what General Reiker suggested."

General McGinnis crossed his arms. "So what exactly do you mean? Just give them better weapons and body armor?"

"No, Ross," said Pilsner, chuckling and shaking his head. "He suggested we take the 1st OAD, and we convert them to become the 1st Orbital Ranger Division. They're already battle-hardened, seasoned soldiers and know how to fight. We'd run them through additional SF training, to include giving them the NLs and some physical enhancements. That'll give us time to train a second Ranger division from scratch, and it'll free up our Deltas for more specialized SF missions."

"Well, old buddy, it sounds like you've already made the decision. Haven't you?" asked McGinnis with a hint of sarcasm.

Pilsner smiled gently as he gave a slight shrug. "Now that we've talked about it, I guess we have, unless you can offer up a really good alternative."

None came to McGinnis's mind. "Just make sure you chop another division to me from AG2 and plus-up my ranks. I need my army at one hundred percent way before this next campaign begins. Oh, by the way, when is the timeline on this next battle?"

"Between twelve and fifteen months is what I've been told to plan for," Pilsner said.

The conversation was much more cordial after that. They finished their drinks, a bit more slowly this time, and had a late dinner together before they parted ways.

****

Two Weeks Later
1st Orbital Assault Division

There was nothing Sergeant Pauli Smith hated more in the military than standing in a parade ground with thousands and thousands of other soldiers, sweating in the heat as they waited for some general or colonel to speak to them all. Sometimes these events were for a special award ceremony or change of command. Today, no one knew what it was for. That could mean one of two things: something exciting was going to happen, or they'd just drawn the short end of the stick to some new tasking. In either case, they'd been standing in formation as a company now for fifteen minutes.

Don't lock your knees, don't lock your knees, thought Pauli.

"When's this guy going to show up?" chided one of Pauli's soldiers softly to no one in particular.

"Hey, who says it's a guy? It could be a woman," one of the female replacement soldiers added.

"Knock it off, people," said Pauli, just loud enough so that his squad as well as the squads nearby could hear him. "This isn't the time or place for smoking and joking. Keep your thoughts and opinions to yourself until this dog-and-pony show is done." The last thing Pauli wanted in a group formation like this was for his platoon to start making too much noise and attract the first sergeant's attention.

Following the last campaign, they'd gotten a new first sergeant. He was a real ballbuster of a soldier—a total by-the-book no-nonsense training Nazi. Instead of chilling and relaxing during the four-month trip back to New Eden, he had had them drilling hard in the simulators or at the rifle range. Then they'd conduct ship boarding and clearing operations. This first sergeant didn't seem to realize they had completed their tour of duty and were headed home for some rest.

A group of military officers walked up to the small stage in front of the division. It was hard to see from his position—being the first battalion, first brigade of the division, Pauli's unit was positioned on the far left. His company, Alpha Company, was the farthest to the left, so they really had a hard time seeing the center of the formation and who all was there. Fortunately, they had a couple of twenty-foot screens on the far sides of the formation, which did help.

"Division! Atten-Hut!" a voice boomed over the sound system.

A second later, a single individual walked up to the lectern to speak. He was flanked by a couple of civilians and several other high-ranking officials. As Pauli watched, he realized it was General Ross McGinnis getting ready to speak, not the division commander.

"Good morning, soldiers! It's a great day to be in the Army, isn't it?"

"Hooah!" came the single-word reply every soldier gives when a high-ranking officer asks a question.

"I'm here to speak with your division about a couple of things. First, we have eight medals we're going to be awarding to highly deserving recipients. Two are for the Medal of Honor; they'll be presented by Governor David Crawley in place of the Chancellor, who could not be here. The other three are for the Distinguished Service Cross, which I'll be personally awarding. With that, Sergeant Major, why don't you come forward and read them off. When we're done awarding these medals, I have a special announcement for your division I wanted to personally share with you."

The sergeant major, who ironically had to be half a foot shorter than the general, walked up and called everyone to attention. He then read off five names and called them forward. Yogi, who was standing behind Pauli, poked him in the back.

"Pauli, wake up," Yogi barked. "Get yourself up there."

Pauli hadn't even realized they'd called his name. He immediately started making his way towards the stage. Like everyone else being called up, he was a bit stunned. As he looked out at the entire division, he couldn't believe that of all the soldiers out there, he was being singled out for this award. He felt ashamed—he had just been doing his job, and he'd survived when more than half of the two squads he'd been in charge of hadn't.

When the award presentations were done, Pauli made his way back to his company. As he walked past Captain Hiro, the man smiled and nodded. Even that ornery hard-ass of a first sergeant gave him an approving smile and nod as he took his place in front of First Squad, Second Platoon.

General McGinnis then began his special announcement. "This new war we find ourselves fighting is proving to be a tough one. That said, we've never lost a battle against the Zodarks. That's a feat even our more advanced allies can't say they've achieved. The Zodarks and their Orbot patrons have proven to be fiercely tough adversaries. As everyone knows, the Army is broken down into two key functions. We have the regular Army, or as they like to call us, RAs. Then we have Special Forces, or Deltas. Both of us perform different missions in this war. Right now, our Special Forces brothers are doing a lot more fighting and dying per capita than we are. Their numbers are thinning out faster than they can be replaced, which is why we see a lot of C100s being integrated into their units.

"A few weeks ago, I had a conversation with General Pilsner, the Army Chief of Staff. He told me they're creating a new Special Forces unit to pick up part of the Deltas' mission, so they can get back to their more specialized roles. This new unit is going to be called the 1st Orbital Ranger Division. Like the 75th Ranger Regiment of old, this new division will augment the Deltas and carry out more of their direct-action missions and work hand-in-glove with them.

"General Pilsner told me that the 1st Orbital Assault Division has been chosen to take this mission on. As such, in two weeks, the division is going to be renamed the 1st Orbital Ranger Division. Now, this is an even tougher and more dangerous mission than the division has done in the past. And like all Special Forces units, there are requirements to be a part of it. First, you have to volunteer to join this new division. That includes the Special Forces reenlistment contract, which I might add is a very long reenlistment contract. Second, you will have to go through a selection process just like the Deltas. So, just because you belong to the division now doesn't mean you'll stay with the new division. Third, anyone who doesn't want to join this new Ranger division will be reassigned to the new 1st Orbital Assault Division that'll be built up to take the place of your unit that's leaving."

General McGinnis paused for a second as he surveyed the soldiers in front of him. "This is a unique opportunity to be a part of an entirely new Special Forces unit. But please understand, this unit will be seeing a lot more action than the regular Army units. The likelihood of being injured or killed in this new unit is much higher than if you just stayed in the RA.

"So what's going to happen next? Over the next two weeks, everyone in the division is going to be medically screened to see if you can make the cut to join. Then and only then will you be asked if you'd like to stay in the RA or transition to Special Forces. Don't take this decision lightly; take a day or two and think about it. As a matter of fact, today is Friday. As the Army Group commander, I'm going to give you all a forty-eight-hour pass to consider this decision. When you come back Sunday night, be ready to make a declaration of what you'd like to do next."

General McGinnis went on for a few more minutes, then the division commander talked briefly before they were dismissed.
****

Sitting on the veranda of a restaurant overlooking Lake Geneva, Pauli sipped on the glass of water the waitress had just brought him. The cold liquid felt good as it ran down his throat to his stomach. He closed his eyes and lifted his face up to the three suns, letting their warmth soak into his skin.

"You all right there, Pauli?" asked Yogi. "Are ya expecting that beautiful waitress to come over here and plant a big kiss on you or something?" he chided good-naturedly and then proceeded to down half his beer.

Pauli laughed as he opened his eyes. "No, I'm not waiting for her to give me a kiss. I'm just taking in the sun. This last day has been amazing.

A few-hour hike through the woods to see that waterfall, a short dip in the lake, and now this. What more could I have asked for?"

"Um, how about getting laid? That's about the only other thing that'd cap off a perfect day for me," Yogi said, laughing to himself.

Pauli shook his head. "And you wonder why you're single."

Feigning a hurt look, Yogi countered, "It's not like any of us have been around civilians we could date. You know the captain and Top frown on that inside the company."

Chuckling, Pauli replied, "Frown on, sure. Stop, not so much. But, yeah, I get it. For us, it's best if we don't have a girlfriend or anything that we're tied to. You see how hard it is on the married soldiers. I can't imagine having a kid and not seeing them for two or three years as we move around the galaxy like we do. It'd be too tough."

Yogi nodded, then turned serious again. "This Ranger thing, are you going to join it or still go to Delta school?"

Pauli had been mulling it over all weekend. Since they had arrived on New Eden, he'd been given an official start date for Delta selection. It had been a dream of his for years to join Special Forces. This new opportunity with the Rangers, though, was filling him with second thoughts.

"I'm thinking long and hard about it, that's for sure," he finally said.

"That's what she said," Yogi countered, trying to control his laughter.

"Damn, dude. I'm trying to be serious here and you're busy cracking jokes." Pauli kicked his friend under the table.

The two laughed for a few minutes until their waitress came back over with their food. They'd both ordered a sixteen-ounce Andoran steak, cooked medium with a red wine reduction sauce, twice-baked potatoes, and green beans cooked in bacon fat. The smell was divine, and the dish looked so appetizing.

"Oh, man. This steak looks amazing, Pauli," said Yogi as he used his hands to waft more of the hot steam up to his nose. The two of them dug into the meal, slicing off modest-sized pieces as they got down to business.

There weren't a lot of steers on New Eden yet. They were still bringing them over and growing the cattle population. But they had found another animal they'd named Andora as a good substitute. The animals were huge, about twice the size of an American buffalo, so the amount of edible meat on them was sizable. They were also in great abundance on the planet. Even better, the Andora was a very lean, protein-rich meat with other essential minerals and vitamins in it—to the point that many considered it a miracle meat. Needless to say, Andora ranching was starting to become a new cottage industry on the planet.

"So, back to my question, what are you thinking, Pauli? Are you going to stay?" asked Yogi as he held his fork in one hand and his steak knife in the other.

Pauli swallowed some of his twice-baked potatoes. "I'll tell you in a minute, but what are you going to do?" he said, turning the question back on his friend. "Are you staying in the RA, getting out at the end of the stop-loss, or staying in to join the Rangers?"

"I'm staying," Yogi responded, speaking with his mouth full, which really irked Pauli. "I'm going to join this new Ranger unit the SF is creating. I know I complain about the Army, but honestly, I really enjoy the friendships and comradery. I also know what these bastards are capable of, and I want to do what I can to keep them away from my family. Back home, I'm the oldest of seven kids. Like you, I joined at eighteen. The rest of my siblings are six years younger than me and on down. By staying in the Army, I can hopefully prevent my brothers and sisters from having to join. As long as I'm in, with that new family cap policy, the Army can't draft any of my siblings."

"What's the family cap?" asked Pauli, leaning forward. "I hadn't heard of that."

Yogi seemed surprised by the question. "Basically, the government has said one out of every four kids in a family can be subject to the draft. That way, no one family could end up bearing too much of the burden of serving the Republic. It's the only deferment they're making in the draft. So, because my parents have seven children, I'm the only one that could be drafted. None of my little brothers or sisters have to worry about being drafted so long as I'm still in."

Pauli nodded as he finished his potato. "That's pretty neat that you're doing that for your brothers and sisters, Yogi. I hope they realize how special a big brother they have to do that for them."

Yogi laughed. "Oh, they do. They ask me every year if I'm still planning on staying in or what I'm planning on doing. None of them want to get drafted. Well, let me take that back. My youngest sister, she's like ten. She wants to serve. She wants to fly those F-97 Orions. I got her a drone version for Christmas, and it's all she talks about. My mom wasn't too happy with me getting her that toy—you know, wanting the baby of the family to always be safe and never go off to do anything dangerous and all. But, Pauli, I thought you had brothers and sisters? I'm pretty sure you've shown me some pictures before."

Pauli nodded as he took a couple sips of his beer. "Yeah, I do, but they're much younger than me. After I was born, my mom wasn't able to have any more biological kids. When I left to join the military, my parents started over and they went into the business of adopting unwanted babies. You know, when a woman is on her way to an abortion clinic to terminate a pregnancy, they'll try to talk to the woman and convince her to keep the baby, and they'll adopt it."

"Really? How is it we've been friends for almost seven years, and I never knew that about your parents? Oh, and how exactly does that work? I hadn't heard about people doing that before." Yogi finished off his steak and started in on the green beans.

"I guess we don't talk too much about our families or home life, I suppose," said Pauli. "What my mom usually does is when she sees a woman approaching one of the facilities, she usually offers the woman a fifty-dollar gift card to Starbucks if the woman will give her five minutes of her time. They talk, and my mom usually convinces them not to go through with the termination. My parents help support the woman financially during the process. When the baby is born, the legal adoption paperwork is drawn up and completed. Then my parents raise the baby like it's their own. So far, they have five little ones they're raising, so my brothers and sisters are ages six on down."

"Wow, that's amazing, Pauli. So, not trying to change the subject, but tomorrow is our last day of this pass. I'm going to meet up with an Andoran rancher tomorrow and talk about possibly investing in his ranch. Would you like to come with me?"

Pauli was a bit taken aback. He hadn't known Yogi to be into investing or things like that, but then they'd never really talked about it.

"Um, maybe. What can you tell me about it?" Pauli asked as he finished off his steak.

Yogi smiled. "I found out about it from an old high school friend of mine. He managed to get a residency permit for New Eden, so he lives here now. He and two other friends I've known since high school bought a ten-thousand-acre plot of land forty or fifty kilometers outside the city.

They're building a large ranch to cultivate Andoras to be sold and shipped back to Earth. He was telling me it was going to be one of the hottest industries in the future."

"Damn, that does sound interesting," said Pauli. "What's the catch? I mean, what are they after?" He sat back in his chair, stuffed to the gills.

"Money," Yogi answered. "They need a lot of capital to get going. They've spent nearly all their cash on acquiring the land and getting it built up— you know, fencing, barns and stables, things like that. Next, they need to get a slaughterhouse built and then cultivate the land better. They have a few thousand acres of timber that needs cutting down so they can turn the land into fields for the cattle. They're trying to raise thirty million RDs to get fully operational."

Pauli let out a soft whistle at the number. That wasn't a small number to raise. RDs weren't like the old American dollar. Now that precious metals were becoming more plentiful from asteroid mining, the Republic had backed all currencies with it. The pay soldiers received was actually pretty good in comparison to what it used to be half a century earlier. Being deployed on a campaign for sometimes years at a time with nothing to spend your money on also meant a lot of soldiers had money to invest or burn on stupid things like fast cars they'd hardly ever drive.

"What's the rate of return on this investment?" Pauli asked.

Smiling, Yogi pulled out his tablet and opened a file up. "They're paying a ten percent dividend on your investment each quarter. So it's decent. However, if you're willing to forgo the dividend, it can be reinvested and grow your stake in the company. They're doing a stock valuation in a month to determine what the company is valued at. That's how they'll ascertain the stock price. Every three years, they'll do another stock evaluation. So basically, you want to buy up as much stock in the company as you can now before they do their second valuation. Once they do that, we'll be able to see how well our investment has done."

"Damn, Yogi. You've really put a lot of thought into this," Pauli remarked, shocked. "How much are you going to invest?"

"I've saved nearly all my pay in the Army, so I'm going to put most of it in with them," Yogi said, reviewing his tablet. "I think that comes out to a hundred and eighty thousand RDs, give or take. I mean, I'm keeping twenty-five percent of my savings, but I'll throw the rest of it their way."

Pauli thought about that. He'd managed to keep the enlistment bonus for SF—all the guys joining the Rangers were getting bonuses. All told, he was sitting on around three hundred and twenty thousand RDs. "OK, Yogi. You've sold me. Let's go check out this place tomorrow. If I like it and they're legit, I'll probably do something similar to what you're doing. But in the afternoon, before we have to report back, I'm meeting up with another company about investing with them. You might like them as well. They're a small outfit that provides a specific piece of technology to Tesla. Without their component, the hovercar doesn't work and they've got a minimum twenty-five-year patent on the technology, so they should be making money for a while."

"Really?" asked Yogi, his left eyebrow raised. "How did you find out about this?"

"Oh, you know. I did some asking around a few weeks ago when I saw a hovercar for the first time. A captain over in the battalion S4 was telling me about it. He linked me up with someone from the company that was handling their investor relations. The only trick was you have to invest a minimum of one hundred thousand RDs to get in on it."

"I like it, diversifying," said Yogi. "Let's do it. We'll go hit both places tomorrow before we have to sign back into the company."
****

"Sergeant Major, you wanted to see me?" asked Pauli.

"Actually, the three of us wanted to see you," Captain Hiro interjected. "Take a seat, Smith." Pauli's first sergeant and sergeant major were both seated next to him.

"Sergeant Smith, I know you've just recently received your orders for Delta selection and are probably eager to start your transition to them," Captain Hiro began. "Is there any chance we could convince you to stay here with us as the division transitions over to Special Forces and this new Ranger unit they want to turn us all into?"

"I know I'm new to the battalion," Pauli's first sergeant said, "but I'm not new to the Army. I've seen your record and I've observed you training during our cruise back to New Eden. You're a natural-born leader, Smith. You soldier well and you know how to motivate and take care of your people. I like that about you. I know I come across as a hard-ass. I was doing that to test you guys and get a better feel for how well you NCOs handle and fight as a unit. I agree with the sergeant major.

181

We'd like to keep you around if possible. What can we do to make that happen?"

Pauli was a little surprised. He rarely ever talked to these two. A soldier didn't usually talk to the battalion sergeant major or company first sergeant unless they were in trouble.

"I thought about this all weekend," Pauli began. "For the longest time, I wanted to be a part of Special Forces. I knew I had to wait until my enlistment was done before I could join, so I did. I was even more excited when I was given a training slot. But this opportunity to still join Special Forces and be an Army Ranger…that sounds damn cool to me. So, to answer your question, yes, I'd like to stay on and be a part of this new unit we'll be creating."

Both senior NCOs smiled happily at his answer.

"Excellent, Smith. See, Top? I knew we could count on him. Smith's been with the unit for more than six years. He's loyal as hell to the company," the sergeant major said.

Pauli sat there, just soaking it up. Not that he chased that kind of praise—he just wasn't used to getting it from the senior NCOs, so when they did give it, he wanted to lap it all up.

"I agree, Sergeant Major," said the first sergeant. "So, Smith, here's the next deal. You're going to stay as squad leader, but we're also making you the assistant platoon sergeant. If Master Sergeant Dunham doesn't switch over or he ends up getting transferred to another platoon or company, we will promote you up. We both want you to know that you're on a very short list of sergeants who'll make the next grade when a slot opens up, so don't do anything to screw it up between now and then. Keep your nose clean and continue to kick ass like you've been doing. OK?"

"Yes, First Sergeant, you can count on me," Pauli replied jovially. He was happy to be staying and even more glad the top two NCOs in the unit thought so highly of him.

"OK, Smith, dismissed. Get back to your squad and figure out who's going to stay or go. We need to start running those staying through the selection process. We've got a lot of work between now and then that needs to happen."

Chapter Sixteen
A Date with Destiny

Cobalt
Messier 31

"Are you nervous about this meeting?" Pandolly asked Ambassador Chapman and Admiral Hunt.

The three of them were standing near the observation window, staring at the enormous but stunning Gallentine planet as their ship approached it. The space around Cobalt was abuzz with activity. Hundreds of smaller ships were moving in and out of orbit. Some were docking at the gigantic and incredible station that wrapped around the entire planet like a ring. Others simply jumped away to far-off places unknown.

Chapman and Hunt stood speechless, taking in the overwhelming scene. It was unlike anything any of them had ever seen before. The station that wrapped around the planet was incredible, beyond imagination. The planet didn't look like a planet at all. Nearly the entire surface of Cobalt, except for the oceans and a few spots here and there, was covered by cities. In the darkness of space, the lights glowed brightly. On the day side, the cities still shimmered with light as the sun refracted off the buildings' surface.

"*Should* we be nervous about this meeting, Pandolly?" Hunt pressed.

"No, I do not think so," the Altairian replied flatly. "I know Ambassador Chapman has been eager to learn more about them. This will be your chance. The Gallentines are eager to meet you as well. When we introduced your species to them and told them about your exploits up to this point, they were very impressed. It is one of the reasons why they are agreeing to meet with you."

"I take it this isn't a standard request," Hunt commented. "They don't normally meet with the other races within the alliance?"

Pandolly shook his head softly. "As a matter of fact, the Gallentines have never met any of the other species in the Galactic Empire. That is why I requested that you not tell anyone else. They have left the growth and development of the Milky Way alliance for us to manage. Their requesting to meet with you in person like this is a great honor—"

Hunt interrupted, "I thought you were introducing them to us in exchange for the Republic withdrawing our proposal to attack Tueblets?"

"Yes and no, Miles," Pandolly replied. "You have many questions and many good ideas, but you lack the understanding of the bigger picture. The Gallentines have been interested in your species since we first introduced you to them. However, when we presented your plan to attack Tueblets to them, they were intrigued enough that they insisted on specifically meeting you, Miles, in person. I asked to bring Ambassador Chapman along so she could learn more about them for your people. This may be the only time you are allowed to see or meet the Gallentines, so I would like you to have as many of your questions answered as possible during this trip."

"Pandolly, what can you tell us about this station?" Nina asked with genuine curiosity. "It appears to wrap completely around the planet."

"It does wrap around the planet. It took many hundreds of years to build. Now, as you can see, it is an integral part of their planet. Multiple space elevators connect it to the surface below. Various parts of the station have different functions: some are used for shipbuilding, some for regular commerce, some for living quarters. The planet, as you can see, is very densely populated," Pandolly explained.

"How many people live on Cobalt?" Nina inquired.

Pandolly turned to face her. "I am not sure of the official count. The last I was told, the population was somewhere close to sixty-two billion. Cobalt is the center of the Galactic Empire. It is the heart and soul of an alliance that spans multiple galaxies and thousands of planets."

Hunt shook his head at the information. He couldn't fathom something so massive. To think, his people had only been a spacefaring people for less than two hundred years, and now he was about to meet a species that had been traveling the stars for tens of thousands of years— a species so advanced he couldn't even wrap his head around what they could do.

An hour later, their ship connected with the station and they began the process of boarding it. When their little group left the Altairian ship, they found two people waiting for them. One was Altairian, the second Gallentine.

It was the first time Admiral Hunt had seen a Gallentine in person. Although he had seen pictures, nothing compared to meeting a species for the first time. Hunt immediately noticed that their skin color came the closest to the stereotype he'd always heard of "little green men," but it was really more of an olive color. Their high foreheads led up to a head full of stringy hair that matched their skin tone. Their eyes were olive-colored as well, punctuated by irises that were bright blue. The Gallentines were a bit taller than humans, but not quite as tall as Zodarks; Hunt knew people that were this tall, even if they were outside the norm. The Gallentines were a bulky muscular species, with seven fingers and two opposable thumbs on each hand—Hunt hoped he never found himself in battle against this species.

The alien stepped forward toward them, unafraid. "Hello, Admiral Miles Hunt, people of Earth. My name is Velator. I will be your official Gallentine ambassador and guide during your visit to our planet."

Despite Pandolly's briefings, Hunt was still unsure of the exact protocol to follow when meeting a Gallentine. "Thank you, Velator," he responded. "It is a pleasure to finally meet you, and your people. I believe we will learn much from each other during this trip."

"I believe you are right, Admiral Hunt," Velator responded warmly. "We were most impressed with your plan to defeat the Zodarks. Let us spend a few days giving you a tour of this station. It is important for you to understand the history here, and how it has become an anchor for the alliance. It wasn't until we built this station more than a thousand years ago that we became the dominant power in the Andromeda galaxy and the other nearby galaxies. Please, if you will follow me, I will take you to your quarters. Once you have had a short while to settle in, I will give you a tour and explain more of our history and culture to you.

"After our tour of the station, you will have a better understanding of our people. Then I will take you down to the planet. From there, I have arranged for several briefings to take place to give you additional knowledge of the Galactic Empire: the territory we control, some of our adversaries, and the importance of the Milky Way to the Empire. Then you will be given a short audience with the Emperor. You will join him and his chancellor for a private dinner. The following day, you will return back to Altairius Prime with a new task given to you by the Emperor himself."

This last piece of information caught Hunt by surprise, but he kept his excitement and questions to himself. There would be plenty of time to ask more questions. Right now, they were in receiving mode.

Later that day, Velator guided them through part of the station that led to the shipyards they had seen on their approach to the station. During their transit to the yard, Miles, Nina, and Ethan had seen more than two dozen different species of aliens. All the species interacted as if it wasn't unusual to see so many different alien races cobbled together. Through the use of the universal translator embedded in his inner ear, Miles was able to understand everything spoken by each of them.

A short while later, they reached an office and entered it. Whatever was written on the door was in a language Miles had never seen before. When they entered, there were six Gallentines working at several stations. There was also a large window that overlooked a large assembly line inside a drydock facility.

Velator explained, "This is the first stage of a ship's construction. Whether military or commercial, they all start in this part of the factory. Now, why am I showing you this?"

The Gallentine let the question hang there for a second before he answered it. "I am showing you this because, like your race, we also use robotics and machines in our daily lives and in the building processes of our society. But we found a way to integrate machines into the process without replacing our people. As you would say, we have kept a 'human in the loop,' so to speak. This is important and I am going to show you, over time, why it is important and why I am teaching you this lesson."

The group stayed there for a few minutes, observing. Miles whispered to his son to make sure to take copious notes. This would aid in the audio reports they would create at the end of each day, which they'd use to put together a comprehensive report to send back to Earth later on.

Several hours later, after dinner, they spent a significant amount of time learning about the history of the Gallentine people: who they were, when they had first discovered space, when they had first united as a people, and then their expansion into space. This discussion lasted well into the evening. It was nearly morning by the time they were escorted back to their living quarters. They could only sleep for a few hours before they'd be picked up for the next day's activities.
****

When Miles got back to his room, he took forty minutes to compile his notes on what had transpired during the day. Then he collapsed on the bed. When his alarm woke him up three hours later, he felt like he'd been hit by a truck.

When Pandolly knocked on his door to collect them, Velator was there with him. There was a robot there with him, holding a serving tray and three glasses of brownish-black liquid.

"I know the contents do not look appealing," Velator said with a hint of amusement. "The taste, however, should be more than good enough for you. This drink will invigorate your mind and body for the remainder of the day. It should help you in processing the rest of today's events."

The three humans shared a nervous glance. Then Ethan grabbed the glass and chugged. Seconds later, his entire demeanor perked up. "Wow, this stuff is great! Is there any way we could program this into our food replicators? This stuff is awesome," Ethan said, to the amusement of Miles and Nina, who then downed their own glasses of the liquid.

Velator smiled. "I will certainly give you a data chip with the information on it for the food replicator. But first, let us continue with the day's events. There is much more we will pass along to you than just this."

They spent the rest of the day touring the various sections of the station. Admiral Hunt felt like he was drinking from a firehose, even with the knowledge booster. That evening, they began a long lecture on the alliance: who all was part of the Galactic Empire, what galaxies were part of the GE and how many races were part of it. This was perhaps the most interesting information Miles had ever heard. It was more fascinating than anything the Altairians had shared with him to date. It also explained a lot about why the Altairians had been reluctant to move forward with his mission proposal. Pandolly was right; there was much about the alliance they did not know.

Velator asked Miles a question. "Do you remember yesterday, when I told you we have found a way to integrate machines and humans without replacing one or the other?"

Miles nodded. "I do. You said you'd explain later on why that was important."

Velator nodded. "More than eight thousand years ago, our people used to be allied with the Collective. Back then, they were a regular species, like you and me. They were biological beings capable of intelligent thought and emotions. They were truly humble and a unique species to be friends with. For thousands of years...we were comrades.

187

"Then one day, it all changed. Around the same time, we had been pursuing AI and machine automation, but the Collective took it one step further. You see, they had been chasing what you call 'God' or the 'Creator.' It had been a single-minded pursuit of theirs for hundreds of years. The more advanced they became, the more they searched for evidence of this god or creator of the universe, until one day, one of their researchers concluded that the only way they could know God, could truly be one with Him, was to transcend their physical bodies and consciousness. They believed if they transcended, they would become immortal, just like God is."

Hunt consciously had to close his open mouth. His jaw had hung open. *Transcend their bodies?* he wondered.

"One day, it dawned on them how to do this. How to go beyond their physical bodies and the limits they have to becoming one with God, in a way, to become demigods themselves. This is when they transitioned from biological beings to machines—but not machines like your synthetic humanoids. They found a way to take their individual consciousnesses from their biological bodies and upload them into a single electronically-networked consciousness."

Holy crap, thought Hunt in horror.

"When they did this, the many became one. We witnessed the most horrific destruction in our history. An entire race, an entire society, destroyed itself as they stripped themselves of their bodies and everything that made them unique, individual, and different. This is when the Amoor, as they were called prior to the transcendence, became known as the Collective. In the span of years, we saw an empire that spanned more than fifty planets and sixty billion people disappear as they transcended—"

Nina interrupted to ask, "What happened to their physical bodies?"

Velator didn't seem the least put off by her interruption. He faced her and said, "They died."

"How does this transcendence work?" Ethan asked. "How were they able to convert their entire society into this electronic version of themselves, and what happened to those who didn't comply?"

Velator studied Ethan for a long moment before he replied, "Your father was right to bring you, Ethan. You are a smart and perceptive individual. I am glad you came. As to your question, the Amoor built a machine that an individual lies down or sits on. Equipment was attached to their bodies, and over a period of several hours, their entire consciousness, what you might call a soul, was recorded and then uploaded into the Collective. Once this process was complete, the physical body was administered a drug that ended its existence. At that point, the individual would only reside within the Collective—"

"But what happened to those who didn't want to do this?" Ethan pressed.

"It was compulsory, from what we were told. Once an individual's consciousness joined this Collective, they became part of what is called a Hive. Each of their planets has a central Hive, a nerve center that stores their consciousness. Their ships and starbases operate the same way. Those that chose not to join the Hive were separated from those who did. The Amoor did not want to pollute the Hive with the dissent of those who did not join willingly. Those individuals were later assimilated by force into what the Collective now calls Legion. In our language as in yours, Legion means many."

No one spoke for a moment as they digested what Velator had just told them. Then Miles recapped what he had just learned about the Collective and Legion to make sure there were no misunderstandings. At the end, he verified, "Was that accurate?"

Velator smiled at their Altairian ambassador. "You were right, Pandolly. They are a bright species, considering how long they've been traveling the stars."

Velator turned back to Miles. "Yes, you summarized it well. Do you want to know what they use Legion for, or have you already figured that out?"

Ethan answered this question, although he probably should have waited for his father, the admiral, to do it. "Legion is used to assimilate those who do not willingly join the Collective."

The Gallentine nodded his head in approval. "Exactly, very astute. This is why the Collective is so dangerous. Their message of transcendence is very seductive, and very destructive. Each new species they encounter either joins their ranks or become assimilated into Legion."

"If that's the case, then why is the Collective not assimilating the Orbots, or the Zodarks, or any of the other races that make up the Dominion alliance?" Nina countered.

"That is a good question, Ambassador. Right now, our best guess is that the Collective is not ready to do this yet. When the Amoor began this process of transcendence, it took their species nearly a hundred years to complete. At least, the peaceful transition took one hundred years. During this time, they forbade any procreation. They focused primarily on assimilating the youth and the elderly. Then they created a version of your combat Synths, which became their enforcer. It phased out their actual military. During this transition, the part of their society that did not want to assimilate attempted to break free of them. They considered what was going on a genocide of their people.

"At this point, a civil war broke out. The Collective, using the shared knowledge of billions of Amoor, was terribly effective at waging war. Then, the war turned truly ugly. The biological side of their society used atomic weapons and cyberattacks to try to defeat the Collective. In response, the Collective, essentially a super-advanced AI now embodied by these incredible killing machines, resorted to cyberweapons and nuclear weapons themselves. This began a twenty-year campaign of terror on both sides. At one point, we were going to intervene. Then we received a warning from them that intervening would not be in our best interest. So, we sat on the sidelines and watched in horror as a society of over sixty billion people destroyed itself."

"When the war ended, the Collective disappeared from space interactions with other species. They stayed within their borders for nearly five hundred years. They spent that time rebuilding their society, their infrastructure, and their industry. When they emerged from their self-imposed isolation, they assimilated some of the smaller spacefaring worlds. At first, it was within their galaxy, the Cygnus galaxy, which neighbors our own. For several hundred years, we did not realize what they were doing. They moved slowly at first, then very quickly."

Miles stopped Velator. "How do you mean they moved slow, then fast?"

"What they do is send an emissary to the species they have their eye on. If it is a species that will help them in their quest to know and understand the Creator, then they will offer them the opportunity to transcend and join them. If they refuse, then they are assimilated into Legion. You see, to continue their journey to reach God, or even one day become God, species need to *want* to transcend. They have to want to be a part of this journey. Without a desire to do so, they would pollute that effort."

"If that's the case, then why do they keep assimilating races into Legion?" asked Miles. "I mean, at this point, they have to have billions of beings from multiple species assimilated into Legion, and all these consciousnesses are essentially loaded into combat robots, or combat Synths as we call them."

"This is my fault, Admiral. I did not do a good job explaining," Velator said, holding up one of his hands. "When the Collective encounter a species that does not want to assimilate, they do not then go on to forcibly assimilate everyone right off the bat. They assimilate a very small percentage of their new adversary to gain the insight and information they need to better fight against the rest of the society they are now at war with.

"They then wage a genocide on their enemy, eliminating every remnant of them. Like a logger or tree cutter clears a forest, they extinguish all the living beings on the planets they capture and can then populate the planet with their own beings. But truth be told, they are nothing more than machines at this point, so they are not really populating these newly conquered planets with their own people so much as they are establishing servers to host themselves on. It's this enormous network of servers and communication nodes that allows the Collective to be everywhere and nowhere at the same time. It's also how they continue to build their knowledge in their continued quest to become like God.

"This is why they are so dangerous. They are everywhere and nowhere. That is why, when you presented your plan to knock the Zodarks out of the war, we felt compelled to meet with you. The plan is brilliant, and it would likely work. The only flaw in your strategy is that it would most certainly attract the Collective to the Milky Way galaxy. That is not something your galaxy is ready to handle yet."

"That still doesn't answer my question about why the Collective has allied themselves with the Orbots or the Zodarks," Miles pressed.

"Yes, the Orbots and the Zodarks. The Collective is still expanding. Right now, they have nearly conquered their entire galaxy. They have just invaded two other galaxies. They have also just invaded *our* galaxy. We are heavily engaged in battle with them right now. Thus far, we have managed to contain them, but that may not last. As to the Orbots and

Zodarks, the Collective has astutely cultivated some allies in the various galaxies to assist them in their quest to find or become God. They have recruited these allies with the promise that one day, they will be allowed to transcend into the Hive and join them. Until that time, they are giving their allies advanced technology and huge swaths of territory to claim as their own. If they encounter an adversary that is too sophisticated to defeat or they are on the edge of defeat, then they will send the Legion to assist them.

"In the thousands of years we've been fighting the Collective, they've only dispatched Legion to four galaxies in which their allies were fighting. In each case, the result was the same: most of the galaxy was destroyed, becoming just another part of the Hive."

Miles shook his head. It was more than he could process, and it made his head swim. He knew it must be doing the same to Nina and Ethan as well.

"Velator," said Miles softly, "how do we defeat this Collective, then? You've been fighting this war against them for thousands of years, as you say. Surely there must be a way to beat them. Please tell me you haven't been fighting this war with no hope or idea of how to win."

Velator considered his response for a moment before responding. "We have thought about this for a long time. We have explored many different strategies as well. The strategy we have been employing up to this point has been one of attrition. We identify where they are building their ships or their mining operations and we take them out. We continue to chip away at their communication nodes and the server farms they establish in the various systems they have conquered. The strategy has worked thus far. It is not the fastest approach, but it has had some success."

"Why not infect them with a computer virus or wage a cyberwar on them?" Ethan questioned.

"We do that when we are able," Velator replied. "You must understand, at this point, the Hive is an extremely advanced super-AI—far more advanced than anything you can comprehend. The challenge with a cyberattack or virus is creating one that is clever enough to break through their own firewalls and then damage the Collective before they are able to identify what is happening and stop it."

"If the Collective is one giant AI, how do they manage and fight their ships?" Ethan asked.

Velator smiled at the question. "Ethan, they may be an AI, but they still have physical functions that need to be performed on a ship, like repairing damage sustained during battle, launching a boarding party, or other tasks that require arms and legs. On each ship, they have a collection of humanoid and sometimes quadrupedal machines that will be loaded with the consciousness of an appropriate person with the knowledge and skills needed to fix the ship or accomplish specific tasks. It is the same with their ground combat operations. The big difference, though, is that, when someone like you or me dies, our souls or beings are received by God—or maybe they are not. Either way, our existence in this universe ends. When their mechanical body dies, their consciousness is downloaded into what we have come to call an Ark."

"An Ark?" asked Miles.

"When the Collective goes into a battle, whether between large groups of warships or ground forces, an Ark ship is usually nearby. When one of their ships is destroyed or a soldier is killed, their consciousness is uploaded to the Ark's servers. When the Ark returns to a Collective system that has a Hive located within it, the Ark's servers are refreshed and the consciousness of those lost during the battle are transferred to the Hive, and they live on."

"So if this Ark ship wasn't nearby, then the consciousness of those lost during a battle would be gone forever?" asked Ethan.

Velator canted his head as he sized Ethan up. He turned to look at Miles. "Are all your military officers as sharp as your son?"

Smiling at the compliment, Miles countered, "I'd like to think so. Then again, I think he got more of his mother's smarts than mine."

Velator laughed at the comment. "To answer your question, Ethan, yes. They essentially die; at least their consciousness ends. This is why you will always see the Collective fleets traveling with an Ark ship."

Ethan pounced on that revelation. "Velator, if that's true, then your answer to fighting the Collective is to target their Ark ships. As soon as your ships engage them in a battle, you focus your entire effort on taking out *those* ships, forcing them to withdraw rather than risk losing the consciousnesses of those involved in the battle."

Velator shook his head, deflating the younger Hunt's optimism. "Do you think a superior race like ours, one that has been at war with the Collective for as long as we have, has not tried that? We have, and on some occasions we have been able to destroy one of their Ark ships. You were correct in your assumption that, without an Ark ship present, their fleets do tend to retreat rather than risk losing their consciousness. However, these ships are not only heavily protected, they are veritable tanks in battle. They can absorb incredible amounts of damage before they are destroyed. And usually, when they are in danger, they will simply jump away."

Velator paused for a moment before he continued, "The Collective is not an easy adversary to fight. They are cunning, and they are ruthless. They are also numerous. Then again, perhaps you humans are just what we need. New blood and a new set of eyes to look at the problem."

For the next six hours, the five of them continued to talk about the Collective, the Hive, and Legion. It was a lot of information to absorb, but it was the last chance they had to talk with their Gallentine host before they transferred to the planet surface to take a brief tour of the capital and meet with the Emperor.

Chapter Seventeen
Fleet Operations

New Eden
RNS *George Washington*

Admiral Chester Bailey sat facing Captain Fran McKee and Vice Admiral Abigail Halsey. He knew Abigail wasn't going to like what he was about to do.

Tough luck—she'll get used to it, Bailey thought.

"Fran, I'm sorry for stopping you from going on leave for a few days while I flew out here. What I need to tell you is best said in person, and frankly, I wanted to be the one to give you the news."

Bailey noticed Fran squirm a bit in her seat, unsure of what was coming next.

He fished in his pocket for a small black box, pulled it out and handed it to Fran. She took the box and opened it slowly. Then her eyes grew wide as she realized what was in it and what it meant. Her entire life had just changed, and she knew it.

McKee wiped a tear away. "I-I don't know what to say, sir. I never thought I'd become an admiral. Heck, I didn't even think I had enough time in grade as a captain to be an admiral."

She was clearly taken aback by the promotion. Abigail sat silently, not saying anything at first. She had argued against Fran's promotion to admiral. Unlike in the previous navy before the reorg and the unification of the militaries on Earth, there weren't a lot of admirals or generals in the military anymore. When one made these lofty ranks, there were typically few others. It was part of the Republic's effort to consolidate the top tier of the military and force out the less-qualified admirals and generals. They were, after all, building a wartime military. Many of those selected for grade reduction were also offered the option of an early retirement. If they chose to stay, they might one day earn back that rank, but they also might not.

Bailey smiled as he got up and moved over to stand next to Fran. "Here, let me help you pin them on. Let's get these eagles off those collars and get these stars on." He fiddled with the ranks for a moment until they were in the right positions. He then took his seat opposite her.

Abigail finally chimed in. "Congratulations, Fran. You've done a great job as the task force commander on the last two campaigns."

McKee smiled. "Thank you, Admiral. That means a lot coming from you."

Admiral Bailey was aware that Admiral Halsey had sour grapes over how rapidly some of the younger officers had moved through the ranks. McKee had only crossed the twenty-two-year mark in the Navy. Halsey, on the other hand, had served forty. Halsey had told him some of the other captains and task force commanders should have been promoted because they'd spent more time in grade and uniform.

Chester noticed the subtle interplay between the two women. "You know why we're promoting you, Fran?"

Admiral McKee didn't reply right away, which forced him to do the talking.

Chester leaned forward as he spoke. "I promoted you above many of your other peers for two reasons. You're aggressive as hell and know when to push your people and your ships, and you're a natural-born leader and tactician. When you got back from the last campaign, I read several reports from the Primord fleet admiral. You impressed him with how you fought and defeated those Orbot ships. I also received a report from the Empire, and the war council headed by the Altairians also commended you for your action. They named your maneuver during the last battle the McKee Maneuver and plan to train their own fleet commanders to execute it in future battles against the Orbots. They told me when Admiral Hunt returns to Earth, he'll be bringing a special award to present to you on behalf of the council."

Halsey bristled a bit at the accolades heaped on her subordinate. It was, after all, her overall fleet that had led the assaults. Since Bailey could tell that Halsey was a bit annoyed by what he'd just said, he quickly added, "Abigail, the council also told me that you will be receiving the same award for your action and leadership in the two campaigns."

He could see her relax a little bit. "Abigail, Miles will be returning to Earth at some point in the near future," Bailey added. "When he does, unless you're opposed, I'd like to select you to take his place on the war council on Altairius Prime. Like his tour, it would be roughly a three-year stint, but it'd get you out of New Eden.

"Now, if you *don't* want to go, I'd completely understand. As a matter of fact, Admiral O'Neal is opting to retire rather than stay on for another stint as the fleet operations chief. If you took that position, it would have you working back on Earth with me in my old position. You'd effectively become the second-in-command of the Space Force if you chose to accept the position. However, before you make your decision, understand this: the fleet operations chief position means you would likely never command a starship again. You would likely never command a fleet either. The Ops position is a staff position—a vital position, but an Ops position nonetheless."

Admiral Bailey practiced considerable restraint as he made this offer, but it was hard to hide the twinkle of excitement in his eyes that betrayed his pride in his vice admiral. Abigail was completely taken aback by the offer. If she took the fleet operations chief position, it meant a fourth star. If she took the war council position, though, it meant a chance to learn more about the alliance and see more of the galaxy.

"Abigail, I don't need an answer right away, and I won't accept one from you right now. It's a big decision; take some time to think about it. I'm going to spend the next two weeks touring some of our facilities down on the surface before I head back to Earth. Please let me know what you decide before I return to Sol."

Halsey nodded. "If I take the fleet Ops position, how long would I be able to serve in that position?" she inquired. "I only ask because, if I remember right, when you held the position, there was no higher tenure."

Bailey smiled at the question; he knew what she was getting at. "It's still roughly the same setup. You'd be getting your fourth star if you take the position. It would, however, lock you into that position for a very long time. I'm not sure if or when you'd be able to take a posting on the war council again. I can't say for certain if they're going to require that position be filled by someone who stays longer or how they're ultimately going to work it out. I know getting your fourth star would mean the world to you. It's something you've worked toward your whole life.

"Frankly, Abigail, you've been my protégé for a long time and I've done all I can to groom you to take my position at Fleet Ops, maybe even as the fleet admiral one day. But, serving on the war council with the Altairians and all the other races would be an incredible experience. If I were in your shoes, I honestly don't know what I'd do. I don't know if I could turn down a prospect like that. To see more of the galaxy and to learn what Miles learned would be a unique opportunity. That's why I'm telling you to take some time to really think about the decision."

Bailey turned back to Fran. "In the meantime, Admiral McKee, you will take charge of the fleet. I know you're two stars below Abigail, but frankly, she was top-heavy for the position. You are now the fleet commander for the second expeditionary force.

"Lieutenant General Ross McGinnis is going to be the overall commander for this next campaign, but you'll be in charge of the fleet operations. I know Ross; he's a good guy, as I'm sure Abigail will be able to attest to. He knows ground combat. Trust him when he asks for certain things, but most importantly, make sure you take care of the fleet and you protect his soldiers. As the new fleet commander, you're not just going to be in charge of your sailors and ships, you're going to be responsible for all of his soldiers reaching the planet. This next campaign is the one we've been asking and training for for years."

They spent the next hour going over the plan to invade the Zodark territory and liberate the Sumerian home world. A sense of satisfaction surrounded the daunting task because they'd been dreaming of it since they'd first learned who the Sumerians were and how they'd been enslaved by the Zodarks.

****

New Eden
Camp Victory
Third Army Group HQ

Admiral Chester Bailey took in a deep breath of fresh air as he stood on the parking ramp. The engine of the Osprey behind him winded down as the pilots finished the shutdown procedure. A few moments later, the man Bailey was there to meet walked toward him.

"Admiral Bailey, it's good to see you again. I hope the trip was pleasant," said Lieutenant General Ross McGinnis as the two men shook hands.

They walked to an SUV that would take them to McGinnis's headquarters. A couple of aides grabbed the admiral's gear and loaded it in the chase car.

"It was an enjoyable trip. Three days of isolation in the warp bubble can do wonders for a person," Bailey said with a chuckle. "How are things going here now that your command is back home?"

The two of them climbed into the back of the spacious SUV. The door closed behind them and the vehicle began to move. The soft and quiet electric engine made it hard to sense they were in motion at all.

McGinnis smiled as he replied, "As they say, Admiral, there's no place like home. Everyone is settling in and enjoying the downtime before the start of our next campaign. In a few months, we'll begin the work-up regimen prior to loading everyone back up in the ships again."

Bailey nodded in approval, "I'm glad to hear you're giving everyone some R&R. That was a very long and brutal campaign your army just returned home from. What's the status on the formation of the new Special Forces unit, the Rangers?"

McGinnis shrugged his shoulders. "Eh, they're coming along. Like anything new, there are some growing pains. We gave everyone in the division a full thirty days of R&R before we started the medical augmentations. They're still in that phase right now. They have another two weeks until they'll be cleared to begin the first phase of the physical training and conditioning, which I'm told is the most difficult."

The vehicle turned a corner and continued down a wide four-lane road toward another section of the base. Most of the construction on the place had been completed since Bailey's last visit more than three years ago.

"How's the recruitment been going, Ross?" asked Bailey. "I heard it got a little bumpy."

Ross tilted his head. "At first, it appeared like we were going to have the entire division join. I'm not sure what changed, but about thirteen percent of the soldiers opted to stay in the regular army. When I saw which soldiers opted not to join, it made sense; nearly all of them are on stop-loss. Most of them have between eight and twelve months of service left in the RA. I suspect they're just worn out and ready to leave."

Admiral Bailey sighed. "Let me ask you something, Ross. I don't want to keep people on stop-loss any longer than needed; however, the Altairians have given us some high numbers for the Army to keep. As you know, your Army group is the only one that's combat-ready for these campaigns. We're nearly ready with Fourth Army. First Army has to stay on Earth, and Second Army has to stay here. How would *you* approach this problem of raising the numbers we need and getting them all trained?"

Every now and then, Bailey liked to throw a tough problem at his subordinates to see what they came up with. He'd often found ideas that way that might work better than his own.

As the vehicle pulled up to the headquarters building, McGinnis said, "Let's finish this conversation in my office. It'll give me a moment to think about it and give you a better answer."

The two of them got out and headed in.

A couple of minutes later, Bailey took a seat in one of the chairs in McGinnis's office and waited for an answer to his question.

McGinnis cleared his throat. "Here's what I would do, Chester. I'd take all the soldiers that are on stop-loss and transfer them to First Army back on Earth. These soldiers have been through hell. There's no reason to keep deploying them knowing damn well many of them may end up getting killed. They've served their country, it's time to serve them now. Because my Army group is sadly the only one that's combat-ready and slated to deploy again, ask for volunteers from across the other groups to see if anyone wants to transfer. If they don't, then yank the best soldiers from those groups and send them here."

Bailey snorted at the solution as he shook his head. "You're going to ruffle some feathers with that approach."

McGinnis shrugged. "Like I care. My soldiers have been fighting and dying on one campaign after another. It's not like any of these other soldiers or officers are making major sacrifices. They can suck it up. Better yet, they can deploy in our stead."

McGinnis was a bit hostile in his response, but Bailey knew he was right. McGinnis's soldiers had done more than their share. It wasn't right that they were the ones being asked to carry so much of the load. Every time Bailey would get another army group brought up to one hundred percent and ready to redeploy, McGinnis would send over a casualty report and Bailey would have to take fifty or even a hundred thousand soldiers from another group and ship them over to McGinnis. His army group was like a meat grinder, constantly demanding more and more soldiers.

"Ross, I like your idea. I'm going to talk with General Pilsner, and we'll do it. You make a good point about the soldiers on stop-loss. They deserve better from us, and it's up to us as the senior leaders to do our

best to take care of them. Now, for the real reason I'm here. Let's talk about Operation Arrowhead Ripper…"
****

New Eden
Fort Roughneck
1st Battalion, 4th SFG

Colonel Bill "Wild Bill" Hackworth read the mission brief given to him by General McGinnis with a bit of skepticism and scorn.

"You look like you just chewed on a lemon, Bill," McGinnis commented.

Hackworth reached for his spit cup and spat some of his chew into it. He knew it was a dirty habit. Still, he wanted that nicotine fix. If they wouldn't let a person smoke anymore, then he damn well would get his fix from his chew.

"I'm not sure the mission can be done, sir," Hackworth finally commented gruffly.

"You're Special Forces. Work your magic. Make it work," McGinnis countered, not giving an inch.

Hackworth snorted. "It isn't that easy, sir."

McGinnis lifted an eyebrow at that. "Really? Do tell."

"First, how are we going to infiltrate the system? Second, how are we going to insert our teams without drawing the attention of the Zodarks? Third, how are we going to communicate anything we find or discover back to the fleet? Unless there's some new techno wizardry I haven't been made aware of that'll solve some of these problems, this mission won't work."

The regular Army general stared at Wild Bill for a moment. "If those problems were solved, could you accomplish this mission?"

Wild Bill paused, calculating. "All right, General, here's the deal. *If* you can get my teams into orbit undetected, and *if* you can provide us with a means of communicating off-planet to the fleet what we're finding on the surface, then, yes, I think the mission is doable."

"I think it's time you take a short ride with me," General McGinnis said with a mischievous smile. "Admiral Bailey has made some new toys from DARPA available to us for a mission like this. Oh, and before you allow skepticism to take over, you should know General Trevor Morton already signed off on adding the new equipment to the SOF inventory."

Hackworth chuckled at the mention of Morton, the head of Special Operations Command out of Tampa, Florida. "Well, General, why didn't you mention Trevor had some new toys for me? That changes everything."

"Bill, I don't have to tell you everything," McGinnis replied with a laugh. "Besides, I wanted your unbiased honest opinion of this mission before I told you squat about the new toys. You told me what I needed and was hoping you'd say. Now it's time I show you some gadgets that might make this mission possible. I need a blunt assessment once you've seen them to know if this is going to work or not. Let's head to the flight line. We need to take a little trip to the DARPA facility, where the stuff's being kept under wraps."

The two of them went to the flight line to take a short flight to a small facility tucked a few hundred miles away from anything on the planet. The location gave the R&D team plenty of space to test some cool stuff without prying eyes.

The flight to the secret squirrel facility went smoothly. The pilots flying the Osprey were based out of there, so they knew exactly where it was. When they came around a set of ridges, the R&D facility suddenly appeared out of nowhere. The base was wedged against the side of a ridge that appeared to extend from a nearby mountain range. It had a runway and roughly two dozen buildings scattered about the place. There was also a paved ramp leading up the ridge and several large closed doors, hiding something within.

Hackworth turned to the general. "I had no idea this place was even here," he said as they descended.

"No one does. That's how they want it."

"Who runs the security for it?"

"Morton has a team from JSOC handling it along with a contingent of C100s. Heck, even Walburg Industries has a small shop here. Maybe we can get them to give us a tour while we're here, beyond what they're already going to show you," the general offered as the Osprey settled on the parking ramp.

The two of them got out. There was no one here to greet them, at least not right away. Then two figures walked out of a nearby building.

The facility director, a colonel, and the R&D director, a civilian, walked up to them and guided them into the building.

"Colonel Hackworth—I was told you were briefed on Operation Arrowhead Ripper and had some questions about the insertion of your people and their ability to communicate once on the ground?" said the R&D director. His name tape said "Bob," but Hackworth doubted that was his real name.

Bob continued to explain, "I believe we have some tools that might be able to address some of those concerns. If you'll follow me, we'll talk over your coms challenge."

As Colonel Hackworth followed Bob into the room, he perked up at all the sophisticated gadgetry that surrounded them: tiny man-portable satellite antennas, new drones, and unrecognizable communications equipment.

The R&D director, Bob, picked up a cylinder. "This, Colonel, is the RD2 advanced communication system. It's a two-part system specifically built for Special Forces to allow you to operate deep behind enemy lines and still communicate with the fleet or other forces as you need to."

"OK, Doc—you're going to need to explain that a bit further before I'm willing to put my people in harm's way with it," Hackworth responded skeptically.

The civilian politely proceeded to explain how it worked. "As I said, it's a two-part system. This part is the actual com satellite. The launch tube is one meter in length and ten centimeters in diameter. This piece here is the fuel source. When you're ready to launch the satellite, you extend the legs like this. Then you attach the satellite to the base like this. Fully assembled, it stands about two meters tall. Once you've activated it and synced it to your coms unit, either in your HUD or the handheld device it comes with, then you launch it."

The civilian continued to explain how it worked for a few more minutes to assure Hackworth the device could place a very small satellite in space. "Once the unit is in space, it has the ability to stay in orbit for up to a year before its fuel cell runs out. Once that happens, it'll slowly lose altitude and eventually fall back into the atmosphere—"

Hackworth interrupted, "OK, Doc, you've convinced me you can get it into space. How does it send and receive data without being detected?"

"We're actually using a microburst transmission process based on Orbot technology we recovered from the last campaign over planet Rass," Bob explained. "When it's time to insert your unit, there'll be a spy ship lingering in the system. That's the ship that's going to receive your transmission and forward it on to the fleet."

Hackworth admired that this R&D team had come up with some innovative toys. He never would have imagined they could create a portable satellite launcher and system. This totally solved not only this communication problem but a host of other coms problems they'd experienced in the past.

"OK, sir, you've solved my coms problem," he admitted. "Now, how are you going to insert us without getting caught?"

"Follow me, Colonel," Bob responded. "We're going to head to the hangar. We've got something new to show you, and I think you're going to like it."

The group walked down the hallway and then took an elevator down a couple of floors. When they reached the bottom, they got out and boarded a tram. Wherever they were going, it was apparently underground and far enough away from the building they needed to take a tram.

"If you don't mind me asking, what else is this building used for and how protected is it from space?" inquired Hackworth.

Bob glanced at the military soldier sitting next to him as if calculating how much he should share.

Colonel Hackworth wasn't sure who Bob was or what unit he was from. If he was in Special Forces, their paths hadn't crossed. Hackworth found that kind of hard to believe considering he was entering his seventy-second year in SF. Hell, he'd been in the military since the last Great War, so he knew damn near everyone at this point. If they hadn't done that major reorg a few years back, he probably would have had a few stars on his collar.

Hackworth had to withhold a snicker—he knew exactly why he didn't have those stars. It all stemmed from a fundraiser at Senator Chuck Walhoon's reelection cocktail party in Houston thirty years ago.

I never should have gone to that stupid party, Hackworth chided himself. *I was just wallpaper dressing for the senator in the first place.* Walhoon liked to surround himself with soldiers and war heroes when he knew there'd be a TV camera or his rich donors would be around. But

Hackworth had been on assignment to the senator for a few months and had just wrapped up his assignment, so when Walhoon had invited him to the fundraiser, he had agreed.

Wild Bill Hackworth had partaken in his share of free drinks and regaled many of the senator's donors with some epic war stories before he caught sight of one of the most beautiful women he'd ever seen. Heads turned wherever she went, and she was absolutely stunning in that classic red dress.

Feeling slightly inebriated from his liquid courage, Hackworth had asked the gorgeous maiden to dance, and she'd said yes. After a second song together on the dance floor, they'd excused themselves to the terrace to talk.

"I hate my father's fundraising events," she'd confessed. Walhoon's daughter, Crystal, complained that she was only there to be eye candy for the old goats who donated money to the campaign.

After he'd served as her shoulder to cry on for a little while, she'd led him off to Senator Walhoon's office in the mansion that constituted the man's home. When they had closed the door, she'd practically assaulted him, kissing him all over. Before he could process what was going on, she had his zipper down and was working him over. She then pulled him over to her father's desk, where she pulled up her dress and lay back, waiting for him.

Hackworth didn't hesitate. The two of them had been going at it on the senator's desk for maybe five minutes when he thought he heard some voices. Before the two of them could react, the senator opened the door to escort a couple of his special donors in for a private conversation—only to find Hackworth there with his pants down to his ankles and his daughter with her dress pulled up on the edge of the desk and her legs on his shoulders.

Needless to say, Wild Bill Hackworth had been passed over for general officer selection five times since. It was impossible to get selected for general or admiral without the Senate Armed Services Committee signing off on it. As the chair of that committee, Senator Chuck Walhoon was never going to sign off on Hackworth making general, and frankly, Hackworth was fine with it. He liked being at the operational level.

Bob broke back through his trip down memory lane. "Colonel, I can't tell you everything we do here. But suffice it to say, we do a lot of

205

R&D type work for the war. As to how protected this place is, well, nothing's completely safe. If they want to take us out, I'm sure they could find a way. However, we didn't make it easy for them, that's for sure."

The tram came to a halt. When they walked into the underground hangar, a ship came into view. Wild Bill let out a soft whistle. It was a sleek vessel, twenty or thirty percent larger than the Ospreys they normally flew around in.

"*This* is how your soldiers will infiltrate. It's a specially modified version of the Osprey we're calling Nighthawks," Bob explained as they began walking around the outer shell of the craft. "Thanks to some miniaturization help from our Altairian allies, we've shrunk the FTL drive down to work on this ship. You'll be able to jump from one gate to another and travel through without the aid or help of a mothership. As you can see, the floor of the Nighthawk is two meters high. This constitutes the engineering room for the FTL drive and the interplanetary propulsion. It also has its own gravity generator, so despite its size, you won't have to deal with that challenge during the trip."

As Hackworth ran his hand along the exterior of the hull, he had to admit, it was one attractive ship. He was eager to see how it was set up inside.

Bob continued his explanation of the Nighthawk. "Now, we don't have an official cloaking system, so we came up with the next best thing. We made it virtually invisible to the naked eye. We also coated it in a special radar-absorbent material to further minimize its signature.

"The Nighthawk isn't built to be a warship, so it's not loaded up with weapons. You do still have the same thirty-two smart missiles that Osprey carries, along with the two fifty-caliber machine guns on the sides, and we beefed up the chin-mounted gun to a five-barreled 20mm rotary gun. But I think you'll like how we organized the interior of the ship."

Bob led them around to the rear of the ship. It had an extended ramp to compensate for the extra size of the undercarriage of the ship. The group climbed up into the craft.

"The rear of the ship has been outfitted with a depressurization room, so your teams can organize themselves in here for an orbital jump or spacewalk. As we enter the main cabin, this section has been converted to become an equipment locker for your weapons and gear. Here," Bob said as he pointed to four simulation pods, "we put these in so your team can continue to train while en route to the target. Next, we have a modified washroom; you'll have two showers and two toilets."

"This is a pretty tight space, Bob," Hackworth said as he surveyed the ship's interior. He tried to imagine one of his teams living and working in this ship.

Bob didn't shy away from Hackworth's assessment. "It is," he admitted. "It's meant to get your guys from point A to point B. It's not meant to be a luxury cruise."

Hackworth laughed. "Sounds great, Bob. I'm looking forward to having you on the trip with us."

Bob held up his hands up in mock surrender. "I get it, Colonel. The space is tight. Ideally, you'll fly in a mothership to get you closer to the target before you'll board the Nighthawk and continue the rest of the way there. The unique thing about the ship is its interior design. We modularized it, depending on the type of mission your units are on. This allows the ship to have a lot more functionality than it otherwise might have. As you can see, we've configured this ship so it can hold a crew of four and up to twenty soldiers. I'm not going to lie and say it'll be comfortable. It'll be cramped. But it will get you to the target."

No one said anything for a few seconds as Hackworth walked around more of the ship.

Bob finally added, "Once you arrive on station, you have two options. Either you can enter orbit and land the ship on the ground, or you can do an orbital insertion and have the ship fly away to a safer location and wait to pick you up."

Hackworth turned to look at Bob. "I take it this is only possible because of food replicators and the miniaturized FTL?"

Bob nodded. "Exactly. Those two things now make specialized craft like this possible. Mind you, Colonel, this will be the first time we'll be using this ship on a long mission like this. So far, we've only tested it on a few places near New Eden. Operation Arrowhead Ripper will be the first real test of the ship."

Hackworth took in the information as he walked around the reconfigured Osprey. This was going to be tight. He didn't like it one bit. He knew his soldiers weren't going to like it either, and they'd be the ones stuck in here for months.

He observed that the Nighthawk had a section with seven bunks for sleeping, a table big enough for everyone to sit at and two food replicators. There was a small kitchen for cleaning dishes and other functions. The whole design reminded Hackworth of those old-fashioned RVs, only this one would have to hold a Special Forces unit for months as they transited to the planets each unit was assigned to.

There is no way we can fit twenty-four people in this ship, thought Hackworth. *They'd go nuts.* Maybe they could rework this with a much smaller team and some C100s.

"So, Colonel, will this work for your snake eaters?" asked General McGinnis. "Can we get some of your teams inserted onto those Zodark-controlled planets?"

Wild Bill thought about it for a moment. He scanned the Nighthawk one more time before turning to face the general. "I don't like it," he said bluntly. "I think it should be a bit bigger if we're seriously considering this thing for long-term Special Forces missions. We can't just cramp people into a confined space like this for months and think it won't cause problems. That said, for this specific mission, I think we can make it work."

Hackworth turned to the DARPA civilian. "Bob, there's no way in hell twenty operators and four crew are going to fit in this thing for months on end to travel to the target," he said forcefully. "No way, no how are they going to stay sane all cooped up in this small space. Reconfigure it for a six-man team and two-man crew. Find a way to stuff six C100s in it. They can stay shut down, so they aren't in the way. But we're going to need to create some more living space and room for them to stretch out in here. Remember, these are SOF—they like to train and train constantly. You can't have them packed in so tight they can't move. This setup would be fine for a day or two, but we're talking about months of travel to reach the objective. I also recommend we maybe configure one ship to be our crew ship and turn the other ship into a coms ship. You know, bring extra com drones and satellites so we can ensure we have a good link in place to pass information from the surface to orbit, then from orbit to the gate and beyond."

Bob nodded and made a few notes on a tablet he had with him. "We'll start on it right away. I think we can get the second bird spun up the way you want it configured without too much hassle. If you don't mind, Colonel, I'd like to ask you some additional questions about what you think would make for a better Special Forces ship. Admiral Bailey has tasked us with either turning this Nighthawk into one or working with you guys to figure out what'll work."

Hackworth nodded in approval. He liked this idea a lot. If it could influence what the ships his guys would have to use would look like, then he'd love to be involved in that conversation. As they worked to make the 1st Orbital Ranger Division operational, his snake eaters would get back to their more conventional SOF-oriented missions and less of these direct-action ones that had been costing them so many operators.
****

Captain Brian Royce and Major Jayden Hopper reviewed the mission brief. This was clearly a SOF mission, no doubt about that. It was also an impossibly difficult mission and one none of them had ever done before.

Colonel Hackworth finally chimed in, "I know it's a tough mission, but this is what you Deltas train for—a deep-behind-enemy-lines recon mission."

"That's an awfully small ship for such a long journey," Captain *Royce* countered.

"I'm not going to lie and say it isn't. I've seen it up close and in person. It *is* small. The first version they proposed would have packed twenty of you in that ship. I told them that was out of the question and we dropped it down to just six, plus four crew to fly it."

"Well, you're the mission commander," Major Hopper said to Royce. "You think you and a team of six can get it done on the ground?"

That was the big question. Truth be told, Royce wasn't sure. In theory, sure, they could probably make it to Sumer and maybe even land this Nighthawk on the surface. But could they operate on the planet as well developed as Sumer and not get detected or, worse, handed over to the Zodarks? That was the real trick. They needed to gather real-time intelligence on the enemy presence down on the surface and what kind of popular support they could expect from the locals once the invasion started.

Royce gave it some careful consideration and then an idea popped into his head. A slight smile crept across his face as he replied, "Yes, sir, we can get it done."

Gaelic Outpost in the Belt
Non-Aligned Space

Liam Patrick sat at the desk carved out of an asteroid. It had been a gift from a mining company that had transferred their base of operations from the Mars Orbital Station or MOS to their little fiefdom out here in the Belt. Many outfits had rebased their operations on the GO or Gaelic Outpost. The tax structure Liam had implemented out here allowed the miners to keep a good portion of their earnings while still giving Liam the financial resources to provide for their people.

As a matter of fact, business had been so good out here the last five years, they had moved forward with their plans to build a massive extension to their carved-out asteroid. On the outer edge, they had started construction on five plateaus on which to construct these new cities. The new domes would range anywhere from six square kilometers to upwards of twelve. Along the edges of the smaller domes, the base height was one hundred feet. On the larger plateau sites, the tops of the domes would reach heights of one thousand, three hundred feet. This would give them plenty of space to build large skyscrapers and structures that would house many tens of thousands of people. Once the five new biospheres were built, they'd increase the population of the Gaelic Outpost by more than two hundred percent. They'd have the largest human colony outside of Mars and the Moon.

Liam looked at a sketch of the new cities. *We still need more room to grow*, he thought. *We need access to our own habitable planet to colonize.*

Not everyone agreed with him. There were many who would rather stay out in the Belt, where they were free to do as they pleased. Liam, however, had bigger plans than just being a pirate-turned-leader of the free people of the non-aligned space. He wanted to build an entirely new society, unencumbered by the trappings of Earth and its history.

"Did you read that request from Rorsh?" asked his partner, Sara Alma, as she walked into his office and sat down opposite him. "You know, that Polish shipbuilder that wants to lease some of our new construction bays."

Liam furrowed his brow. "I don't think I saw that one. When did it come in?"

Sara smiled and shook her head. "Nice try, playing dumb, Liam. You know, if you want to be the station chief and head of the NAS, you're going to need to stay on top of things like that."

Liam shrugged and gave her a weak smile. "You going to tell me about it or make me dig around for their message and proposal?" he asked.

Sighing, Sara tapped away on her tablet for a moment before she found what she was looking for. She hit a key and the message was displayed in a floating text box on the center of the desk between the two of them.

"Going to make me do all the work for you, aren't you?" she asked coyly, her Irish lilt especially strong in that moment.

Blushing at the rebuff, Liam started reading the proposal. "They want ten slots?" he asked, practically shouting. "That's half the new slots we're completing with the new yard expansion." Sara motioned for him to keep reading. "Whoa, they're wanting a fifty-year lease. Willing to pay one-third of that lease upfront, right now."

Sara smiled and put her hands on her hips. "See what you missed by not reading your mail? It's a good thing I'm nosy. You would have missed the deal of a century, Liam."

"Yeah, I guess so. That's a lot of money. Do you have any idea what they're wanting to use the slots for? Like what kind of ships they're wanting to build?"

Sara shrugged her shoulders. "No idea. I'm sure you could ask. You know, we're one of the few places with a shipyard that isn't dedicated to wartime production. If I had to guess, I'd say they are probably looking to build transports. There are hundreds of millions of people who want to move to New Eden or Alpha Centauri."

Liam shook his head at the mention of war production. He'd allowed them to get roped into that several years ago as part of his unofficial drug deal to have the charges against him and his company wiped away. In exchange for their independence in the Belt, they had to produce up to ten frigates at a time. There was no letup, no quota, just ten frigates constantly under construction. As soon as one was complete, they'd start laying the hull for another one. Each slip was knocking out frigates at a pace of one every three months, for a total of forty frigates a year. Out of that lot, they'd been able to keep a total of eight to form up their own navy and self-defense force.

"I'll approve Rorch's contract," he told Sara. "Send them a private note and ask them what they're looking to build. It's not a requirement of me signing off on their deal, I'm just curious what's going to be built in our yard."

"Done," Sara replied. She was all smiles now that her business had been taken care of. She did, after all, run the shipyards, so keeping that side of the business growing was critical to their continued economic growth. The yards provided upwards of forty percent of all jobs on their station.

Standing up, Liam stretched his back. "Walk with me," he said, holding out his hand. "Let's head down to the promenade."

The two of them walked out of the room that functioned as their governor's office and headed down the walkway that led to the shops, restaurants, and bars that made up the downtown of this little bit of paradise they'd created.

As they walked, some birds chirped while a handful of them flew from rooftop to rooftop or to some of the trees and other shrubs they'd taken the time to cultivate inside the carved-out asteroid. Making sure they had enough greenspace inside the facility was important. The clusters of areca palm, snake plants that were also known as "mother-in-law's tongue," gerbera daisy plants, Douglas fir and spruce trees all helped to create the necessary green spaces to maintain their delicate ecosystem, made to support life.

Along the walls of the massive city and in a couple of strategically placed parks were clusters of bamboo stalks. Over the years, many of them had grown to be thirty centimeters wide and now reached some twenty-eight feet into the air. They could actually reach as high as ninety-eight feet in some places on Earth. The bamboo plants were important to the station's carbon sequestration or carbon dioxide removal process. The station did have the necessary backup machines to perform this function should they need it, but they wanted to place their primary focus on natural oxygen generation.

The two of them walked to a restaurant that claimed to serve the best Indian food in space. Considering they were the only Indian restaurant this far away from Earth, that statement was probably accurate.

"So, what's on your mind, Liam?" Sara asked as she placed her order.

Liam sighed before he spoke. "I've been looking at the project to build the new habitats and expand the base. I just wonder sometimes if we might be better off trying to secure a habitable planet of our own. We know there are thousands of them out there. I'm sure there must be one out there we could lay claim to. Then we could expand without having to worry about the vacuum of space."

Sara smiled, not saying anything right away. She let him talk. She'd been with Liam now for nearly thirty years. He wasn't a big talker, but when he did want to talk, she let him.

"What is concerning you most about the expansion?" she asked.

"If we build the biospheres on the outer shell of our asteroid, I'm concerned they won't be protected enough in case a meteor comes through the area or something hits the dome hard enough. If that thing cracks, we're talking about thousands, tens of thousands of people that could be killed."

She ran her fingers through her hair. "Why would it crack, or better yet, why would something hit the dome? Between the defensive turrets we've anchored around the place, the early-warning radars, and the type of material we're building it out of, shouldn't it be safe?"

Liam took in a breath before he explained. "Yes and no. OK, so on the outer shell of our asteroid we've carved our little kingdom out of, we're going to have these large flat plateaus we'll be building the new biodomes on. Each plateau is between eight and twelve square kilometers. We're building some metal flooring to shore up some areas and expand the plateau base in others to give us a larger area to build on. Here's my concern—all of these areas are also going to be piped into our artificial gravity system. Our asteroid is actually going to have a slight gravitational pull to it because of what we're doing. Now, this might not have been a problem when the bulk of our habitat was *inside* the asteroid, but when we start construction of biospheres on the outer shell, it's going to naturally attract objects—objects that will impact against the outer shell of the biosphere."

Sara nodded. "I see what you mean. Wasn't this problem identified before we began construction of these outer plateaus a year ago?"

Liam's expression turned sour. "It was. I just learned a week ago about a biosphere just like the one we're building suffering a breach on one of Jupiter's colonies. Our plan was essentially built around theirs. The artificial gravity caused some nearby rocks and debris to rain down on the dome. Fortunately, they were still in the construction phase, so no one was living in it at the time. A couple of construction workers were killed, though, when they were sucked out into space."

Sara gasped as her right hand moved to her mouth. Accidents in space happened. Still, they made you realize how fragile humans were out here. The slightest mistake or misstep could result in immediate death.

"Tell me they have a solution to solve this?" she pleaded.

Liam nodded. "They think they do. Right now, the dome is approximately three feet thick. It's exceedingly durable. It'll even stop a single 20mm magrail slug. What the company that's building that Jupiter colony is proposing is to double the width of the material. They also want to weave in a second titanium-wired mesh into its construction. Instead of the wired mesh only being on the inside to provide its shape and support, they're going to add a layer to the outer portion."

"It sounds like it'll be pretty solid, but that will be damn costly and time-consuming," Sara commented.

Liam snorted at the assessment. "It doubles the costs of the domes and triples the time needed to build it. This is why I was saying it'd be nice if we could just lay claim to our own moon or planet and not have to deal with this. I mean, we're going to be stuck building places like this for generations if we opt to really grow our new society out here in the Belt. I almost wish we could just use this place to fund our colonization of a new world instead."

Sara reached across the table and grabbed his hand as she looked him in the eyes. "Maybe you are right, Liam. In the end, your idea might make more sense. Let's file this in your 'good idea bin' and keep exploring it as the opportunities arise. You and I both know the only way we're going to get to claim a new planet all to ourselves is if we go out there and find one.

"I think if you want to pursue this idea, then we should create our own exploration ships and go find one. With the war going on between the Republic and the Zodarks, they're going to be focused on that for a very long time. While that's happening, let's keep building our own little society out here and position ourselves to lay claim to our own planet. This new shipyard is going to bring in an enormous amount of new revenue to our fledgling government. The new biospheres you're building will enable our population to reach a million people."

She sat back and chuckled. "Now, if you don't mind, I want to eat my food before it gets cold," she finished with a grin.

Chapter Nineteen
Rangers Lead the Way

New Eden
Fort Roughneck

"What do you think of the new armor, Pauli?" Sergeant Yogi Sanders asked as the two of them went through the process of setting their rigs up the way they wanted.

Pauli smiled. "I like it. It's going to take some getting used to, but I like the idea of being able to get back up after a blaster shot to the chest."

"I think the armor is going to be a lot easier to use than these new augmented bodies they've given us," Yogi commented. "I think I could still use another month of physical therapy before I'll feel comfortable. Learning how to use this neurolink is proving to be a royal pain. I sent a rather embarrassing message to the guys in my squad the other day."

Pauli laughed—he'd done the same thing to his guys and he'd received more than a few awkward messages from them as well. One of the female soldiers in his squad didn't realize that the fantasy she was running through in her mind of a couple of the male soldiers was being transmitted to the rest of the squad. Fortunately, that was as far as it had gone.

"I hear you there, Yogi. Just give it another couple of weeks. We'll have this stuff figured out. I talked with one of our Delta instructors the other day. He told me it took many of them a few months to fully figure things out. I'm sure the more we use it, the more comfortable we'll get with it." He stretched to stand taller. "But, hey, let's get moving. We don't want to be late to formation. It's our platoon's turn to get a peek at that new infantry assault vehicle the Army's being given."

The two of them headed out the door and off to the motor pool. After nearly a decade of war, the Army was finally fielding them with an honest-to-goodness infantry fighting vehicle.

Joining the rest of their platoon mates, Yogi and Pauli waited around until they were told they could go in and see the new vehicle. A few minutes later, an Army major and a couple of civilians walked through the door of the large building and made their way over to join them. The major took a couple of steps towards them and called them all to attention.

The squads formed up, and their platoon leader took his position at the head of their formation.

"Good morning, everyone. My name is Major Jiao Kaihe. These other two gentlemen are from DynCorp and Norinco. They have teamed up to provide us with this incredible new infantry fighting vehicle. Some of you may not have known this, but the vehicle saw limited combat action on both Intus and Rass. That allowed us to work out the bugs in the system and further refine some last-minute features.

"In a moment, we're going to take you guys inside to check it out, let you guys have a chance to crawl around it and get a feel for it. Once you've had a chance to look it over, we'll head over to the classroom, where we're going to go over the specifics of the vehicle and how to operate it. Starting tomorrow, you guys will be put through a driving course on how to drive it and use its weapon systems. The vehicle itself is going to function as either a platoon or company headquarters vehicle or command-and-control operations center."

The major from the former Asian Alliance paused to let some of what he said sink in before continuing. "As you all know, we're now officially the 1st Orbital Ranger Division or ORD. That means we need to be able to operate as an independent assault force outside of the regular Army. The Deltas are the scalpel; we're the short sword. We need to punch above our weight at every unit level in the coming engagements. This vehicle is going to allow us to do just that, so it's important that you all know how to operate this vehicle and effectively use it. With that said, let's go ahead and show you guys the newest weapon of war."

Pauli smiled at the pep talk, and so did most of the soldiers in his squad. After months of training on how to use their new bodies, they were finally getting the chance to see some of the new toys the Army had been quietly creating.

As the doors to the large building opened up, they all caught a glimpse of this new tool. "This, soldiers, is the DN-12 Cougar," Major Jiao explained as the soldiers began to approach the vehicle. "It's a ten-wheeled amphibious-capable modular armored vehicle developed in a joint collaboration between DynCorp and Norinco. Because it's a modular vehicle, it can be outfitted as a direct infantry fighting vehicle, which is the variant you're looking at, or outfitted with a Howitzer to provide mobile indirect fire support. It also has an antitank variant, equipped with additional smart missiles or a 130mm direct-fire autocannon. There is also a battlefield logistics version, which allows it to transport large quantities of supplies across rough terrain and under hostile fire to provide medical support with its makeshift hospital variant."

Everyone was acting like a bunch of excited children at Christmas as they looked over the new vehicle. Many of the soldiers ran their hands across its armored shell while they walked around it, talking excitedly amongst each other.

"How many soldiers can this thing carry?" shouted Yogi, a question many of them had.

"In the infantry variant, it has a crew of three and a troop bay of sixteen fully loaded-down soldiers. It has two drop seats, so technically, you could transport two additional passengers if you had to. This vehicle was specifically built to transport an entire squad into combat or move you guys around a planet or moon."

Pauli walked around to the major. "Is this the kind of armament the infantry variant will be equipped with?" he asked.

Major Jiao smiled and nodded. "It is. The variant you are looking at has a turret that carries sixteen smart missiles. As you can see, just above the driver compartment is a remote-controlled single-barreled M91 heavy blaster, just like the ones your machine gunners carry. Just above the rear hatch is a second M91 to provide coverage for the rear side of the vehicle. Both guns can be operated by the vehicle commander, who sits behind the driver compartment—or they can be operated by the driver or assistant driver. This configuration allows the vehicle to provide close-in air defense, antitank/vehicle protection and direct-action offensive capabilities to support your squad in combat."

One of the other soldiers yelled out another question. "What kind of speed and range does this thing have when it's fully loaded down?"

"That's a good question, soldier. We'll go over more of that in the classroom. But suffice it to say, the cruising speed of the vehicle for optimal battery use is one hundred kilometers per hour. It has a maximum speed of one hundred and ninety kilometers per hour, but at those speeds, you'll chew through the battery pack pretty quick. As to range—at cruising speed, it has a range of five hundred and ten kilometers. If the vehicle is in heavy combat and you're doing a lot of starting and stopping, then we think the range will likely be closer to three hundred and twenty kilometers.

"The great thing about the vehicle is it comes with its own solar panels. This allows a squad, platoon, or company to operate on their own for long periods as they can independently recharge their own vehicles. This is what makes the vehicle so valuable as an IFV. A company of these can operate outside the FOB or the main operating army for weeks or months without needing any additional support. You're more likely to run out of smart missiles than you are energy for your batteries. The vehicle also has multiple recharging ports to allow you guys to recharge the batteries for your blasters."

Many of the soldiers let out a soft whistle as the major continued to give them the specs and capabilities of their new toy. It was a remarkable all-around vehicle—exactly what they had been needing since the start of this war with the Zodarks. Pauli was pretty confident if they had had this vehicle during the outset of the war, they probably would have lost a lot fewer people than they had.

"OK, everyone. Let's make our way into the classroom. We have a lot to teach you all about your new tool and weapon. This is going to be a game changer for the Army," the major declared as he guided them to the classroom. The two contractors from DynCorp and Norinco would then do their part of introducing them to the vehicle and how to operate it.

****

Later that evening at dinner, Lieutenant Atkins placed his tray of food in front of an empty seat opposite Yogi and Pauli. "There you clowns are. I've been trying to find you guys."

"Whatever it is, LT, it wasn't me," said Pauli jokingly. "Yogi did it."

Yogi jabbed Pauli in the ribs, countering, "Hey, Pauli tricked me. I had no idea she was your girlfriend."

"Hey, cut the crap," Atkins shot back, narrowing his eyes as he looked at the two jokers. "Be serious for a minute. I need to talk with you guys about something."

Yogi and Pauli sat a little straighter in their chairs. "Sorry about that, sir. We're listening," Pauli said for the both of them.

Seeing he had their undivided attention, Atkins began to explain why he'd tracked the two of them down. "Our company has now finished phase two of our training. As you both know, phase three is a bit looser. We have to start identifying the more specialized training we want the different squads and platoons in the company to receive. When we enter phase four, that's when we have to put all those different training pieces back together for our final training exercise."

This was the part of the training all the soldiers had been looking forward to—the chance to really start specializing inside of Special Forces.

"OK, so here's the deal. Everyone has to go through the orbital high-altitude, high-open jump program. From what I've been told, soldiers either love it or they hate it. In either case, it's a requirement for graduation, so tell your squads they'll have to suck it up. Once everyone's graduated that program, one squad's worth of soldiers has to become proficient in how to use that new DN-12 Cougar. They'll learn how to use every variant of the vehicle and its various weapon systems. They'll also learn how to pack its chutes, so the vehicle can follow us in an orbital HAHO jump if required. No idea how they made that possible, but they did, and it's why each platoon has to send a squad's worth of soldiers through its advance training program.

"While they're going through that course, a squad's worth of soldiers needs to go through the advanced demolition and weapons training," Atkins continued. "This group will learn how to use and maintain Zodark and now Orbot weapons since we captured a bunch of them during the Rass campaign. The remaining two squads will be sent through some additional combative and weapons training courses— basically, a lot more training on how to use a variety of knives, pistols, and other weapons. Then they'll have to go through a few dozen training simulations using those newfound skills."

"Damn, LT. Phase one, the medical stuff, took us four months to get through," Yogi griped. "We just finished three months of phase two training. Now we're going to have *three more* months of this before we even start phase four, and that block of training is six months?"

Special Forces school had been hitting a lot of the soldiers hard. Pauli knew this was going to be a tough program. He'd been mentally psyching himself up for the full-on Delta school, which was a thirty-six-month program. The toned-down Ranger training was still sixteen months. The only good thing about the long training program was it meant they weren't available for any campaigns that might arise—at least not until they were operationally ready to deploy.

Lieutenant Atkins finished his food and softened his tone a bit as he looked at the young sergeant. "Yogi, I know this is tough. I'm sure everyone is questioning why they signed up for this new unit. But here's the deal. Whether we like it or not, we humans are stuck in this new war. It's a war of pure survival or extinction, with little middle ground. None of us wanted this, but here we are. If we don't figure out a way to win this war, it could mean humanity is either wiped out or enslaved like the Sumerians. Right now, the Republic has been given an incredible gift. You want to know what that gift is?"

Pauli thought he knew, but he wanted to let Yogi answer this one. He knew his friend had really been struggling the last month or so with everything that had been going on.

Yogi sighed in frustration and then shook his head to Atkins's question.

"We've been given *time*, Yogi—time to prepare for the coming storm. The other day I had the opportunity to sit in on an officer call with the division commander. He's going through the training with us as well. He told all of us that the Republic was going to go on the offensive. We aren't going to sit around and wait for the Zodarks to attack us and we aren't going to fight battles that won't lead us closer to victory against the Zodarks. When the division completes our training, we're going to go liberate the Sumerian home world. Their planet sits in a star system that leads down a dead-end star chain, according to the stargate maps. Our intelligence tells us there are close to a dozen habitable planets and moons down that chain. We also learned there are five planets with humans on them—all slave planets to the Zodarks. We're going to go liberate them and add them to the Republic."

Atkins paused for a moment as he let Yogi take in what he'd shared. "I know the training is tough, Yogi. But we've all survived multiple orbital assaults. We'll get through this too. Now, you guys figure out what training your squad members want to complete and have a list ready by tomorrow evening. We start the new training phase on

Monday. Once it's completed, the platoon will re-form back up, and we'll complete the final phase of training before we're deployable."
****

New Eden
Fort Roughneck
1st Ranger Division

"That's a lot of Cougars," the staff officer commented.

The front ramp of the T-92 Starlifter had lowered as two columns of the new infantry fighting vehicles drove off. The drivers parked them in neat rows along the parking ramp. They'd be inventoried and checked for damage and then driven over to their new units.

Brigadier General William Darby stood on the flight line with his hands on his hips as he watched the large cargo transport being offloaded. For the last month, they had been receiving their long-awaited shipment of vehicles and the new infantry assault rifles.

The venerable M85 rifles were being phased out for the newest version, the M1. A new century had dawned since the last rifle had been created, so the designers had started over with a new model number. The M1 was still equipped with the over-under barrel like its predecessor; the big improvements to the rifle came down to its increased hitting power and size. The new rifle was going to be four inches smaller. The blaster now had a stun setting, and the magrail had an increased power option designed to penetrate the Orbots' body armor and the newly improved Zodark armor.

The biggest change coming to the Rangers and the Army in general, however, was definitely the new Cougars. The DN-12 modular infantry assault vehicle was going to give the Army a lot of flexibility they currently didn't have. Mainly, it would allow them to become more independent of the fleet instead of relying on it to move them from point to point.

When the war with the Zodarks had begun, the military hadn't really had a combined arms function. The vehicles and weapons they'd had had been built to fight each other, not conquer and capture foreign planets and deal with the Zodarks. The drawn-out fight to capture New Eden and then the immense reliance on the fleet for the Intus campaign had really laid bare the inadequacies of the Army.

222

"You ready to head back to the office, sir?" asked the staff officer as the last vehicle drove off the transport.

General Darby turned to the young lieutenant. "Yeah, let's head back. I've seen what I wanted to see."

Ten minutes later, they arrived at the building that constituted the division headquarters building. When Darby walked in, he saw that General Ross McGinnis was waiting for him.

"Ah, there you are, General. Someone told me you went down to the flight line," McGinnis commented as Darby and his staff officer walked in.

Darby would normally be surprised to see McGinnis waiting in his office, but the staff NCO had sent a message ahead to let them know he was waiting there for them.

"Just checking on some of the new equipment coming in. What can I do for you today?"

"I wanted to talk with you about the coming Sumer campaign," said McGinnis. "We're less than six months out. How do you feel your divisions are coming along?"

Darby took a seat as he answered, "They'll be ready. I think these new weapons and equipment are going to make a difference."

"Let's hope so," said McGinnis. "We honestly have no idea if the Sumerian people are going to be hostile to our presence and side with the Zodarks or side with us. Things could get real ugly if they choose the former."

"What do we know about the planet? Do we have eyes on it yet or intelligence from the surface?"

McGinnis shook his head. "Not yet. The Deltas are going to be landing a team on the surface soon. We'll have a better idea of what's going on once they arrive."

"Any idea when that'll happen?" asked Darby, leaning forward.

"They're spinning up a team for it right now," McGinnis replied. "I suspect they'll leave soon to start their recon. I think they're taking one or more of the original Sumerians we liberated on this planet with them as local guides. I suspect they'll need to get them trained up and then they'll head out."

Darby nodded. The more information they had on the planet, the people residing there, and any possible enemy resistance that might await them on the surface, the better prepared they'd be to handle them.

"Sounds like a plan, General. I suppose we'll continue to get ourselves ready on this end. Do you know how big an operation this will be?"

McGinnis smiled. "Big. We're bringing the entire Third Army on this one. Once we liberate Sumer, we'll planet-hop down the entire chain until we've secured all the habitable planets along the way. From there, we'll establish a new series of forward outposts and begin fortifying the stargates and the systems against counterattack."

Darby grinned at the news. *Finally, a mission worth dying for—a campaign that'll actually make a difference in the overall war effort.*

Chapter Twenty
Behind Enemy Lines

New Eden
Fort Roughneck
Alpha Company "Ghosts"

Captain Brian Royce reviewed the company roster and selected the five individuals who'd be coming with him on this mission. Technically, he should be sending one of his lieutenants—he was, after all, the company CO. But Major Hopper hadn't shot down his plan to go himself, so he was all in. Truthfully, Royce probably had more experience in Special Forces than damn near anyone in the battalion, so it made sense for him to lead this mission. It could also end up turning into a first-contact event, so having someone with a bit of rank would help.

Next, Royce scanned the battalion personnel files, searching for one particular individual. *Ah, there you are,* he thought. *Hosni—well, he's now officially Lieutenant Hosni.*

Hosni was one of the original Sumerian prisoners they'd liberated on New Eden a little more than twelve years ago. Following his multiyear debriefing, Space Command had given him a couple of choices. He could attend any university he wanted in order to learn about Earth and go on about his life as a regular civilian, or he could join the military and help liberate his people from the Zodarks.

Hosni had chosen the hard path. He had told Admiral Bailey and Chancellor Luca he'd like to serve the Republic and do whatever he could to liberate the Sumerian people. After making that difficult decision, he'd been sent to Space Academy in Colorado Springs. After four years at the Academy, Hosni had opted to go the Army route, as opposed to the fleet route. He'd spent a year learning to become an intelligence officer, then Big Army had sent him to learn psyops. Following the schools the Army had wanted him to attend, Hosni had applied to and been accepted to Special Forces.

For the next three years, Hosni had gone through selection, then the medical augmentations and enhancements before he'd completed all of his necessary qualifications. His service jacket showed he'd just been assigned to the 4th Special Forces Group a few weeks ago. It was a very long and hard road Hosni had chosen to follow, but now he was about to put all those skills to good use.

Royce made a note to have Lieutenant Hosni summoned to his office ASAP. He also clued Major Hopper in on the request so he could be present as well. Next, Royce found two other individuals perfect for the mission, Private Beth Chandler and Corporal Iris Wells.

Royce didn't have a lot of women in his company. Heck, the battalion didn't have a lot of women in it as a whole. Most but not all women pursued service in the fleet. Flying starships around the galaxy seemed to generally be more appealing than being a soldier. Being a Delta versus a regular Army soldier, well, that was an entirely different breed of woman who wanted to pursue that path.

Using his neurolink, Royce summoned the two women to his office. He also told his first sergeant and his XO to join him for the meeting. Royce's XO, a woman as well, was tough as nails and knew how to soldier well.

It was time to get his leadership team brought up to speed on this new mission and the fact that he was going to be gone for an extended period of time. It meant his XO was going to have to step up and take charge for a while. This was a good opportunity to prove she was ready to take command of her own company.

****

"At ease. Please take a seat," Captain Royce said to the two female soldiers standing in front of him.

As they sat, Royce pulled up an image of the Sumerian home world, Sumer. "I've summoned you both because you've been selected for a top secret mission," he announced. "I'm not going to lie to you and tell you this will be easy; it's going to be a tough mission, and there's a chance some or all of us may not come back. That said, this mission is crucial to the war effort."

The two soldiers looked at each other with a twinkle of excitement in their eyes and then back at him. "We're ready, sir. What's the mission?"

Royce smiled at their eagerness. *They don't care what it is, they want in.*

"We're going to insert a recon team on Sumer. You, along with three others, will be on the team, which I'll be leading. We're going deep behind enemy lines with no help from the fleet or anyone else. I need to know now if either of you has any hesitation. I'm making this a voluntary mission. You do not need to come if you feel someone else might be a better fit."

Both soldiers shook their heads. They were on board; they wanted in.

Royce smiled. "OK, good. Then I'm glad to have you on this mission. We're only gonna have five Deltas on this mission and a couple of terminators. I'll be relying on you ladies a lot. So, right now, I want you both to go next door and spend the next several hours reading over the mission brief.

"Private Chandler, as the mission coms specialist, effective tomorrow, you will spend a week at a different base, learning a new coms system we will take with us on this mission. I need you to learn everything you can about this new coms gadget. Make sure you know how to troubleshoot it, take it apart and fix it or whatever else you think you need to know. If the coms system breaks, you'll need to know how to fix it. It's going to be our only way to communicate once we're on the ground. If it goes down, our mission is essentially over. Got it?"

"Yes, sir. You can count on me," she replied crisply.

Captain Royce turned to the other female soldier. "Corporal Iris Wells, I understand from your service jacket you have a knack with languages?"

"Yes, sir. I studied linguistics in college. I'm fluent in six languages on Earth, to include Arabic and many of its different dialects. I also have a working understanding of the Sumerian language, which we now understand is a variant of ancient Chaldean. It's related to Arabic, Amharic, and Hebrew, which I'm already fluent in," she explained without hesitation.

"Damn, that's impressive, Corporal," Royce replied. "I can barely speak English, and you've got me bested with six other languages. I truly do marvel at folks like you who can understand so many different languages."

Her cheeks flushed slightly. "My father and mother were diplomats, so I grew up living in embassies around the Middle East and in the Balkans. I guess it just comes naturally to me."

"I like it. In any case, you're going to have one of the toughest jobs on this mission. You and two other people on our team will be our linguists. While I think we have a solid working understanding of their language and our universal translators can generally understand what they're saying, we're going to be bringing two native speakers with us. Once they're read on to the mission, you will be teamed up with them during our train-up. I want you conversing with them in their native tongue nonstop. I need you to develop a flawless working knowledge of Sumerian. You need to be able to speak it fluently in their midst, because in all likelihood, the three of you will be doing the recons of the Sumerian planet. You're going to be our eyes once we're on the ground. Understand?"

Corporal Wells lifted her head a bit as she suddenly realized the implications. They weren't just going down to the planet to observe from a remote location—he was sending her in amongst them.

"I understand, sir. I've been casually studying the language for a while, but I'll dig into it now. If I'm not mistaken, I believe we just had a Sumerian join the battalion. A Lieutenant Hosni?" she inquired.

Royce nodded. "You are correct; we did. I haven't seen Hosni in years, but I know him. I was on New Eden when we liberated him. As a matter of fact, once he's been read on to the mission, he'll be coming with us. The two of you will have plenty of time to talk and improve your language skills."

Captain Royce paused for a moment before dismissing the two soldiers. He still needed to meet with Hosni and then convince the brass that he really needed to take Hadad as well.
****

The following day, Royce was walking back to his office when he saw a lieutenant standing nearby, waiting for him. As he approached, the lieutenant snapped to attention.

"Lieutenant Hosni, reporting as ordered."

"At ease, Lieutenant. Come on in," Royce said as he led the two of them into his office. "You caught me coming back from lunch."

Captain Royce walked around his desk and took a seat. He didn't think Hosni remembered him. Heck, it had been nearly eleven years since they'd last seen each other.

"Lieutenant, we met many years ago. Back then, I was a master sergeant. I was part of the team that liberated you from the Zodark camp."

The lieutenant smiled slightly. "I thought I recognized the name, but I didn't want to assume. With all the recent battles and the high casualties, I wasn't sure if you had made it. I'm glad you have."

Royce shrugged his shoulders. "It's not for lack of effort on the part of the Zodarks or the Orbots, I'll tell you that. But, yes, I'm glad to still be alive and kicking."

Hosni chuckled at the comment. "I'm glad you're still alive. I had hoped I'd get to see you and Major Hopper again. I still remember talking with you guys after we boarded the *Voyager*. You asked me if I wanted to be a soldier like you and liberate my people. Well, it took me longer than expected, but here I am."

Royce smiled at that memory from so long ago. "I'm glad to have you here, Hosni," he replied. "Hey, when it's just us—please, call me Brian. Now, back to why I called you here. I'm putting together a deep reconnaissance mission, and I need you on it. I know this will be your first real Delta mission. Still, I need your language abilities and your background as a Sumerian for this particular mission."

Hosni nodded as he took in the information.

Royce continued, "Our team is going to insert on the Sumerian home world. It will be a small team, roughly six of us. We will be on our own and deep behind enemy lines for an extended period of time. Are you ready for something like this?"

Hosni smiled. "I am. But you do remember that I was a slave to a Zodark NOS, right? I have never been to Sumer, and I know nothing about the planet or its people."

"That's true, but you're still a native speaker of the language. You also have a deeper understanding of the Zodarks than anyone else I know. We will need that. Our mission is to scout certain areas of the planet to find Zodark facilities and any planetary defensive weapons. We Earthers may not know what they look like if they don't match what we've seen on Intus and Rass. We also need to locate a suitable drop zone for the assault force that'll allow us to capture and secure key government and military installations quickly.

"Ideally, we want them to welcome us with open arms as we liberate them from the Zodarks; however, if they're intent on staying part of the Zodark Empire, then we may have a fight on our hands. In either case, we're going to capture the planet as it's going to be a springboard for further invasions of Zodark-controlled space. So, we're going to need as much intelligence as we can acquire."

"Have you thought about bringing Hadad with us?" Hosni asked. "Or maybe that other woman, Satet? They are both from the capital city. They'd probably be able to guide us around the area a lot better than I can."

"I have thought about that," Royce replied. "I'm having a meeting with Colonel Hackworth to discuss it. Hadad is currently working for Governor Crawley. I'm not sure if he'll want to come with us or if the Governor will allow him to. Hopefully, they'll allow him to come, but if they don't, we'll do our best to figure it out on our own. As to Satet, I'd love to bring her, but she's married now and is a university professor. The Republic now has her teaching Sumerian language and culture classes to help us better understand the Sumerian people."

Hosni nodded in acknowledgment. "OK, Brian. So, what do we do while we wait to see if Hadad is going to come with us? Is there any specialized training we should be preparing right now?"

"There is," said Royce with a nod. "Work on getting to know the rest of your teammates. We're also going to be incorporating a number of new types of surveillance drones on this mission. Everyone's going to need to pitch in on how to operate and use these things effectively. I'll be the mission commander, but we have four others. If Hadad can come, then he'll make six.

"If he comes, then we're going to have to spend some time teaching him how to conduct an orbital HALO. That can be a tricky jump, so we'll be practicing it ourselves a handful of times from the new ship we'll be using for the mission. We will make a few practice trips in this new ship. I have a feeling it has some bugs that'll need to be worked out before we're stuck on it for months on end."

Chapter Twenty-One
An Emperor's Mission

Cobalt
Gallentine Imperial Palace

Rear Admiral Miles Hunt was in awe of the palace as they approached it. They had flown in a small hovercraft vehicle out of the center of the city toward the imperial palace, located on the outskirts. It was positioned along an ocean, one of the few planetary features not covered by the continuous city that wrapped around the entire planet.

Pandolly interrupted his private thoughts. "This is a great honor being bestowed upon you, Miles. I hope you understand how incredibly rare this opportunity is."

Hunt turned to the Altairian, who had become quite the friend and mentor over the years. "I appreciate that, Pandolly. I feel my people owe this opportunity to you. You've taught us so much. Had the Altairians not intervened in our war with the Zodarks, there's a good chance my people would either be slaves or dead."

"If there is one thing I have learned from my years of interacting with you and your people, Miles, it is not to underestimate you humans," Pandolly replied. "Of all the races of people we have encountered, humans are by far the most clever and resourceful. The technological leaps and bounds your species has made in the last thirteen years are beyond impressive."

Pandolly fidgeted a bit. *Is that nervousness I detect?* Hunt asked himself.

"When we reach the outer chamber to the emperor's private chamber, you and Ambassador Chapman will enter on your own," Pandolly explained. "Your son, Ethan, and I will join you for dinner."

Once the vehicle came to a halt on an outer parking pad, the four of them got out and headed into the palace. A set of guards snapped to attention as they approached. Miles and Ethan were wearing their military dress uniforms, medals and all. Nina had an elegant formal outfit on as well. The three of them were dressed to impress.

As they approached the antechamber that led to this private meeting, Ambassador Velator appeared. "Hello, Miles," he said, a little less warmly than his previous greetings. "In a few minutes, I will escort you to meet with the Emperor and some of his key advisors. When we walk into the room, you will be required to approach the emperor and stop three tensils from him. That's approximately three of your meters. The Emperor will approach you, and he will extend his right hand to you. You will drop to one knee and then take his hand in yours and kiss the imperial ring. The Emperor will then return to his chair, and the two of you will take your chairs.

"The Emperor will spend some time talking with you before he'll bring in his advisors. They will quiz you on matters they would like to ask you about. When this is done, we will move to the dining hall for a formal state dinner. Your son and Pandolly will join us for this dinner. Do you have any specific questions for me before we go in?"

During the last few days, Miles had learned that Ambassador Velator was a very precise man. He provided very detailed information and liked the itinerary to run on a very precise timeline. He was a very meticulous individual, as all Gallentines appeared to be.

"No, Mr. Ambassador, I believe I understand what's expected of us. Thank you for allowing our people the opportunity to meet with the Emperor," Miles said calmly. He might have managed to portray composure, but internally, Miles felt like a kid on his first day of school—unsure of everything that was about to happen. Butterflies swirled about in his stomach.

"Excellent. Pandolly, we will see you later today. Miles, Ambassador Chapman, if you'll follow me in," Velator replied before leading them through the massive double doors of the anteroom.

When they entered the room, Miles shook his head, in awe of the grandiosity. It wasn't gaudy, but at the same time, it had the appropriate amount of decorative touches to communicate to those entering the hall that someone important resided here. The Emperor sat on a throne on a raised platform at the end of the chamber. Along the edge of the room were large, ornate columns. There were guards positioned periodically throughout the chamber, armed with a type of rifle Miles had never seen before.

Along the walls of the room, windows provided natural light, and a strange light emanated from the ceiling. There were some flags with strange markings on them hanging on the walls—Miles assumed these must represent some of the factions of their Empire.

As they approached the raised platform with the throne, the Emperor stood to greet them. He proceeded to walk down toward them. "People of Earth—Admiral Miles Hunt and Ambassador Nina Chapman—it is truly an honor to meet you both."

As the leader of the Empire approached, Miles and Nina dropped down to a knee as they had been instructed. The Emperor held his right hand out to them. As instructed, Miles reached for the extended hand and saw a large rectangular ring with the seal of the Gallentine on it. He kissed the seal as he'd been taught and then waited for Nina to do the same.

When this part of the protocol had been completed, the Emperor turned around to head back to his throne. Some people appeared from the side of the room, holding two very comfortable-looking chairs, which they brought forward for Miles and Nina.

"How would you like me to address you?" the Emperor asked. "Shall I call you by your formal military rank? You may address me as Your Majesty, a term I am told was also used on your own planet many centuries ago."

Miles smiled that even the most powerful man in the universe would take the time to ask such a question. Miles could already tell he was going to like him.

"Your Majesty, my friends call me Miles. You may call me Miles or by my formal military rank, whichever pleases you." Miles was doing his best to be as agreeable and amenable as he could. This was an incredible opportunity to meet the head of the Empire, and he was determined to make the most of it.

"I am pleased you feel we can be friends. I would like nothing more than for the people of Earth to become good friends with me and the Gallentine people. I shall address you as Miles, and you as Nina," the Emperor said, welcoming his two guests.

"Please, take a seat. We have much to talk about. I want to get to know you both as individuals and as a race," the Emperor said eagerly as he sat forward in his chair, truly showing an interest in them.

For the next two hours, the Emperor asked Miles and Nina a host of questions about Earth, their people, and themselves as individuals. The Emperor asked about their families and what it was like for them growing up. Both Miles and Nina had grown up after the Great War of the 2040s. The economic and physical devastation of that war had obviously impacted them as people. The Emperor was keen to learn what had caused the war and how it had ultimately ended.

Miles regaled him with tales of how the two warring sides had developed autonomous killing machines and then, later, how those machines had gone rogue and threatened the very existence of each side. The Emperor told him this story paralleled what had happened with their former friends, the Amoor, who would later go on to become the Collective as they left their biological bodies in search of transcendence.

The Emperor talked at length about his concern that the Collective was growing at a rate that, in time, would make them impossible to defeat unless a way to triumph over them was found soon. It was during this conversation about the Collective that the Emperor brought in several of his advisors to join their conversation.

One subject the Emperor's advisors asked Miles about was his plan to seize control of the Zodark world Tueblets. They were extremely curious about why Miles had chosen that particular world when there were so many closer worlds and systems that could be seized more easily.

Miles explained his current frustration with the Altairian strategy—how he felt they were waging campaigns that were losing tens of thousands of people without bringing the war any closer to victory. Miles told them about the strategic importance of Tueblets and how its capture and the fortification of the surrounding stargates would cripple the Zodarks. He explained how he would then work on dismantling the Zodark Empire and either force them into surrendering or suing for peace. Once that had been achieved, then the Alliance would put its entire effort into defeating the Orbots.

The Gallentine advisors dissected the plan in many different ways. They asked Miles a lot of probing questions about how he would handle the war in the Milky Way galaxy, what he'd do if he were in charge of the war, and how he'd handle dealing with the Orbots and, ultimately, the Collective. Miles's plan for dealing with the Orbots was simple— remove the Zodarks as a pawn they could use. Isolate them, then wage a total war on them across all of their systems while seeking the knockout punch that would remove them from the war.

The longer the conversation went on, the more Miles felt like this was turning into a job interview more than an exchange of ideas or a "get to know you" meeting. When they had been talking for nearly three hours, the Emperor finally asked, "What is the biggest factor holding your people back from being able to wage the kind of war you want to wage to defeat the Zodarks and then the Orbots?"

Miles felt this was a bit of a loaded question but did his best to answer it truthfully. "Aside from the war council and those who lack the will or the vision to see victory—technology. We've done a lot with the technology we have. But at the end of the day, we're facing off against a technologically advanced foe that has more ships, more resources, and more ways to defeat us."

"If you could be given one piece of technology to change the course of the war, what would it be?" asked one of the Emperor's military advisors.

Miles wasn't sure how to respond right away. He asked for a moment to think about it. When he was ready, he replied confidently, "Wormhole technology." At this point, Miles figured that the Gallentines had offered the opportunity to make such a request, and he was going to go for it. "While our warships are inferior to the Orbots', we've found ways to leverage the technology we do have to defeat them. What we lack is the ability to travel from one system to another the way they can, or for that matter, the way the Gallentines and the Altairians can. If we had the same wormhole travel technology as the Altairians, we could deploy our forces faster and keep the enemy off-balance."

That same military advisor then asked for clarification. "You mean our wormhole generator? The ability to create a portable wormhole that other ships in a fleet can use as opposed to just the single ship generating the wormhole?"

Miles nodded. "Yes, exactly. The Altairians have used that technology with our fleets a couple of times, but not nearly as often as they could have. For example, when our forces assisted the Primords in capturing Intus, it took our naval forces five months to travel to the battle. When we assisted the Primords in attacking Rass, it took our forces another four months to reach *that* battle. When the fighting was over and we redeployed our forces back to New Eden, it took four and a half months for them to reach our staging planet. This was more than an entire year we lost in transit, just moving from one battle to another."

"You are saying if you had this technology, then you could have moved your military force from one battle to the next with little time between battles?" the Emperor asked, summarizing Miles's point.

235

"Exactly, Your Majesty. That's the key to defeating the Zodarks and the Orbots," Miles replied. "We need to keep them off-balance. We need to keep them constantly trying to guess at what we're doing next, where we're going to strike, and how many forces we're going to hit them with. If we were provided this technology, then I am confident our human fleet could make the difference in the war. Heck, we might even be able to defeat the Zodarks on our own without any help from the Galactic Empire. Humans are natural warriors; we just lack some of the technology needed to make us truly deadly in this war."

There was a short pause in the conversation as the Emperor leaned over to talk privately with a couple of his advisors.

While they were talking, Miles whispered to Nina, "What do you suppose all of these questions are about?"

"They've been interviewing you," Nina replied softly. "What they are interviewing you or us as humans *for*...I can't say yet. Judging by the questions, I'm getting the vibe that maybe they aren't happy with how the Altairians have been managing the war. It appears the Alliance has made more progress in this galactic war since we joined than they have in more than a hundred years."

Miles snorted at the suggestion. "It sure seems that way. With all the Altairians' technology, I'm truly surprised they haven't been able to defeat the Orbots or the Zodarks yet."

Before the two of them could talk amongst themselves any further, one of the Emperor's advisors asked, "Miles, do you believe the war between the Zodarks and Orbots can be won quickly?"

"That depends on what you define as quickly," Miles countered. "The Altairians have been fighting them for nearly a thousand years."

"That's a good point," said the Emperor, seemingly amused. "That is also a problem we want to address. We are pleased with how the Altairians have cultivated and grown the Empire in the Milky Way galaxy, but their warfighting abilities are lacking. They have been at war for nearly two thousand years with the Orbots and then, later, the Zodarks. This war never should have lasted so long. We consolidated the Andromeda galaxy in less than four hundred years. We've consolidated three more galaxies in another thousand years. Our Empire now spans four and a half galaxies, yet the war in your home galaxy threatens that. The Zodarks and the Orbots need to be defeated—"

Miles was afraid to interrupt but did so anyway. "Excuse me, Your Majesty. Each time we've proposed a strategy or campaign to end the war or bring it to a swift conclusion, the Altairians and others bring up the threat of the Collective coming to the Orbots' aid. Is that true? Would the Collective come to their aid?"

One of the military advisors spoke. "That depends. The Collective might. Right now, their attention is focused elsewhere, and it likely will be for many years to come. They are focused on a couple of galaxies on the far side of the universe. It is the opinion of many on this council that the Collective would probably stay away. If they did attempt to intervene, it would be a limited engagement meant to restore the balance of power back to the Orbot side. However, if the Collective did appear in your galaxy, we would also dispatch ships to fight them."

A short pause ensued before Miles asked, "Your Majesty, what can I or the people of Earth do to assist you in defeating the Orbots and the Zodarks? What can we do to end this war swiftly for the Alliance?"

The Emperor stared deeply into the eyes of the humans, as if searching their souls. Two of his advisors leaned in and whispered something to him. He nodded and then smiled. "I would like humans to defeat the Orbots and their Zodark pets. I realize you cannot do this in your current technological state. However, you have proven to be the warrior class we have been seeking. As such, we are going to do something the Altairians may not like or agree with. We know they provided you with some technology and are currently assisting you in building a new fleet of warships. We would like the current class of warships they are helping you build to be the last you construct. We will provide you with direct military assistance to lead the Alliance to victory in your galaxy."

The Emperor continued, "We will provide you with the wormhole technology. We will provide you with the blueprints and technology to build your own orbital ring like the one we have around our own planet. This will enable Earth to become a dominant military and economic superpower in the Milky Way. It will take you many decades, maybe even a hundred years, to build, but once complete, it will become the economic engine for your people.

"My military advisor will tell you about the ship we will give you," the Emperor said as he nodded for the person to speak.

"We will give you a Gallentine Titan," the advisor explained. "This ship is equipped with a wormhole generator. It will enable you to move entire fleets at a time to battle the Zodarks and Orbots. The weapons on the ship are more powerful than anything the Zodarks or Orbots currently possess. The Titan is the largest capital-class warship in our fleets. This ship turned the tide of the war against the Collective in our favor. If a Collective ship ever did attack inside your galaxy, the grand Titan would be more than capable of destroying it.

"Giving you this ship will immediately change the balance of power in the Milky Way. In addition, we will give you the designs to build our standard battleship and destroyer-class ships, so you can build them for your own purposes. It will take you years if not decades to build these warships and learn how to use them properly, but they will turn the tide of the war in your favor."

Miles couldn't believe what they were offering. He didn't know how to respond. Based on his interactions with the Altairians, he hadn't expected a response like this at all. He stammered, "I-I don't know what to say. I wasn't expecting such a gift as this from you, Your Majesty."

The Emperor stood. "I like to believe I am a good judge of character. I have listened to you speak and answer questions for nearly six of your hours. I believe we have found the warrior class we've been searching for to conquer the Milky Way. Admiral Miles Hunt, I am charging you and the people of Earth with defeating the Zodark Empire and the Orbots. I am charging you with consolidating power in the Milky Way galaxy. The Altairians will work with you. They will administer and manage the galaxy for you. They have the technology, infrastructure, and ability to do these tasks exceptionally well—but *you* will lead the war council and the military force for the Empire in the Milky Way.

"I am going to issue you one of my imperial seals," he said. He made a sort of snapping motion with his hand, and an aide came running up with a box to hand to Miles. "You will speak on my behalf in the Milky Way, and all military matters and decisions will now reside under your command and control. You will be answerable only to me and my war council from now on.

"You will be required to send periodic updates on your operations and provide us with reports on the outcomes of your military actions. From time to time, we may summon you back to Cobalt for in-person meetings. These are nonnegotiable.

"I need you to understand something, Miles. I am entrusting you with a lot of power—that power comes with responsibility. You and the people of Earth are answerable to us, the Gallentine Empire, now. I am your Emperor; I am your supreme ruler. You may keep your governing systems in place, but know that your people are now and forever going to be my subjects. You will fall under our protectorate, but you also fall under our rules. Do you accept this position?"

The Emperor expectantly waited for Miles's response while patiently gazing through him to his core. The Emperor's offer caught Miles off guard. Miles didn't believe he had the authority to commit to this, but he didn't feel like he could say no, either.

Sheepishly, he turned to Ambassador Chapman. "Nina, a little help here. Can I even say yes to this?"

She seemed flustered by his question. Finally, she nodded, apparently not sure what else she could do at this moment.

Miles turned to face the Emperor. "Your Majesty, on behalf of the people of Earth and the Republic, I agree to your request and proposal."

The Emperor smiled softly. "Very well. You are now Viceroy Miles Hunt, the Supreme Military Commander of the Milky Way's Imperial Army. We will now head over to the state dinner and announce this deal to the others. Special instructions will be sent back to Altairius Prime with Pandolly."

This is going to make for an interesting war council back on Altairius Prime, Miles mused. He wondered how he should handle this with his two new bourbon-loving friends. There were so many angles to this game of 3-D chess. *One step at a time,* he told himself.

"The three of you humans will be staying here on Cobalt a while longer," said the Emperor, breaking into his thoughts. "We have much to still talk about and teach you before you take command of your flagship and return to Altairius Prime. When you return, you will need to reorganize your local war council how you see fit—we can talk more about this later.

"Come, let us dine and enjoy each other's company as we announce our newest Viceroy."

Chapter Twenty-Two
Rise of the Republic

Cobalt Prime
Imperial Palace

When the dinner had ended, the Emperor asked for Pandolly to stay behind. The humans left to return to their quarters back inside the city.

Ambassador Velator took Miles, Nina and Ethan aside and explained, "Starting tomorrow, you will move to a different facility where you'll spend the next several weeks learning more about the Empire and the Collective. You will also receive some advanced training on how to use and operate the Titan ship being given to you. This is not a ship that humans can readily operate. It is too advanced and too complicated; you'll need to receive specialized neuroimplants and training on how to use them with the ship itself.

"When you travel back to the Milky Way, a crew of Gallentine naval officers will accompany you. They'll gather the humans on the Altairian home world that aren't staying behind and take them back to Earth. From there, they will work with our new partners to train a human crew to man, repair, and fight the ship—this will take at least a year of intense training."

Ambassador Velator continued, "The plan will move rapidly once you return to Earth. A lot of technology will be given to you, along with a lot of training on how to use and implement that technology.

"A total of four thousand Gallentine advisors will be traveling with you on the ship and will remain on Earth for the foreseeable future. These advisors will assist the humans to prepare to take over military command of the Milky Way forces. Until further notice, no further military campaigns beyond the Harran campaign to liberate the Sumerian people will take place while the military and Alliance reorganization are underway."
****

The following day, Pandolly met with Miles and Nina for an hour. He went over his conversation with the Emperor. Pandolly said he'd convey the personal message from the Emperor back to his own leaders.

The group then separated, with Pandolly going back to his ship and the Earthers staying on Cobalt for a while longer.

Miles wasn't sure if Pandolly was mad or relieved that the Altairians would no longer be in charge of the war. The Altairians rarely showed any emotion, so it was hard to read him. Miles suspected the Altairians would be more than mildly put off by the idea of the humans taking over the war function of the Galactic Empire.

Some of the other members on the council might also feel they would be better suited to lead—but at the end of the day, Miles didn't care what they thought.

They had their chance to end this war, and they blew it, he thought.

Miles was the one who wore the ring with the imperial seal on it. He was the Viceroy and the man with the commission from the Emperor. Come hell or high water, Miles was going to push this Galactic Empire hard. He was going to listen to his Gallentine advisors and spend the next couple of years building and preparing. He'd institute a complete top-down retooling and training of the Alliance. When he was done reorganizing the fleets and battlegroups, the Zodarks and Orbots wouldn't know what hit them.

****

Two Weeks Later

"Are you ready to see your new ship?" asked Ambassador Velator as their shuttle climbed up into the sky.

Miles nodded and a wide smile spread across his face. He felt like a little kid being told he could finally open his Christmas presents.

Ethan was joining him for this trip as well. They were taking a small shuttle up to the ring station. The ship they were being given command of had just come out of the shipyard, so it was brand-new.

"How big is this ship?" asked Ethan, clearly also excited. "What size crew does it take to man and operate?"

Velator turned to the younger Hunt. "The *Freedom* is the seventh ship in the Titan class. The ship's operations are largely automated, so it can theoretically run with a very small crew—at least that's what I've been told. When we land on the ship, you will meet the ship's captain. He will work directly for you, Viceroy Hunt. He will take orders from you as if you were the Emperor himself, and so will his crew. They will spend as long as it takes to train a human crew to take their place, and they will stay on as your crew as long as you want them to."

Miles nodded in approval before asking, "How many Gallentine crew will I have on the ship?"

"The minimum number I was told would accompany you is five hundred. The ship itself, however, can carry substantially more. The captain will explain more to you when we dock."

As their shuttle rose out of orbit and approached the ring station, Miles and Ethan saw dozens, maybe even hundreds of starships and warships of different sizes and styles docked there. Some were undergoing repairs while others were clearly shells still under construction. Still, many appeared to be ready for battle.

When they came around a bend in the station, Miles saw three massive extensions on the station that didn't quite make sense. Just as he was about to ask Velator about it, one of them began to separate from the station. It wasn't an extension of the station at all—it was a ship—one so enormous it resembled a small station in its own right.

Miles turned to his Gallentine friend. "Velator, what kind of ship is *that*? It's as big as a space station."

Velator smiled and his chest slightly puffed out with pride. "That, Viceroy, is the flagship of the Milky Way fleet. It is your new ship. This, Miles, is the *Freedom*."

Miles's eyes got a little wider as he shared a glance with his son, Ethan, who was as wide-eyed as he was.

"How big *is* this ship?" Miles managed to gasp out.

"In your units of measurement, the *Freedom* is fifteen kilometers in length, one kilometer in width, and one kilometer in height. As to further specs of the ship, I again will defer to the captain, who we'll be meeting once we dock."

A minute later, their shuttle pilot said they were receiving a message from the ship's captain, who had granted them permission to land in the port-side shuttle bay. As their shuttle neared the landing bay, all Miles could do was marvel at this monstrosity of a ship. It was enormous, far bigger than any starship he'd ever seen. As a matter of fact, this ship was larger than the John Glenn Orbital Station above Earth. It was larger than any *station* he'd ever seen.

How do you even get around on a ship this size? Miles thought in awe. He imagined that it would take more than an hour to just travel from one end of the ship to the other.

As they approached the entrance, Miles saw a yellowish shimmer in front of the landing bay. Then they were inside the ship.

Miles gazed out the front window, taking it all in, while the pilot maneuvered them to one side of the landing bay. The inside of this ship was overflowing with rows of shuttles, starfighters and other spacecraft as far as the eye could see.

"The captain and some of his officers are here to meet you, Viceroy," Ambassador Velator said as he pointed to a row of Gallentine military personnel lined up on deck.

Miles felt a bit awkward about all of this. It seemed odd that a superior species like the Gallentines would have placed hundreds of their own sailors under a human's command. Hell, him being made a Viceroy felt strange. He couldn't imagine what people were saying on Altairius Prime and the war council. Miles anticipated an uncomfortable conversation in a few days when they arrived.

The pilot deftly landed the shuttle, making sure to place the entrance in front of the military formation that was waiting to greet them.

Once they'd docked, the shuttle door opened with a slight hissing noise. As Miles prepared to walk down the ramp, he took a deep breath. He appreciated that the Gallentines' biological bodies functioned best in the same atmospheric conditions as a human. He didn't have to wear a breathing device or keep using one of those inhaler-like contraptions he'd have to keep near him on an Altairian ship.

Ambassador Velator leaned in. "Don't be nervous, Miles," he said softly. "They are professional soldiers, just like you. They know their duty. They were given personal orders by the Emperor himself a week ago. Each of them considers it a great honor to have been selected to serve under you, the Viceroy and military commander of the Milky Way forces."

Miles smiled. Velator's comments did make him feel a bit better. He didn't want them to feel like he was somehow usurping their chain of command or like they had been placed under the command of an inferior species.

Ambassador Velator walked down the shuttle ramp toward the formation of soldiers. There were probably two hundred of them on either side of the path leading to the captain of the ship, who was standing at attention with a couple of his officers near him.

When the ambassador reached the flight deck, he stood to the side and waited for Miles to join him.

"This is it, Dad. Don't trip on your way out. It'd make for a bad impression in front of your new command," Ethan jested as he attempted to calm the butterflies in his dad's stomach.

Miles snickered. "I look that nervous?" he asked.

Ethan shrugged. "Kind of. I figured you could use a little levity right now. Go on, you don't want to be late to your own party." His son had a big grin on his face. This was exciting for him, too. They were the first two humans to come aboard any Gallentine ship, let alone command one.

Miles lifted his head a bit as he walked down the ramp of the shuttle. As he left the ship, the entire assembly of troops came to attention. As Miles came abreast of Ambassador Velator, the two of them walked to the captain and his leadership team. When they got within a few feet, the captain snapped off a crisp Gallentine salute, a closed hand brought to one's chest and then extended forward. It almost resembled what Miles knew to be the Nazi salute from World War II history. He made a mental note to talk with them about that later.

"Viceroy Hunt, my name is Captain Wiyrkomi, of the clan Ishukone. It is a great honor for us to serve you, the Viceroy, in this grand war. I look forward to working with you and teaching your people everything there is to know about this warship," he said confidently as he puffed his chest out a bit.

"It is a pleasure to meet you, Captain Wiyrkomi," Miles replied. "I am honored by the Emperor's selection of you and your men to serve on this ship with me. The Emperor has sent only his best soldiers and sailors to serve with us. I am confident that together, we will make the Emperor proud."

They spent a few more minutes talking as the captain introduced some of his senior officers. He then led them down two rows of the soldiers standing in formation, while giving Miles a short introduction to some of them and explaining what some of their jobs were. In addition to the five hundred sailors, one hundred and ten Gallentine soldiers were accompanying them to act as personal security for the Gallentine sailors until a human crew and security forces could be trained.

When the introductions were done, Captain Wiyrkomi led them up to a small briefing room. Miles, Ethan, Ambassador Velator and the senior leadership of the ship spent a bit of time getting to know each other before they got down to business. Hunt wanted to make sure they knew he was serious about ending this war with the Orbots and the Zodarks. He also laid out his expectations of the crew and of the captain as well.

Aside from operating the ship, for the time being, they were to spend as much time as possible with their human counterparts to impart as much knowledge and information as possible. For now, Miles was intent on running a dual-species crew. He wanted them to all work on learning from each other and strive to get along.

Miles then asked for the captain to provide him and Ethan with a detailed overview of the ship, how it worked, and what made this ship so special in comparison to the rest of the Gallentine fleet. There had to be more to this ship than just its sheer size. Miles wanted to understand the strategy behind why the Gallentines had built a ship so massive as the *Freedom.*

"First, I need to show you how we get around on a ship as large as this one," said Captain Wiyrkomi. Miles had been curious about this, especially after he'd learned that the ship had more than thirty-two decks in some sections of the ship. In addition to the elevators and stairs, a series of tram lines ran along the entire spine of the vessel. The system ran like a subway system on Earth. The ship had four color-coded sections denoting specific sections. Depending on which area someone needed to travel to, they would get on a specific-colored line. If they were at the front of the ship and needed to get to the rear, they hopped on one line, and if they needed to get to the middle, they hopped on a different line.

The tram system functioned very similarly to how a hyperloop system worked on Mars, the Moon, Earth, and now New Eden. One could travel from the front of the ship to the rear in under two minutes, which greatly reduced the travel time needed to move from one end to the other.

As the Gallentine captain finished showing them how to move about the ship, Miles decided to get back to business. "Captain Wiyrkomi, can you explain what makes this warship so different and so much more powerful than other Gallentine warships?" he asked.

"The *Freedom* is more than just a battlewagon or a weapons platform—although it has plenty of weapons," Wiyrkomi said with a smirk. "What this ship offers that many others do not is that it acts as an orbital base when it jumps into a system.

"On either side of the ship are two extendable platforms that can extend as far as half a kilometer from the ship. These four platforms are mobile docks: other warships and freighters can dock there to transfer people or equipment between the *Freedom* or each other."

The captain then told them about the ship's fighter and bomber complement. The *Freedom* had a total of ten flight bays: five on either side. Two were near the rear of the ship, one in the middle, and two near the front. A Gallentine squadron was broken down into twenty-four spacecraft, and the *Freedom* carried a total of twelve hundred fighters and four hundred and eighty bombers—that worked out to fifty fighter squadrons and twenty bomber squadrons. The ship also carried six hundred shuttles for the ground force it carried.

Since this ship acted as a floating station and base of operations, it also carried a large contingent of soldiers. A total of forty-five thousand could be carried on the ship. When the ship was fully crewed, it had a complement of nine thousand. This was only possible because so much of the ship had been automated. The crew still performed vital duties on the ship, but the fleet crew was primarily there to make sure the ship was operating the way it was supposed to, although they'd be sent in to take over if the automated systems went down or there was a problem. The majority of the large crew manned the flight operations for the ship, which were substantial.

Miles's head was swimming with the information being shared. He had so many questions he wanted to ask. He had to calm his mind and remember that he didn't need to learn everything about the ship during his first meeting with the captain and the crew.

"Captain Wiyrkomi, how soon until the ship will be ready to head to Altairius Prime?" Hunt asked.

"The crew and our required supplies are aboard and ready. The advisors will start arriving tomorrow. It'll take about four days for all of them to make it aboard. We should be ready to go in six days," the captain replied.

Hunt nodded his head in approval. "Excellent. When Ambassador Chapman is done with her meetings tomorrow, have her brought aboard.

Since we have some time before we'll be leaving, could you arrange for some briefings for myself and Lieutenant Hunt? I'd like to have a three-hour block of instruction in the morning, another block in the afternoon, and then a couple-hour tour after dinner of the different sections of the ship each day."

"Certainly, Viceroy. I've taken the liberty of setting the ship's time to human standards. We've also spent the last several weeks training the crew on how to understand it in comparison to our own. I believe the crew has a good understanding of your units of time. With that said, we can start the first briefings tomorrow at 0800 hours if you'd like?"

Hunt smiled at the initiative this captain had already shown. "That would be great, Captain. Thank you for taking care of that. It was an adjustment when I arrived on the Altairian home world. Getting used to their units of time was not easy. I suspect it hasn't been easy for your people either."

The captain shrugged. "We are soldiers and sailors; we make do. If I may, Viceroy, I'd like to take you on a brief tour of the bridge to meet some of the officers operating it. Then I'd like to show you to your quarters and allow you some time to get comfortable and acquainted with it. This is our first time having humans on any of our ships—we'd like to know what we can do to make your living arrangements and facilities more suitable for humans before more of your people come aboard. Because we're still docked on the ring station, we can have the modifications made while the rest of the crew is brought aboard."

"That is a great idea, Captain," Hunt replied. "Let's take that tour of the bridge. Then let's prepare to make history." He had a renewed sense of excitement and energy he hadn't felt in a very long time.

Chapter Twenty-Three
Recon Prep

New Eden City
Alpha Company "Ghosts" Deployment

"Whoa, wait just a second—you want me to travel back to Sumer with you?" Hadad exclaimed in a scared tone. "You do realize I am a civilian, right? People on Sumer know me. They may recognize me. I'm supposed to be in some Zodark penal colony—If they see me alive, they'll know something is wrong. They may harm my remaining family that's still there."

Colonel Hackworth interceded before anyone else could. "Hadad, I get it, you're afraid of being discovered and something happening to you again. That's normal. We'll do everything we can to make sure that doesn't happen. But there isn't a better person for this mission than you. At some point, we're going to have to know if the Sumerians are going to side with the Zodarks or look to us as liberators. You are probably the *only* person that'll be able to help us make that determination. The lives of millions are going to rest on that."

Captain Royce quickly added, "Hadad, I was part of the Special Forces team that liberated you from a Zodark camp on this very planet. I remember your stories about how the Zodarks had enslaved your planet, your people. You told us about the tributes and how you had no idea what was happening with those people or the children being taken. Well…we know what's happening to them—they're being used as slaves and bred to be foot soldiers for the Zodarks and the Orbots.

"You told me, you told us, you wanted to do what you could to liberate your planet, to free your people. This is your chance. I need your help. I can't do this mission without you—will you help me liberate your people? Will *you* liberate your people?"

Colonel Hackworth nodded in approval. The two military soldiers returned their gaze to Hadad.

Hadad was visibly struggling with this decision. He was obviously scared about the mission now that he'd been filled in on more of its details. He'd initially agreed to join, but now, he was having second thoughts.

Governor Crawley, who was also in the room with Hadad, reached over and placed a hand on Hadad's shoulder. "I know you're nervous," he said. "That's to be expected. If you don't want to do this mission, I'm sure they can find another way to make it work. But this is your chance to liberate your people. You have a unique opportunity, Hadad—don't let it slip through your fingers because of fear. If that's all that's really holding you back, I'm sure these men have ways of helping you overcome that."

The governor gave the soldiers a nod and sat back. A good minute went by with no one saying anything, just silence. Finally, Hadad spoke. "Can you maybe help alter my appearance, so it'll be less likely I'll be recognized?"

Royce nodded. "We can. We can also teach you how to overcome your fears. I promise you this, Hadad—you will feel a sense of liberation once your people are forever free."

"When we land on the surface, what exactly will you want me to do? Why is it so important that I come with you?" Hadad asked.

As the mission commander, Royce explained the importance of Hadad being on the mission. They needed his knowledge of the capital city and the planet. They needed his understanding of the geography and culture as they looked to identify targets for the invaders and landing zones for the soldiers should the Sumerian people side with the Zodarks.

This mission was the first human-led, human-only mission since Earth had joined the Empire. There was a lot of pressure to make sure it went off without a hitch. The Earthers were also hell-bent on showing the Galactic Empire a well-planned and executed campaign. No one in the Republic leadership was happy with the haphazardness of the Empire's current campaigns. A lot of people had been killed because missions weren't properly planned or executed.

Hadad finally responded to Captain Royce, "OK, I'll do it. When do we start training, and when do we leave?"
****

New Eden
Fort Roughneck

Captain Royce stood in the front of the training room as he went over the mission. He paid special attention to Hadad, who was the only nonmilitary person coming with them.

"Once we approach Sumer, we're going to look for a suitable place to set down on the surface. Ideally, we want someplace near the capital city but also away from any developed areas, where the ship could be discovered. We're going to slip into the planet's atmosphere with our new stealth ship, the Nighthawk."

A hand rose before Royce could get any further into the mission brief. It was Hadad. Looking at the civilian, Royce motioned for him to speak.

"Sorry to interrupt, Brian." Hadad insisted on calling him by his first name. He wanted to make sure everyone knew he was a civilian along for the ride and not a soldier. "If we set down too far outside of the city, how are we going to get to the city?"

Smiling briefly, Royce replied, "We'll either walk or look for some sort of public transportation. Do they have any trains or busses we might be able to leverage?"

"Actually, they do have a rail line that connects some of the outer cities directly to the capital," Hadad confirmed. "If we don't set down too far away from some of them, the walk shouldn't be more than ten to fifteen of your miles. I think the bigger challenge for us might be money. That's going to be hard to come by, especially without a hand chip."

Captain Royce furrowed his brow. "Hadad, I think this is the first I've heard of this. What is this hand chip you're talking about? Is this going to be a problem for us?"

Hadad was about to say something, then paused for a second as if trying to remember something from a long time ago. "Just as I was being exiled from Sumer, our society was transitioning to a chip that would be embedded in one's hand. This chip would essentially become your electronic wallet and digital file. It was something new the Zodarks had insisted on all Sumerians having—a way for them to tightly monitor and control our activities. Identifying subversive activities and anything that could undermine their control of us was a top priority of the Zodark leadership on the planet."

One of Royce's soldiers chimed in, "Sir, it's possible that we could snatch a person or two and remove their chips and reinsert them into our teams that'll be exploring the city. This might give them immediate currency and a free pass to walk through the capital. At least for a day or two, until it was obvious that those citizens had gone missing."

Royce thought about that for a moment. It wasn't a bad idea. They'd need to make sure they brought some medical equipment designed to do that. They'd also need to limit the number of times they went exploring in the city. This wasn't something they'd be able to do often, not unless they wanted to kill the people they were taking the devices from.

Sighing, Royce looked at their lone medic for the trip. "Why don't you pack some extra equipment needed to remove a chip like what Hadad mentioned and reinsert it into the team members that'll be exploring the city?"

Captain Royce then continued on with the rest of the mission brief. A key piece of equipment they were bringing with them was the new surveillance drones. They had a couple of variants. Some were high-altitude drones that ran on solar power—these could stay aloft indefinitely, assuming they didn't get detected and destroyed. That was, of course, a possibility, but they had taken a lot of precautions with them. The outer bodies of the drones had a fiberoptic skin, capable of mimicking their surroundings. They were also coated in a special radar-absorbent material, designed to make them as stealth as possible. While aloft, a drone would soak up all sorts of electronic emissions until its stored memory was full. Then it would compress the file down into tiny data packages that would be sent via a short burst transmission back to the Nighthawk.

They had other drones that would look to infiltrate the Zodark and Sumerian government buildings and any military installations they could find. All the data would be sent back to the Nighthawk, where Royce and two of the other Deltas would analyze as much of it as possible with the ship's onboard AI. Twice daily, the information would be transmitted to the lone stealth satellite they'd be deploying prior to their landing on the surface. The satellite would beam that information to the Nighthawk's sister ship that would be hiding in one of the many asteroid belts throughout the system. Every couple of days, they'd drop a coms drone that would zip the collected data through the stargate back to a frigate waiting in the next system. Steadily, the information would be relayed all the way back to New Eden and the Third Army's intelligence group.

It was a rather complicated mission, and they had taken significant precautions not to be detected by the Zodarks. However, if they wanted real-time intelligence about what was going on down on the surface of a Zodark-controlled planet, this was really the only way to make it happen. Once General McGinnis's command felt they had enough information, they'd order the nearly five hundred thousand soldiers assigned to Third Army to load up in the transports, and the fleet would begin the journey to the planet Sumer to liberate humans from the insidious enslavers, the Zodarks.

****

Zodark-Controlled Space

Two weeks—that was how long they'd been cooped up in this damn ship. It was one thing to be cooped up in an orbital assault ship. Those ships were big—big enough you could go for a run or stretch your legs out. On an orbital assault ship, there were plenty of other people to talk to. But this thing...the Nighthawk...was cramped—and that was putting it kindly.

With the flight crew of four and the six of them, it was a tight fit, with virtually no room to spread out. The only saving grace they had was the four simulation pods. Aside from the standard military training they had to carry out each day, Captain Royce had allowed each person a certain amount of personal time in the sim pods.

Everyone needed to relax and unwind. For one person, maybe that involved a sim of sitting on a beach in the Maldives—for another, it could be sitting in the stands at the Super Bowl, watching their favorite team play. Whatever it was, it was their time to spend how they saw fit.

Corporal Wells looked at Hadad. The two of them had been speaking almost nonstop in the Sumerian tongue since they'd met. She was doing her best to learn the language but also to understand what it was like on his home world. What were the people like? What did the place look like? Was it an advanced society like their own, or more so? But now they had moved on to the strategy of the mission.

Hadad explained that they would need to find one female and two male Sumerians to temporarily detain so they could commandeer their ID chips and blend in with society. There were some potential problems: one of the Sumerians could have a movement restriction listed on their biometric chip, or they could have insufficient funds on their chip to purchase a train ticket or pay for food or other items they might need to purchase.

Captain Royce had overheard their conversation and joined them. "Hadad, before we decide who to detain, is there a way for us to check their biometric chip in advance to know what their credit balance is or if they do have a movement restriction?"

Hadad thought about that for a moment. "I think there probably would be. The larger issue we're going to have to contend with if we go that route is the security protocols the Zodarks may have placed on the biometric chip."

"Great, a new wrinkle in the plan," Corporal Wells muttered. She hadn't spoken very loudly—however, everyone heard.

"Hadad, before you left Sumer, were you aware of any resistance groups?" asked Lieutenant Hosni. "Any kind of subversives operating against the Zodarks?"

Damn, why didn't I think of that? Royce asked himself.

Hadad leaned back. "If there was, that group would have been under heavy surveillance by the government, not to mention the Zodarks themselves. While they don't have a standing army on the planet, they still maintain a security garrison in the major cities or industrial centers. It's more than large enough to control the planet if they sought to. You have to keep in mind, when the Zodarks took away our ability to leave our star system, they also dismantled our military. They allowed us to maintain an internal security force, but their weapons were strictly monitored. They couldn't develop weapons that would one day tip the balance of power away from the Zodarks. That's why one of my colleagues turned me in—they believed what I was working on could have, as you humans put it, a dual use."

Corporal Wells chimed in, "I still can't believe they would just send you to a penal colony for something like that. You seem like too smart of a person to just throw away like that."

Hadad shrugged before replying, "When I was on Earth, I spent a lot of time studying your history. I wanted to try and understand you as a people. When I got to your twentieth century, I read about your World War II and then the subsequent Cold War. I see a lot of parallels to what your people did during that period between your history and what was happening on my own planet. I read that in 1930s Germany, the government there would strip incredibly smart and business-savvy individuals of their rights because they were Jewish.

"Then I read about this other country called the Soviet Union. They used to abduct all kinds of people who spoke out against the government and send them to gulags or penal camps, much like what the Zodarks did to us on New Eden. You see, even though our societies have developed on different planets, it would appear our histories are not as far apart as they may appear. The Zodarks are like your Nazis and Soviet Union put together. They have built a government on Sumer over the last hundred years to resemble what those countries must have looked like during those time periods. So if there was a resistance, as you put it, then the likelihood of our finding them is going to be incredibly low. Worse, if we did find them, chances are they would be under so much surveillance, we would likely be discovered if we met them."

"Well, you guys may not like my approach," Private Chandler said, "but I say we abduct one of these Sumerians so we can see firsthand how these biometric chips act. For all we know, there could be some sort of security feature that sends an alert if it's removed from where it's embedded. If that's the case, then we're going to have a host of other problems to deal with."

"One issue at a time, folks," said Royce. "Let's get on the planet first. Then we'll solve the next problem."
****

Two Days Later

"Captain Royce, we're approaching the stargate now. Let your people know we're about to jump," the pilot announced.

Royce turned to his people. "OK, folks, this is it—the moment of truth. When we come out the other side of that gate, we'll either be able to make a break for it or be dusted by whatever Zodark ship is waiting for us."

One of the sergeants laughed. "A great attempt to boost morale," he joked.

Moments later, they jumped. It took them a moment to travel through the wormhole connecting one gate to another, but once they were through, the pilot let them know it was clear. Their luck had held out once again. The two Nighthawks set course for the nearest asteroid belt to begin their initial intelligence gathering.

For the next five days, they'd float in a mostly listening mode as their suite of electronic equipment soaked up everything that was happening in the system. Once they had a better sense of who was in system, then they'd begin their approach to the planet Sumer and look to identify a suitable landing site.

Captain Royce walked over to the copilot, who was sitting at a station with a headset on while looking at a computer monitor. "What do you have for us, Lieutenant?"

Pausing what he was doing, the officer took his headphones off. "It's strange, sir. When the Viper came through this system nearly ten years ago, the electronic traffic was practically off the charts. We had communications being sent between the mining colonies, starbases, and Sumer. Right now, I'm hardly showing anything. It's almost like it's all disappeared."

Royce didn't like the sound of that one bit. This wasn't matching the profile they should be seeing.

"Do you think we'll start to get more data in another day once some of the other signals start to return?"

The lieutenant shrugged his shoulders. "I mean, it's possible. But regardless of what electronic pings we shot across the system, we should still be picking up their own traffic. By any standard, this system should be hopping with radio chatter and ship traffic. It's the main reason the Nighthawk has been painted with the specially designed material it has— so *we* wouldn't get detected if they started scanning in our direction. But right now, it doesn't appear there's anyone out there to scan us."

Leaning in closer so no one else could hear, Royce asked, "Is it possible something happened on the planet or with these colonies?"

"That's exactly what I'm starting to think," the lieutenant whispered back. "I recommend we head towards the two known colonies on Hortuna and Tallanis. We should detect something there. If not, then maybe we'll find signs of what might have happened."

Royce nodded. The two of them spoke with the pilot, who concurred and set a new course. They'd head towards the first colony on Tallanis; it was closest to their position.

Not wanting to rattle everyone, Royce kept the information they'd discovered to himself and told the flight crew to do the same for the time being. Once they approached Tallanis, they'd hopefully start to find some answers.

It took their ship nearly a day to get within sensor range of the first colony, Tallanis. From everything they knew about the place, it had been a deep-space mining colony the Sumerians had settled nearly two hundred years ago. Hadad had told them that at the time of his exile, the colony had had a population of around twenty-nine million.

It wasn't a hospitable planet. The colonists mostly lived underground or in domes on the surface. Because of these factors, the colony had never taken off like the one on Hortuna, which had closer to a hundred million people.

Royce walked up into the flight deck. "Have we found any additional signs of life?" he asked.

The lieutenant operating their suite of electronic equipment turned to look at him. "On the contrary—we're starting to find more details about what may have happened, but I'm afraid it's not looking very good."

Royce closed the door behind him, walked the rest of the way in and took a seat.

"OK, why don't you explain what you've found and what you think it means?"

The pilot turned around in his seat to join the conversation. "Captain, at this point, we don't know a lot as we'll need to get closer for some of our more detailed sensors to give us a better assessment. But what we can tell you with confidence is it appears some sort of battle happened. I can't tell you exactly when, but it likely wasn't recently. The sensors are detecting a lot of debris floating in orbit of Tallanis, and we're detecting ship fragments indicative of a space battle. As we get closer to the planet, we'll likely find more fragments and maybe some additional information. With your permission, Captain, I'd like to take us in closer. I'd also like to have our sister ship, the *O'Brien*, stay behind, just in case it's a trap. Once we discover a bit more of what's going on, we should probably send our first com drone back to the fleet."

Royce nodded in agreement. It was a sound plan. If something had happened to the Sumerian home world, then they needed to send that intelligence to the fleet ASAP. If the system was open to the taking, then General McGinnis and Admiral McKee would likely want to grab it before it was reinforced by the Zodarks.

The closer they got to the planet, the more debris they detected. The planet was still silent. It was unclear if there was life on it anymore. They'd know more as they moved into orbit themselves. What was clear was that something tragic had happened, and a lot of people appeared to have died.

What exactly happened here? Royce asked himself in horror.

Finally, Royce broke the news to everyone else. Hadad probably took the news the hardest. Everyone he had known and loved was in this system, and right now, it appeared they all might have died.

When they finally slipped into orbit, they saw the ruins of the space elevator, an important piece of infrastructure for a mining colony as it allowed the Sumerians to move refined materials from the surface to orbit to be transported back to Sumer. It had sustained a lot of battle damage. Part of the station's outer rings had been destroyed, and the inner ring was torn open in several places. The center part of the station had sustained a lot of damage, given the scorched markings on the hull.

"How's it staying in orbit if it's lost its ground tether and power?" asked Royce. He was a soldier, not a fleeter, and space operations were out of his domain.

"I don't think they've lost all power," said the copilot, pointing to something. "Do you see those lights on in some of those windows? I mean, the rest of the station looks dark and dead, but that's clearly light coming from those areas."

"Good eye, Tom. I completely missed that," the pilot said. He then turned to face Royce. "It's possible some people survived on the station, and if they were able to maintain any sort of power, they were probably able to keep the station from falling out of orbit."

The pilot paused for a second. "Sir, I know this would break all our protocols and give away our position. But if there is life still on that station, then I recommend we try to make contact with them. Perhaps we can be of assistance to them. Maybe they'll be able to tell us what happened."

The two other crewmen nodded in agreement. "Sir, I think we should hold off," the copilot countered. "I'm not saying we shouldn't contact them, but we should wait until we've explored Hortuna or even Sumer. We should gather more information before we alert anyone to our presence in the system."

Royce turned to the pilot. "How far away are we from Hortuna and Sumer?"

"We're three days' travel from Hortuna, then we're just eighteen hours to Sumer. Those two are much closer together. But this would also mean lighting up our MPD engines and not going with the stealth system. If we use the stealth system, you can multiply those travel times by three."

Royce hadn't thought about the engines. That was a new feature the Nighthawks had. They had a dual thruster system. One was the traditional MPD thrusters the other warships and transports had. The other was significantly slower, but it was essentially undetectable, at least by anyone other than the Altairians.

Royce blew some air out of his lips. "What's the likelihood anyone's alive in this system? I mean, if we light up the MPD thrusters, is there actually anyone out there with the capability to detect us?"

The two pilots looked at each other and shrugged. They couldn't offer him any information on that front.

As much as Royce wanted to maintain their radio silence, they also needed answers. Then an idea dawned on him. "Bring us in closer to the station. Let's try and find a hatch or a way we can gain entry to it. Perhaps there's a way we can maintain radio silence and still get the answers we need."

For the next couple of hours, they maneuvered themselves in close to the station. Even in its damaged state, it was still a large structure— maybe not as large as the John Glenn back on Earth, but it wasn't far off. It took them the better part of a day, but eventually they found what was likely a service hatch on a section of the station that looked like it was connected to the part that appeared to still have power.

Fortunately, the Nighthawk still had the same undercarriage docking hatch and the ability to conduct a hostile boarding if necessary. This would allow them to anchor themselves over top of the hatch to create a seal and then cut their way in. While the pilots were getting them into position, Royce had his guys suiting up and getting their gear ready.

Twenty minutes later, the Nighthawk was properly positioned. Royce turned to his senior NCO, Sergeant Peterson. "Why don't you cut us a path in?" he said. "Let me know when you're ready to kick the door in, and I'll help you clear the area before we let the others in."

Peterson nodded. He and Royce had served together for coming up on fourteen years, since their first foray onto New Eden. Peterson had been a private back then and Royce a master sergeant. "On it, sir," he replied with a smile.

He grabbed his cutting equipment and went to work. It took Peterson just five minutes to cut the seals on the service hatch free. He sent a message through Royce's neurolink that he was ready. Royce told Corporal Wells to follow him. The three of them would move in and clear whatever lay on the other end of this service door.

They readied their new M1 rifles and prepared for whatever might be on the opposite side of the door. Peterson nodded to Royce that he was ready. When Royce nodded back, Peterson pushed the cut-out door inwards and to his left, using it almost like a shield as he pushed into the room.

Royce was hot on his heels, his HUD scanning what was in front of him and then the rest of the room. It was empty. There was no one there waiting to greet them. Better yet, they appeared to be in some sort of sealed chamber. If this truly was a service door, it made sense that it would be connected to a sealed chamber to allow for pressurization and depressurization.

Peterson moved to the next door. He looked at the keypad—it was still lit up. If it had power, then there was a possibility people were still alive on this thing.

Peterson held a hand up as Royce started to move closer to it. "I'm going to see if our locksmith can gain entry for us. If it can, we won't need to cut our way through."

He pulled out an eight-centimeter-by-thirteen-centimeter black device and placed it over the keypad. He hit a couple of buttons on the device, bringing it to life. His HUD then sent instructions to the device. It synced up with the keypad and began the process of crunching the numbers to find them the right code that would open the door.

It took the tool all of two minutes to pop the lock. When it did, they heard a slight hissing noise as the seal between the two rooms was broken. Readying themselves, they prepared to venture into the station, not knowing if they'd be welcomed as rescuers or attacked as hostile invaders.

"Breaching," Peterson said over their secured coms net.

He pushed the door open and swung his M1 and body in a sweeping motion from the front to the left as he moved to clear his sector. Following directly behind was Royce as he swept from directly in front of him to the right. Following Royce was Corporal Wells, who advanced forward.

"I got bodies!" shouted Sergeant Peterson as he moved to clear his sector.

"I've got them on my side as well," shouted Royce in reply.

"All clear," Wells said. Her path wasn't as long, essentially the fifteen feet directly opposite the service hatch.

"What the hell happened here?" Peterson said in a soft voice as he looked down at the dead bodies. Some were slumped against the wall; others were strewn about on the floor.

"There's so many of them," Wells added as she too began to look around in shock.

Something isn't right, he thought in horror. Dropping down to a knee, he examined the body of a woman on the ground. Her skin was bluish, her eyes glazed over.

"They look frozen," commented Wells.

"That's because the ambient temperature of this place is around zero degrees," said Sergeant Peterson.

Royce shined a light over the woman's body and saw her abdomen and chest area had been shot by a blaster. Moving to another nearby body, a man, Royce saw this person had several large gashes across his chest, frozen blood surrounding his body.

"Peterson, Wells, what do these wounds look like?" Royce asked as he saw them examining bodies themselves.

Wells was the first to speak. "If I had to guess, the gashes or slashing wounds look like what I've seen those Zodark short swords do. I still have nightmares about what I saw them do to some of the RA guys we were helping out during the Rass campaign."

"I was going to say the same thing. The burn marks look like blaster wounds, probably from one of their blasters," Peterson added.

"How much you want to bet the drones will show us more of the same across the rest of the station?" Royce asked. "Oh, Wells—get those drones launched. I want to see what else we can find before I tell Lieutenant Hosni to bring the others." He stood up and walked toward a sign mounted on the wall.

Corporal Wells stood up and pulled a couple of Dragonfly drones from her vest and tossed them in the air. They came to life instantly, speeding off in different directions. Once they took off, she detached four more of the little speed demons and released them as well. They needed to figure out what part of the station still appeared to have power. Not knowing how long ago this attack had happened, they had no way of knowing if anyone was still alive.

As the little drones zipped down their paths, their radar and video feeds were transmitted back to their HUDs, giving a real-time picture of what they were seeing. Right now, the only images they were receiving were of a lot of dead bodies.

"Sir, look at Dragon Two. I think we found our proof of what happened here," Wells explained.

She pulled up the image of the drone that was loitering over the dead body of a large figure. Sure enough, it was a Zodark corpse. Its large frame, four arms, jet black hair, and bluish skin told them all they needed to know. For whatever reason, the Zodarks had gone on a killing spree in this station.

Peterson walked up to Royce. "Sir, you think the colony on the surface is going to be the same as up here?"

Royce just shrugged. He honestly had no idea. He hoped not, but it was appearing more and more likely that this entire system might be just like this station.

"Here, sir. I think we found something," said Corporal Wells.

Royce pulled up the images of the drones on his HUD. "What am I looking for, Wells?"

"Pull up the video for Dragon Four," she indicated. "Using the thermals, I detected a heat source. It appears we have some survivors cooped up in this section. I've told the rest of the Dragonflies to switch to thermals. It'll be the fastest way to find more survivors. No one could survive in this cold without an EVA suit or a compartment with climate control."

Royce saw exactly what she was pointing to, so he sent a quick message to Lieutenant Hosni to bring the rest of the team into the station. He also told them to expect bodies—lots of frozen bodies.

"Wells, see if you can have Dragon Four switch over to X-ray. I want to see beyond the heat of that wall and know if we do in fact have people in that room. We need to start figuring out who is still alive and where they are."

"Yes, sir. On it."

When Lieutenant Hosni arrived with Hadad and Private Chandler, Royce told Sergeant Peterson and Private Chandler to stay put. "You're going to guard the path leading to the Nighthawk, just in case there's a Zodark still alive on this place, or a band of survivors decide they want our ship," he explained.

"The rest of you, follow me," Royce announced. "We're going to see if there are survivors, and if we can get them to talk with us and tell us what happened here." He began advancing towards Dragon Four's position.

The further they walked into the station, the more dead humans and Zodarks they found. There were scorch marks on the walls of the corridors and side rooms, and most of the doors had been either left open or blown open. An intense battle had been fought here.

When they reached the room that appeared to house survivors, the ambient temperature outside the closed doors was significantly warmer than anywhere else in the station. They also observed that the bodies nearby had been carefully moved and placed along the sides of the hallways. It was clear someone had left the room after the battle.

As he walked up to the door, Royce observed a camera mounted above the center of it. A small red light was on, letting him know it had power. Royce signaled for the others to stage on either side of the door while he attempted to make contact with whoever might be inside.

Extending his hand as he balled it up, Royce pounded three times loudly on the metal door. His loud banging echoed throughout the hallway.

At first, they didn't hear anything. Then, the drone's X-ray camera spotted action on the opposite side of the door.

"We've got movement, sir. Looks to be three individuals...no, make it nine individuals now," Corporal Wells called out. She was watching the drone footage a lot closer than Royce, who was trying to keep his focus on the door in front of him. He needed to be ready to bolt or move in the blink of an eye if the situation required it.

Wells, can you tell if any of them are armed? Royce asked over the neurolink.

Yes, it looks like at least two of them are armed. I'm not sure with what, though. I can't make out that level of detail.

Using the translator in his HUD to speak Sumerian, Royce called out loudly, "I am Captain Brian Royce of the Republic. We mean you no harm. We have come to help. We can provide food, water, and medical services if you need them."

"That certainly did something, sir," said Wells. "I can see them talking animatedly with each other. Whoa—a large group of them just showed up. Some of them appear to be armed. Many of them look to be unarmed."

"OK, you guys stay ready in case they decide to attack me," Royce ordered. "As a matter of fact, switch your blasters to stun. If we have to fire, I'd rather knock them out than kill them unless we absolutely have to."

Reaching down to the selector switch on his own blaster, Royce changed the setting to stun, hoping he wouldn't need it. They needed answers to what had happened here, not a shoot-out.

A voice from somewhere broke the stillness of the hallway, asking, "Who are you?"

"I am Captain Brian Royce," he replied, continuing to use his HUD translator to speak Sumerian. "I am a member of the Armed Forces of the Republic. My team and I were dispatched to come to your aid. Who is in charge of your group?"

Another moment of silence occurred before they got a response. "I am Belshazzar, the person in charge of this station. I am afraid we have not heard of this 'Republic' you speak of. What race of people are you, and where are you from?"

Royce snorted at the question. He knew the easiest way to explain would be to just take his helmet off so they could see that he was human. "Hadad, prepare to translate for me."

Hadad nodded and stepped forward to stand next to Royce. When he removed his helmet, Royce could feel the cold air on his skin. The temperature around this part of the station was close to forty degrees—above freezing, but by no means warm. Looking to the camera, Royce stated, "I am human. Just like you. I come from a different star system than yours and from a different planet, a place called Earth."

There was a moment of silence before Belshazzar spoke again. "How do we know you are not working with the Zodarks?" he asked. "They have other human pets, slaves and soldiers that work for them."

Captain Royce lifted his chin up as he spoke. "My people have been at war with the Zodarks for the last fourteen years. We have fought many battles against them, to include liberating the mining colony you call Clovis. We now call it New Eden."

A slight hissing could be heard as the large scorch-marked doors opened in front of them. As the light from the room poured into the hall, a wave of heat washed over Royce's face.

"Please, come inside," a man in uniform said as he motioned with his arm for them to come in. "We can talk more inside the security of this room. But, please, keep your weapons lowered."

Everyone stay frosty, heads on a swivel, and follow me in, Royce said over their neurolink. He knew Hadad didn't have one, so he whispered the same message to him. He was also the only one of them who was unarmed—he wouldn't carry a weapon no matter how much they'd asked him.

In the room, a group of maybe thirty Sumerians stood in a half-circle, staring at them. Some of them wore uniforms and were armed, but many were not.

A man stepped forward. He appeared to be older than the others. "My name is Belshazzar. I am the person in charge of what remains of this station and our people. You said you have food, water, and medical supplies? We are in need of all these things. We have been sending out distress signals for months—at least until our communications relay was destroyed."

Royce spoke but had to wait on Hadad to translate for him. He explained his people spoke a different language. He told Belshazzar he was going to place his helmet back on so he could use the translator built into it. To further set them at ease, Royce sat down Indian-style on the ground, placing his rifle next to him on the ground. The others did likewise, which seemed to ease the tensions with the guards a bit.

"Belshazzar, we do have food and medical supplies. One of my soldiers here is also trained as a medical technician. But first, can you tell us what happened here? Where are all the Sumerian people, the ships, everything?"

Belshazzar looked down at the floor briefly, as did everyone else in the room. When he looked up, he had a burning fire in his eyes and sorrow written across his face. "Everyone is dead…butchered by those Zodark beasts."

"What do you mean, *everyone* is dead? That can't be! There are millions of people," Hadad burst out.

Belshazzar turned to Hadad. "You speak our language flawlessly. You sound like you are from the capital."

Hadad nodded, his cheeks reddening as he apparently realized he'd spoken out of turn. Captain Royce was supposed to ask the majority of the questions. "I am also a Sumerian—and, yes, I am originally from the capital. I used to be a researcher in Sumer. When it was discovered I was working on something that could be turned into a weapon, I was banished—turned over to the Zodarks, who shipped me off to Clovis to work the mines and eventually die. Then Captain Royce and his soldiers, they liberated my camp and the others on Clovis. Then they fought many hard battles against the Zodarks and defeated them. They removed them from Clovis and now claim the planet as their own."

Some murmuring and whispers could be heard from the crowd. Several of the guards held their weapons a bit tighter, as if suddenly realizing the potential threat these three soldiers and this civilian posed.

"Is this true?" asked Belshazzar. "You have fought and defeated the Zodarks?"

"My soldiers and I have fought many battles against the Zodarks, and, yes, we have won many of them," Royce confirmed. "My people are still in a war with them that continues to this day. We are also part of a much larger alliance—an alliance called the Galactic Empire. It's led by another alien raced called the Altairians. They're an even more advanced race than the Zodarks."

"You said your name was Captain Royce?" Belshazzar asked hesitantly.

Royce nodded slightly. "My given name is Brian. My surname or family name is Royce. My military rank is captain. My soldiers call me Captain Royce, but Hadad and other civilians just call me by my first name, Brian," he explained.

Nodding in understanding, Belshazzar smiled warmly at him—the first time he'd smiled at the Earthers. "Then it is a pleasure to meet you,

Captain. Did you really hear our distress call, or were you traveling to our system for another reason?"

This old guy is smarter than he looks, Royce thought.

Royce detached the small voice translator device from his helmet and took it off so he could see them, and they could see his face and eyes. He felt this explanation would come across better if they could see his facial expressions.

Taking his helmet off, he held up a small device. "This device is called a universal translator. When I speak in my own language, it will translate my words into your own." Pointing to just behind his ear, Royce explained, "Inside my inner ear is another device that allows me to understand everything you're saying. I wanted to take my helmet off so we can talk as friends, as fellow humans, and not as foreign soldiers."

Belshazzar smiled and nodded at the gesture. The guards who were still standing also appeared to relax a bit.

Using his neurolink, Royce told the others they should also take their helmets off, so the Sumerians could see them and their faces as well. This was a first-contact mission now. They needed to gather as much information as they could, and that required building trust and doing so swiftly.

"You have a woman soldier," commented one of the Sumerian guards.

Corporal Iris Wells smiled as she proudly replied, "Our people have many women soldiers. My name is Corporal Iris Wells. I'm originally from Topeka, Kansas, on Earth. I have been serving in the Army Special Forces for eight years."

Some of the female Sumerians appeared surprised, but also pleased to see a strong female soldier like her.

Captain Royce proudly explained, "In our society, all people are treated as equals. They are given equal opportunities to grow as a person and excel in whatever pursuits they may choose. That is why our people, our government, is called the Republic. Our government is a representative republic, meaning we hold elections, and it's through those elections that our government is formed and the laws that govern us are created."

"Wow, that is a unique system your people have developed," Belshazzar commented. "I am sure Hadad has probably explained to you how our people are governed," he said, pointing to the Sumerians. "Our leaders—if you can call them that—are selected by our Zodark overlords." Belshazzar paused for a moment before he added, "It didn't use to be like that. There was a time when we Sumerians used to rule ourselves without the Zodarks. Heck, there was a time when we and the Zodarks actually lived in peace together. I mean, I wouldn't say it was the best of relationships—they still demanded their tributes—but they didn't rule our people with an iron fist like they have the last two hundred years."

Royce let the man talk for a little while, explaining their society and people to him. While Royce knew a lot about the Sumerians already, he still enjoyed hearing more about their people. He sent a message to Sergeant Peterson for him and Private Chandler to bring enough MREs to give all thirty-three survivors a meal, along with some water and the med kit.

"Belshazzar," Royce said, attempting to regain control of the conversation, "can you tell us what happened on the station and the colony below? When did all of this take place?"

Belshazzar sighed as he nodded. The old man looked like he had known he was going to have to explain this to them at some point but had been doing his best to avoid it for as long as he could.

"I am not sure of your time standards or how you judge time, but the situation with the Zodarks and our people started to turn bad approximately six tannals ago," Belshazzar said.

Hadad interrupted to clarify, "Six tannals is approximately twelve years."

"Thank you, Hadad. Please, continue, Belshazzar," Royce said, "And please, call me Brian."

Smiling, Belshazzar continued, "Six tannals ago, the Zodarks told us that a wild band of workers at the penal camps on Clovis had somehow risen up and killed many guards at one of the camps. We had no idea what that meant, why they were upset about it, or why they were directing that anger towards us. None of us even knew where Clovis was, and we had no ability to travel there. But when this happened, the Zodarks clamped down harder on our society.

"There were some small pockets of subversive groups out there among the Sumerians, but they were loosely organized, and their numbers were small. However, when it was learned that the prisoners in one of the mining camps had overthrown and killed their Zodark guards, the perceived invincibility of the Zodarks suddenly evaporated. These subversive groups began to grow, and they also became even harder to track and uncover," Belshazzar explained.

"I am not sure when this happened, but one of our people learned from a Zodark that their soldiers and fleet had lost control of Clovis. The Zodarks that told our people about this explained it was lost during a major space battle between an elder race the Zodarks have been at war with—that it wasn't the Sumerian prisoners who defeated them. Still, the sudden realization that the Zodarks could be beaten gave us hope that they could be defeated here in our home system. These rebellious groups grew like wildfire. No matter how hard the government tried to suppress them, holding trials and even public executions, their numbers continued to grow."

"I'm not sure of the man's name, but someone on Hortuna, our other colony in the system, invented a rudimentary laser blaster," Belshazzar continued. "It's similar to the one you see our guards here use. This was something we were not allowed to have. Not even our security forces were allowed to have blaster weapons. The Zodarks gave us a stun weapon that, when fired, disables someone for a short period of time. That was the only weapon we were allowed to have, and it was only used by our security forces."

Royce and his people sat listening with bated breath, enthralled by what they were hearing. Just then, Sergeant Peterson and Private Chandler arrived, bringing with them several boxes of MREs. They didn't have a lot of MREs on the ship; their primary source of food was their replicators.

The Earthers passed out the food and water, explaining how to open and heat them the MREs. The survivors eagerly ate the food, commenting to each other how good it was.

As they ate, Royce asked, "So what you're saying is when your people realized the Zodarks could be defeated, some people began to find ways to create new weapons that could take them on?"

The old man nodded as he finished the last of his MRE. "Exactly. You see, we couldn't use the stun weapons the Zodarks had given our security forces. Those weapons could be turned off by the Zodarks. We had to create our own version. But they couldn't be built on Sumer. There was too much surveillance, and frankly, when the Zodarks offered a bounty for anyone who turned in a member of the resistance, or someone who was working on something that could be construed as a weapon, it became nearly impossible to develop such a thing on Sumer.

"So a small group of people began to develop it on Hortuna. You see, Hortuna is a big planet, just like Sumer. But it also has high mountains with snow on them. If there's one thing the Zodarks do *not* like, it's cold temperatures and snow," he said with a slight chuckle. "A small cave was turned into a weapons lab, away from prying eyes. That's when they developed our blaster weapon. It was small and relatively easy to disassemble and reassemble, so it could be smuggled more easily. It was also easy to mass produce with the technology we had. But this wouldn't be enough—even if we could kill a few dozen or even thousands of Zodark soldiers, we had nothing that could take on their warships.

"That's when someone came up with the idea of hijacking one of their vessels. Looking back on it, it was a terribly silly and stupid idea, one that ultimately cost the lives of tens of millions. But these resistance fighters seemed hell-bent on their cause no matter the consequences. There was just no reasoning with them," Belshazzar explained glumly.

"So what happened?" Hadad asked, desperate to know what had happened to his own family.

Belshazzar turned to Hadad. The sadness in his eyes was palpable. "They called it the Day of Liberation, but it was anything but liberation. All across Sumer, Hortuna and even here on Tallanis, these resistance fighters rose up and attacked the Zodarks everywhere they could. Zodark stations across the colonies and on the home world were attacked by these resistance groups. But the main attack focused on my station here.

"At the time, I was completely unaware of what was happening. We had three Zodark ships docked here: two were transports taking on refined materials from the mines below, and the other ship was a cruiser. We normally don't see cruisers or battleships in our system, so I believe the resistance thought this was their best chance at capturing a warship.

"When the attack happened, it was lightning fast. Faster than I thought a poorly trained group could execute. The resistance was able to storm the Zodark ships and fought an intense battle on board. In less than twenty minutes, they had seized control of the station, isolating me and my staff in this portion of the station. I am not one hundred percent sure what transpired next, but they did manage to take control of the Zodark ships. Shortly afterwards, they left the station and went about attacking the other Zodark ships in the system.

"Our computer monitors provided news reports of fighting taking place all across the colonies and Sumer. Zodark soldiers fought fiercely against the resistance fighters while the central government pleaded with the resistance to lay down their weapons before more people were killed—"

Royce interrupted to ask, "When did this uprising take place?"

Belshazzar replied, "Approximately one tannal ago."

OK, so two years, Royce thought as he did the conversion in his head.

"Is that when the Zodarks attacked your station?"

Belshazzar shook his head. "No, that came later. After about a week of fighting against the Zodarks, the resistance did eventually win. They captured many Zodarks and paraded them through the city. Many people spat on them, hit them with rocks and rotting food. For about two weeks, everyone thought we had rid ourselves of these beasts.

"Then a large fleet arrived at the stargate. Our three stolen ships were promptly destroyed. When the fleet moved through the system, they systematically destroyed all our ships. Our small freighters and transports, shuttles…everything. When they reached our station, they landed a boarding team, which systematically killed everyone they came across, even people trying to surrender. We locked ourselves in here. One of my staff came up with the quick idea of dropping the temperature in the place so the Zodarks would either leave or believe the station had been severely damaged.

"We even vented a couple of sections of the station before the automated safety features kicked in and restored pressurization to the station once again. By this point, the Zodark soldiers had left the station. We watched in horror as they bombarded part of the colony below. Then they launched waves of landing ships to the surface. When we saw what was happening…it was horrible." Belshazzar had to stop for a moment. He wiped away some tears as he sought to regain his voice.

Many of the other Sumerians were also crying; a couple of the women fell apart emotionally and started weeping and sobbing. A man held one of them as the two of them cried together.

"They murdered everyone, Captain Royce—I mean, Brian. They did make a distinction when it came to the children, though. If a child looked like it was under the age of six tennals, then the Zodarks separated them from their parents, oftentimes killing the adults right in front of them.

"The children…were carted off to their shuttles to be taken up to the larger ships. I think the Zodarks must have thought we were dead or would die soon as they did nothing to cut off our access to the colony below or simply blow us up. Perhaps they wanted us to watch, knowing there was nothing we could do to stop them. For the rest of the day, we watched on the monitors as marauding groups of Zodarks moved from one habitat or section of the colony to another, butchering people with their blades and their blasters. In some instances, we saw them ripping people apart with their talons. As my staff turned on their home cameras to check on their families and spread a warning to just hide, we realized we were too late in many cases to warn them."

The woman who had been crying in the arms of one of the men stood up defiantly, with tears still streaming down her face. "When we saw the attack begin on the colony below, I attempted to contact my husband to warn him of what was about to happen. By the time I was able to get our own coms situation on the station repaired so we could talk to the surface, the Zodarks had already arrived and were causing chaos," she recounted.

The woman paused for just a second, then steeled herself to continue sharing her story. "Once I was able to access the cameras in our housing unit, groups of Zodarks were busting down the doors to people's homes and going inside. What I saw…" The woman moved her hand to cover her mouth as another woman stood up next to her, comforting her. "I saw those animals eating my husband alive, joking and laughing with each other as they cut his stomach open and ate bits of him while he screamed for mercy. I had to listen to my Isiah, tears streaming down his cheeks, plead for them to just kill him to end the pain," she said, her burning hatred for the Zodarks evident in her voice.

Even Captain Royce, as battle-hardened as he was, felt his stomach churning at this point.

"He must have sensed I was watching him on the cameras or that the event was being recorded, because before he died, he told me to avenge him and save our children. When it dawned on the Zodarks that our children must still be in the house, they tore the place apart until they found them in our hidden safe room. They took our four children and showed them their father, ripped apart and dead. They told them that this is what happens to those who defy them, who dare to challenge them. Then they took my babies to a transport apparently filled with children.

"That was nearly a tannal ago. I haven't seen or heard from my children since then."

Belshazzar stood up and hugged the woman briefly before turning to face the soldiers standing before him. "As you can see, it has been very tough on our people here. It took their fleet several days to travel from this colony to Hortuna and then Sumer, where they repeated the process. I have no idea what has happened to Sumer. When our communications relay was destroyed, we lost all communications with the capital and everyone on Sumer. Then we lost communications with Hortuna. The last transmission I received from them was from my fellow station manager over there. He told me the Zodarks were on a rampaging killing spree unlike anything he'd ever seen or heard of. He also told me that just like here, they were taking all the children with them."

Royce and the other Earth soldiers sat there in stunned silence. They had heard and even seen the atrocities the Zodarks had inflicted on others during the many campaigns they had fought, but still, hearing stories like this always reminded them of why there could be no peace with these insidious animals.

"Belshazzar, has your group been trapped on this part of the station since the attack began?" Royce asked.

The man nodded. "Unfortunately, we have. When you made your appearance, we were actually down to our last few weeks' worth of food. We still have the ability to create water, but after scavenging the station, we have essentially run out of food options. But, Brian, you still haven't answered my original question. What brought your people to our system? You have saved our lives."

Royce took a deep breath in as he prepared to give their side of the story of why they were here. "When we liberated the prisoners on Clovis, we learned about your star system and your planet Sumer. We freed nearly five hundred Sumerians on the planet, who have gone on to tell us much about your people and planet as well as the Zodarks. Several years after our victory in the Rhea system, where Clovis lies, we sent a small scouting ship to your system. It spent several days observing the activities in your system and learning what it could about the Zodark presence. Our scout then traveled down the stargate chain to visit the other planets along this dead-end system. It was during this scouting expedition that an elder race known as the Altairians first made contact with us.

"We were brought into a new alliance, and from there, we spent the next eight years fighting alongside them, defeating the Zodarks and some of the other species that fight with them," Royce explained. "My team and I were sent here to Sumer to establish an intelligence-gathering operation. Our political and military leaders had determined we should remove the Zodarks permanently from our system and then move to liberate the remaining systems down this dead-end star system chain. There are six other systems with a total of eight habitable planets and moons within them. Some are occupied by other humans, while the others appear not to be inhabited."

He paused for a second while they appeared to take in what he was telling them. "Our team was going to infiltrate your capital and assess your people to see if they would side with the Zodarks or look to us as liberators when the time came. That was until we saw what had happened here and opted to stop and investigate."

Belshazzar asked, "Were your people planning to invade our system?"

Royce tilted his head slightly as he replied, "I suppose that's one way to put it. We thought of ourselves more as liberators, coming to free your people from the Zodarks, than as a conquering army. Our hope was to bring your people into the fold of the Republic, our human-led alliance. We would look to integrate your people, economy, and system into our effort to defeat the Zodarks as we liberate more human-populated worlds from these beasts."

The older Sumerian nodded in approval, as did everyone else. "I am not sure what kind of condition the rest of the system is in right now," he said. "For all I know, the other colonies and the capital may be in flames, or they may be doing fine, just under a heavier Zodark presence. We have not had contact with anyone for many months. What I can tell you with certainty is whatever is left of our people on the planet below would likely view you as liberators, saviors sent to save us from these animals."

For the next hour, they spoke more about what might lie down on the surface. Try as they might, they were unable to reestablish their communications link with the colony on the planet. For his part, Royce called over to their sister ship, the *O'Brien*, and had them compile what they had learned up to this point and send a com drone back to the fleet to let them know that their primary mission had changed.

The Sumerians used what little power the station had left to get the hangar bay operational. Both of the Nighthawks were able to fly in and land. They couldn't fit everyone in either spacecraft, so they opted to leave most of them on the station with additional food and water along with some medical supplies.

When the Sumerians asked about security in case more Zodark soldiers showed up, the Earthers introduced them to the C100 combat Synths. They would leave four of them behind, with strict orders to protect the remaining survivors. Belshazzar and one other survivor from the station would travel with Royce and his team in their Nighthawk while ten others would travel in the other Nighthawk.

****

Once everyone was secured, they headed down to the planet and the colony there. Having the proper access codes, Belshazzar was able to get the hangar doors to open so they could land inside the facility. When they left the ships, they searched for additional survivors. For the next day, they saw nothing but death. Everywhere they turned they saw countless bodies. The Zodarks had been meticulous in their slaughter.

By the end of the first day, they hadn't encountered any survivors— that wasn't to say there weren't any, they just hadn't been able to find any during their limited time on the surface. Captain Royce was determined to get back on track with their mission. They needed to check on Hortuna and then Sumer and see if the Zodarks had committed a genocide of the Sumerian people, or if there still might be survivors. He was praying there were survivors. The Sumerians used to number somewhere around twelve billion people spread across three planets and two moons in their system.

As they traveled to Hortuna, Royce ordered the pilots to go active with all their sensors—there was no reason to act stealthy at this point. They needed answers.

With their active sensors going, they started getting a much better picture of the system. The space elevators that used to operate over two of the moons, Hortuna, and Sumer, were all silent. Where there had once been hundreds of shuttles, transports, and ferries moving about the system, now there was nothing—nothing but the scattered wrecks of countless spacecraft.

When they eventually neared Hortuna, it became apparent that the place had been utterly destroyed. The starbase that had been near the planet was nothing more than debris, chunks of what had once been a large structure. The space elevator had been completely destroyed, with the orbital platform falling back into the planet's atmosphere.

There were huge scorch marks where cities had once stood. Without going to the planet directly, they couldn't search for survivors, and Royce and his team just weren't equipped for that kind of mission. After being on station for a couple of hours, they opted to head to Sumer, dreading what they'd likely find.

As they approached the capital planet of the Sumerian people, Captain Royce thought it reminded him of New Eden or Intus. From out in space, the planet looked beautiful—at least until it started to come into better focus. That was when they started to see the damage on the surface.

Hadad poked his head into the pilot's section of the ship. It was the first time he'd seen his home planet in more than twenty years.

Royce watched a tidal wave of emotions roll across the man's face. He'd finally come home, with the real possibility of seeing his family. Then his eyes registered the scorch marks on the surface and his entire countenance and demeanor changed.

He turned to Brian, tears running down his face. "Is it possible my family could still be alive down there?"

Royce didn't know what to say. He felt himself starting to get choked up with emotions. Hadad was a friend. To see the man hurting like this pulled at his heartstrings.

Royce bit his lower lip as he tried to respond but stopped so he could choke back his own emotions. He was Special Forces; he wasn't supposed to cry. He reached over and placed a hand on Hadad's shoulder. "I'm not sure. It's possible. But I promise you this—we'll sure as hell find out."

From the Authors

I hope you've enjoyed this book. If you'd like to continue the action of the Rise of the Republic Series, you can order your copy of *Into the Chaos* on Amazon You can also tear into our newest military thriller series—*Monroe Doctrine: Volume I* is available on Amazon.

If you would like to stay up to date on new releases and receive emails about any special pricing deals we may make available, please sign up for our email distribution list. Simply go to https://www.frontlinepublishinginc.com/ and sign up.

If you enjoy audiobooks, we have a great selection that has been created for your listening pleasure. Our entire Red Storm series and our Falling Empire series have been recorded, and several books in our Rise of the Republic series and our Monroe Doctrine series are now available. Please see below for a complete listing.

As independent authors, reviews are very important to us and make a huge difference to other prospective readers. If you enjoyed this book, we humbly ask you to write up a positive review on Amazon and Goodreads. We sincerely appreciate each person that takes the time to write one.

We have really valued connecting with our readers via social media, especially on our Facebook page https://www.facebook.com/RosoneandWatson/. Sometimes we ask for help from our readers as we write future books—we love to draw upon all your different areas of expertise. We also have a group of beta readers who get to look at the books before they are officially published and help us fine-tune last-minute adjustments. If you would like to be a part of this team, please go to our author website, and send us a message through the "Contact" tab.

You may also enjoy some of our other works. A full list can be found below:

Nonfiction:
  Iraq Memoir 2006–2007 Troop Surge
  Interview with a Terrorist (audiobook available)

Fiction:

The Monroe Doctrine Series
Volume One (audiobook available)
Volume Two (audiobook available)
Volume Three (audiobook available)
Volume Four (audiobook still in production)
Volume Five (available for preorder)

Rise of the Republic Series
Into the Stars (audiobook available)
Into the Battle (audiobook available)
Into the War (audiobook available)
Into the Chaos (audiobook available)
Into the Fire (audiobook still in production)
Into the Calm (available for preorder)

Apollo's Arrows Series (co-authored with T.C. Manning)
Cherubim's Call (available for preorder)

Crisis in the Desert Series (co-authored with Matt Jackson)
Project 19 (audiobook available)
Desert Shield
Desert Storm

Falling Empires Series
Rigged (audiobook available)
Peacekeepers (audiobook available)
Invasion (audiobook available)
Vengeance (audiobook available)
Retribution (audiobook available)

Red Storm Series
Battlefield Ukraine (audiobook available)
Battlefield Korea (audiobook available)
Battlefield Taiwan (audiobook available)
Battlefield Pacific (audiobook available)
Battlefield Russia (audiobook available)
Battlefield China (audiobook available)

Michael Stone Series

Traitors Within (audiobook available)

World War III Series

Prelude to World War III: The Rise of the Islamic Republic and the Rebirth of America (audiobook available)

Operation Red Dragon and the Unthinkable (audiobook available)

Operation Red Dawn and the Siege of Europe (audiobook available)

Cyber Warfare and the New World Order (audiobook available)

Children's Books:

My Daddy has PTSD

My Mommy has PTSD

Abbreviation Key

AG1	Army Group One
AG2	Army Group Two
AAR	After-Action Report
AI	Artificial Intelligence
ASAP	As Soon As Possible
C100	Combat Synths
C-FO	Commander, Flight Operations
CHU	Containerized Housing Unit
CO	Commanding Officer
DARPA	Defense Advanced Research Projects Agency
EVA	Extravehicular Activity (suits made for being outside a spaceship)
EWO	Electronic Warfare Officer
FID	Foreign Internal Defense
FOB	Forward Operating Base
FOBBIT	Duty stuck at the FOB (reference to how the Hobbits stayed in the Shire)
FRAGO	Fragmentary Order
FTL	Faster-than-light
G2	Intelligence Officer
GE	Galactic Empire
GO	Gaelic Outpost
HAHO	High-Altitude, High-Opening
HALO	High-Altitude, Low-Opening (jumps intended for stealth)
HUD	Heads-Up Display
IFV	Infantry Fighting Vehicle
IRR	Inactive Ready Reserve
JSOC	Joint Special Operations Command
KIA	Killed in Action
LT	Lieutenant
MOS	Mars Orbital Station
MPD	Magnetoplasmadynamic
MRE	Meals Ready to Eat
NAS	Non-aligned Space
NCO	Noncommissioned Officer

NL	Neurolink
NOS	Zodark admiral or senior military commander
OAB	Orbital Assault Battalion
OAD	Orbital Assault Division
ORD	Orbital Ranger Division
PA	Public Address
PSYOPS	Psychological Operations
QRF	Quick Reaction Force
R&D	Research and Development
RA	Republic Army
RAS	Republic Army Soldier
RD	Republic Dollar
RTO	Radio Telephone Operator
RV	Recreational Vehicle
S1	Personnel Officer
S3	Operations Officer
S4	Supply
SAW	Squad Automatic Weapon
SF	Special Forces
SFG	Special Forces Group
SOCOM	Special Operations Command
SOF	Special Operations Forces
SOP	Standard Operating Procedures
SW	Sand and Water (missiles)
VIP	Very Important Person
WIA	Wounded in Action
XO	Executive Officer

Printed in Great Britain
by Amazon

33226763R00155